Death

at the

Reunion

A Haydn and Speaker Mystery

September 2018

Death

at the

Reunion

A Haydn and Speaker Mystery

Reed Browning

To Peggy
In thanks for your tireless
campaigning for Kendal and your
kindness toward me —
Reed

Deernasus Publishing

ISBN: 978-098-56065-2-7
Library of Congress Control Numbeer: 2018907681

Book production by Tabby House
Printed in the U.S.A.

Cover design by Keith Saunders
Marion Designs

Deernasus Publishing
219 Kendal Drive
Granville, OH 43073

Dedication

For Susan, my wonderful wife for the past fifty-five years. From Vienna to Ohio, we've had fun. And much fun lies ahead.

1

Monday, June 4, 2001

Knowledge of all human activities in the past, as well as of the greater part of the present, is . . . knowledge of their tracks.[1]

Connie Haydn jotted the declaration down in his chapbook and picked up his breakfast coffee cup. A trained philosopher, with a fondness for Hume, Connie often spent intellectual downtime reading the methodological reflections of historians. Marc Bloch, whose *The Historian's Craft* he was currently engaged with, represented the height of mid-twentieth-century French historiography; and since David Hume, a luminary of the Scottish Enlightenment, had been in this time a well-regarded historian, Connie was trying to figure out what Hume might have made of Bloch.

Both men—and here is what attracted Connie to their thinking—insisted on the paramountcy facts, on the need to root all conclusions about humankind in the firm ground of empirical evidence. Connie had initially been drawn to Hume's historical work by the realization that the method underlying his exploration of England's past illuminated the elegant power of his analysis of human reason. But then over the past year, as Connie had found himself unexpectedly engaged in detective work, he had come to appreciate the affinity between the criminal investigator and the historian: the reliance that both placed on the ferreting out of facts. Or, to use the image of Bloch, on the finding of tracks. *Had he chosen another line of work*, Connie thought, *Marc Bloch might well have been a star of the Sûreté*. Diverted by that thought, he leaned back in his chair to gaze contentedly through his dining nook window at the stand of pink dogwoods glowing in the morning sunlight.

A ringing phone interrupted this meandering revery. Leaving the book on the crumb-covered breakfast table, Connie made his way to his barebones living room and dropped himself into a brown easy chair before picking up the receiver. A passing glance at the digital clock calendar confirmed that it was June 4. He was curious about who would be phoning a retired professor at just a few minutes after 9:30 on a Monday morning.

"I know you're an early riser, so I won't apologize for calling." Connie immediately recognized the voice of Shrug Speaker, Connie's collaborator in the recent trio of crime investigations. "I've got an invitation I hope you won't refuse." Shrug paused for effect, then continued. "So here's the tease. There may be murder afoot. Are you game for what could become another bout of sleuthing?"

"This is serendipity," Connie chuckled, explaining that his mind had just been savoring memories of their detection successes.

"Good. Then it's entirely appropriate that I'm inviting you to a conversation. I won't say any more right now. It's better to let Bryan explain. But I hope you'll find his tale irresistible." And a half an hour later a curious Connie Haydn drove his tan Buick Regal into the driveway of the two-story brick home of Bryan Travers, a fellow resident—though in a more upscale neighborhood—of the small city of Humboldt, Ohio. *It's wonderful*, Connie mused as he got out of the car, *to be retired and healthy. To be free to seize any passing conundrum that happens to pique my curiosity.*

Bryan Travers, a man of about forty, met Connie at the door, introduced himself, thanked him for coming, and led him into a large den, where Shrug and a fourth man were standing. Shrug promptly introduced Connie to Cole Stocker, a nattily dressed, well-toned, and markedly handsome man in his sixties. Travers invited his guests to take seats on the porch, and then, since the others had obviously been waiting for Connie's arrival, moved immediately to his point. "I've invited you two here"—he pointed to Connie and Shrug—"because I think my father may have been murdered." He paused briefly, to let that remark sink in. Then, after fumbling a moment with a piece of paper in his hand, he continued, speaking directly to Connie. "And because I want to be up-front about what I'm doing, I'll say right off—though I'm sure you know what I'm up to—that I'm hopeful you and Shrug will be willing to look into Tony's death."

Connie tried to appear impassive. Yes, he was curious. But he knew his role in this situation. For the moment he simply nodded his readiness to have the meeting proceed.

"My father," Travers began, "died three years ago, at the forty-fifth reunion of the Humboldt High class of 1953. At the time, the death seemed accidental—and it was certainly ruled as such. He was seventy-two years old and he . . ."

"Seventy-two?" Fearing he had missed some important point, Connie sought an immediate clarification. "At a forty-fifth high school reunion? Seventy-two? That doesn't seem quite right."

"Yes," Travers quickly agreed. "It sounds odd, I know, but it's true. And it's a bit complicated. You see, he'd been born in England in 1926, and by the time he came to Humboldt High in the fall of 1951 he had already served in the British army, first in France during the Big One, and then later in Malaya."

"Okaaay." Connie was speaking slowly. "That answers one question. But it raises a new one. What was he doing, a Brit in his mid-twenties, attending a high school in rural Ohio?"

"Yes, that would seem odd too, wouldn't it?" Bryan Travers hesitated briefly and then offered what he called the short answer. "He was the beneficiary of a program that Humboldt College had created during the war to invite lads who'd served in the Crown's forces, including Canadians and Aussies and Kiwis, to come to the States for a college education. In a few cases, if the former soldiers weren't academically ready for college but showed promise, Humboldt College placed them in high school here, and supported them there, too. Tony fell into that category."

Connie noticed that Bryan Travers, though he spoke with no trace of a British accent, occasionally used British locutions.

"And that's how it happened that Tony finished high school in 1953 at the age of twenty-seven, with Shrug and Cole among his Humboldt classmates."

Connie's eyebrows lifted. Of course! That bit of information allowed other pieces to fall instantly together. The class of 1953 was Shrug's class. He and Cole Stocker and the dead man had all been classmates.

"Amazing," Connie mumbled. "About the program, I mean. So ahead-of-its-time. Sorry to have interrupted, but this background is fascinating. I hope you'll fill me in some day."

"Oh," Travers declared, "I plan to. If you and Shrug agree to help out, that's *exactly* what I plan to do. You'll need all the background I can give. So jump into my story anytime you want. There are many aspects of Tony's life that are unusual."

Connie replied that he'd try to contain his curiosity for the time being, recognizing even as he spoke that he was already yielding to the prospect of hearing more about this life that had been unconventionally led and (perhaps) criminally ended.

The basic tale of the death of Bryan Travers's father was fairly simple. The body of Tony Travers had been found on Saturday, June 4, 1998—"three years ago today"—at the bottom of a high school staircase during the Saturday evening reunion festivities of the Humboldt High class of 1953. Since Tony Travers was known to have been in poor health, and since there was no witness to his fall, the coroner determined that the death, officially caused by the head and neck injuries sustained when he had bounced down the stairs, was accidental, probably the result of his having stumbled or lost his balance.

At the time Bryan Travers had accepted that verdict unquestioningly. And why not? His father, who had moved back to Humboldt in 1994 to be near his son, had been a sick man, suffering from heart trouble, emphysema, high blood pressure, weakness in the legs, and a tendency to become faint-headed. Not that his ailments had soured him. He was cheerful and upbeat to the end. He did not describe his afflictions as burdens. In fact, to underscore his insouciance, he had defiantly continued smoking. "And he was particularly excited by the prospect of seeing old friends at the reunion." Thus the facts of the death seemed quite simple: a man with so many serious ailments ("Did I mention that he needed a cane to walk around?") might be expected to die at any moment. "That's why," Bryan Travers explained, "it was easy to accept the sudden death as both a tragedy and a mercy."

Connie flinched slightly at that familiar usage. It involved comparing incommensurables, and always left him wondering whether the presumptive beneficiary of the mercy, if somehow empowered to render a judgment, would really share the self-serving opinion of the living.

For almost three years Bryan Travers had had no reason to question the verdict of the authorities. But then, a scant three weeks prior to their present conversation, and serving as the trigger for it, Travers had been foraging through the boxes of papers left him by his father and come upon a note atop a pile of letters in one box. At that point he handed Shrug the piece of paper he had been quietly twisting. Shrug read it through twice before passing it on wordlessly to Connie.

The text on the sheet was brief, and Connie read it aloud: "If your life is in danger, you should go to the police. They can protect you. For God's sake, Tony, don't delay. This is serious. Take care." Connie then handed the sheet around. As all could see, the handwriting was in block print. There was no date. The signature was "Less."

When no one seemed ready to speak, Bryan Travers resumed his tale. He had interpreted this note to mean that his father had been threatened by some unknown person. He didn't know who

Less was; he'd never even heard his father mention the name. And a cursory survey of the many documents his father had gathered over a lifetime of correspondence-collecting had revealed no Lesters or Leslies.

"Though I might have missed one, I'd be the first to admit," he added. Since his father had died at the reunion, Bryan Travers had quickly decided that the murderer, if murderer there was, was probably one of the people in attendance. "And that's why I contacted Cole," he added, nodding to the hitherto silent fourth person in the room.

"What Bryan wanted to know," Cole Stocker promptly declared, his deep voice coming in right on cue, "was whether I still had the videos we took of the reunion activities. I did, of course. We'd used them to make a commemorative tape that was sent out to all class members. But I still had the originals. And like Bryan, I thought the note suspicious. Or maybe I should say 'peculiar.'" He stopped, as if to reflect on what he'd just said. Then he turned to Connie and began again, but less formally. "Oh, I'm sorry. I should have explained what I'm doing here. I'm the president of the class of 1953 for the 1993–2003 term. There's no big deal in being class president, for no weighty responsibilities are involved, aside from spurring the planning of reunions every five years. But it means by default I'm temporary class archivist. And I do have the tapes Bryan inquired about. He and I looked at them last night."

"You're still ahead of me, Bryan." Shrug needed assistance and turned back to the host. "Why are these tapes so important? They don't show Tony being murdered, do they?"

"No, that would be too much too hope for. And I don't really know whether they're important at all," Bryan admitted. "But if someone in the class killed Tony, then something on the tapes might provide a clue." An embarrassed smile flickered across his face. "I know, I know." He held his hands up before him. "It's just a hunch, a hope. Maybe I've seen too many TV shows. But I looked at them last night, and Cole has examined them too and we think one of them might be very helpful."

"How so?" asked Connie.

"The main one," Bryan began, but Stocker interrupted him.

"There are two tapes," Stocker stated, clearly accustomed to taking the lead in meetings. "The one that Bryan calls 'the main one' covers the whole dining area for the whole evening. It's much more valuable than the other, which spends the whole damn night focused on those of us at the head table." He paused, apparently to let that distinction sink in. "The great value of the main one, at least as both Bryan and I see it, is that it shows people leaving and entering the room. Tony left the room shortly before his death, and, if we can identify others who were out of the room at the same time, then. . . ." He seemed to expect a response. But when neither Shrug nor Connie said anything, he added, with slight irritation, "Don't you see? It gives us our list of suspects."

Shrug heard the "our" and tensed at his classmate's patent effort to insinuate himself into any investigation that might ensue. But he allowed that Stocker's idea about the tapes might be worth pursuing. "You really ought," he said, addressing Travers, "you really ought, you know, to talk with the people who make solving crimes their business. I can vouch from experience that George Fielding, our local sheriff, is a good man."

"I'm glad you put it that way." Bryan suddenly swung around to address Shrug and Connie directly. "It's your 'experience,' as you put it, that leads to today's meeting. The only thing right now that I would be able to show a law officer or a sheriff is an undated note from an unidentified correspondent. Do you really think that's enough to get them to throw time and energy into reinvestigating the death of a seventy-two-year-old man that the authorities have already adjudged accidental? I don't. And I suspect you don't either." He paused, and neither Connie nor Shrug felt like challenging his summary of the situation. "Besides, as Cole reminded me— no, I'll put it more forcefully: as he *suggested*—the class of 1953 already had its own, as he put it, 'Sherlock Holmes.'" He nodded to Shrug. "Cole has followed your career over the past year." His gesture indicated that he was including Connie in the reference. "He thought I might ask you two if you'd look into this matter. And if you're wondering why I'm getting in touch with you now rather than last week or next month, it's *not* because today is the third anniversary of Tony's death, though that's an interesting co-incidence, but because the four class officers are currently in Humboldt for the annual class planning meeting, and they're available for a conversation about the reunion three years ago—if, of course, you're interested in helping out and think such a conversation would be useful." Unable to capture a consistent tone, Bryan was alternately imperious and importunate.

But he needn't have bothered. Connie and Shrug found themselves staring bemusedly at each other, their inclination to cooperate in the proposed project palpable in their eyes and body language.

"I think," Shrug began, with modest hesitation, just in case he was misreading his friend's expression. "I think we're at least willing to poke around a bit before coming to a final decision about whether we believe we can be useful."

Connie nodded his assent to that cautious formulation.

"Oh, thank you, thank you." Bryan's gratitude was unmistakable. "I'm at a loss otherwise. It could be there's nothing at all to be uncovered. But I'd feel very odd—no, I'd feel unfilial—if I didn't make some sort of effort to find out what this note was about. And of course I'll give you the boxes of Tony's letters to check through."

Shrug thanked him for that offer, noting that, even if they were only tentatively proceeding, it would probably be useful to sort through the writings as quickly as possible. "Two points need to be made right away, however, before we get away from ourselves." He was shifting into business mode. "First, we can talk to some of your classmates who were at the reunion. See if they remember anything of interest. We can look at the tapes and examine the boxes of correspondence. But if none of this seems to give us any reason for proceeding, we'll report as much and drop the matter. There would be no point in wasting our time or inflating your hopes."

Travers opened his mouth, but Shrug raised a finger to silence him even before he spoke. "Second, if we do go ahead, and if the investigation requires travel, we will bill you for our travel. Is that okay with you?"

Shrug had expected at least a brief moment of hesitation, but Travers accepted the terms immediately. "Of course. That's fine. Tony went all over the world. You might conceivably wind up having to fly to Hong Kong or Sidney." Connie and Shrug stared at each other, astonished. "But I assumed as much. Yes, of course I'll pay for any travel your investigations take you on. Nothing else would be acceptable. And I'll pay for your time, too."

"We'll see about the matter of 'time' later," Connie chipped in. "Shrug and I are still very much amateurs. Whether our time will be worth anything to you is yet to be determined. Besides, this is our hobby. People don't ordinarily get paid for pursuing their hobbies. So," he glanced at Shrug to be sure he wasn't presuming too much on his friend's generosity, "we'll settle for travel reimbursement, for now." Shrug nodded his concurrence.

"Since you're willing to poke around," Travers said abruptly, "I need to impose on you for another immediate favor."

Connie and Shrug gave him their attention.

"Since the class committee is in town only through tomorrow, I'm guessing you'll want to find a way to talk to them." Bryan Travers was visibly uncomfortable in forcing the time issue in this fashion. "And if you do, then I think you'll want to have seen the tapes before you meet the class officers. Which means—and I'm sorry to be so pushy—you really need to see at least the main one this afternoon. Is that okay? I mean, does that make sense?"

Connie was willing to expedite matters, and so he said that he could readily manage a viewing that very afternoon if Travers thought it would be useful. Shrug concurred, noting bromidically that there was no time like the present. Then, with the modalities settled upon, the four men allowed their conversation to shift to more casual and, as it turned out, biographical topics. Cole Stocker explained, for Connie's benefit, since Shrug knew about his classmate, that he was an orthopedic surgeon working in Columbus, that his wife Loretta Szek, not a Humboldt High alumna, was a Columbus-based litigator, and that they were co-leaders of the Christian Marriage Association, a group of married couples who met weekly for the systematic study of the Bible. "We hope we're making our own modest contribution toward the encouragement of fidelity to Christian principles to strengthen Christian marriage," he declared with a hint of smugness. (A devout Episcopalian, Shrug immediately nodded his approval of the enterprise.) Bryan Travers, younger by a generation than the three other men, explained that he was a free-lance graphics designer who, after briefly sampling life on both coasts, had gravitated to Humboldt in 1991 because the town offered a collegiate atmosphere and because his father had praised it. "I tended to heed what Tony said."

When no questions arose about Connie or Shrug, the friends privately concluded that Travers and Stocker had done whatever homework into their backgrounds they had deemed necessary before inviting their assistance. At 11:30, with the energy for small talk waning, the four men broke for lunch, agreeing to regather in two hours at Shrug's house to examine what the video tapes might reveal about the activities of that fatal evening three years earlier to the day.

Shrug Speaker's Victorian living room provided comfortable seats for the four video viewers. A large television screen dominated one end of the busy room and a grand piano dominated the other end. Cole Stocker remarked that he would need to leave before four for a conference in Columbus, but that until that time he was entirely at the disposal of Connie and Shrug. (*This man speaks in clichés*, Connie found himself thinking, almost simultaneously kicking himself for the cheapness of the reflection on a man who annoyed him.) As Stocker prepared the main tape for viewing, he explained (chiefly to Connie, who was unfamiliar with the physical layout of the high school building) that the class of 1953 had gathered in the old high school gymnasium on Saturday evening, June 4, 1998, for a reception, a dinner, and a variety of planned postprandial exuberances that had unhappily been cut short when Trish Ridgway had run into the room to report that she had discovered Tony Travers's body. "You'll see," Stocker declaimed, "her dramatic entrance on the tape."

He then returned to the fact, which he clearly thought significant, that there were *two* tapes, both taken from fixed cameras. One had been focused remorselessly on the head table and dais. It showed (he explained) only the four class officers, who rarely left their seats, and various other class members, who came to the front to contribute speeches, songs, or exhortations. He opined again that he thought that tape unlikely to be useful, even though it provided him his alibi (he gave a mock bow) and so, time being limited, he proposed viewing the main one first. Taken from a camera mounted aloft at the far end of the improvised dining room, the main tape captured virtually the whole scene. This was particularly important, Stocker declared, because Tony Travers could be readily identified on this "main tape," and so it was possible to see when he left the room for the last time and to calculate who was out of the room at the same time. This reasoning struck Connie as flawed, but he decided to hold his questions until he had seen the film.

With that introduction, the tape was inserted into the VCR player, the television set was turned on, and the showing began. Shrug's memory of the commemorative disc that all classmates had received several months after the reunion was quite imperfect, but at least in its edited form—with commentary, juxtaposed with still photos and a musical sound track—it had suggested vitality. The tape that was now running on the screen was in color, of course, but dull, filmed from a static spot above the diners; and by effectively including all forty-seven classmates in attendance, plus the spouses and partners of the few of them who had brought companions, it gave an impression of visual incoherence as the class members sat, rose, ate, and squirmed.

Although the lens made the figures rather small, most seemed plausibly distinguishable. Connie pointed proudly when he was able to pick Shrug out, his full head of gray hair, a tendency toward pudginess, and a preference for dull sports jackets being invaluable clues. More to the point, Bryan quickly identified his father. Clearly older and lamer than the others, Tony was seen leaving the room for a brief moment early in the taping. But he resumed his seat at his table soon thereafter.

Connie and Shrug noted immediately that the film appeared to offer two grand advantages to would-be investigators like themselves: it gave a clear view of the only door that allowed entrance or egress, and it included the clock that sat above the doorway. In principle, anyone who arrived or left would be seen, and to each arrival or departure a time could be attached. A steady trickle of persons, seeking bathrooms, smoking opportunities, hallways for stretching their legs, or quiet away from the din, demonstrated the validity of the principle.

"Why," Connie asked, "was there only this one door for exiting the room? That sounds unsafe and probably contrary to regulations, especially for a school."

Stocker paused the film. "You're right, of course. And actually there was and is a second door," he explained. "It led directly to the outside of the building. So the room conformed to code. But the door wasn't used that evening because we had placed the head table with the dais in front of it, making it hard to get to. And to further discourage using it, we'd hung celebratory ribbons and streamers across it. All this was deliberate, to keep the weather at bay, in case it was a rainy evening. Though in fact the weather was fine. Of course the door wasn't locked; that would have been reckless. If a need for a prompt exit had arisen, the door could have been used as easily as the main one."

When no further questions came, Stocker resumed the showing. "We can zip through much of this," he said after a bit,
"because Tony is in view and clearly still alive. This is just to
give you a taste of what the film is like." Stocker then pushed
the FF button, and the reunion figures started zipping about like
swift, jerky puppets. But when the clock on the dining room
wall reached 8:05, Stocker slowed the tape down, and the silent
figures resumed their normal strides. The class was soundlessly
singing songs from the old days, and within minutes Tony again
left the room. Bryan signaled the importance of the moment by
quietly remarking that "he doesn't come back." Connie quickly
jotted down 8:10 P.M. as the time of his departure, and Stocker
paused the video.

"As I see it," he announced, "here's the situation at this point.
If Tony was murdered, and if the murderer was a classmate, then
the only people of interest are those who were out of the dining
room during Tony's absence. They are our list of suspects." Connie felt another twinge of annoyance at Cole Stocker's patent effort to shape the start of any investigation that might occur, but he
couldn't really disagree with his logic.

Shrug offered refills to his guests while the tape was in pause
mode and asked what struck him as a basic question. "Why do we
have to assume that the murderer—*if there was a murderer*—was
a class member or a person who accompanied a class member?
Couldn't a total stranger have entered the building during the
evening?"

Bryan Travers began to reply, but Stocker interrupted to explain that, while that possibility couldn't be ruled out completely,
it was unlikely, since the class of 1953 had had sole use of the high
school that night, adding that their responsibilities had included
establishing a security system that would keep gatecrashers out.
"It was in our contract, and to make sure we fulfilled our duties, we
hired a person to serve as gatekeeper. I can't recall the woman's
name, but it was Craig Brownlee who worked these arrangements

out with school officials, and you can get the details from him if you feel you need them."

Shrug was privately confident that they would certainly need these details and made a mental note to contact his classmate Craig Brownlee to get a fuller explanation of the methods the class had used to assure compliance with the contract.

"Okay," said Connie. "Why don't you just get the tape rolling again. And at this point you two" (he nodded at Shrug and Stocker) "are going to have to do some identifying. Bryan and I will sit back and enjoy your efforts. For if these people are to constitute, as Cole puts it, our 'list of suspects,' we'd better at least be accurate about who we put on the list." Connie wondered if the irritation he felt was audible in his voice. He said he'd keep track of names and times during the window of opportunity—*and to think I accuse others of cliché-mongering*—and he nodded to an impatient Stocker to press the PLAY button.

Although the elapsed real time was only twenty-one minutes— 8:10 to 8:31—it took Stocker and Shrug far longer to identify those who came and went, in part because, as the viewers quickly realized, they needed to backtrack to well before 8:10 to take into account those in attendance who had left the room before Tony Travers did, but whose absences overlapped with his. Eventually, however, after much fast-forwarding and fast-rewinding, Connie's list contained eight names. Happily, all were classmates, not spouses or friends.

Freddy Kramer was already out of the dining room when Tony Travers left. He returned at 8:16, six minutes into the period of interest.

Sonya Klepper, now Sonya DeLisle, was also out of the room when Tony left, and because she never returned, she was absent from view for the entire period.

One of the Grunhagen twins—either Bonny or Bunny—left at 8:14 and returned at 8:22.

The other Grunhagen twin left at 8:17 and returned with her sister five minutes later.

(Connie realized he couldn't distinguish between the two women, and asked if they were more easily differentiated in person. "Not really," was Shrug's quick reply. "If they become focuses of attention, we may have an interesting problem on our hands.")

Denny Culbertson left the dining room at 8:20 and returned at 8:28.

Eddie Moratino also left at 8:20 (but about ten seconds after Culbertson) and never returned.

Amanda Everson left at 8:21 and returned with Culbertson at 8:28.

Trish Ridgway, now Trish Wilson, left at 8:26. Her return at 8:31, distraught and out of control, and alerting the class to Tony Travers' death, triggered general confusion in the dining room and brought the period of interest to a disorderly but memorable conclusion. (Connie was struck by the redness of her hair.)

Attaching names to the sometimes shadowy forms that moved rather blurrily on the screen was not always easy. Sonya Klepper (as the viewers insisted on calling her, preferring the usage of high school days to the nomenclature of marriage) and Eddie Moratino proved particularly resistant to identification. But in the end Shrug and Stocker felt confident they had gotten the roster of "suspects" right. Ultimately Connie read the names off to them, with the time line of opportunity, and they agreed that it was right.

Shrug could not shake his doubts. "This has been fun, but not to put too fine a point on it. . . ." He hesitated, then moved ahead. "Isn't this whole exercise a bit too much like some English country house murder mystery from the 1930s? Straight out of Agatha Christie. There's an unexplained murder (though here of course we don't know that any foul play was involved at all). It's a situation that artificially confines attention to a sharply delimited set of suspects. The operating presumption is that careful investigation will reveal how some dastardly deed from the past—the theft of a diamond, perhaps, or the betrayal of a friend—has led some otherwise respectable person to commit a heinous crime." He set the mocking tone aside. "Isn't it just too cut-and-dried?" He turned to Connie. "I appeal to my friend. If we've learned anything this past year, isn't it that crime and criminals are complex and that they run in twisting, muddy paths? The sheer neatness of the puzzle we've described here violates the complicated texture of reality."

Bryan Travers spoke up before Connie, asking the obvious question. "What are you proposing?"

"Only this, I suppose." Shrug was suddenly meeker and more forbearing. "That we leave our minds open to the possibility that, even if we have a murder here, someone unconnected with the upstanding Humboldt High School class of 1953 might have been the perpetrator. In fact, I wouldn't be surprised if it turns out that that's what happened, if, of course, there really *was* a murder." He turned to Stocker, who was already preparing himself to leave for his appointment. "After all, Cole, however well-laid-out Craig Brownlee's security plans for the evening of the dinner were, I can't help but think that someone bent upon killing Tony Travers could have found some way to insinuate himself into the building. We weren't security pros. We weren't expecting anything nefarious. Excepting Freddy Kramer, none of us, as far as I know, has had experience in law enforcement. So why aren't we just a bit more suspicious of our cabined assumptions than we're proving to be?"

"Here's my quick answer," Bryan Travers interjected, annoyed at Shrug's unexpected raising of doubts. "We're working with what you call our cabined assumptions because there's no place else to turn right now. If the murderer—let's say for the moment that Tony *was* murdered—if the murderer wasn't a classmate, indeed, wasn't one of those *eight* classmates who was out of the dining room when Tony was, then the murderer might be any one of over 250,000,000 people in the United States. The latter alternative obviously invites dropping the investigation. So why not start with the far more confining assumption? It gives us a plausible starting point. And what have we, or I guess I should say *you,* got to lose, except time?" Travers's passion momentarily froze the room. "Besides," he added, "if your and Connie's examination of my father's papers turns up a possible murderer, we can adjust the focus of our search for suspects. But right now we don't *have* any outsiders."

"Spoken like a disciple of Ockham." Connie grinned. "Besides, I know my friend Shrug better than you two do. He didn't say he was withdrawing from an investigation. He just expressed a doubt about our assumptions. And no sane man believes it's inadvisable to reassess assumptions at regular intervals." Shrug nodded in grateful approval, and so Connie continued. "So we're still on board. And that means," (he snatched Stocker's elbow as the physician was going out the door) "that we *would* like to meet with the class officers tomorrow. Can you arrange it?"

Stocker pulled away and winked playfully at Travers. "Already set up. Lunch tomorrow at the Porcupine Grill. Twelve o'clock. Bryan's picking up the tab." Having imparted that information as telegraphically as possible, he dashed to his car.

"Well," said a surprised Shrug, turning to Bryan Travers, "you've certainly got our investigation choreographed."

"I want you to succeed." The terseness of the reply and the blankness of the tone struck the friends as apt and telling.

"I understand." Shrug was trying to let Travers know he wasn't irritated at his preparedness. "But we need much more background on your father. May we meet with you still again this evening?" Then realizing he hadn't consulted Connie in making that suggestion, he turned sheepishly to his friend. Connie's nod put Shrug at ease. Travers concluded the matter by confirming he'd be happy to see them at 7:30.

"Just tell us about your dad. We'll jump in if we have questions. And we're sure to have a lot more of them when you've finished." Connie Haydn was hoping to encourage Bryan Travers to free-associate himself into the life of his father.

The three shirtsleeved men sat on a patio behind Travers' home in the early evening. They looked out at a spacious backyard which turned at some imperceptible boundary into the equally lush backyard of the neighbor who owned the home behind Bryan's. Beer was the libation for the occasion. Shrug Speaker, as was his wont, sat with pad and pencil, ready to scribble down any information that caught his attention. Connie Haydn, trustful as ever of a capacious memory that was both analytic and synthetic, followed his usual practice of relying on his mind. When Bryan seemed uncertain how to launch his description of his father, Shrug offered useful counsel. "With biographies, it's usually best to start at the beginning."

"That sounds right," Bryan replied. And the narrative began. Anthony Travers had been born in Prescott, England, in 1926. His family was "self-styled working class, though I think in America we'd call it lower middle class, or maybe just middle class." Tony didn't much care for school. "He later told me he found it, and I quote, 'fucking boring,'" and so he leapt at the chance to join the army early in 1944. "He said His Majesty's Forces offered wider opportunities for his brand of hell-raising." He was stationed in France, and though in later years he never spoke much about the details of campaigning against the Germans, he often assured his son that the great General Sherman had been right in his broad assessment of war. Nevertheless, there must have been something about military life that appealed to Tony, for he reenlisted after the war and served in Malaya as Britain tried in the postwar period to cling to its many imperial outposts. "He didn't return to England for any significant period of time until about 1950 or so."

Shrug asked if Tony had received any professional training of consequence, either in civilian life or in the military. Bryan didn't know. Connie inquired whether Tony had brothers and sisters. "No," came the quiet reply. "Just like me, he was an only child."

Tony's great break had come in 1951, when he won a coveted scholarship to attend Humboldt College and, in his case (because he needed additional preparation), Humboldt High School. "Throughout his life he was grateful for this opportunity. He thought it a fine example of American generosity."

Connie inquired about the program, which he had never heard of despite years of service on the Humboldt faculty, and Bryan explained that the college had created it during the war with the goal of bringing to the Humboldt campus young men (and occasionally women) who had served in the armies of the British crown in the struggle against the Axis powers. "The remarkable thing was that the college paid for the care and maintenance of those winners who still needed a little high school work to prepare for college." Still puzzled, Connie then asked how Tony had qualified, since he had been, self-admittedly, a poor student. "Oh, he may have been a calamitous pupil," Bryan said proudly, "but he wasn't dumb. Not remotely dumb. And he had used his leisure time in East Asia to bone up on subjects he'd sloughed off on in school. He told me later that his application exam had been the 'most uneven' the judges had ever seen. He was off the charts on geography, for example, but also off them—in the other direction—in math."

Tony had spent two years at Humboldt High before graduating, as a twenty-seven-year-old classmate of Shrug's and Cole Stocker's, in 1953. He then attended Humboldt College, graduating in 1957 at the age of thirty-one with honors in History. "He never spoke a whole lot about either experience, but I know he treasured both. Tony was, in many ways, a very taciturn kind of guy—not exactly the caricatured stiff-upper-lip Brit, but rather a person of deep emotion who did not like being ambushed by his feelings and who had therefore mastered techniques for containing them." This flash of psychological analysis caught both Connie and Shrug by surprise.

After college, Tony had begun a peripatetic life. Bryan didn't know the sequence of locales he visited, nor could he be confident his list was complete. But he recalled Tony talking of time spent in such exotic places—"that's how they seemed to me: exotic and mysterious"—as Hong Kong, Moscow, Sidney, Kuala Lumpur, Johannesburg, Harare, Khartoum, the Falklands, and Baghdad. He also traveled a lot in the States and in Britain. "He had an insatiable Wanderlust." Shrug noticed that he pronounced it as a native German would, "and led an exciting life."

When Connie asked what Tony did for a living during these years, Bryan replied with visible embarrassment that he didn't know. "Tony must have been good at his jobs, for—and *this* I can soon show you—he made money. But what these jobs were remains a mystery to me." Connie and Shrug exchanged puzzled glances.

At this point in his account, Bryan suddenly smiled. "You're probably wondering where *I* came from." Connie offered an encouraging nod, and Bryan continued on this new tack. "First off, you need to know that Tony had a powerful sex drive and had many lovers during his lifetime. Did you know that for my thirteenth birthday gift he asked a thirty-something-year old female friend of his to seduce me? He said it would help me grow up."

The friends' silence showed they did not know how to respond to this surprising disclosure, and so Bryan returned to his basic subject. Tony got married four times, to Mary, Linda, Pat, and Judy in turn. "My mother is Linda, and I was born in 1963, but Tony didn't stay hitched to any of his wives for very long." Bryan hadn't seen much of his father when he was growing up, and for reasons that Bryan couldn't fathom, when the two men became reacquainted in the 1990s, Tony preferred to reminisce about his lovers than to talk about his wives. "He said that every man has one great love in his lifetime—and that's what he called his own great love, 'the Great,' like Catherine the Great, I guess—and he said that that love must be treasured above all other things. But who 'the Great' was, I don't know. He never told me her real name, and of course I never asked." (Connie wondered why Bryan had included "of course." But he said nothing.)

Shrug inquired about Linda, Bryan's mother, and was told that she now lived in California with her second husband and that Bryan visited her occasionally.

"Tony was a man of many gifts," Bryan said, resuming the central story. In fact, by his son's slow and deliberate account, Tony was incredibly smart, indefatigably resolute, astonishingly brave, superhumanly strong, remarkably resilient, infinitely adaptable, endlessly imaginative in devising solutions, and therefore a natural leader. As Bryan elaborated on each virtue by citing several exemplifying anecdotes, Connie and Shrug came quickly to realize that the rhapsodical son had fallen victim to hero-worship. And while that trait in itself was not exactly reprehensible in a son, it had the effect of casting doubt on the reliability of his descriptions and analyses. Connie recalled that Marc Bloch had cautioned against totally trusting any witness.

Tony's life had changed in the late 1980s when his health showed its first signs of decay. First came diabetes, then high blood pressure, then prostate cancer. About 1991 he suffered a minor stroke. Meanwhile, arthritis ravaged his knees, and emphysema, a product of years of smoking, led him to suspect that he would die of lung cancer. "But the affliction that most distressed him was his fading vision. He had cataracts, which were correctable, and macular degeneration, which wasn't. He had become a great reader at some point in his life, especially of works about animals, and he felt keenly the prospect of losing his access to his books. That was the only regret I ever heard him express about his afflictions. He feared the prospect of losing his ability to read books."

Lifelong readers themselves, Connie and Shrug were quick to acknowledge the tragedy of losing one's eyesight.

In 1994 Tony had returned to Humboldt, buying a small house about ten minutes' drive from Bryan's. Father and son saw each other regularly though not extensively thereafter. "He was a private man, and he may have been assembling his papers to write his memoirs. But sometimes we'd share thoughts over beer and wine, and he would unexpectedly open up. It was during those four years at the end of his life, when we were both living in Humboldt, that I learned most of the things about him I'm passing on to you now. But he didn't mention getting threats. So I'm sure he didn't tell the police." Bryan described Tony's last years as happy. "He loved life and accepted the early onset of the disabilities of aging with a startling composure. And to the end he remained a defiant smoker. Did you know a partially smoked cigarette of his was found by his body? He died while enjoying the charms of nicotine."

"Were you yourself ever married?" Shrug thought his query, though apparently unexpected, quite apposite.

"Yes. Geraldine and I got divorced about ten years ago. No children. But in my case, the divorce wasn't grounded in the kind of sexual high-spiritedness that made my father a man unsuitable for monogamy. No, in my case, we just came to loathe each other." The voice was soft, the tone resigned; and Shrug, who knew the stoniness of life before divorce, dropped the subject.

Resuming his chief topic, Bryan explained that Tony's death, while unexpected, had struck him in retrospect as predictable. Though he continued to miss the company of his father, he hadn't grieved long. And as for the will, it had brought a real surprise. First off, the size of Tony's estate—more than $3,000,000—was far larger than his modest living arrangements might have suggested. Bryan had been given no idea that his father was such a wealthy man. Second, its distribution raised questions. None went to any of his wives, three of whom, Bryan believed, were still alive. Instead, half went to Bryan himself, "making me, I guess, a suspect," he said, in a wan effort at humor. The other half was divided equally between the Alliston Home for War Veterans in Britain and "Chucklehead Clancy." The last term brought odd stares to the faces of Connie and Shrug, and Bryan quickly explained that no one had ever figured out whom that term referred to. Tony's lawyer in Humboldt, a man by the name of Axel Berlin, had made out the will in 1994 and had asked Tony to clarify the identity of this strange beneficiary; but Tony, whether talking with attorney or son, had remained resolutely and puckishly silent on the matter.

"He enjoyed his games," Bryan said, by way of explanation. As a result, even after the proper portion had gone to the Alliston Home (a hospital where Tony had recuperated after an injury incurred in Malaya), and a bit over a million and a half dollars to Bryan himself, about $800,000 of the estate still remained undistributed. Of his own portion, Bryan then added, he had given half to his mother.

By the time this recital of a swashbuckling life was over, night had come upon Humboldt. Sitting in the dark, fortified by their drinks, the three men returned systematically to some of the topics Bryan had discussed, with Connie and Shrug seeking clarifications or amplifications. They learned the name of his local physician. ("Dr. Lydia Trench. Tony always liked his health care pros to be women," Bryan added.) They secured an acknowledgment, grudgingly extended, that Bryan had no way of knowing if Tony was being reliable in his lively tales about his adventurous career. And Bryan apologized again for the vagueness of his knowledge of the sources of his father's money. "I know very well," he said, "that a globe-hopping life like his, marked by a casual indifference to convention, might easily have generated all sorts of incidents that could serve as grounds for a later murder. But I just don't know where he went or what he was doing in all these exotic places." When asked if he could supply the names of any of Tony's local friends, Bryan admitted that he didn't know of Tony having any. "He was a private person," he said, by way of explanation.

Toward 11:00 P.M., under what Shrug took to be the solicitous twinkle of Capella and Vega, and moved more by curiosity ("Chucklehead Clancy" resisted relegation to background storage in Connie's memory cells) than by a conviction that they could be authentically useful, Connie and Shrug confirmed that they would start an investigation into Tony Travers's death.

They explained that they'd be a little slow in getting their inquiry launched because Connie had committed himself to attending a conference on Kant that was to be held in Ann Arbor on Wednesday and Thursday of the current week, and Shrug would be out of commission from Friday to Sunday, recuperating from surgery for an inguinal hernia scheduled for Thursday. ("Modern medicine has made this procedure a 'minor' one," he explained, his voice conveying his skepticism.) But they pledged their best work and promised to keep Bryan Travers fully informed.

"I think," said Shrug, as they were leaving, "that I'm speaking for Connie when I say that we're not exactly optimistic about securing results you'll deem totally satisfactory. After all, it's far from clear that your father died from anything other than the premature encroachments of senescence; and it's even less clear that we'll be able to find plausible mechanisms and grounds for murder from among the detritus of his extraordinary life. But we'll try. And if we conclude there's no evidence of anything untoward–that there's no 'there' there–we'll quickly let you know." Under the circumstances, this carefully worded declaration was the firmest commitment they could make.

1 Marc Bloch, *The Historian's Craft*, trans. Peter Putnam (New York: Vintage, 1953), 55.

2

Tuesday, June 5, 2001

The Porcupine Grill sat atop a gentle hill about two miles south of Humboldt. Once a sleazy bar patronized by restless youths, it had been sold in the early 1990s to an ambitious young couple and reborn as an attractive restaurant offering a wide variety of what its newspaper ads styled "elegant dining experiences." The affluent of Humboldt dined there regularly. As Connie and Shrug parked next to the restyled building right at noon on Tuesday, June 5, they speculated about the expenses the new owners must have incurred to transform the structure and reputation of the establishment. "By the way," Shrug whispered as they entered the restaurant, "I'm not going to drink any alcohol today, but I very much hope our guests will." He winked and patted his notebook.

Brian Travers had reserved a table for the luncheon meeting, and when the two friends were escorted to a pale blue lounge, three people rose to greet them. They recognized the informally dressed Travers and the suited Cole Stocker, but only Shrug recognized Cheryl Bollinger, whom he greeted with a brief hug. In introducing her to Connie, he explained that she was the treasurer of the class of 1953.

"I bear fiduciary responsibility for the princely sum of $278," she noted. Shrug added that she had been the outstanding female athlete of the class. When Connie inquired, she said that, yes, she was the founder of Bollinger's Health Club, the town's only exercise and training facility; and further conversation revealed that she now spent much of her time in Hilton Head, golfing as frequently as the weather allowed. She was tall, blonde, trim, and well-spoken, and Connie concluded that she was a woman who had paid full attention to her health and appearance throughout what must have been an active life.

The quintet settled into comfortable chairs in the otherwise empty lounge. As a new round of drinks arrived, the two final guests hurried in, full of apologies. Stocker introduced them to Connie (and to Travers, who was also meeting them for the first time) as Dirk Glass, the bald, pudgy, and bespectacled class secretary; and an earnest-looking Gertie Heintzelman, "though we knew her as Gertie Werner," he added. Heintzelman, he explained, had been the chief organizer and record-keeper for the 1998 reunion.

"This," said Stocker, with an authoritative sweep of his hand, "is the steering committee for the class of '53."

Shrug was delighted to see his former classmate, Dirk Glass, again and, to ease Connie into a conversation with him, immediately commended Glass for his labors at keeping the class members informed about each other. It was clear to Connie that Glass was a man not comfortable with praise, for the bland-faced secretary quickly deflected the commendation by crediting his wife for most of the work. As Connie talked with him further, he learned that in 1992 the secretary had taken early retirement from an executive position in a small southeastern Ohio coal company to move back to his family dairy farm, located about ten miles southwest of Humboldt. When Connie asked about his high school days—the theme of the luncheon meeting, after all—he learned that Glass had founded a student-run radio station.

But even as he chatted with the class secretary, Connie heard enough of the nearby conversation that Gertie Heintzelman was having with Shrug and Stocker to know that this woman's career had something to do with higher education. His curiosity piqued, he made a point of sitting beside Heintzelman when the septet was finally led to their secluded table in the adjacent dining room. He soon learned that she was an educational lobbyist in Washington,

D.C., living in Herndon, Virginia, with her husband, a retired industrial engineer. A self-assured woman of medium height, who wore her gray hair in a bun, Heintzelman spoke more rapidly than Midwesterners usually do, jovially passing along tidbits of inside-the-beltway educational gossip that Connie, an outsider when it came to the politics of education, savored. But her prognosis for the future, whispered in her husky voice as dinner plates were cleared and Stocker was calling the meeting to order, was not meant to be cheering. "Despite its rhetoric, the Bush administration will probably not be very friendly to higher education in the one area where it counts—money."

After Stocker shushed the table with a mock scowl and Travers, the youngest person in the group, thanked his father's classmates for being willing to help, Shrug assumed direction of the conversation, summarizing the discussion of the previous day and taking care to make clear that he was not entirely confident that a satisfactory conclusion could be reached. He explained that he hoped the class committee might talk about the eight "classmates of interest," what the diners recalled of them in high school, but equally important, what they recalled of them at the reunion.

Shrug had deliberately refrained from resorting to Stocker's freighted term of "suspects" to identify the eight names on his list, but his clumsy circumlocution served chiefly to elicit smiles and chuckles from an audience that was not to be gulled by gingerly speech. "Finally," he said, by way of trying to move past his misstep, he set forth a ground rule: "I'll introduce names in alphabetical order, so as not to tip my hand about who I really think dunnit." He winked broadly. "That means" (he removed his glasses to read his list more closely) "we're worrying about Denny Culbertson, Amanda Everson, Bonny and Bunny Grunhagen, Sonya Klepper, Freddy Kramer, Eddie Moratino, and Trisha Ridgway." From the raised eyebrows and occasional guffaws that the list provoked, Shrug and Connie gleaned that the "classmates of interest" were unlikely to be dullards.

As first one up, Denny Culbertson was a perfect choice. The very mention of his name, or rather the recollections of his reunion "antics" (the word was Glass's), brought groans and sighs to all who had been present in 1998.

"He's gone hippy," was Bollinger's contribution.

"He's found religion," added Heintzelman.

"He's a health nut," muttered Stocker.

Each class member tossed out at least one anecdote about Culbertson, and it was only when Connie began posing clarifying questions that a pattern began to emerge.

Denny Culbertson had been a smart and hard-charging high school student. He often wore a jacket and tie in school—"today he'd be called a dweeb," Bollinger suggested—and his grim determination to secure good grades had left him without many friends. After graduating from Humboldt High, he had gone on to Yale and Tuck Business School, and subsequently to a career with one of the major airline companies. At the twenty-fifth reunion in 1978, the only previous class event he had attended, he had struck people as nothing more or less that the eighteen-year-old Denny twenty-five years deeper into self-absorption. "His conceitedness bordered on the offensive," Heintzelman said. "His attire was meant to radiate power, and he made little effort to hide his sense that he thought himself better than the rest of us."

But shortly thereafter Culbertson found Jesus. The man who came to the forty-fifth reunion in 1998 was "born again." He had resigned his executive position. A bicycling enthusiast, he had organized a group called Cyclists for Christ, used gatherings of bicycling friends as occasions for evangelizing, and cycled all the way from Pittsburgh to attend the reunion. He now sported a ponytail and a beard, and he wore casual and colorful shirts and moccasins, all with a bow tie! His cheerfulness was relentless, "Especially so," noted Glass, "because it served his determination to convert us all to his own brand of Pentecostal Christianity." His wife Loraine, who had undergone the same remarkable transformation as her husband, seemed to be as committed as he to the cause of celebrating the Holy Spirit. And by their accounts, they had raised their children to share the same joy in Christ.

"I have met many religious nuts in my day," Heintzelman declared, "but never someone as smart as Denny. And with that Tuck training, I'll bet he's good not only at preaching but also at managing the business side of religious outreach." Shrug winced during parts of this conversation but held his tongue.

When the moment was opportune, he brought forward the next name on the list: Amanda Everson. The reaction could scarcely have been more different.

"She was a stitch," Heintzelman said.

"That gal always knew how to dress," Bollinger added, simultaneously flicking her blond hair out of her eyes. "She actually got away with wearing a yellow skirt to the reunion."

"She'll be hard to contact, though," Glass added, "for she's living in New Zealand now, with her daughter or granddaughter." As Connie listened to Glass's remarks, he found himself fascinated by the size of the man's wiggling wattle.

That remark, confirmed by Heintzelman, led the chuckling officers to envision their style-conscious classmate trying to "jumpstart Kiwi couture." But when they set about trying to assemble useful facts about her post-high school life, they came up surprisingly short. Though she now used her maiden name again, they knew from the brief entry in the class's book of reunion bios that she had been married and widowed, that she'd lived in Houston for a while, that her husband had had some connection with Enron, and that she'd raised two children. Still, Heintzelman offered the possibility that, of all the classmates who attended the reunion, Everson had changed least over the intervening forty-five years.

Connie tried to pull the rambling remarks together by suggesting that Amanda Everson sounded like a person who, unlike Denny Culbertson, was simply a fuller version of her high school self.

"That's not wrong, Connie," Stocker replied, "but it's not quite right either. This was the first reunion she'd ever attended, and I think we were all struck by how certain traits we vividly recalled—her strong, cheerleading personality, her interest in looking good, her kindness—were still evident; while others, and here I'm thinking especially of her love of music and singing, were gone completely. But as our comments have made clear, she retained that note of self-confidence that helped define her in our minds. She had loads of memories from high school days, and they all seemed to be happy."

Glass said that "of all the female classmates, sorry, ladies," (a nod toward Bollinger and Heintzelman) "she had borne the indignities of time best."

"That's a good way of putting it," Bollinger suggested, poking her finger lightly into Glass's oversized stomach. "Though maybe she's had some surgical assistance." Connie had been wondering the same about Cheryl Bollinger but said nothing.

"Let's move on to the Grunhagens, Shrug," Stocker suggested. "If you want colorful stories, that's where they're to be found." The rush of laughter that swept the table suggested that the reminiscers were qute ready to swap some rowdy recollections.

"You need to know," Stocker said quickly to Connie, "that Bonny and Bunny were identical twins who gloried in their identicalness. And who still do!"

Heintzelman jumped in. "That's why, when you first mentioned their names, my initial thought was, 'Hey, guys, if Bonny and Bunny are involved, you'll *never* get to the bottom of this crime.'"

When Connie looked briefly puzzled, she elaborated. "If either of them did it, the other can supply an alibi."

The picture that slowly emerged from the eager sharing of lively anecdotes was of identical twins, best friends from their childhood to the present, living as much as possible in a world of their own construction. Bonny (who's real name was Stephanie) and Bunny (really Heather) had not been raised to mirror each other. Their parents had in fact tried to promote their individuation. But the girls would have none of it. Once they had come of an age to choose their own school clothes, they had preferred wearing identical dresses, blouses, shoes, bathing suits, hair styles, and glasses. When one got braces, the other followed. In high school they had found it easy to trick new teachers into confusing them for each other. As far as any of the class officers could recall, the only significant time they had been separated was during their college years, when Bonny had attended Michigan State while Bunny had gone to Ohio State. But after that four-year experiment in leading separate lives they had come back together and settled in Humboldt, at first with their parents and later on their own.

"And they've spent the last forty years here in town," Shrug explained, making his first contribution to the colloquy.

"How can it be that I've never heard of, or noticed, this remarkable duo?" Connie's puzzlement was genuine. Humboldt was not a small town. He certainly didn't know everyone. But still, over the course of thirty years he might have expected to have at least *heard* of this strange pair.

"Don't blame us, Socrates," Bollinger teased. "They've *been* here. Maybe you've just been too much in the clouds." The remark was probably not meant unkindly, but Connie knew that it had elements of truth in it. For even though he liked to think of himself as a practical man, he recognized that, as someone not inclined to socialize, he was always in danger of withdrawing into scholarly seclusion.

"What's even more astonishing," Stocker added, "is that, if anything, they've grown more alike over the years. Not only do they live together and dress identically, they've now developed the habit of finishing each other's sentences and talking to each other in a cryptic private language of their own. It's unnerving. They've attended every reunion I can think of, and each time I see them, the blending has become more pronounced."

When Connie asked whether they had ever had jobs, Heintzelman explained that they'd been successful air hostesses for many years. "It was one of the few exciting jobs a woman could reasonably aspire to enter back in those days." When he finally inquired about husbands—and he suspected he knew the answer—Bollinger confirmed his speculation by saying that neither had ever been married and that most classmates assumed they were lesbians. (Shrug stored that remark away, since he knew, but Connie didn't, that Bollinger herself had never married.)

"They have a wonderful array of flowers and bushes around their house," the hitherto-silent Glass unexpectedly interjected, "and they write a weekly garden column for the *Humboldt Herald & Examiner*. It's one of the reasons I subscribe to the paper."

"What can you tell us about Sonya Klepper DeLisle?" With time passing, Shrug felt the need to push the discussion onto the next name. The initial answers, however, turned out to be variations on "not much." The group shared tales of a quiet woman who was eager to show anyone who was interested—and many who weren't—photos of her grandchildren.

"She didn't understand the rules of the road on these matters," Heintzelman gently explained to Connie and Shrug. "It's okay to pull out photos of kids and grandkids, but only if someone asks."

Then Glass threw out a remark that briefly brought discussion to halt. "I think she dated Tony Travers in high school."

"Oh, surely not," Bollinger said after a moment. "He was older than all of us and, let's say, experienced, while she was, well, probably virginal. That's an unlikely pairing."

"I know it sounds unlikely," Glass replied, "but I'm sure I recall her mooning about him."

Bollinger laughed. "There's a big difference between mooning and dating. A lot of us girls thought him quite a—what did we say back then?—A he-man?" Her dismissive chuckle suggested that she found the memory of the word distasteful. "But as for dating him, I suspect he wanted more action than many of us would

38

have been willing to give." Shrug noticed Stocker throwing a quick, dark glance toward Bollinger.

"In any case, it might be worth asking her, Shrug," Glass continued. "She lives just over in Richmond, Indiana. She's a widow now, but she used to be a teacher right here in Humboldt."

"Of course," said Shrug abruptly, slapping his forehead in the conventional gesture. "I should have remembered. She taught Marilyn in high school. English, I think." Marilyn, he quickly elaborated for the uninitiated, was his daughter, who had graduated in the 1980s.

"Or maybe social studies," Heintzelman suggested. "I recall having a conversation with her when I was first trying to get up to speed on the problems facing education in America. She turned out to be what I've come to call a 'conscientious apologist.' She assumes the blame for herself when her students don't perform as well as she had hoped they would."

Conversation returned to the attitude of the girls of the class of 1953 to the British "war hero" in their midst. "We were sure he'd been a hero," Heintzelman explained to a bemused Connie. "I think he tended to date casually. I sure don't recall any serious relationships."

"Our parents wouldn't have stood for them," Bollinger added.

"If he had close friends in those days, male or female," Glass declared, "they must have been older." And with that remark, which had a ring of closure to it, Shrug again played the master of ceremonies, directing their attention to Freddy Kramer.

"What a little shit!" Bollinger muttered, not quite inaudibly.

"Let me explain what Cheryl means." Cole Stocker moved quickly to interpret the unexpectedly sharp remark. But by his account, which four nodding heads reinforced, the description had not been far off target. Kramer had left town after high school to pursue a career in law enforcement. He had returned occasionally for reunions in the early years, but had stopped attending sometime after 1963. Then in 1980 he had moved back to Humboldt, embittered at having lost a policing job in some southern city. His attendance at the forty-fifth reunion, marked by one unpleasant encounter after another, was his first appearance at a class function in several decades.

In high school, Bollinger explained, Kramer had been awkward, gangly, and given to unpleasant episodes of wormy ingratiation. His classmates had been surprised when he chose law enforcement for his career, for he hadn't seemed the type.

"I took it," said Heintzelman, "to be an effort to remake himself." And all agreed that he was certainly now a different man, but far from a better one. Two marriages had failed. His career had burned out, and he seemed to be living on an early pension. He had withdrawn into self-pity. And in tones of anger and contempt he blamed everyone else—especially black people—for his woes.

"For example," said Glass, "he told me that he'd been passed over in the police force in Charlotte, North Carolina, in favor of an African-American who'd gotten a lower score on some test. He said something about it being impossible to feel at home in his own country any more. He was a *very* bitter man."

"And do you remember," added Bollinger suddenly, "how he was no longer 'Freddy'? He insisted that we call him 'Fritz.' He seemed to think it was a manlier name. What a joke!"

As Connie listened to the discussion, his mind wandered and two contrapuntal strands of thought began playing their way through his mind. One emerged from the prominence of German names in the conversation. Bollinger, Grunhagen, Klepper, Kramer, Stocker, Werner. To which might be appended the names of two of the assembled septet, Haydn and Heintzelman. This summoning up of surnames reminded Connie that the city of Humboldt had been founded around 1850 by Forty-Eighters who had fled the failed revolutions in their German homelands. With their commitment to free men and free soil they had made Humboldt a staunch supporter of the party of Lincoln during the Civil War. And although many other groups had arrived in the subsequent century and a half, the German impress still lay heavy upon the town—in place names, in business names, in the names of prominent citizens, and even perhaps in the sturdy spirit of self-reliance that, to Connie's despair, made the small city a continuing stronghold of Republicanism.

The competing strand of thought emerged from the unexpected intrusion of race into the conversation. Connie knew that a small number of African-Americans lived in Humboldt. He himself had two black acquaintances on the Humboldt faculty. Both he and Shrug counted George Fielding, recently elevated to county sheriff, as a friend. And Shrug turned often to the black rector of Trinity Episcopal Church, Allan Clark, for spiritual counsel. But more to the point, Connie knew that Shrug's high school class had contained four or five African-American members. Yet as he thought back over the conversation of the day or the reunion video he had viewed, he realized that black class members were neither seen nor mentioned. *That says something,* he mused. *I guess growing up black in Humboldt must not have been easy.*

The realization that Shrug had moved discussion to Eddie Moratino pulled Connie's wandering mind back to the topic of the day. And Glass's opening remark of, "What a nice guy!' seemed soon to encapsulate everyone's opinion.

A class clown in high school, Moratino had matured into a genial, self-effacing senior citizen who was, of all things, a trader and specialist in East Asian art. The reunion anecdotes of his classmates reinforced each other. Although Moratino could be induced to briefly discuss his travels along the East Asian coast, he wound up revealing little about his life, for he had the gift of getting others to talk comfortably about themselves. Even more important, he never asked intrusive or embarrassing questions. And although he was obviously wealthy, nothing in his manner suggested a desire to draw attention to his material condition. He was, in short, a man at ease with himself, happily living inside his body; and there was no reason to believe that his decision to attend his first reunion in forty-five years had been grounded in anything other than a simple eagerness to see old friends.

"He grew into full adulthood more successfully than any of the rest of us," Stocker commented. "No signs of envy or pride or prurient curiosity. I can't think of a less likely murderer in the class of '53."

"Nor of any classmate who changed more dramatically over the intervening forty-five years," Heintzelman added. "Even Denny and Freddy—oops, Fritz" (she smiled)—"strike me, now that I think about it, as less transformed than Eddie."

"And an interesting consequence of all of this," Bollinger chipped in, "is that the high school nuisance who couldn't stop talking about himself wound up being a remarkably private man. He talked more about his hobby as a piano tuner" (Shrug's ears perked up at this unexpected disclosure) "than about any family he might have. In fact, do any of you know if he's ever been married?"

No one did. And the ensuing silence suggested to Shrug that, given the passage of time, he needed to shift the group's attention to the last name on his list: Trish Ridgway, now Trish Wilson.

"Ah yes," said Stocker with a note of pleasure in his voice. "Trish the dish."

Shrug was uncertain whether anyone else noticed the thickly indecipherable glance that Bollinger shot toward Stocker at that moment, but to Shrug it suggested that there was an element of electricity in the relationship between the class president and the class treasurer.

"All the boys called her that," Glass explained.

"And the girls, too," Heintzelman added. "She was what we then called 'easy.' I don't know that she ever dated Tony Travers, but she was the kind of Humboldt High School girl he probably would have liked."

Glass interrupted the snarkiness. "Well, remember, she really did some constructive things later on." And as the classmates pulled up their fragmented memories of various moments from Ridgway's nontraditional life, the portrait that emerged spoke to a strand of adventurousness uncommon among female graduates of Humboldt High in the 1950s. She'd organized an all-girl rock band in the 1960s to entertain American troops stationed in Korea and Japan. Later she'd served on the Humboldt Planning Commission. And still later she'd formed the excellent garbage company that provided Humboldt with the trash removal system that had won some sort of "best in Ohio" citation. All concurred that Ridgway had made her mark.

"And you know, guys," Stocker suddenly declared, "if anyone had a reason to dislike Tony it was Trish. Remember the fortieth reunion! What a fool she made of herself."

Prompted by that remark, all of the five participants in the 1993 event contributed anecdotes to a narrative that, as Connie silently assembled it from its various strands, conveyed a picture of a woman both unhappy and out of control. The class committee of that year—"not us," Bollinger was quick to note, "our predecessors"—had decided that they would present an award to the class member who had, in the words on the plaque, "Contributed Most to Society." Trish Ridgway coveted the award and believed that her record of service virtually assured her of securing it. But the class officers had chosen Tony Travers instead, commending him for helping—again quoting the plaque—"to defend freedom against the Nazi menace."

"When Tony's name was announced," Bollinger explained, turning to Connie and Bryan Travers, "Trish went ballistic. She was already drunk, and now she started ranting about how she was the one who had deserved it, that getting drafted into an army didn't require any initiative, that men always got a free ride anyway. She shouted and, if I remember right, staggered a bit. It sounds funny as I tell it now, but at the time it was gut-twisting—for her, presumably for Tony, and certainly for all of us obliged to watch."

"And drinking has remained her problem." Glass's quickness in further elaborating the story of Ridgway's complicated life showed that her capacity to fascinate had not abated. As reunion anecdote piled on reunion anecdote—and there were lots of them, for Ridgway had attended regularly since the twentieth—the woman who had constructively served American troops stationed overseas and the residents of her hometown, and who had also thrown a memorable public tantrum, became transformed into the pathetic figure of a boozy attention-getter.

"At the forty-fifth her hair was red," Heintzelman declared, "not amber but Buckeye-scarlet. And her clothes were, well, sophomoric. It was as if she was trying to go back to a Hollywood version of high school forty-five years ago—a tight pullover sweater, prominent boobs, a plaid skirt, and penny loafers. And she still nursed her grudge, talking about how unfair it was that she'd been denied the award five years earlier. It was gruesome."

"And wouldn't you know it. She's the one who discovered the body!" Stocker's remark brought silence to the room.

Shrug knew what thought sprang to everyone's mind at that moment and he didn't want it to be openly discussed. So he used the silence to bring the luncheon to a close. "It's 2:30. You all have things to do, and Connie and I have a lot to think about. So I'm going to exercise my authority as convener and declare these informative proceedings at an end." He thanked the class officers, as did Bryan Travers; and he told them there was no need to treat their lunchtime conversation as a matter of confidence. In making that remark he knew he was merely bowing to reality, but he had the additional motive of hoping that he might actually prompt some rumor-mongering in town. "Who knows," he explained, "what kinds of information might get stirred up?"

Shrug then went to the men's room, leaving Connie, who was still feeling like the stranger on the occasion, to watch in silence as the four members of the class committee, having bid him goodbye, left together, chatting amicably. Bryan Travers, after settling the bill, stood briefly alone, meditating (Connie presumed) on whatever forty-somethings wonder about when confronted with the stark reality of the world of sixty-somethings.

When Shrug returned, Travers had left, and the two friends decided, as was their wont, to seize the moment. So they followed lunch with a drive over to Humboldt High School to allow Shrug, whose memories of the eventful evening three years earlier had been enlivened by several conversations, to show Connie what the layout of what Connie was calling "the scene of the maybe-crime" looked like. After all, summer vacation had begun and there would be few people in the building.

They parked in the school lot, and Shrug then guided his friend toward the building. "It's a larger structure now than when I was in school, but its core remains intact." They secured two visitors' passes at the main office, and Shrug led Connie through the precincts of a building he had known so well in his youth. The tour gave Connie a much clearer sense of the movements that the class committee had described. They reconnoitered the room where the dinner had been held, they visualized how the cameras had been situated, and—of particular importance—Connie noted how the one internal exit from the dining area opened onto a confluence of paths that allowed an exiting person to choose any of three directions to walk in: down hallways to the left or the right, or straight ahead to what appeared to be a refurbished atrium and entranceway. "I doubt that this arrangement would meet construction code for a new building today," he commented.

"And since," Shrug added, "this is a school building, I'm surprised it's even tolerated. I guess that shows how little you and I know about State of Ohio building codes." With that, the friends returned to their car and drove to Shrug's house, where they discuss their opinions and options.

"Well, my friend, that's quite an impressive set of classmates you have." Connie delivered this judgment as the two friends were settling down in Shrug's living room. Meanwhile, they shifted their soft drinks, snacks, and notepads around on a card table. It had become their habit to regard these moments when they would take stock of their investigations as their "War Councils," a term they adapted from the usages of the Clinton White House. The information-gathering of the past two days had given them much to consider, and experience had taught them that they were spending their time wisely when, at intervals, they paused to test each other's thinking.

"Are you talking about the class committee or the whole class?"

"Both. The committee, for its vigor at an age when, as we both well know, aches and stiffness and the inroads of lethargy and complacency are not uncommon. And the class, for the range of its biographies. Quite a crew."

"Well, I'd be willing to bet that some sort of crude Darwinian principle explains the former. The fittest are the ones who will accept leadership roles. And their number is doubtless diminishing in a class approaching its seventies. As for the class as a whole, well I really doubt that they're any odder or more diverse or—face it—more interesting than any other set of fifty people who knew each other as teens but moved after that into the full array of career opportunities that life in America offers. Since *The Origin of Species* seems to be on my mind, I'll just add that I share Darwin's astonishment at the spectrum of diversity. Only, in my case, it's *societal* diversity that astonishes."

"I've also been thinking about my own high school class," Connie explained, "and what they've done with themselves. And the shameful answer is I don't know. You're lucky in that way. You've stayed in touch with old friends. Living in Humboldt all your life, you can shift from past to present with comfort."

This observation arose from Connie's heart. The son of a naval officer, he and his parents had moved often as he was growing up. As a consequence, he supposed, he had placed a high evaluation on "feeling at home" for as long as he could remember.

"You ought to try to contact some of your old friends." Shrug meant well by the advice. "But not quite yet, of course. For right now we have work to do." He hoisted his glass in a token of comradeship.

Connie reciprocated—it was a gesture of understanding they often resorted to—and the two friends turned their minds to the topic of the hour, quickly agreeing that they had heard nothing to suggest that a crime had actually been committed. "Though that merely means, I suppose," Connie added, "that no one jumped out of the video, pointed a finger at himself, and said, 'I killed him; arrest me.'"

Ignoring his friend's foray into silliness, Shrug immediately voiced what he called "his basic concern. I'm still struck by the artificiality of the situation we're creating. I suppose much of fictional crime detection is like this. You delimit the number of suspects and then examine each of them in turn. But in this case the analogy of the British locked-door mystery is very inexact, largely because we have no reason to believe that the door to the school was anything close to locked. Especially if some intruder really wanted to break in and kill Tony. That's why I keep worrying that by restricting our scrutiny to the eight classmates who were merely unlucky enough to be out of view of the cameras when Tony Travers went to take a leak, we are probably missing the chance to identify the intruder who actually killed Tony—if, that is, he *was* actually killed. For which, as we've just agreed, we have not a shred of evidence. Isn't an investigation launched in such bleak circumstances likely to be inconsequential and a waste of time?"

"*Likely?* I don't know. But possible? That's for sure. So maybe it's time for you take a leap of faith." Connie's invoking of a Kiekegaardian motif was designed to tease his friend, a committed Christian. "After all," he continued, "we're not professional law enforcement folks. So we have the luxury, if we want, to play the closed-room game for a little bit. We've enjoyed detecting in the past. Here's a chance to have fun again."

Shrug smiled. "I like that. So I guess I didn't need much persuading. Maybe all I really wanted to do was to go through the motions of clearing my conscience. And now I've done it. So I'm happy again."

"Well," Connie chuckled. "That was easy. Makes me wonder about the quality of your conscience though."

Since Shrug himself often fretted over his conscience, he simply cleared his throat. "I suggest," he then continued, "that we proceed by dividing the eight suspects. Okay, I know I'm yielding to Cole's terminology, but it's the easiest one, by dividing the eight suspects between us. You take responsibility for contacting four. I'll take the other four. What do you think?"

"I think I've got a better idea. You know these people; I don't. They'll talk more openly to you than to me. Or even if they don't, you'll have lots of memories and contextual information through which to interpret and maybe challenge what they say. I don't. It would be silly to put me on an assignment that you're much better qualified for. So why don't you tackle all eight of them—which I guess means interview them—while I'll start seeing what might be gleaned from our documentary evidence."

"You're referring to the boxes of Tony's correspondence?"

"Sure. If 'Less' and 'Chucklehead Clancy' are ever to be identified, that's the place to start. Also, if Tony had any enemies—and we know, even apart from the possible circumstances of his death, that he must have—the memorabilia boxes are the likeliest places to get leads about their identities. But I also think the high school yearbook of the class of 1953 could be helpful. Not only because it will reveal your class in its days of youthful innocence but also because, if your class was like mine, the remarks that friends wrote to one another might suggest relationships we've heard nothing of. I know Bryan has his dad's yearbook; I'm sure he'd lend it to us. And if it's all right with you, I could look through *your* copy too. Who knows where hints might lie."

"A brilliant idea, my friend. You've been thinking this problem through."

"I do my best." Mock humility adorned Connie's face. "And I can do even more while you're giving the third degree to the suspects. I'll check out the newspaper account of Tony's death, to see if something unexpected gets mentioned. I'll check with Dr. Lydia Trench, to see if she'll talk about her late patient. I'll visit Axel Berlin, just in case Bryan didn't put the right questions to Tony's lawyer. I'll tell George Fielding what we're up to, and maybe, if we're lucky, he'll share whatever information his office might have about the death. I'll stop by the county records office to see what Tony's death certificate says. And of course, I think we should invite Abe to help us in Internet-searching about our suspects. I think he'd be delighted to work his magic again." "Abe" was Abe Steinberg, archivist at the county library and, by virtue of an unlikely background in spycraft, an adept at the art of pulling useful arcana from the Web. His assistance had proved invaluable in past investigations.

Shrug promptly assented to the plan. He relished the prospect of talking with his classmates, some of whom had once been good friends of his; and he was already testing out conversational ploys in his mind that might unlock the secrets held by these various interlocutors. "I've discovered my flair for subterfuge in my old age," he chuckled to Connie, "and so I approve wholeheartedly of your wise division of labor. Adam Smith would be pleased." (If Connie's eighteenth-century hero was David Hume, Shrug's was Hume's friend and fellow Scot, the great political economist.) "And since the crazy Grunhagens, the dislikable Fritz Kramer, and the erratic Trish Ridgway all live in town, I may be able to get my interviews going even before my short hospital break. In the case of the others, I'll probably have to use the phone. But I'll write them first. We might well decide that we want to take a failure to reply as a sign of something to hide." At that point, hearing the excitement in his voice, he laughed. "Isn't it fun to play detective again!"

The remark about the hospital led Connie to inquire about Shrug's upcoming surgery. "I'll just be in overnight—two nights actually, since I go in tomorrow evening—and Marilyn will come to stay with me for a few days until I'm mobile again." Shrug knew that Connie would be pleased to hear that his daughter would be in town for a few days. "I'll have lots of time to give thought to our investigation. Maybe some heavy and concentrated thinking will pay off. What about your Kant conference?"

Connie told how he would be driving to Ann Arbor the next morning, returning late on Thursday. "It's a long trip, but it will be fun to see some of the few remaining Kant-hands again—we're a dwindling tribe, you know—and besides, I've been asked to comment on one of the papers." He took a long draught of his Coke. "Have you noticed," he began again, indicating by his tone that he was changing the subject, "that even as we talk about playing games, we're getting more professional and confident with this detective business? In the past we've always been slow and self-conscious about calling our enterprises 'investigations.' But not with this one. And this time, for the first time, and thanks to you, we've actually set down rules for compensation, at least for travel. If we don't watch out, pretty soon the Second-Best Club is going to have to get itself licensed." That reference warranted another raising of the glasses, for the two friends had long used the term self-referentially in joshing recognition of Speaker's status in Cobb's shadow and of Haydn's in Mozart's.

"What do you think of our eight suspects?" Shrug finally asked the question that both men had hitherto avoided. "We heard quite a bit about them yesterday and today. Do any loom large for you?"

Connie replied indirectly. "I don't think any of the so-called 'possible motives'—gossip, by and large—that came up at noon today is likely to be relevant. So what if Sonya Klepper had a crush on Tony almost half a century ago! That strikes me as harmless. I'd even say, so what if Trish Ridgway resented Tony's winning of the silly class award! I know, I know. She rushed into the dining room saying she'd found the body. Very dramatic. And so it's just possible to imagine her *creating* the body she'd found. But that scenario doesn't ring true. Her life story says she's a constructive person. She releases her emotions through rants, not violence. And for that reason, if she had murder in mind, she'd take aim at the people who *chose* Tony, not the recipient himself."

"I don't think you're giving enough attention to that very heavy fact that she's the one who actually found the body." Shrug spoke with unexpected seriousness. "We know she's volatile, which undercuts your implication that she would be a calculating killer. And what better way to muddy up an awkward situation—like, say, having suddenly killed someone—than to come in screaming about what you've just discovered."

"But that doesn't make sense," Connie rejoined. "If the crime was premeditated, like we think it probably was, then her volatility (as you put it) is irrelevant."

"Maybe so. But if it's my turn to provide impressions of the suspects, I have to start by saying that I don't place Trish among the 'improbables.'" He paused, thinking over what he'd just said. "Yes, that's it. I've clumped our eight suspects into two categories—the 'improbables' and the . . . well . . . the 'slightly more probables.'"

"Interesting classification," Connie remarked. "As if everyone falls into nine and nine-and-a-half on a scale of one-to-ten. But I'm listening. You are, after all, the only person who attended the reunion whose views I still know nothing of."

"Well," Shrug continued, feeling the prick of Connie's remark, "my improbables are Sonya Klepper, Fritz Kramer," (Connie stirred at that surprising inclusion), "Amanda Everson, and Denny Culbertson. And I'll tell you why."

Connie noted that Shrug was not so much relating his memories of the reunion evening as fusing memory and impression into tentative assessments. But he chose not to interrupt.

"I know we can't prejudge these things. Our first impressions have often enough been wrong in the past, and we don't have much to base first impressions on right now anyway. But there you have it. If I were a betting man, I'd put my money on one of the other four."

"But did you talk to your four 'improbables'? Do you remember anything about conversations with them?"

Shrug hesitated, and then decided to keep his replies complicated. "Yes, I recall talking to them, or at least to Sonya, Amanda, and Denny. But you know how memories are. I should have jotted mine down at the start, for now they're polluted by hearing the recollections of my classmates. And that's confusing to me, for in some ways, with some of the suspects, I think the sketches we've heard aren't quite congruent with mine."

"They're not always congruent with each other," Connie remarked, beginning to see some humor in the situation, "so please go ahead. This is getting interesting."

"Okay. Let's take Sonya and Amanda. Speaking today, I would have to say that Sonya did strike me as unusually quiet that evening, distracted maybe, and Amanda did strike me as quite attractive for someone her age, though rather vacuous in conversation. So to that extent I agree with the others. But I recall additional, free-floating snippets. Sonya, for example, enjoys crossword puzzles. I wonder if that's important. Amanda enjoys hiking. That might be important. None of this is startling, I know. None of it is ominous. So I don't think I'm much help. But at least my portraits have their novelties." He hesitated, then added a coda: "yet my impressions probably don't count for much. And in any case, these two women don't strike me as murderers."

"I never knew you'd be such a tentative, insipid, self-doubting witness. And your conclusion is unrelated to your rather sparse evidence." Connie offered the remark through slightly narrowed eyes, half-jokingly but half-puzzled. "Did you deliberately avoid talking to Freddy?"

"In a way, yes, I suppose I did. I can't reconstruct my state of mind as the evening began. But time was limited, I didn't much care for him, and so he would not have loomed large on any list of people I'd hope to see. As for the rest, I guess his path and mine never crossed, at least as far as I remember."

"Then why include him with the 'improbables'? Everyone seems to agree he's dislikable."

"That's just it. He's so caught up with himself that I find it hard to see why he'd want to kill someone."

When Shrug stopped, Connie could only remark, "And I, my friend, find it hard to see what your assessments are grounded in. What about Denny?"

"Here's where—and I want to choose my words carefully— here's where, though I can see what my classmates were talking about, here's where my judgment is most at variance from theirs." Shrug proceeded slowly, with Connie giving him the time he needed. Shrug's difficulty, it emerged, was that, as a practicing Christian, he didn't like the readiness of the wider culture to cast enthusiastic believers as cultural freaks; but as a member of that wider culture, he knew full well that a religious vocation attracted the self-glorifying and the crooked as well as the devout.

"Denny spoke to me of his uncertainty about how to represent his convictions in meetings like our reunion. He disliked the possibility that he was coming across as a nut, but he feared the reproach of his conscience, should he pass up an opportunity to testify to the Truth. Me—I almost always wimp out. But Denny doesn't. And the fact that he could be self-reflective on the subject makes him seem to me—I know this is another nonsequitur—makes him seem an unlikely murderer. Besides, he's got this theory that you can read a person's character by knowing how he flosses his teeth."

Connie didn't know how to respond to that remarkable comment, and so he simply looked sympathetically quizzical.

"I realize it sounds odd," Shrug continued, "but that's his view. And I suppose it could have merit. After all, dental hygiene must say *something* about a person."

"Just let me know if he gets his research findings published. That's when I'll try to catch up on the theory." Connie's tone was less sarcastic than bewildered. Despite three decades of friendship, he had never been as privy as at this moment to the processes of Shrug's intuitive methods. But he couldn't suppress a last word ("Flossing?") as he sought to push past yet another nonsequitur and regather his aplomb.

"How about the other four classmates, the ones who are more suspect in your eyes? The 'slightly more probables' was, I think, your graceful term."

Shrug smiled. "I've already explained my feelings about Trish Ridgway. And I need to emphasize again that this whole exercise isn't as easy as I'd thought it would be. In many cases I like these people. In every case I know them."

"Spoken like a human being. Now put your detective hat on. Your intuitions have always been useful to our work. They're more reliable than mine. And so I'm listening to your intuitions, and respecting them, even as the philosopher in me despairs of the disconnect between your reasoning and your gut feelings."

"But my intuitions aren't always right." Shrug's apologetic reply was subdued.

Rather than agreeing or disagreeing with his friend, whose state of mind continued to puzzle him, Connie decided to try to move the conversation along by providing Shrug with a target. "The Grunhagen twins seem a puzzling duo," he opined. "In fact, Cheryl Bollinger's remark sticks in my mind. They really do present the potential of a classic murder-mystery situation." But as he set the stage, Connie began shifting into the abstracted tone he adopted when he was talking more to himself than to anyone else. "Bonny or Bunny might have killed Tony, knowing that in a pinch, her sister could contrive an alibi. In fact, if murder there was, has *already* provided a potential alibi for her. Now *why* one or the other might have done it is a separate question. Maybe we'll find a motive. But for the moment, all we've got is the prospect of a delicious conundrum. I hope we can clear them early on. Do you have any relevant memories?"

"The two sisters strike me as slightly artificial, like delicate plants that can survive only in a well-tended greenhouse, protected from the elements. And I'm not just thinking of their apposite fondness for gardening when I say that. They're . . .? What's the word I want?"

Connie suggested "fragile," but Shrug shook his head.

"No," he finally said, finally pulling up the term he'd been groping for, "they're symbiotic—they're frighteningly symbiotic."

"You make it sound like a disease. Care to explain?"

Shrug told of sisters who shared such a degree of interdependence that, in his sketch at least, it sat somewhere between the unusual and the pathological. "And yet I like them. So my gut tells me they're good people. But they're certainly very unusual. And so quite unlike bland Sonya and bland Amanda."

Connie said nothing, expecting his friend to continue his analysis of the Grunhagens. But Shrug shifted directions. "And then there's Eddie Moratino. He merits attention, and for two reasons."

"Oh?" Connie could think of nothing else to say.

"Well, first, he revealed so little about his life. Everyone describes him as adroitly taciturn about his private life, and it was my experience with him too. And I pushed a bit, because I knew his life had been more exciting than mine, and I wanted to hear about it and about how it had affected him. But he was very deft at fending off queries. He's a man who is determined to keep many secrets. Even his brief bio in the reunion's booklet of biographies is startlingly non-revealing. He's quite practiced at keeping the nosey at bay."

"Sounds like a healthy attitude to me. I hope your second reason has more weight."

"Well. . . ." Shrug was hesitant, suddenly aware that his case for being suspicious about Eddie Moratino was considerably less than substantial. "I think it's interesting that his work has taken him to a part of the world that Tony Travers knew. Even about *this* part of his life—his work—he wouldn't say much. I guess I can understand a person trying to cloak his psyche. But his career? That's odd."

"Maybe he's just shy," Connie suggested. "You're being uncharacteristically judgmental today, even for you."

"You asked for my views. I'm offering them: unvarnished, untidied, gloriously inconsistent. And I guess there's a third reason too. After all, consider what that *work* of his is. Trading in ancient artifacts. That sounds like the kind of work that, if movies can be trusted, might get one in contact with the seamier elements in the commercial world. What do you think?"

"That you've seen *Raiders of the Lost Ark* once too often. And what are you getting at? That Eddie and Tony's paths crossed in some sinful oriental city and that they came away with a dreadful secret? Or that one betrayed the other? Or. . . ?" Connie stopped with a smile.

"It's not impossible," Shrug mumbled. "And remember, one or the other might have been a government agent."

"Now you've been reading entirely too much Graham Greene." Connie was laughing. "Eddie Moratino sounds like a perfectly nice guy to me."

"You may mean John Le Carre. But no matter. I yield to your sounder sense of human character." Shrug paused and fingered his drinking glass. "Now for an interesting question. Do you think we should regard Bryan Travers as a suspect? After all, he inherited Tony's estate. And we only have his word that he didn't know the size of it."

Connie hesitated before replying. "Like Eddie, he doesn't look suspicious to me. And we certainly have an obligation to keep him vaguely informed, since he's paying the bills and might still be able to come up with the names of some local people with whom Tony became friends after returning to Humboldt in 1994. Still, just as a general rule, I think we ought not make him privy to our reflections. For you're right about one thing for sure: if the question is *cui bono*, so far there's only one answer. He's the one who had something to gain. So let's keep him in mind."

"What we're looking for," Shrug suddenly interjected, "is a German augmented sixth chord."

"Oh?" Connie was genuinely puzzled.

"You'll recall," Shrug explained, "that in music theory there's a chord called a dominant seventh. It leads, with a naturalness that seems almost inevitable, to a nice tonic chord. That comfortable progression is very common." He walked to the piano to play a chord of G-B-D-F followed by a chord of C-G-C-E to demonstrate the point. Meanwhile, Connie settled back indulgently, giving Shrug the same sort of tolerant attention that Shrug afforded to him when he started talking about baseball. Besides, he had already heard Shrug talk about the dominant-tonic sequence. He sensed he now had a chance to widen his knowledge of music theory. "As we gather facts about our suspects," Shrug continued, "in just about every case they will lead to the conclusion of innocence. So innocence equals a tonic chord." He played the sequence again.

"And the German whatever?"

"There's also a chord called the German augmented sixth. It is created by exactly the same keys on the keyboard as the dominant chord, but it is used in very different circumstances—the fact that it's spelled differently proves that—and leads . . ." Connie's puzzlement was genuine. "Wait? Chords are *spelled*?"

"Yes, you twit. And don't interrupt me when I'm on a roll and expounding." He smiled broadly. "And leads not to a tonic in C major, but to a two-chord sequence that ends in the very different key of B major." Connie was lost. "In the context of a piece of music," Shrug continued, "the musical purpose of either of the two identical *keyboard* chords—dominant seventh and German augmented sixth—is very unlikely to be missed. And, or maybe I should say *though,* since the dominant-tonic sequence is much the more common of the two, we expect the G-B-D-F chord to be followed by the C-G-C-E chord." He promptly repeated the sequence at the keyboard. "Very mellifluous. That's a typical dominant-tonic progression in the key of C. However, if I hit the same dominant seventh notes" (he did so) "and then progress so" (he played an F#-B-D#-F#) "we've moved into the different tonal universe of B major." He quickly demonstrated this fact by playing an F#-A#-C#-E chord followed by the patently tonic B-F#-B-D# chord. *"Voila!* It's not the sequence we expect. But it doesn't sound wrong. It just surprises. Ain't that a miracle?"

"And your point, maestro?"

"For one of our suspects, the facts we gather may turn out to constitute a German augmented sixth rather than a dominant seventh. The facts will resolve naturally enough, yes, but still unexpectedly, and point a finger of guilt."

"I'll take your word for it," said a bemused Connie.

Then Shrug got serious. "I wish we'd inquired more about Tony Travers himself when we talked to the committee. We got so caught up in their views of the suspects that we neglected the guy who died."

"You're right," Connie observed. "Though I heard enough to give me the impression that the class committee didn't feel warmly toward him. Respectful, for sure. But unwilling to welcome him as a friend." He paused, reconsidering his words. "Or maybe what I mean is that none of them was himself a friend of Tony's. Is that odd?"

"I wasn't close to him either," Shrug replied. "He was a nice enough guy. We didn't shun him. But he was older and had different interests. And he'd actually been in war. So I don't think it's odd that the others had little to say. He was simply a friendly stranger in our midst." Shrug then changed the subject. "Will you try to uncover anything about Tony Travers' pre-Humboldt life?"

"Fortunately," Connie replied, "that's probably the one area in this matter that we don't have to worry about. If he was killed by a member of the class of 1953, the motive has to lie either in some misadventure that occurred in high school or, likelier, in something that happened subsequently. Besides, that pre-Humboldt life is a life spent out of the U.S.A., largely beyond our capacity to recover. The principle of parsimony tells us to place our energies elsewhere."

"And what does the principle of parsimony tell us about chess this evening?" Shrug's remark brought the War Council to a quick close, for Tuesday evening meant Chess Club, and while neither Connie nor Shrug was likely to give any grandmaster a sleepless night, they both took their struggles across the sixty-four-square board very seriously. Which meant that they needed to repair to their respective kitchens if they were to get their evening suppers under their belts in a timely manner. And so, with lots of investigative procedures agreed to but few answers secured, the friends dropped the subject of Tony Travers to prepare themselves for entering the world of Capablanca and Alekhine.

3

Wednesday, June 6, 2001

A pious man, Shrug almost invariably ended his Wednesdays by attending the midweek service of Evening Prayer at Trinity Episcopal Church. As he rose on this particular Wednesday, he immediately recalled that once today's evening service was over, he planned to enter Trinity Hospital in preparation for his hernial surgery scheduled for early the next morning. In ordinary circumstances Shrug did not pray for himself. But he believed in a loving God, a caring Father who knew a petitioner's self-concerns, and he was therefore confident that when those worries were irrepressible (as he was now finding his own to be), there would be no point in trying to pretend that his Father in heaven did not know that he was fretting about his own problems.

Still, he had for days been determined not to allow brooding to induce paralysis, and so even as he prepared his bacon-and-eggs breakfast on June 6, with CNN's business summary in the background, it was gratitude rather than anxiety that defined his mood— gratitude over his success the previous evening, not at chess to be sure, but at least in lining up immediate interviews with several local classmates. He wasn't surprised at this readiness to talk, for he had learned over the past year that when a local investigation was afoot, curiosity might drive people—occasionally even guilty ones—to make themselves available to the interrogator's probings. And so a full schedule lay before him: chats with Trish Ridgway, the sisters Grunhagen, and Fritz Kramer, followed by dinner with his daughter Marilyn, attendance at Evening Prayer, and entry into the hospital. He offered his Father thanks that activity, duty, and love afforded such strong reefs against the waves of undue self-solicitude.

Shrug had spent his professional life as an investment counselor. In the process he had developed a robust equity portfolio which, to the astonishment of friends, he had unexpectedly liquidated barely two years earlier. The bulk of the wealth had gone into trusts for his grandchildren. With much of the rest he had bought life annuities for himself. And he retained a small "stock pot" as a hobby he could "play with." His explanation for the conversion—puzzling at the time but looking increasingly percipient in light of the recent volatility in the market—had been that he wanted to maximize security. His needs as a single man past sixty-five were relatively modest, as the only indulgences he allowed himself were frequent attendance at concerts and occasional trips to Europe. Besides, shedding stocks made life just plain easier. Shrug had always enjoyed his work, which allowed him to provide authentic assistance to many financially unlettered people while affording him professional reasons for studying the multifold intricacies and marvels of the Market. Most of his friends found this cerebral interest unfathomable. But Shrug didn't care. He had long since concluded that he would live his life by his own lights; no alternative principle seemed sustainable in the long run.

At 9:30 A.M., armed with his notepad and dressed informally for the forecast warmth of a June day, he pushed the bell at Trish Ridgway's front door. He tried to recognize the tune that chimed his arrival, but before he could pull "Bless This House" up from his memory banks, an overly made-up Ridgway welcomed him, and, while guiding him to the back porch, bombarded him with cheerful and inane chatter. "So good to see you again, Shrug. You've aged so well." (Shrug knew that remark to be a lie.) "And you seem to have gotten along so well after your divorce. But I still sometimes wonder if you get lonely. I think a man needs a woman's presence, don't you?" *Ah*, he thought, *the inevitable subject—of-*

ten innocent but sometimes the advance tip of a complicated agenda. "How is that wonderful daughter of yours—Margaret, isn't it? Or Melinda? She grew up so well, didn't she? Oh, I wish I were better with names." Even under the miasma of a thick perfume, Shrug detected the unmistakable odor of mouthwash covering up alcohol. *It's only 9:30 in the morning.* He was astonished.

Ridgway offered him a seat at a glass-covered porch table and pulled up her own chair directly opposite him, where they could look each other in the eye. Ridgway was wearing an aquamarine blouse that contrasted attractively, Shrug thought, with her shoulder-length brown hair. He also thought that it could only be because she was curious about the rumors of possible foul play at the class gathering that had swept through Humboldt the previous evening that she then promptly abandoned small talk and asked about the business at hand. Shrug explained that he and Connie had agreed to look into the cause of the death of Tony Travers at the forty-fifth reunion, on the off-chance that it hadn't been an accident. He watched her carefully when he spoke Tony's name, but it provoked no alteration of facial expression that he could detect. He explained that he was turning to her first because she had discovered the body—a convenient half-truth. He did not mention that he had heard tales of her resentment over the choice of Tony as recipient of the class award eight years earlier.

"It was a terrible evening," she began. "I'll never forget it." *A banality*, Shrug thought, *that has the advantage of almost surely being true.* Her lips twitched as she told her story. How she had left the dining room because she was feeling nauseated "from overeating." How she had vomited before reaching the ladies' room. How she had felt anger and shame over soiling her outfit. How she had hoped to find fresh air, away from her classmates. How that search for an exit door had led her to a dim and empty stairwell where she had found Tony's body. "I bent over him, and I was pretty sure he was dead. His eyes were open—like in the movies—and his head was lying at a strange angle on his shoulders. Like a cattywampus picture."

"What did you do then?"

"I wanted to be resourceful, but I think I just screamed. No one heard me, of course, so I had no choice but to run back upstairs to the dining area. They'd been in the process of singing, and the party was getting rowdier. And I still felt pretty shitty. But I ran in and broke it up with my screaming. Yes, that was my contribution to the evening. I broke up the party." She let out a giggle.

Since Shrug now had Ridgway's "alibi"—one of his private goals for the conversation—he wanted to get her to talk about other classmates, and especially the suspects. But he felt he couldn't switch gears too abruptly, and so he let her ramble on about the experience of discovering the body. It was obviously a tale she was delighted to relate. It was when she contrasted this experience with the happiness of the earlier part of the reunion evening that Shrug felt he had his opening.

"What do you remember about our forty-fifth bash? What memories stick out in your mind?"

Ridgway gave him a briefly puzzled look but then began telling of an evening of drinking, conversation, and flirting. None of the persons who had been assigned to her table were of interest to Shrug, but before asking about the reception that preceded the dinner he endured a tale of how Benjie Kostelanitz had groped Ridgway's leg even with his wife seated just to his right. That prompt brought back a new catalogue of memories, with the drinking antics of Cynthia Kleist and Tommy Blisting leading the list. (Shrug recalled that Blisting had recently died of cancer.)

After mentioning several other irrelevant classmates, Ridgway brought up Eddie Moratino. "He was *sooo* nice. And he's rich, too. He's met a lot of famous people over the years and owns several expensive cars. I think he's gay, but boy, I wouldn't mind traveling around the world with him. You know what I mean?" Ten minutes and three classmates later, she recalled the Grunhagens. "They're even harder to tell apart now than they were in high school. It's almost as if they'd gotten some cosmetic surgeon to match up their facial lines, wrinkle on wrinkle. But green was a poor color choice for their dresses that night. They're just weird; there's no other word for it. Weird. I can see why neither of them ever got married."

By natural step her memory turned next to Amanda Everson. "Now there's a well-maintained chick! She said that when she'd been an agent for romance novel writers she'd learned the importance of looking good, but to tell the truth—and I'm sure you'll remember—she was known for dressing well, even in high school."

Ridgway's serendipitous interest in fashion led her quickly to another suspect. "By way of total contrast, there was Denny Culbertson! Do you remember his outfit that evening?" Without waiting for an answer, Ridgway raced into an extended description of Culbertson's attire. "The bow tie was red! Can you believe it? And he had a red handkerchief crisply folded in the breast pocket of his blue shirt! Of course, he was deep into Jesus, and I suppose that means he was slightly off his rocker. He kept talking about finding the truth. Did you know he'd found Jesus on a trip to the Holy Land? He's just plain loony. See what I'm saying?"

As 10:30 approached and Ridgway began to slow down, Shrug realized that if he was to get comments on all the suspects he would need to become more directive. "Did you see Fritz Kramer that evening?"

"So it's him you're really interested in, eh? I can't say I'm surprised. He's one mean hombre. I stayed away from little Freddy, now little Fritzy. I've never felt comfortable in his presence."

Shrug didn't press the point. "How about Sonja Klepper?"

"Oh, she was born to be a grandmother." Ridgway said nothing more, and Shrug concluded that the remark had not been meant as a compliment.

"How about Tony himself?" Shrug decided he couldn't dodge the question. "I seem to remember your sounding off at our fortieth about him winning the award that evening." He stared hard across the table at his hostess.

"Why Mr. Speaker," she drawled, "how ungracious of you to mention a lady's embarrassing moments." A startled Shrug detected no sense of self-referential irony in the imitation of a southern belle. "Yes, I was rather unguarded in my remarks on that occasion. But I quickly got over it, and apologized to poor Tony."

So, thought Shrug quickly, *that's going to be her story. Okay, I'll let it ride for the moment.* He began making his I'm-about-to-depart remarks. But as he rose just a few minutes later, Ridgway grabbed his left hand in her right and said she hoped he'd come by again. Then when he thanked her for her help, she replied that after divorcing John Wilson, she had decided to resume her maiden name. As he made his way to the door, she said, "don't be a stranger." Most startling of all, as he turned to say good-bye on the front porch, she blew him a kiss. Shrug felt a powerful wave of relief as he closed his car door and began his escape down Ridgway's driveway.

Bonny and Bunny Grunhagen lived in a large old house on a hillock just north of Humboldt. Shrug arrived at their home right at the appointed time of 11:00. He couldn't help noticing that the landscaping was imaginative, colorful, and eye-catching. A lush, emerald green lawn. Large, showy blanket flowers, maroon in the center, with rays of red petals tipped with gold. Brilliant white coneflower blooms. Clusters of the cheery yellow of Coreopsis. Buttercups, cyclamens, and jonquils. Pruned yews outlining the base of the house. *Their landscaping*, he thought, *is a work of art.*

After spending a moment to admire the colorful patterns, he rang the bell. Almost immediately the door flew open, revealing two women, gray-haired and clad largely in blue, who might easily have been one person standing next to a mirror. Each had short, identical hair stylings, each sported yellow-and-red pendant earrings, and each wore yellow-framed glasses perched on identical pug noses.

"Please, Shrug . . .," said Bonny.

". . . come in," said Bunny.

Even with almost half a century of intermittent familiarity with the ways of the Grunhagen sisters, Shrug found the sight of them in their full duplicative glory a bit unsettling. Over the years he had learned who was who, though so subtle were the cues that allowed him to do this that he would have had difficulty specifically identifying them. Bonny took his left arm, Bunny his right. And as they guided him into their entertainment center, replete with an enormous television screen, a wide array of electronic equipment, and shelves of books about flowers, they continued their linguistic table tennis.

"This is . . ."

". . . so exciting."

"Tell us why . . ."

". . . you think Tony was killed."

Shrug could not help being disconcerted by this stereophonic conversation. But he reminded himself of his task—eliciting information—and, thus steeled, pled ignorance as to whether Tony had been murdered and then provided the sisters with just enough background to make his interest in the death of a classmate seem warranted.

"How chilling it must have been . . ."

". . . to receive a death threat."

They simultaneously turned to look at each other and trembled.

Shrug did not know whether they were mocking him. All he could do, he concluded, was persevere. And since he had not been happy with the time-wasting results of his laissez-faire approach with Trish Ridgway, he decided to be more heavy-handed in querying the Grunhagens.

"I'm interested in what you remember about the reunion evening and in particular about Tony Travers. But even before that, I'd like to ask you about some specific classmates." He tried to read their thoughts. "If you don't mind." He worried that he would let their impassive expressions overawe him.

"Oh, we'll be happy . . ."

". . . to share our memories."

"It's in a good cause . . ."

". . . isn't it?" They smiled benignly.

On Tony, however, they were uninformative; neither knew him well, and they didn't recall talking to him that evening. On Fritz Kramer, they had much more to say, with most of their memories reinforcing the rapidly emerging image of Kramer as a dislikable misanthrope.

"He's a sexy, sullen bastard," Bonny volunteered. (Shrug thought the adjective "sexy" a bit surprising.)

"Did you know," Bunny added, "he took a course in German history at OSU Mansfield and . . ."

". . . that's when," Bonny said, without missing a beat, "he began to insist on being called 'Fritz'."

Shrug asked how they knew this, and they replied that Kramer had told them.

"When?" Connie asked.

"Oh," said Bunny, "we occasionally . . ."

". . . see him in this small town."

They fell silent, perhaps defensively so, and Shrug decided not to pursue the Kramer matter at the moment and asked instead about Amanda Everson. They recalled her as being too loquacious, with a slightly artificial ("uppity" was Bunny's word) accent, but they shared the general conclusion that she still dressed smashingly.

As for Denny Culbertson, he dressed, in Bonny's phrase, "idiosyncratically." The term reduced both sisters to convulsive giggling.

"We didn't talk with him very much," Bonny explained, after catching her breath, "for . . ."

". . . we keep away from Jesus freaks." Bunny's term again set the sisters to giggling.

When Shrug introduced the subject of Eddie Moratino, the sisters' tone became more respectful. They had much to say, and were particularly impressed that he was knowledgeable about flowers and had met both the Dalai Lama and Nelson Mandela.

"And he has had some hair-raising . . ."

". . . medical adventures in his life."

The basis for that unexpected assertion was a story he had related during a conversation with the two sisters and Amanda Everson. When Everson told of injuring her leg while hiking in the mountains, fifty miles from a hospital in either direction and unable to secure help, Moratino had listened solicitously but then told of coming down with stomach pains deep in the field in Kenya and ultimately submitting to a rather *ad hoc* appendectomy, with liquor as his only anesthesia.

"That shut . . ."

". . . Amanda up."

The Grunhagens said they couldn't recall talking with Sonya Klepper. *She seems to have been so bland*, Shrug thought, *that nobody recalls much about her. I wonder if that's significant.* And as for Trish Ridgway, they bluntly declared that after her misbehavior at the fortieth reunion, they had made a point of staying away from her. But they then spoke, not without sympathy, of her difficulties with alcohol, of the meanness of her former husband, and of her skill as a bass clarinetist. It turned out that they rather liked her after all.

The conversation about Ridgway left Shrug with the dilemma of how to pose the important "alibi" question. Ridgway had solved it for him by volunteering her story of the vomiting. But the Grunhagens had said nothing about their absence from the room during the window of opportunity. Since Shrug's inclination, when he couldn't think of an indirect way of phrasing questions, was to plow ahead, he chose to jump in when the Grunhagens ran out of reflections about Ridgway. "You two," he said, "left the room shortly before Tony's body was discovered. Do you recall why?"

Bonny and Bunny looked at each other in disbelief and started giggling again.

"You mean . . ."

". . . we're suspects?"

Shrug was delighted that they took the question as an occasion for amusement rather than as an insult.

"I don't remember . . ."

". . . and neither do I, but . . ."

". . . if I had to bet, I'd say . . ."

". . . we were doing what little girls need to do,"

". . . for it sure beats hanging out at the beach." And now came gales of laughter.

Shrug could no longer contain his curiosity. "It's extraordinary how you two seem to participate in the same consciousness. It means that an outsider like me has trouble tracking where your thoughts are coming from or going. Are most identical twins like that?"

Somewhat to Shrug's surprise, they were pleased to talk about their shared life. No, they said, it was rare for identical twins to be as cognitively connected as they were. Rare, but not unheard of. Even as children they had noticed that they often thought alike. The same sense of humor. The same taste in clothes and music. The same approach to problem-solving. The same skepticism about humankind. The same casual, live-and-let-live attitude toward life. By the age of eight they were each other's best friend. And that bond had made the later decision to live together very easy. Living together in turn had intensified their habit of finishing each other's sentences. It had become, they confessed, a kind of game with them; they were practiced at it—it had become second nature— and they knew it rattled those they were talking to.

"We know too . . ."

". . . that people think . . ."

". . . we're lesbian."

They seized each other's hands and laughed.

"But we're not."

"Oh no, we're lustily hetero."

"We just like . . ."

". . . to shake men up."

The whole conversation had certainly left Shrug feeling somewhat shaken up, and since it was a bit past noon and he needed to leave anyway, he chose this moment to thank them for their readiness to help out and for the good spirits in which they'd taken his questions. They wished him well and guided him back to the front door just as they'd earlier steered him to his chair. As he left the front porch he briefly enjoyed another view of their colorful yard. But as he subsequently walked toward his car he could hear the resumption of laughter inside. *The strange, private world of the Grunhagens is certainly a jolly place.*

Fritz Kramer's home was most definitely not a jolly place. When Shrug ran the bell at half past one, Kramer swiftly opened the door and, barely allowing Shrug to say, "Hello, Fritz," declared, "Don't think I had anything to do with Tony Travers' death. Hell no. I admired him. He had the balls to join an army and fight in a war. That's more than can be said for almost of the cowards in our class. And that includes you, too, Shrug. No, I admired Tony. He acted on sound Nietzchean principles. He showed that he had courage."

Shrug was stunned. He had not expected Kramer to be one for mincing words, but this verbal onslaught was astonishing. Though Shrug hadn't accused him of anything, he clearly had no desire to let unvoiced suspicions fester. And the rebuke was not without its sting. For although the Korean War was winding down when the class of 1953 graduated, the army had still needed men, and the draft law was still in force; and yet, so far as Shrug knew, not a single member of the class—including himself of course and Kramer—had joined the armed forces.

Ignoring the disorder of the living room Kramer led him into, Shrug replied that he wasn't accusing anyone—a remark that brought a dismissive smirk to his host's face—and had asked to talk with

Kramer only because he was a class member who was resident in Humboldt and who had attended the reunion. Though, Shrug added somewhat awkwardly, he hoped Kramer wouldn't mind saying where he'd been during his absence from the dining room. With that remark, Shrug took a seat on a captain's chair.

Kramer laughed as he also sat down. "I'm not obliged to tell you anything. Besides, how the hell should I know? I can't recall what I did every minute of that evening. Maybe I needed to take a piss. Maybe I just wanted some fresh air. Maybe I was so fed up with the pablum that passes for thought among our classmates that I felt the need to escape their babbling. Maybe all or none of the above."

Shrug was not surprised to learn that someone as unpleasant as Kramer hadn't spoken with many classmates that evening. "I was seated with Brenda Smith, Ollie Brush, Sonja Klepper, and Peter Tinker. What a hopelessly dull and unimaginative group. Chatter about grandchildren, church activities, saving the whales, helping the homeless. I know those are all things you probably think are good. But to me they're just banalities—the sludgy by-products of group-think among mediocrities. What dull people they must be if that's all they can chatter about."

Biting his tongue, Shrug asked specifically about Klepper, the only name on that list that really interested him. Kramer laughed. "She was like the rest of them. Empty-headed. End of story."

Shrug wondered to what extent Kramer was merely trying to *épater les bourgeois*—to impress. He had no doubt that Kramer held the views he expressed. But he detected as well an element of delight in Kramer's declarations. *Even in his bitterness*, Shrug thought, *he manages to squeeze some fun out of life.*

"Now as for Tony," Kramer suddenly added, "he was different. Not just because he was older but because he was made of steel, not jelly."

"Oh, you talked with him that evening?"

"No, not really. We would have talked. I wanted to but it just didn't come off." His voice fell away. Shrug noticed that the subject of Tony Travers was not only oddly close to Kramer's mind but also capable of disconcerting him.

Shrug trotted out some other names. To his mentions of Amanda Everson and Trish Ridgway, Kramer shook his head. "Don't recall speaking to them at all." Of Denny Culbertson he was contemptuous, concluding his brief character sketch by dismissing him as "a fool for accepting the slave morality of Christianity." *This guy is inebriated with Nietzsche.* (At that very moment Shrug noticed that Nietzsche was a prominent author on Kramer's bookshelves.)

Only Eddie Moratino warranted a full analysis. "You won't like this, Shrug, but I have to tell you the truth." Kramer's tone was suddenly very earnest. "Eddie is soft—the very antithesis of Tony— and an example of the kind that is unfit for long-term survival." *So now we get our Nietzsche through a Darwinian filter.* "Of course, he's into artsy things."

Shrug found himself becoming very annoyed with his host as the litany of Moratino's flaws poured out. "Did you actually talk with him?" he finally asked.

"Just a bit. A *boooring* guy."

At this point curiosity and irritation drove Shrug to pose the question that had been forcing itself into his consciousness from the inception of the conversation. "I'm sorry to be so blunt, but why do you choose to come across as so bitter and angry a person, Fritz?"

"You think I'm jaundiced, eh? Or playacting?" The tone struck Shrug as confrontational.

"No, but sour maybe . . . and more important, with dialogue that is slightly contrived."

"Well, let me tell you then." Kramer now rose, revealing a stomach larger than Shrug had been imagining and a limp that Shrug hadn't recalled from reunion days. His voice was brasher and yet quavering. "I've been a victim of what the media call 'affirmative action' but what should be called a 'help-the-unqualified program.' We can't talk honestly in this country any more. The herd mentality of the demos imposes its stultifying censorship on all original thought. That's how the Constitution got subverted." And with that acerbic introduction, Kramer told of how, when he'd been on the Charlotte police force, he had lost seniority and the perks appertaining thereto because the city council, in its wisdom, had wanted to hire more "Negroes." Kramer's voice was rising. "Shit! They were dumber than me. They didn't know the handbook and rules like I did. They didn't know the city like I did. But they got the preferred slots and I got . . . dumped. Wouldn't you be sour?"

Knowing nothing of the practices of officer selection in Charlotte, Shrug had no idea whether the complaint had any merit whatsoever. But he found it easy to believe that any law enforcement organization unfortunate enough to find itself saddled with someone as disagreeable and angry as Fritz Kramer might welcome an opportunity to shed him, even at the cost of a long-term pension obligation. Rather than express that judgment, however, he confined himself to thanking Kramer for explaining the reason for his sense of bitterness. Although he was curious whether Kramer had sought employment elsewhere after the Charlotte debacle, his distaste for the conversation led him to conquer his inquisitiveness. *If it becomes a matter of importance*, he thought, *I can ask later on*. So he rose much sooner than he'd planned for, apologized for intruding on Kramer's afternoon, and quickly made his way to the door.

"As I suspected," Kramer said sardonically as Shrug opened the door to leave, "you can't take the truth very well. So you run away. That's okay. Most people can't. Look, I'm unusual. And I know it." Then, as an apparent afterthought, he asked if Shrug planned to see the Grunhagens. When Shrug replied that he'd talked with them that very morning, Kramer smiled in mock-graciousness and said that he bet they hadn't told him that Bunny had dated Tony on a serious basis in high school. He then slammed the door. An astonished Shrug stared at its blankness.

"What a jerk," Shrug said half-aloud, after he had started his car. But he stored away the closing remark as worthy of fuller attention: if true, it raised the question of why the sisters pretended to have little interest in Tony Travers? For the moment, however, his chief sensation was weariness. He thought back on Connie's remark about the extraordinary range of life-trajectories the members of the class of 1953 had experienced. Fritz Kramer's was one of the most striking. But unlike so many other classmates, his life experiences had not nurtured maturity. Shrug understood his situation to be, at a generalized level, a sad one, inviting compassion. But he found it hard to feel much sympathy for a man immured in a self-pity that was grounded in a truculent scapegoating and a bastardized Nietzscheanism. *Allan Clark would urge charity upon me, but even he might find it hard to think good thoughts about Fritz Kramer.* On that reflection, he returned home to finish preparations for Marilyn's visit.

As Shrug settled into his old-fashioned armchair later that Wednesday afternoon, waiting for Marilyn's arrival, he had his first opportunity to mull over his conversations of the day. Even at this early moment in the investigation, he found his brain oddly bifurcated. One part of it continued to tell him that the very presupposition of the inquiry—namely, that the "murderer" had to be a classmate—was ungrounded. It seemed implausible on its face, and smacked too much of contrivance to satisfy his sense of what he could only call "the sloppy esthetics of crime." But the other part of his brain pushed him ahead, as the sheer joy of trying to untangle a human mystery began again to reveal its astonishing force. Besides, what choice did they really have? *It's not* logic *that's making a "cozy" of this mystery,* he thought, *it's necessity—the need to envision a strategy of investigation that was feasible.*

The four "easy" contacts had now been made. The remaining four suspects lived further afield—and in the case of Amanda Everson, in New Zealand. Shrug hoped he would be able to talk with them by phone, but he had decided as soon as he had been designated the contact-person that he would approach them first by letter, and in that way set them up for a call.

He pulled a pad from his desk drawer, jotted down a few organizational notes, and then moved to his computer to compose the core of his letter. Although each epistle would be carefully individualized, allowing him to give space to discussions of experiences or interests he shared with each recipient, the heart of each would be identical. Striving for a balance between informality and clarity, and using the passive voice whenever he wanted to leave agency obscure, he quickly pasted together his crucial paragraphs of explanation and inquiry.

> I'm writing you on a matter of business, however. You'll recall that our reunion festivities of three years ago came to an abrupt end when it was discovered that our classmate Tony Travers had died at the base of the northeast tower stairwell. At the time, we all concluded that the death had been the result of a tragic accident. But recently evidence has come to light that suggests that the death might—and I do emphasize might—have been a homicide. I know that sounds awful, but it's true.
>
> At the request of Tony's son Bryan, the class committee has agreed that Connie Haydn and I should look into the events of that night. You may already know Connie. If not, he is a retired Philosophy Professor from the college. He and I have had some success over the past year in making sense of several old crimes. I'm writing letters to a number of classmates who were out of the dining room at about the time Tony left the dinner for the last time, in the hopes that you might remember something about the evening.
>
> So here goes. I hope you'll be willing to answer three general questions in your letter of reply. 1) Do you recall anything about the reception and dinner on the evening of June 4, 1998, that might now, in light of the

possibility of foul play, seem odd? 2) Do you recall
anything about Tony from that evening? Did you, for
example, talk to him? 3) Can you recall what took you
out of the dining room while the class was singing, and
whether, while you were out, you saw anything peculiar? Finally, I'd like to give you a phone call to explain
and discuss all this, and so I'd be grateful if you'd send
me your phone number, in case it's changed since the
reunion book appeared.

Shrug knew from a lifetime of letter-writing that all correspondence could be improved. But he also knew something of the law
of diminishing returns. And so, muttering to himself with a chuckle
about the words he had been tempted to use—"a failure to reply to
this missive makes someone a prime suspect"—he set about wrapping his essential core with four personalized contexts; he included
his own phone number; and by 5:30 he had letters ready for evening
posting. One for Denny Culbertson in Pittsburgh. One for Amanda
Everson in Dunedin, New Zealand. One for Sonya Klepper in Richmond, Indiana. And the last one for Eddie Moratino in New York
City.

Shrug then moved to his piano to relax, as his clumsy fingers
played over the manifold wonders of Schubert's B flat Major Sonata. His digits were as inept as ever, but the mysterious sweep of
the music exercised its unfailing power. Schubert held a special
place in Shrug's heart. He supposed—it was, after all, the "correct" opinion—that Beethoven's piano sonatas were a grander aggregate achievement; certainly he could understand how one might
make that claim. But deep in his heart he gave primacy of place to
Schubert. For melodic inventiveness. For harmonic boldness. For
the sheer pianicity of the works. For the scope of the composer's
structural vision, especially in the late sonatas. *But what does "late"*
mean for a man who died at thirty-one? For Shrug, music was
more than a source of solace or joy or excitement or intellectual

stimulation. No, for Shrug, music was akin to life itself. And no composer's music was richer with the pulsations of life than Schubert's.

———

Marilyn Speaker arrived shortly after 6:00 P.M. She was the single most important entity in Shrug's world. Religious faith had always come easily to Shrug, and so the proving of God's existence had never struck him as a particularly useful intellectual activity. But *if* it should ever turn out to be necessary to demonstrate the reality of a loving deity, one of the strongest proofs, he had long believed, was the force of love between parents and children. (Connie, he knew, being versed in Darwin, thought ruminations of this sort a bit daft.) Shrug and his ex-spouse had gone their separate ways many years earlier. And while the peripatetic Julia had spent those three decades testing various men for their suitability as bedmates, Shrug had raised Marilyn. He understood that his life had been immeasurably more rewarding than his former wife's.

Marilyn and her father hugged. Shrug asked about Guy Andrews (her husband) and their children, Brandon and Gretchen. Marilyn asked if he was packed for the hospital (he was), and then, after a quick supper, they drove to Trinity Episcopal Church, taking their seats with about a dozen other worshippers just as Evening Prayer began.

Lord, I have loved the habitation of thy house, and the place where thine honour dwelleth. Shrug found all the introductory options that the Prayer Book made available to Allan Clark attractive, each in its own way. But this verse from the twenty-sixth psalm struck him as particularly apposite, focusing as it did on his role as a guest in his Father's house. Unable to dislodge the looming matter of his surgery from his mind, he prayed that the surgeon's hands might bring healing, adding his wish (as he always explicitly did when he prayed for himself) that God's will, not his own, be done. The invitation to the prayer of confession brought its usual dilemma: Shrug was never able to regard his heart as being sufficiently *humble, lowly, penitent,* and *obedient* (especially obedient!). But, as always, he struggled on through the text, knowing that howsoever imperfect his stance might be, the rector would respond to that imperfection with assurances that God would bestow *the grace and consolation of his Holy Spirit* on the parishioners. Shrug was grateful that Allan Clark had chosen the "collect for aid against perils" for this particular evening, for, with surgery ahead the next morning, its plea for God to *defend us from all perils and dangers of this night* spoke to his anxiety. The rector's homily, delivered with his unmatchable resonance, addressed the topic of charity, and Shrug found his mind wandering. But the General Thanksgiving pulled him back to his devotional duties. And the wonderful prayer of St. Chrysostom capped the service with an apt reminder that God attended favorably to the prayerful requests of his people. Shrug and Marilyn left the church hand in hand, talked briefly with Allan Clark (who promised to visit Shrug soon after he came home from the hospital), and walked to their car. The early June evening was still warm and bright.

On the drive home Marilyn asked about the investigation for the first time. Shrug knew that she was trying to keep his mind off his imminent hospital visit, but he knew too that she might have some useful ideas about how to proceed. Especially since she had been a student of Sonya Klepper's. But his account of the preceding two days got waylaid almost immediately when he mentioned how his class had been singing the Humboldt High alma mater during part of the reunion dinner.

"Do you remember how the boys used that song to make fun of me, Daddy?"

Instantaneously, a long-forgotten incident came flooding back into Shrug's mind. The Humboldt High alma mater was set to the tune of "Maryland, My Maryland," and in celebrating the devotion that the Lions of Humboldt High felt for their school, it featured the treacly sort of sentiments conventional to the genre:

> To thee we sing with ardent voice,
> Humboldt High, oh Humboldt High.

Such lyrics didn't wear well with time, and Shrug recalled that when the members of the class of 1953 had sung them at their forty-fifth reunion, some of the sillier lines had elicited snickers.

But when Marilyn had been a sophomore in 1984, silliness had not been the problem, for some wiseacre boys had devised what could only be called a cruel alternative to the canonical version of the Maryland state song.

> She is the girl who stokes my lust,
> Marilyn, my Marilyn.
> My mighty sword shall never rust,
> Marilyn, my Marilyn.
> She summons forth my Lion's roar,
> She makes my raw libido soar,
> She is my favorite Humboldt whore,
> Marilyn, my Marilyn.

The words still stung as Shrug retrieved them from their well-tended site in his capacious memory.

Had Marilyn been made of lesser stuff, she might well have wilted under the deliberate effort to bully and humiliate her. But the toughness of Shrug's daughter had been legendary even before her high school days, and since one of her tormentors had been reckless enough to have joined the fray even though he was named Richard, Marilyn and her friends had been swift to devise several apt and devastating ripostes based upon his first name. He was the one who wilted. And so when Shrug first learned of the contretemps, his daughter was already being toasted as the victor in a fray that had caught the attention of much of the high school.

So, yes, Shrug did remember the incident. And his pride in his daughter's handling of it was as strong now as it had been then.

"Do you remember that Mrs. DeLisle had been a big help to me at the time?"

And yes, Shrug immediately remembered that too. Mrs. DeLisle—Sonja Klepper to the class of 1953—had given moral support and strategic advice to Marilyn at that crucial moment. "How could I have forgotten? Of course, she was wonderful to you."

"That's what made her such a successful and popular teacher," Marilyn explained. "That, and her vivid imagination. She had the ability to treat us in an age-appropriate manner. She never tried to be a 'pal,' but she also understood that we usually didn't want to be lectured to, condescended to, patronized, or criticized either. We all—and by that I guess I mean the girls, not the boys—we all had the sense we could count on her. She took our serious problems seriously. She invested a lot of herself in us. The high school lost a good teacher when she left."

Shrug always valued his daughter's judgments of people and events, and so he tallied this remark up as a powerful endorsement of the good sense of Sonja Klepper Delisle. And he suddenly realized that he had missed a chance to add a notably personalized anecdote to the letter he had just mailed. *Well,* he thought, *it will give me something to talk with her about over the phone.*

About twenty minutes later, Marilyn helped Shrug check into Trinity Hospital. Then, leaving him in his bed with a kiss on the forehead and promising to be back by mid-morning the next day, she left him to his thoughts. They were chiefly happy ones. Surgery still lay ahead, of course. But not for the first time he was congratulating himself on having raised such a splendid daughter.

4

Wednesday, June 6, 2001—Saturday, June 9, 2001

With Ann Arbor and Kant beckoning, Connie rose much earlier than Shrug on Wednesday. He wanted to be on the road before 7:00. As he wolfed down a cereal-and-coffee breakfast, he recalled the dream that his alarm clock had interrupted only a few minutes earlier: a vision of fictive college days in which he had frantically struggled to find his way across a sprawling and unfamiliar campus to take an exam in Arabic, a subject he had never studied. It was his recurring variation on the classic academic's nightmare.

The dream set Connie to reflecting again about his life in the academy. Though ultimately quite satisfying, his career had not followed the path he had once charted for himself. True, it had begun spectacularly, with an appointment in Philosophy at Stanford. But reality had intruded when he was denied tenure. So in the late 1960s he had accepted a job offer at Humboldt College, a small liberal arts school in rural Ohio, unusual amid the aggregation of denominationally identified colleges in the Buckeye State chiefly because of the fiercely secular ethos that the institution had embraced from its birth in the nineteenth century. There was no church affiliation for Humboldt College. Indeed, no college chapel and no department of Religion. Instead, it cast itself as a redoubt of uncompromising reason within a national landscape of benighted colleges standing for varieties of theological obscurantism. Despite this commitment to raw rationalism, however, among American colleges Humboldt was no great shakes intellectually. It tended to accommodate students who couldn't meet the higher admission standards of Princeton, Williams, Grinnell, Reed, and, yes (he had to admit), instate Oberlin. A few of these entrants blossomed, and some small proportion of these late-bloomers even became Philosophy majors. But in general Connie had not had a truly outstanding student to work with during his entire career at Humboldt. This was not all bad, since, he had come to realize, it may have matched instructional competence level to student skill level. For as experience had compelled Connie to acknowledge, though he was a researcher by inclination, he lacked the imaginative reach, the drive, the intelligence, and the creativity that make some people great scholars. He was, he believed, a good teacher for hardworking students, not a shaper of great minds. Humboldt was his proper home.

When Connie reached Toledo (and with the morning now sufficiently launched), he stopped at a Denny's restaurant to get a coffee and place a call to Abe Steinberg back in Humboldt, hoping, actually, assuming, he could recruit Steinberg's assistance in this matter of Tony Travers. The director of the county historical museum, Steinberg had known Connie and Shrug for many years and had helped them in earlier investigations. He enjoyed burrowing among documents and on-line sources for relevant information, having an imaginative gift for such excavations; and he was very knowledgeable about computers, belonging in fact to an informal club of retired intelligence personnel who challenged one another with difficult data digs.

"If information is legally or even semi-legally available," he occasionally boasted, "I can find it." Steinberg listened patiently to Connie's explanation of the friends' new investigative undertaking and gladly accepted the assignment of working to fill in the many information gaps in Tony Travers's exotic career. He also committed himself to researching, though less extensively at this early point, the lives of the eight so-called suspects.

"It's the kind of task I relish," he said, "bringing people out of the shadows." And Connie believed him.

The phone call completed, Connie felt he could set the investigation temporarily aside. After all, Kant called. And so for the next thirty or so hours he gave himself over to the peculiar pleasures of an authentic academic conference in a casual academic setting. He saw old friends. He listened to papers from up-and-coming scholars. He heard a few newish takes on old problems. He made his own modest contribution to the formal conversations. During a slaphappy Wednesday evening at a local bar he joined a motley crowd of professional Kantians, untenured novices and crusty old hands, hirsute men and skirted women, all attired as if the 1970s had never ended, swapping impressions about the compatibility of *The Critique of Practical Reason* with both Confucianism and Islam. Above all, as the conference moved relentlessly ahead in both its scholarly and its social channels, he saw how the broader shift of interest in the American philosophical community from epistemology to moral philosophy was affecting the academic study of the works of a man who was a giant in both fields.

Connie felt himself to be a bit of a fraud on these occasions: if truth be told, he was fonder of Hume than of Kant, and he wasn't an important commentator on either. But because he had long since learned to live with his academic limitations, he saw no sense in disguising the fact that he enjoyed the shoptalk and gossip of the academic muster. He exchanged farewells with his colleagues at lunch on Thursday, and it was not until he had passed the city limits on his way home that he realized, almost guiltily, that the name of Tony Travers had not crossed his mind once since he had arrived in Ann Arbor.

That was a situation he rectified that evening. After a phone call to Marilyn Speaker—*Shrug sure has a nifty daughter*, he had often thought—to make sure that the surgery had gone well and that Shrug would be home the next day, he turned his full attention to what he was calling "Tony's stuff." It consisted preeminently of four large, cardboard boxes, each of which was packed with loosely bound clusters of papers. But the term also included the several copies of the class of 1953 yearbook that Connie had collected two days earlier. It turned out that Tony had been a bit of a pack rat. All these materials needed to be examined, but given his exhaustion after two days of driving, pondering, and schmoozing, Connie wanted to begin with a selection that might be likelier to offer entertainment than substance. And so, pulling a bottle of Sam Adams from the refrigerator, he set Tony Travers's copy of his high school yearbook before him.

A quick glance through its pages showed that it conformed to the stiff generic standards and formats of high school yearbooks of the day: there were sections devoted to photos of groupings of faculty members, to photos of student clubs and committees, and to advertisements (gathered at the end), but primacy of space was given to individual black-and-white head shots of the seniors. The book evinced no foreshadowings of the freewheeling layout modes that had swept through the yearbook publication world since the 1980s. Although he was curious to examine the photographs and see how the main players had looked almost half a century earlier, the first thing he noticed, quite accidentally, was that Bunny Grunhagan had been editor of the volume.

It went without saying that all of the suspects had looked young in 1953. But since he didn't know how any of the eight looked in 2001, he couldn't hope to identify specific changes. And he could only wince at the prominence of crew cuts and bangs that the freshly minted high school grads sported in their official photos.

He found Shrug's portrait particularly amusing: short hair, a blazer and tie, large eyeglasses, and a shy smile. The caption under the photo read "He taught us to number our days," and his list of activities included German Club, Chess Club, the Humboldt Players, and National Honor Society. Connie grinned. In general, the boys looked rather goofy, *almost as if they're fourteen rather than eighteen,* and the girls, with their florid permanents and frozen smiles, looked even more alien, like creatures from some Stepford world.

Then Connie got down to work, gathering impressions as he proceeded. Tony Travers, who of course looked older than his classmates, had been a handsome young man, with a strong chin, oddly sensitive eyes, and a high forehead. His picture figured prominently through the book, not only in activity shots—the school newspaper, the soccer club, the choir, the Spanish Club, and the National Honor Society—but also in the informal images of dances, sporting events, and simple horseplay that were interspersed through the pages. From the personal messages that classmates had penned in over their individual head photos, Connie concluded that Tony had moved the hearts of a number of girls, including three of the suspects. Amanda Everson had written, "You've been a good friend who I'll remember forever." Sonja Klepper had said simply, "I hope we'll stay in touch." And Bunny Grunhagen, more opaquely than the others, had exhorted him, "Never forget what Mrs. Dashwood said about Elinor and Maryanne." Connie could find no Mrs. Dashwood on the faculty nor any Elinor or Maryanne among the seventy-odd classmates.

Two of the male suspects had also written in the book. A stern-faced Denny Culbertson penned, "Thanks for all you taught me," while Eddie Moratino contented himself by simply signing his name. Of the suspects, only Bonny Grunhagen, Trish Ridgway, and Freddy Kramer had not left a mark on Tony's yearbook. Freddy, in fact, except for his head shot, seemed absent from its pages, though Connie spent at least half an hour scouring group photos in an effort to find him.

As the evening wore on, fatigue and beer wrought their inevitable consequences. But before yielding completely to his mounting drowsiness, Connie let his mind drift back to his own days of youth. Unlike most of the members of Humboldt High's class of 1953, whose families had lived in the same town for several generations, Connie's peripatetic childhood had denied him an opportunity to develop long-term childhood friendships. He had sometimes attributed his interest in philosophy to the isolation-induced self-reliance of those earlier days, even though, he had to wryly admit, he couldn't remember actually feeling lonely at the time. No, he finally concluded as he settled into bed, his real loneliness, the loneliness that never completely left him, was not a product of his childhood and youth. Its roots lay in that single terrible moment from his immediate post-college days, when the mysteriously lovely woman whose photo sat on his mantel was killed in an auto accident just days before their scheduled wedding. *That*, Connie mused, was the real source of the sense of existential isolation that he had spent much of his adult life holding at bay and that a lifetime of bachelorhood both contributed and testified to. A few minutes later, the arrival of sleep ended the reflective melancholy of the philosopher.

Connie spent Friday morning contacting the three local professionals whose knowledge might be useful to the investigation. Axel Berlin, Tony Travers's taciturn attorney, added nothing new to Bryan Travers's account of Tony's will, though he seemed happy to learn that someone was resuming the effort to identify Chucklehead Clancy. He pleaded ignorance when asked if he knew where Tony's millions had come from.

George Fielding, still visibly pleased at finally being appointed sheriff, expressed amusement at the friends' undertaking. "You guys just can't stop playing at kids' games, can you?" he said, but promised assistance if Connie and Shrug should come to think it helpful. He pulled out a small folder on the death of Tony Travers and after sorting through papers (copies of a police report, a medical report, witness reports, parking reports, and vandalism reports) he confirmed that Tony Travers had not notified authorities of any threats on his life prior to his death. When Connie teased him about the slowness with which his office was entering the computer age, he muttered something about waiting for an intern to do data entry and dismissed Connie with a scowl.

Lydia Trench, Tony's doctor, said that while she could have no useful opinion on whether Tony stumbled, jumped, or was pushed, she regarded him, with his multitude of ailments, as a good candidate for sudden death. "It's astonishing," she remarked, "that a man as smart as Tony would not stop smoking. Cigarettes ought to be banned."

With that declaration ringing in his head, Connie visited the County Records Office to inspect what turned out to be Tony's uninformative death certificate. It listed "death due to broken neck and other injuries caused by falling down stairs."

At noon Connie called Shrug again and learned that his friend was doing very well. "In fact," Shrug said proudly, "Abe Steinberg phoned to ask if he could meet with us to fill us in on the secrets of Tony Travers's life. He claims there are no bombshells, but lots of intriguing turns, and I proposed Sunday afternoon here at my place. *That* should show how healthy I feel. I hope it suits your schedule." Connie was pleased that his friend was feeling so perky and approved of the Sunday meeting immediately. He then spoke briefly with Marilyn, who confirmed that she'd be staying in town to help her dad until Monday, assuring Connie of a chance to see her before she returned to Iowa.

After lunch, Connie paid his regular weekly Friday afternoon visit to Tuscan Court, a care center for the elderly outside of town. Connie's mother Veronica, her memory irretrievably locked into the 1930s and 1940s, resided there, in apparently blissful indifference to the fact that almost fifty years had elapsed since her older son Donald had been killed in Korea. Although Connie experienced the visits with his mother as duties and generally found them depressing, he did not begrudge her the time he spent with her. Nor was she exacting: half an hour almost invariably sufficed. On this day she talked of Lefty O'Doul's generosity, Senator Johnson's rectitude, Mrs. Shelton's wayward nephew, and William Powell's mustache. As usual, Connie participated solely as an auditor, occasionally nodding encouragement or agreement. And also as usual, when thirty minutes more or less had passed, she abruptly thanked "Donald" for coming, told Connie he was a good son, and received a kiss in return. Connie departed her room with his spirit beset, as usual, with sobering reflections on the way of all flesh.

But that mood didn't last long, for a short walk to another wing of the campus brought him to the apartment of his former faculty colleague, Teresa Espinosa. When he was totally truthful with himself, Connie acknowledged that it was probably the prospect of chatting with Espinosa that made his weekly trips to Tuscan Court acceptable. Older than Connie by a decade and hobbled in body (but not mind), Espinosa shared Connie's love-hate relationship with the academy and his taste for faculty gossip. She was, moreover, a widely knowledgeable person whose judgments about people and events merited respect. Most relevantly, she had been on the Humboldt faculty during Tony Travers's college days and might have taught him Spanish.

Teresa Espinosa's door was open. She greeted Connie with her usual enthusiasm and haltingly made her way over to hug him. When he commented on her mellow smile, she explained that the house cleaner had just left her apartment; and that while she was willing to let the teenage girls who helped out at the Tuscan Court dining room treat her as if she had been born during Abraham Lincoln's presidency, she had not yet figured out how to instruct fifty-somethings that they should not speak to her as if she were a slightly retarded adult. "They mean well, I guess," she grumbled, "but I'll be damned if I'm going to let them come to think of me as some 'old dear.'"

"You've been watching too much British TV fare, my old dear. Americans don't talk that way."

"The hell they don't. Besides, British TV sure beats the American-made shows with their pretty faces and contrived endings." She winced from her hip pain. "Please sit down." With that invitation, Espinosa hobbled back to her chair. "This morning I was at a memorial service in the chapel." There was a wistfulness to her voice that immediately caught Connie's attention. "They're common occurrences around here, of course, these memorial services.

This one was for Mr. Quimby, that quiet man who lived down the hallway from me. The staff found him dead in his room several days ago after he didn't show up for breakfast."

"I'm sorry, Teresa." Connie didn't know what else to say.

"You're not much for religion, are you, Conrad?"

"Well, no, not really." She rolled her hand to encourage him to continue. "I lost my faith, what little I had, that is, in college, when I encountered philosophy. In a way, although I'm not a zealot about it, that's one reason why I liked getting a job at Humboldt. It doesn't try to pretend that religious faith is legitimate. It. . . ." He stared hard at Espinosa. "I'm sorry, Teresa. This isn't what you wanted to hear."

"Oh don't be silly, Conrad. I'm a big girl. And I'm a Humboldtian, too. I know all about the arguments against religion. But let's just say this lapsed Catholic may be struggling her way back to orthodoxy."

"I'm happy for you, and I hope you succeed. As you must know, as my friendship with Shrug testifies, I don't regard piety as an obstacle to comradeship." And he gave her a quick hug, allowing the conversation to shift in the direction of banter.

After fifteen minutes of swapping impressions and tales, Shrug moved to the business part of the conversation. He explained that Shrug and he were looking into the death three years earlier of Tony Travers, a graduate of Humboldt High School and Humboldt College; and that, if it turned out not to have been accidental, it just might have been related to something that had happened in the distant days of the 1950s. "He studied Spanish. Did you know him?"

Espinosa, who had been smiling throughout Connie's narration, was silent for only a moment before fulfilling Connie's hope. "I recall him clearly. I'm hesitating because I'm just trying to figure out how to frame my impression. He was," she hesitated, "he was very different from the other college students. Not just older, but made of different stuff. It was as if he'd known pain."

Startled at the unexpectedly psychological character of the portrait that Espinosa's brief reply limned, Connie remarked that, as a veteran of warfare in Germany and the British Empire, Tony certainly *had* known pain "and loss too, I imagine."

"I concede the point. But my impression is of a different order. He wasn't just a juvenile who had undergone experiences that no young person should have to endure. Rather, it was that he seemed wise beyond his years." She put the folder down. "Oh, I'm sorry. That's not it either. I'm not expressing myself at all well today."

"Sounds good to me," said Connie, trying to encourage his old friend.

"I was much younger back then, just starting my teaching career at Humboldt. And he of course was almost a decade older than the regular Humboldt student. We were probably close to the same age."

Connie's ears picked up.

"And, no, Conrad," Espinosa quickly said, her eyes sparkling, "I did not have an affair with him. Although I know it sounds like I was preparing the way for that sort of confession. But I didn't. We weren't even particularly close, and there was, so far as I know, no physical attraction, at least none on my part. But talking with him, about Spanish literature for example, could be a grand experience. He had deep and thoughtful things to say. He had, as I say, known pain. In contrast, all the other students—even the Spanish honors students—seemed callow and silly. Like the teenagers many of them still were. Strange to say, though I haven't thought of Tony in many years, this impression came surging back in on me, in full flood, the moment you mentioned his name." She hesitated, and then, in a patent effort to shift the direction of the conversation, asked Connie to tell her more about the investigation.

Connie was happy to honor the request, but as he recounted what he and Shrug had been doing the past four days, touching even on the Kant conference and the surgery, he was struck by how paltry the evidence of foul play was. "I guess that's not much to show for several days work. Aside from the teasing note signed by 'Less,' it would be hard to make the case that any crime had been committed."

"Oh, I don't know," Espinosa said thoughtfully. "I admit that you haven't come up with much. But that note was not just 'teasing,' as you put it. It was downright ominous. And you've got a lot of people to take account of. Moreover, if you'll let an old lady complicate your task, I think you've been too quick to rule out the possibility of an outsider getting into the high school."

"Now you sound like Shrug. That's his worry, too."

"Well, good for him. Very sensible of him, too. It's just absurd to believe that an amateur security staff made up of an occasional retired farmer or real estate agent or whatever!, could assure that no determined stranger, bent upon mischief, could get into the high school."

"Actually, we still haven't checked with the man who was supposed to be handling security at the school. But point taken. Still, if that's so, we hardly know where to go with an investigation. Who then is a suspect?"

"Everyone. And that's why your work with the memorabilia is so important. Keep at it." Connie realized she was serious.

Ten minutes later, but with that cheerleading exhortation still ringing in his brain, Connie left Tuscan Court, recommitted to the importance of finding clues in Tony's boxes.

——— ——— ———

Connie decided that his first task should be to try to make sense of Tony's finances. He lacked Shrug's enthusiasm and instinct for financial records, but since no one seemed to know how or when Tony had become moderately wealthy, the matter invited attention. Fortunately, Tony's pack rat instinct served the investigator well. By spending half an hour examining checkbooks, Connie learned that Tony had made a substantial amount of money in the late 1960s and again in the late 1970s. Much of it had gone into stocks. Presumably there had once been documents that explained where this money had come from. But for reasons that only Tony had known, his hoarding instincts had not prompted him to retain these documents. Thus Connie could learn only what Tony had done with his income, not how he had gained it. The gap in information was irritating, for Connie had no idea whether Tony had come by his income in the United States or elsewhere, indeed whether it had been gained legally or illegally. But at least he now knew that when Tony Travers moved to Humboldt in the early 1990s, he had already provided more than adequately for his old age.

Shrug turned next to the bound piles of correspondence. One contained letters from army buddies, but even though Connie was initially hopeful about these documents, he soon decided that they were essentially vacuous, reflective in aggregate of little more than the inevitable growing apart of men who had spent eight or nine months of their youth in a circumstance that called for intense mutual loyalty but who had spent all their subsequent decades following very dissimilar life trajectories. Boastful reminders of the pranks, tomfoolery, and occasional small crimes that ease a soldier's tension in a war zone interlarded the correspondence. Reference to sexual triumphs were a staple. Their senses of humor seemed coarse and juvenile. But the only items that Connie thought were likely to be useful were some first names he jotted down. Gene, Graham, Edward, Bruce, Howard, Joe were the letter-writers. *Not a Lester or Leslie among them,* he thought. And then there was someone named Sandy, not himself a correspondent, but the commander of the unit, whose insistence on discipline and intolerance of horseplay earned an occasional rude rebuke. How far Connie might go with this information in the absence of last names seemed rather dubious. But supposing that Tony's full name would be sufficient to identify a unit, Connie set the list aside for work at a later time, if it should turn out that communicating with people Tony had known before he arrived at Humboldt High might have potential value.

The next pile was far more interesting, for it contained a set of love letters, all of them apparently from his post-high school days.

And it supplied as well a new and complete name: Claire Van Tassel. These Van Tassel letters, written from various locations around the world, told of a love affair that had burned bright for more than a few years in the 1960s and 1970s. And even after it had lost its intensity, even after Van Tassel had married someone named Patrick, the two had stayed in friendly contact. Connie was astonished to find at the top of this set an undated letter from Claire Van Tassel to *Bryan* Travers, not to Tony, and offering her condolences to the son on his father's death. Its presence showed that Bryan had added to, *tampered with?,* the collection of memorabilia. It gave an address, not more than three years old, at which Van Tassel could be reached. And it left Connie puzzled as to how a former lover would have learned of Tony's death. Maybe, Connie thought, Van Tassel is "the Great." *Certainly*, he concluded, *she can tell me more about Tony's life during the "missing years" than anyone else we've come upon.*

And so he immediately broke off from his scavenging among the memorabilia to write a note to Claire Van Tassel, explaining that he and a friend were, with Bryan's approval, looking into the death of Tony Travers, and expressing the hope that she would contact him, since he hoped she could help them on a number of points. As he drafted the letter, he noted that if Van Tassel's name was spelled backwards, the first four letters would be LESS. *Is it possible I'm going to kill* three *birds with one stone?* he wondered. But that hope quickly dissolved when he compared the flowing cursive handwriting on Van Tassel's letters with the sturdy block lettering on "Less's." *Ah well, we wouldn't want things to be too easy, would we?*

By 5:30 Connie felt he needed to break off from this scrutiny of correspondence. The amateur historian in him took pleasure from reading other peoples' letters, but his eyes were beginning to ache and his stomach beginning to send grumbles to his brain. "I sure got stuck with the less engaging side of this investigation," he mumbled to himself. "Shrug gets to chat people up, and I get to

93

bore down into dry documentation." But even as he shaped the thought, he knew it wasn't exactly accurate. *After all, I am the professional researcher on this two-man team. I'm the one who has always gotten his kicks in museums, archives, or just curled up with an important book. (Does anyone really "curl up" with books?) So maybe this distribution of labor, which was, after all, my suggestion, really* is *the best one.*

When he asked himself what his survey of 'Tony's stuff' had taught him so far, he promptly made two observations. First, he had found no indication that Tony had heard from any high school classmate. *He might of course have thrown such a letter away. But I doubt it.* Second, although Tony collected many kinds of memorabilia, photographs did not seem to be among them. *That's just plain odd. Who* doesn't *collect photos from old friends? They're probably the most common collectible in the country.*

Connie chased these mental hares as he folded the piles and boxes together again, to await another scrutiny the next day. And by the time he fixed himself a small supper of canned baked beans and a jelly sandwich, his mind was on what lay ahead the next day: a baseball game in Columbus.

During his childhood on the West Coast, Connie had learned the lore of Pacific Coast League baseball from his mother, whose special heroes, which became Connie's, too, were Joe Dimaggio and Ted Williams. Over the subsequent decades, whether in California or Ohio (or elsewhere), he had attended games as often as was conveniently possible, followed the fortunes of various major league teams, and read widely in the history of the game. Friends kidded him that his enthusiasms were Hume and Hornsby, Kant and Cobb, Locke and Lajoie, Aristotle and Aaron. He himself sometimes said he was the only person he knew who could discourse comfortably on the achievements of William James and Bill James. And he knew that at one level the two enthusiasms were products of the same intellectual impulse: a desire to secure as much mastery as possible over the evidentiary legacy (the tracks) of two very different human enterprises that Connie could only hope to be a spectator to. For Connie knew that there was no chance he would write a monumental tractatus, no chance that he would pitch a no-hitter. But at least he could keep alive the memory of the giants who *were* capable of such feats.

And so, on Saturday afternoon, with the investigation still on hold as Shrug recuperated, Connie, armed with sunglasses, sun cream, and an old San Francisco Seals cap, headed off for an afternoon of baseball watching.

The drive to Cooper Stadium, on the southwestern edge of Columbus, took about an hour. Connie felt that the special charm of minor league baseball lay in the proximity to the action that smaller ballparks afforded the fans. It was an added attraction that the Columbus Clippers, a Yankee farm team, generally fielded a competitive team. Just a few years earlier he had seen Derek Jeter perform on this very field. After parking his car and buying a slice of pizza and a beer, Connie made his way to his seat, which (as usual) lay close behind the third base side dugout. Two young couples, a raucous older man, two nuns, and a father with two children were his neighbors.

By the third inning, however, Connie found his mind beginning to play what he called "philosopher's tricks" with him. It all started as an exercise in baseball memory, when Connie began musing about the 1930s, the heyday of minor league baseball in Columbus. It was then, with the blessing of Branch Rickey and under the leadership of Larry McPhail, that the Columbus Redbirds had risen to dominance in the International League. Players such as Harry Brecheen, Paul Dean, and Enos Slaughter had passed through Cooper Stadium.

Then he started thinking about their nicknames: Harry "the Cat" Brecheen, Paul "Daffy" Dean, Enos "Country" Slaughter.

That led to consideration of other delectable baseball nicknames: Johnny "the Big Cat" Mize, "Pistol Pete" Reiser, "Dixie" Walker,

Harry "the Hat" Walker, "Skeeter" Webb, George "Snuffy" Stirnweiss, "Spud" Chandler, "Red" Ruffing, "Peanuts" Lowrey, "Yogi" Berra, "Preacher" Roe.

And finally (the game he was watching was now in its fifth inning), his analytical instinct kicked into high gear, and he began setting up classifications for nicknames.

There were the nicknames that were nothing more than adaptations of first names: Eddie Stanky, Al Simmons, Jimmie Foxx, Phil Cavaretta. Connie postulated, because he didn't have time to test the hypothesis empirically, that this was the most common kind of nickname.

Why am I doing this? he asked himself in the sixth inning. *Oh, of course, I've got "Less" and "Chucklehead Clancy" jostling for attention at the back of my consciousness.*

Other categories of nicknames emerged from his consideration of the evidence. There were those that identified traits, and a trio of "Leftys" came quickly to mind: Grove, Gomez, Carlton. But there was also Spec Shea and Rapid Robert Feller and Whitey Ford and Adonis Terry. Some identified style: "the Yankee Clipper," "the "Say-hey" Kid," "Stan the Man." (*Do those really count as nicknames?*) Others reflected geographical origins: Vinegar Bend Mizell and Arky Vaughan. Some nicknames were humorously descriptive: take "Rabbit" Maranville, for example, or Jesse "the Crab" Burkett. Some were ironic: "Tiny" Bonham had been anything but. Still others, and now the system was reaching second-order significance, drew their effectiveness from their relationship with prior nicknames: Daffy Dean (an allusion to his more famous and eccentric brother Dizzy Dean), Cy "the Second" Young (a name bestowed on Irv Young, when he entered baseball in Cy Young's day), and of course a variety of derivative "Babes," of whom Babe Herman was probably the ablest.

Where am I going with this? he wondered as he rose for the seventh-inning stretch. *It's pointless. But then, lots philosophizing is pointless. Until it suddenly acquires a point. Philosophy is one of those enterprises that defies justification by utility, until it suddenly reshapes a conceptual world.*

Complexity in this taxonomical analysis of nicknames reached its climax with the case of "Honus" Wagner. At first the matter seemed simple enough. After all, "the Flying Dutchman" had been, reflecting nineteenth-century America's cavalier indifference to European geography, a German. "Honus" sounded Teutonic. But then, as Connie culled his memory, he realized that the great shortstop's nickname was a double formation. Though baptized "John," he had earned the sobriquet "Johannes" in deference to his roots. Then this moniker had in turn been truncated to "Honus." And Connie's reflections on Wagner's nickname didn't stop there. *There's an additional oddity here*, he thought. *The nickname derives from the second syllable of the name it replaces, not the first. That's really unusual.*

As the ninth inning started, Connie insisted on self-discipline. *If a subconscious concern with the investigation into Tony Travers's death is what's driving me to obsess about nicknames, then I ought to see if my classification system helps me make sense of "Less" or "Chucklehead Clancy."* But by the time the last batter flew out, and the Clippers walked off the field with a lopsided victory, Connie was forced to acknowledge that his theorizing still left him in the dark. *"Chucklehead" probably describes a trait, but I didn't need nine innings of baseball to figure that out. What I need is a "Clancy," and so far I haven't found one anywhere.* He was waiting for his row to clear out before moving to leave the stadium. *As for "Less," well, what does one make of a nickname like that? Less of what? Less than what? What did someone do to get a nickname like that? No, it must be a truncated name. So I guess I've just got to keep looking for a Lester or a Leslie, or maybe a Lescynski or a Lessig.* Connie smiled to himself as he walked through the ballpark's dark interior into the bright, sunlit parking lot. *I'm just being silly. Too much beer, too little discipline.*

As he approached his car, his cell phone rang. Curious about who might be calling him late on a Saturday afternoon, he almost dropped his car keys while fumbling to extract the phone from his inner jacket pocket.

"Hello, Connie. This is Abe. And do I have news for you!" The voice of the ordinarily placid Abe Steinberg was agitated. "I've been checking up on Freddy Kramer. And you know what? That bastard is a Nazi!"

"He's what?"

"You heard me. He's a Nazi. Like in Hitler and Goebbels and all that loathsome crowd." Connie knew that Steinberg's parents had died in the Holocaust.

"Shit!" Steinberg continued. "It's a good thing we're meeting tomorrow, for I can fill you in on the wretched details. But I couldn't hold off telling you. And in case you didn't make the connection right away, it seems to me that you've now got a prime suspect for the killer of a man who was, after all, a soldier who fought against Nazi Germany. God, how I hate Nazis!"

With that remark, the call ended. And all thoughts of nicknames were gone from Connie's head.

5

Sunday, June 10, 2016

Allan Clark arrived at Shrug's home about 12:45 P.M. on Sunday, shortly after completing the 11:00 A.M. service at Trinity Episcopal. A tall black man, he stood out at any public occasion in Humboldt, a town where African-Americans constituted less than five percent of the population. He had been rector of the church since the early 1980s, long enough to have known Marilyn Speaker as a high-schooler. His life history was an intellectual flight from the doctrinal rigidity of Pentecostal fundamentalism into the capacious if murky arena of Anglican theology, where he stood in the conservative camp. It fitted him for service as both a lively spiritual leader and a rousing pulpit preacher.

The foundations of his close friendship with Shrug had been laid almost twenty years earlier, in the contentions surrounding his candidacy for the position at Trinity Episcopal. As was plain from the start, his race was an issue, and while no parishioner of the almost entirely white congregation of Trinity would own up to racial anxieties, talk of "fitting in" and "cultural gaps" had studded committee deliberations. Then there was his Pentecostalist upbringing, for while he no longer encouraged glossolalia, his preaching style was imbued with the enthusiasm of a man who, when in the pulpit, was in thrall to the Holy Spirit. Finally, and to some, this was his greatest shortcoming, he was politically and theologically conservative. Like most modern Episcopal congregations, Trinity tended to be liberal in its political preferences, as strongly for Carter in 1980 as for Gore in 2000, and squishy in its theological commitments. A rector who had kind words for Republicans and took the dual procession of the Holy Spirit seriously was not, some said, the sort of rector that Trinity needed.

As chairman of the search committee, Shrug had been point man in dealing with these eddies of discontent. Somehow he had seen, through all the tumult, that Clark had what the parish needed: a charismatic personality, a gift for tact, and an ability to counsel the wayward constructively. A political liberal and a theological conservative himself, Shrug was well-positioned to offer a proportioned view of Clark's strengths. He had fought down the merely mean-spirited opponents; he had listened carefully and responded thoughtfully to those who had worried that Trinity was "too culturally European" for an African-American leader; and he had pleaded, usually successfully, with those who threatened to take their contributions elsewhere if the parish chose Clark. In the end, Allan Clark had been called, and the remarkable recent period of growth in membership, vitality, and spirituality at Trinity had begun. Most people had forgotten, in fact, with each passing year a larger proportion of the parish had never known, the months of discord that had preceded Clark's installation. But shared memories of those times were among the bonds that allowed Shrug and Clark to trust each other, and that made Allan Clark, after only Marilyn Speaker and Connie Haydn, the most important adult in Shrug's life.

Clark's formal purpose in making this brief post-service visit to Shrug was to offer the Eucharist to his temporarily homebound friend, an office he quickly completed. As he packed up his home communion kit, Clark mentioned that he had briefly spoken to Marilyn after the early service. "It must have been a grand help to have had her here the past few days."

Shrug nodded his agreement, and Clark shifted direction. "How's your article coming along?" Shrug, he knew, was tackling the topic of the Holy Spirit in the series of essays he was writing to explain the tenets of the Christian faith to a modern and puzzled audience.

"As always happens," Shrug sighed, "it's reached a vexing stage. If Augustine and Aquinas couldn't make the character of the Holy Spirit as an aspect within the Trinity clear, how can I hope to do it? I find I just keep paraphrasing them, and with much less success. And as for Dorothy Sayers' being helpful, she was just imposing an idiosyncratic theory of artistic creativity on God."

"Hmm." Clark stared hard at Shrug. "When people talk of the mysteries of faith," he said slowly, "the nature of the Pneuma has to stand up there near the top of the list. And if you're right about St. Augustine and St. Thomas failing, though I'm not conceding that point, then at least console yourself with the thought that you're in good company." Clark had the gift of saying serious things in settling ways. "But if you'd like me to read over a draft, you can count on me."

Shrug laughed. "You can bet I'm counting on you. The readership of *The Christian Venture* may not be very large, but it's sure to contain some people who are more learned thinkers than I am. Your job will be to save me from all sorts of theological gaucheries."

Clark replied with his deep, warm, resonant chuckle, rejecting the implication that he possessed any notable sophistication in matters of church doctrine. "It's your grammar that I'll be policing, young man." (Clark was fifteen years Shrug's junior.) "Your grammar."

"Well," Shrug continued, "I may seek your editorial eye on another piece, too."

"Oh?"

"Yes," said Shrug with a tentative smile. "Framing an explanation of the Holy Spirit has become a sufficiently daunting task that I've moved back a step. I'm trying my hand at a piece showing the insufficiencies of materialism. It's an easier subject."

Clark laughed aloud. "Your energy and ambition are extraordinary for someone approaching his seventieth birthday."

"Despite your gentle, albeit chiding, undertone, I'll take that as a compliment. Verdi was going strong in his seventies, and I've decided to make him my role model. But Connie and I have also made a pact not to let the bemused smiles of skeptics and mockers deter us from having fun as wrinklies."

As Clark was pulling his sweater on, Shrug mentioned the investigation. "Speaking of Connie, he and I may be back in the hunt. There's a chance that Tony Travers's death three years ago wasn't an accident."

"Who is Tony Travers? Or *was* Tony Travers?

Clark's unfamiliarity with the name obliged Connie to provide a condensed version of the backstory.

"Well at least I've met *Bryan* Travers," Clark commented, when Shrug's account ended. "And I know Trish Ridgeway, who handles our garbage collection. And Cheryl Bollinger, of course, since she sometimes attends Trinity when she's in town. And while I don't know the remarkable Grunhagen sisters, I've heard of them. 'The laughing twins,' or something like that. But everyone else you've mentioned is a cipher to me."

"I was hoping that maybe you were privy to some tidbits of useful information that weren't protected by the secrets of the confessional and that kind of mumbo-jumbo."

"Sorry to disappoint you, but I know nothing, either openly or confidentially. I have no doubt, however, that you and Connie will resolve the matter. Your sleuthing fame has become the talk of Humboldt."

"Maybe. But this current investigation may bring our reputations back to earth. After all, sleuths can't strut their stuff if there hasn't been a crime."

After a brief prayer for continued healing, Clark left Shrug's home to minister to other homebound parishioners while Shrug limped his way into his living room to prepare for his afternoon visitors. A few minutes later Marilyn Speaker returned from a shopping expedition, her arms filled with grocery bags.

"I'm sorry I missed Allan. But at least I saw him after church. And now you're taken care of with food for the next few days,

Daddy. Don't be too active after I leave, and you'll heal real fast."
She needed two more trips to the car to bring all her purchases into
the house. Shrug watched her labors and could only mumble a
silent prayer of gratitude that he had been blessed with such a wonderful daughter.

————— ————— —————

Connie arrived shortly before 2:00, and Marilyn greeted him with
a warm hug. Though she had spoken with him by phone, she hadn't
seen him since her arrival in town. She looked upon Connie not
merely as her father's best friend but as the Speaker *family's* good
friend; a man who was looking after her father and would tell her
the truth about him. She had once worried about how her father
would deal with loneliness, first when she departed for college,
then when she married Guy and moved to Iowa. He had, after all,
been a single parent as he raised her, and she knew she was the
center of his life. That's where Connie fit in. He hadn't supplanted
her, of course; no one could. But he *had* complemented her, and,
by assuring that her father would work to stay engaged with the
whirligig of life even after his "chickling" had left the nest, he had
helped her father realize himself. He made Shrug laugh and appreciate company, providing a counter to the insidious enchantments
of solitude implicit in his love of music and chess and financial
analysis and God.

"You're looking pretty healthy," Connie said, as the invalid
limped around the corner.

"Feeling pretty good, too," Shrug grunted, his gait suggesting
that his words needed to be taken contextually.

Marilyn returned to whatever part of the house she had been
working in, and Shrug and Connie made their way into the living
room. By unspoken agreement, they decided to wait upon Abe
Steinberg's arrival before talking about the case, passing the time
instead by discussing a controversial proposal now before the planning council to debate the construction of a small, private airport
outside of Humboldt. Shrug liked the idea, Connie didn't.

Steinberg arrived five minutes later, his face florid, obviously eager to talk about what he had discovered the previous day. And as soon as the three men sat down, the words came firing out. "Not only is that slimy Kramer a Nazi. He doesn't even try to disguise the fact. He operates a Web site with links to Aryan Nation. It warns of the dangers of Jews, Blacks, Hispanics—anybody who doesn't conform to his white, Anglo-Saxon, Protestant, rural, God-fearing, Loretta-Lynn-loving, beef-eating, beer-swilling, pick-up-driving, toothpick-wielding, NASCAR-attending stereotype." At that point in his Homeric litany Steinberg paused. "Sorry. I got carried away. Sorry." He then went on to explain that Kramer didn't use racial or ethnic epithets. "He wants to be taken seriously, to win people over by his remarkable powers of persuasion. Oh, and he throws in snippets about the glories of the Superman. He's obviously dipped into some Nietzsche Web site sewer . . ."

Connie's eyebrows shot upwards; Shrug, already familiar with this side of Kramer, just smiled.

". . . and pulled out a filthy idea or two, " Steinberg continued.

Connie asked how Steinberg had learned all this about Freddy Kramer so quickly.

"Easy as pie. Just go searching for Fritz Kramer on the Web. He isn't hard to find. He's not hiding. And once you've found him, he guides you through his own pseudo-philosophical writings and points you to others. Oh, you'll just love this guy, Connie."

"How can you be sure he's *our* Fritz Kramer? The country must have hundreds of them." Shrug hoped against all likelihood that Steinberg had forgotten that minor demographic point.

"As I say, he doesn't hide. He gives his e-mail address, and it's the same one that the class of 1953 class list supplies. His self-preservation instinct is strong enough to keep him from supplying his residential address and phone number. No Nietzschean super-heroics there. But there's no doubt that your esteemed classmate" (a nod toward Shrug) "and the man who denies the Holocaust are one and the same slug."

"Sounds like a classic case of the high-school loner turning into the adult sociopath." Connie's voice was low.

The men were silent for a moment.

"I'm not sure," said Shrug hesitantly, "that this information gives Kramer a motive to kill Tony Travers." His companions looked at him inquisitively. "When I talked with him, he praised Tony for having 'balls.' Abe has now shown where this admiration for physical courage comes from. It may not be important that Tony displayed this courage against the Germans. It may simply be important that he *has* it. In Kramer's weird world view, it could be that bravery trumps politics."

Steinberg's reply was terse. "I'm sorry, Shrug, but that's bullshit. Read his writings and see for yourself. He reveres Nazi Germany and, by extension, is very likely to detest anyone who fought against it."

"But," said Connie, "by that criterion, he would treat the United States as a foe, too. After all, we were at *war* with Hitler's Germany. But instead, if I understand the American Nazi types right, they don't want to punish the United States, just 'reform' it."

"You're missing a distinction that seems to me to be key," Steinberg retorted. "He might merely want to correct what he sees as the structural flaws in his native country, even though, for most sensible Americans those so-called flaws are the values that make the country great. But for the particular individuals who actually took up arms against his beloved Hitler there were no extenuating circumstances. To me, it's quite plausible that he would just want to kill anybody he happened to know who had fought against the *Wehrmacht*."

"Why not kill Tony earlier, then?" Connie was curious about how well Steinberg had thought through his speculation.

"Probably because, so far as I can tell, his Nazi-craziness is of recent origin. Or perhaps because it has taken on new urgency in recent years. Or maybe it's that damned Nietzsche again. Hell, I don't know!" Steinberg was exasperated as well as angry. "But in any case, the notion that a present-day defender of all things Hitlerian would want to do away with someone who served in His Majesty's forces during World War II scarcely strikes me as implausible."

"Well," said Shrug, aiming at lowering temperatures, "I need to say that my speculations are often wrong. And it would be very satisfying if it turned out that we could pin a murder on this scumbag. Ah, Humboldt High, what have you wrought?"

"As you can imagine," said Steinberg, looking slightly relieved, "I'm eager to help you guys in nailing this rodent."

"I hope you can keep checking up on the others," Connie quickly added. "Just because Fritzy Kramer has suddenly offered himself up as our favorite target doesn't mean we should forget about the other suspects. It's possible we'll discover that his life as a trafficker in hate is a literary existence, only a way to vent aggression without getting physical about it."

"Bullshit," mumbled Steinberg.

"Connie's been studying psychology in his retirement," Shrug interjected, to no one in particular.

"Well, then," Steinberg said, obviously annoyed but now wishing to join the effort at tamping down frictions, "let me switch to my wider research and tell you what I've found out about Anthony Travers, the man you know as Tony. And here, these will help." Steinberg handed out to Connie and Shrug a set of papers on which he had typed a chronology of Tony's life.

"Anthony Travers was born in 1926, in Sheffield, England. His parents, as you can see, were Thomas and Ellen Travers. I didn't follow through on them, though I can, if you think it would be useful." Steinberg then explained that he hadn't tried to track Tony's pre-American career either. "Connie's instructions were to find out about his life after high school."

Connie nodded.

"When he arrived in the U.S. in 1951 to enter what was in effect his junior year at Humboldt High, he was twenty-five years old. That means he was, on average, about eight years older than his classmates." Steinberg spoke of Tony's high school activities, but since his source had been the same high school yearbook that Connie had consulted, the information was not new.

"After graduating with Shrug in 1953, he entered Humboldt College. No doubt because Connie was not yet on the faculty, Tony was not drawn to any Philosophy courses." Steinberg sketched out a college career that sounded fairly typical: he majored in History, played on the soccer team, ran cross-country, joined the Spanish Club."

"Teresa Espinosa remembers him," Connie interjected. "She was impressed, startlingly so."

Steinberg continued "He was president of the International Students Club, and graduated *magna cum laude* right on time in 1957. Oh, and he was also in the Fencing Club."

"Well, *that* adds a little dramatic dash to an otherwise unremarkable college life," Shrug remarked.

Steinberg explained how he had used the Humboldt College yearbooks and graduation programs (of which the county museum had a complete run) to gather this information. He suspected he could garner more information about Tony's undergraduate days if the friends decided they needed it.

"In 1956, before he graduated, he became an American citizen."

"I'd wondered about that," Shrug said. "Do we know what led him to do it?"

"No. He may have decided early on that wanted to cast his lot with the New World rather than the old country," Steinberg replied. "But all I can do is report a fact, not a motive."

Steinberg resumed the biography, saying that Tony had taken a job with Texaco after graduation. "But after that his employment career became harder to track than I had expected. Still, it's consistent with what his son said about him being frequently out of the country." To Connie's inquiry about how Steinberg got information about a person's past jobs, the former intelligence officer simply said the he had "my ways. And none of them are strictly illegal." The three men laughed at that remark. Connie and Shrug had heard it before.

"Tony got married for the *first* time in 1958." Steinberg's emphasis was not really needed, since Bryan had already explained that his father was the marrying type. This news led the three men into a short excursus on the topic of matrimonial success, a subject neither Connie nor Shrug had any grounds for pontificating upon. It was Steinberg's view that none of the marriages he would soon be mentioning had been happy, that all the evidence from Tony's life pointed to a fundamental restlessness that resided at the core of his being and that stood at odds with the requirements of settledness and commitment which underlay most successful marriages.

"I know," Steinberg continued, "that some couples enjoy climbing mountains together, pulling up stakes every other year, or spending long periods of time apart. But they're rare. Most often, when *one* member of a couple has the restless gene, the other (and it's usually the woman who has this nesting instinct) finally calls it quits. And some restless ones, like Tony, refuse to learn from experience. They just keep trying to find the right mate, often someone quite a bit younger and starstruck, and wind up making a series of spouses unhappy." Although Steinberg, a widower, spoke abstractedly, there was an authority to his declaration that led both Connie and Shrug to wonder what experiences in his own life allowed him to speak so confidently.

"But back to the subject. His first wife was Mary Gillespie, a fellow member of the class of 1957 at Humboldt College. Though remember: even though she was his classmate, she was eight years younger than he." Steinberg added that the couple had divorced less than a year later, in Nevada, and that there had been no children. Humboldt College records showed that she had later remarried. She had died in 1989.

Between 1959 and 1964 Tony Travers had been a free-lance journalist, and his byline had frequently appeared in magazine and newspaper articles from such places as Saigon, Vladivostok, Hong Kong, New Delhi, and Jakarta. "He seemed to make East Asia his beat." The articles themselves were relatively anodyne, tending more toward travel literature than political analysis. The conclusion to be readily drawn from this evidence was that he visited many parts of the world during these years. "But it's just not clear where he spent most of his time, whether he spent much of it in this country, or whether he was rarely in the U.S.

"He married for the second time in 1963, to Linda Dremminger. She's Bryan's mother, and Bryan was born five months after the wedding, which took place in San Francisco." The three men briefly discussed premarital conceptions, noting that perhaps, in the more relaxed atmosphere of the late twentieth century, an unmarried but pregnant Linda Dremminger would have felt no pressure to marry her child's father. Steinberg added that the couple had had no other children and that Tony's second marriage had ended in 1966.

"It's always possible," Steinberg noted, "that Tony *wasn't* Bryan's father—that he married Linda Dremminger for some other reason—say, compassion. I make that suggestion only because, after all, none of the other marriages produced offspring."

"Well, *that* would complicate our task, wouldn't it?" Connie was looking into his coffee cup. "But we can't ignore the possibility either."

"By the time the second marriage ended," Steinberg said, resuming his story, "he was living in Brockton Heights, outside of Pittsburgh."

"I wonder if Denny Culbertson was living in Pittsburgh at that time," Connie remarked, almost absentmindedly.

"It's a big city," Shrug replied, "but the possibility of their getting together is another matter that needs to be checked into."

"Don't know about any of that," Steinberg continued, "but I do know that in 1966 he moved from a house to an apartment. I'm

109

betting that Linda got the house in a divorce settlement. But the important thing is that I can finally pin Tony down to a business activity." And Steinberg explained how, in 1965, Tony had founded Travers Enterprises, a construction company, and how it had prospered under his direction. "He sold it in 1970, but it still exists and under the same name. It's a well-regarded, small company specializing in the building of upscale homes in the Pittsburgh suburbs."

Connie and Shrug shared the conclusion that the success of the company demonstrated that Tony had both an acumen for business and a familiarity with construction activities. "Bryan said he was a smart guy," Connie recalled. "Getting a business to run properly, which is to say, profitably, takes a range of intellectual talents." Connie was not one of those academics who sneered at business talent.

"I'm embarrassed to say," Steinberg continued, "that the next five years of Tony's life are a blank. None of my usual sources give me any tips as to where he was living and working from 1970 through 1974."

"Interpret that for us," said Shrug. "It sounds significant, but is the gap maybe just an artifact of the kinds of records you can get access to?"

"In part, yes. But for someone to disappear completely is strange. For example, he filed no income tax returns." Connie raised his eyebrows at this remark, but Steinberg just plowed ahead. "We know he emerges at the end of the tunnel. So we can't ascribe the silence of the records to his demise. That's a joke! But something happened. And even living abroad, which is what I suspect he did, wouldn't usually explain the lacuna. Unless he lived in some dodgy place like, say, North Vietnam or North Korea or conceivably Cuba. So there's probably some reason to think that he *wanted* to be hidden."

"Well," said Connie, his triumphant tone suggesting he had something of moment to impart. "I don't know *where* he was during these years. But I've got a good idea about *who* he was with, at least for some of time." And he told them the one-sided story of Claire Van Tassel that had emerged from Tony's correspondence. "Obviously she wasn't with him all the time, or she wouldn't have written. But some of the letters have inside addresses, or at least cities of origin. On the assumption that he spent some time with her in these places, it ought to be possible to identify a few of the sites he hid in during the mysterious five years. I'll get the names of those places to you, in case they're useful."

"Actually," Steinberg interrupted, "there's going to be a second five-year gap. But meanwhile, please do send the names and dates on. They'd sure help narrow any search."

"Will do. And please resume your outline of Tony's life," said Connie.

That sketch, as unfolded by Steinberg, revealed that Tony Travers had reappeared in the records in 1975, when he had married for the third time. "The lucky woman," Steinberg explained, "was Patricia Poston, a petroleum engineer. And they got married in, of all places, Butte, Montana." Steinberg had found no evidence of the place of residence of the couple, remarking that "petroleum engineers frequently change work sites." The marriage ended in a Nevada divorce in 1980. Again there were no children. And Steinberg found no evidence of what, if anything, Tony had done to make money during these years.

"Tony remarried very quickly in 1980, to Judy Anderby. The swiftness of the marriage suggests to me that Anderby was probably at least *one* reason for the breakup of the marriage to Poston. In any case, she was a twenty-five-year-old dental assistant, he was now in his fifties, and the wedding took place in Lexington, Kentucky. The marriage lasted three years." Steinberg explained how he was particularly proud of tracking down the information about Anderby's job, and he concluded by reiterating that, like all but the second marriage, there had been no children from this fourth one.

"In sum, he had four wives—count 'em—and so far as I can tell, with the exception of Mary Gillespie, they're all still alive. Maybe they'd be a fruitful source of information about him."

"One thing I suspect they'd agree on," volunteered Shrug, "is that he was a hard man to live with." The three men chuckled lightly.

"Now we come to the longest span of documented employment in his career," Steinberg continued. "For almost eight years, from 1980 to 1987, Tony operated a private security agency in Lexington, Kentucky." Steinberg, who knew something about this line of work from conversations with other former spies, explained what the job entailed. It might, he said, overlap with the kinds of things private investigators did, but at its core it involved guarding things. "To be good at it, you need to know a lot about electronic protection devices, and today, increasingly about cyber-security. So I think you can assume that Tony had a good understanding of how home and business security systems worked and should be deployed. Of course, *when* he got the background is unknown. But it's important to keep current in that kind of business. Even if he acquired some expertise in World War II, that knowledge would have been hopelessly old-fashioned in the 1980s. So he must have been doing *something* to keep his skill set up to date." Steinberg added that, according to his cursory check, the business had been successful. "He sold it for a half a mil in 1987."

"That doesn't quite tally with my cursory examination of his bank records," Connie remarked. "By the evidence *I've* seen, Tony was *not* pulling in a consistent income in the 1980s. And those hidden years in the 1970s on the other hand served him pretty well."

"Well," replied Steinberg, "there's another mystery. I'll revisit the periods in a few days. And I'm sure you will, too."

When Shrug asked what happened to Tony after 1987, Steinberg explained that he entered another blank period. "It's like 1970–74 all over again. We know he was alive. But from 1987 till 1992

I can't find a trace of him. And again I emphasize, becoming completely invisible isn't all that easy. It almost surely doesn't happen by inadvertence."

"Maybe we'll conclude he became a spy, found Eddie Moratino having an affair with Bunny Grunhagen, tried to blackmail them, and was murdered in 1998 for his nosiness." Shrug's remark brought feeble smiles to the faces of his colleagues, who otherwise ignored his weak attempt at humor.

"He reappeared in 1992, when he bought a condo in Princeton, New Jersey. I don't find him employed, and he was sixty-six by then, but it may be noteworthy that the condo was certainly not at the lower end of the scale." Steinberg knew the area personally, and described its residents as an oil-and-water mixture of young, single professionals who worked in New York City or with local technology firms, *and* retired professionals: doctors, engineers, professors, government workers, who were downsizing. "The chief mark of the community is the absence of children. When young women become pregnant, they move away."

In 1993 Tony Travers attended the fortieth reunion of his high school class. "As far as I know," Steinberg noted, "it was the first time he had returned to Humboldt since graduating from the college."

Having no grounds for disagreement, Shrug suggested that "maybe he had been given advance notice. Sure, that makes sense, advance notice that he was to receive the award for serving humankind. Under those circumstances, attending was the right thing to do." Shrug wished he could recall more about the visible state of Tony's health in 1993, for Bryan had reported that his health problems were mounting by that time. But memory failed him.

"My tale endeth," said Steinberg with mock-solemnity, "in 1994, when Tony bought his small home on Cedar Street here in Humboldt and became a neighbor of us all."

Connie and Shrug expressed delight and amazement that their friend had been able to uncover so much about his quarry in so

short a time. He explained a few of his techniques, adding however that practitioners needed to keep some of their tradecraft tricks
confidential. "And it helps to have pals around the country," he
added, winking at the two investigators. His face said that he was a
man who enjoyed having his secrets.

"And what do you make of all this?" Connie asked. "You're
the pro when it comes to interpreting biographical data. We're going to follow up on the time line you've sketched out, trying to fill
in blanks and flesh out facts. But do *you* see hints of matters that
might interest us in this array of information? How do you ap-
praise all this?" With these awkward formulations, Connie was trying to get the ex-spy/museum director to season the facts he had
supplied with suggestions about the lines of inquiry they pointed
toward.

Steinberg rose to the bait of the flattering invitation. He explained that he thought it odd that he couldn't uncover more about
Tony's credit record, especially since he had Tony's Social Security number, "usually the open-sesame when it comes to looking
for records." Steinberg concluded from the paucity of information
that Tony was one of those rare people who prefer not to use plastic and who never borrow. He explained that he was similarly surprised that Tony had avoided appearing before any court in any
capacity in the United States. "All of that suggests," he said, "a life
of carefulness. And carefulness in turn suggests that there are facts
he wants to hide." Steinberg reiterated his belief that three of the
former wives were probably still alive and might be useful sources
of information. And by way of wrapping up his impressions, he
noted again that Bryan appeared to be correct in claiming that he
was Tony's only child and hence his only heir.

Shrug wanted to revisit the gaps in the evidence about Tony's
employment record. "Are silences of this sort indicative of something important?"

"Well, they might hint at engagement in illegal activities," Steinberg replied. "That would certainly be important and is a possibil-

ity that can't be ruled out. But since we know from other sources that he spent lots of time out of the United States, it's easier to account for the silences by positing that he was working in places that fall beyond the purview of American record-keeping."

The afternoon was well advanced by now, and Marilyn had begun hovering just beyond the room, occasionally drifting into sight and obviously ready to intervene and send her father to bed. Taking the cue, Shrug said that he was feeling somewhat sore from the surgery and that it was perhaps time to end the conversation. The friends expressed their gratitude to Steinberg, who in turn reminded them as he left that they needed to "turn the screws" on Fritz Kramer. Marilyn showed him out.

Once they were alone, Shrug suggested to Connie that they meet again the next day for a War Council.

"Will you feel up to it?"

"Absolutely. And we've got lots to talk about now. We can't wait for all the information to come pouring in. We've got to move on such pieces of it as arrive. And Abe has now given us some big chunks to work with."

"Well, aren't you the eager one! But as usual, you're right."

Since Connie had a breakfast meeting with a former student and appointments with his attorney and a barber on Monday morning, the friends settled on 1:30 the following afternoon for their session. Connie then drove home, Marilyn helped Shrug clean up the living room, and after a short evening of television-watching (Shrug drank beer, Marilyn wine) the two retired to their bedrooms. Shrug knew that his daughter needed to get back to her family in Des Moines, and while he would miss her, he also knew that once she had gone, he would feel freer to get out and about, even if haltingly, as Connie and he moved ahead in their effort to find some event or person in Tony Travers's past that might account for a threat and perhaps a murder. Besides, despite his invocation of prudence in reacting to Abe Steinberg's discoveries, he wanted to sink his teeth deep into Fritzy Kramer.

6

Monday, June 11, 2001

Shrug's surgical site ached when he got up early on Monday, but he took two Tylenols with his breakfast, bade Marilyn good-bye, and by 8:30 was turning his attention to his investment hobby. His "pot" wasn't large. But even in retirement Shrug had lost none of his enthusiasm for trying to understand the remarkable phenomenon of equity trading, and his weekly analyses of his position within the wider universe of stock expectations was one of his favorite intellectual pastimes. An enthusiastic capitalist, he savored the concept of "creative destruction," and read Peter Bernstein and Joseph Schumpeter for recreation.

Shortly after ten, as he weighed a rebalancing that would shift the pot away from the pharmaceutical sector and toward petroleum stocks, the phone that Marilyn had plugged in next to his work chair began ringing. Welcoming the interruption, Shrug closed his folder and picked up the receiver.

"Hello, this is Angelina Lopez, Mr. Moratino's secretary, calling from New York. May I please speak to Mr. Shrug Speaker?" Ms. Lopez was businesslike.

"This is Shrug Speaker, Ms. Lopez." Shrug tried to emulate the sobriety of the voice at the other end of the line.

"Good morning, Mr. Speaker. Mr. Moratino called in over the weekend—he's out of the country now—to ask me to phone you to let you know he has, let me see, now; I'm checking my notes, to be accurate, he has received your letter, or, to be more precise, I have read your letter to him, and he will give you a call as soon as he is back."

When Shrug inquired where Mr. Moratino was or when he might return, the secretary became discretion itself. "You may be confident, however, that you will hear from him. Mr. Moratino always fulfills his commitments."

Shaking his head in bemusement, Shrug thanked Ms. Lopez and hung up. *He's probably in Vietnam,* he thought, *trying to find the rubies that Tony stole from him a quarter century ago in the confusion of the American withdrawal from Saigon. At least I can now check him off as having been "contacted." Only three to go.* He then returned to his hobby, concluding that the opacity of Enron's financials was ample reason to shed his small stake in the company.

Shortly after 11:00 A.M. the postal delivery rattled through the slot on the front door. As Shrug bent over to pick up the envelopes, flyers, and magazines that had arrived, he realized his soreness was receding. *I'm beginning to think that Dr. Cassidy was right: that this really was minor surgery.* His sense of relief was palpable, for even though he did his best to put on a bold face when talking with friends, Shrug could never suppress the nibbling fear that, at his age, every pain was the first symptom of some fatal affliction.

Thumbing through the envelopes, he saw immediately that he had received a letter from Denny Culbertson. *Contact number two! Lucky Monday!* He tore the envelope open. The neatly handwritten letter thanked Shrug for his communication, expressed eagerness to be helpful in any way possible with the investigation, and urged Shrug to give him a phone call at his convenience. That kind of invitation, especially after a morning split between assessing financial probabilities and brooding over the absence of evidence of a crime, was too good to pass up. Shrug immediately dialed through to Pittsburgh, unsure as to whether he was phoning a business or a residence.

After two rings, a cheering, "God be with you," came across the line.

Must be Denny, Shrug thought. But good manners prevailed, and he merely introduced himself and asked if he might speak with Denny Culbertson.

"Shrug! It's good to hear your voice. Thanks for calling." Without waiting for an inquiry, Culbertson explained his unusual salutation by saying that he was organizing a "ride-in" at a local women's clinic. "We call ourselves 'Cyclists Against Abortion.'" He added that he needed to stay by the phone on this day to receive messages from "suburban cells." Shrug quickly offered to call at another time, but Culbertson, apparently oblivious to the tone of antiabortion urgency he had just communicated, replied that murder investigations should never be put on hold and asked how he might help. Without waiting for an initial question, he volunteered that he hadn't known Tony well at all. "In fact, as you may recall, I was a bit of a loner in my misspent high school days."

"You're the only person I know who, in retrospect, would call steady academic application a poor use of time."

"That's exactly why I'm in a position to make the judgment."

Shrug then provided what he hoped was enough background to make his coming request seem reasonable. He concluded by asking Culbertson to think back to the evening of the class dinner. "Films of the event have allowed us to identify a period of about twenty minutes when Tony was out of the room before Trish Ridgway came running in shouting that he was dead. I'm contacting all those, like you, who were out of the room for at least some of that time, to find out what you might remember seeing in the hallways." Shrug felt himself wince at the gracelessness of that formulation.

"So I'm a suspect, eh. Fair enough, I suppose, given the reasoning you've laid out. If you say I wasn't in the room, then I can understand why you'd think that."

"You're putting too malicious a twist on what I said. Please just take it at face value. Yes, it stands to reason that, if Tony's death wasn't natural, one of the persons not in the room might have killed him, but it also stands to reason that all the others who were out during the window of opportunity might have seen something that Connie and I could find useful. It's that latter kind of information that we can legitimately inquire about."

Culbertson laughed. "You're pleading too much, Shrug. I understand. I really do. I doubt that I can be useful, for I don't even remember being out of the room. But I understand."

Shrug paused, gathering his thoughts. "Well, if you don't remember leaving the room, let me ask you about your memories of some of our classmates."

"Ah, the other suspects!"

Shrug thought he could hear the smile across the line. But since the implication of his procedure was inevitable, he just moved ahead, mentioning the names of each of the remaining seven slowly and alphabetically. In some instances Culbertson reported no memory of all. "I don't think I talked to Freddy Kramer or the Grunhagen girls. I hadn't really known Freddy in high school, and while I'd had a crush on one of the twins back then (isn't it odd how I can't even remember which one?) I don't think I've talked to them since. They scarcely ever left Humboldt, and I almost abandoned the town."

In other cases, even though he didn't recall conversations from the evening of the reunion dinner, he shared impressions that had arisen from acquaintanceships maintained over the years. Eddie Moratino was an "all-round good guy, someone who has matured into a responsible businessman and has never forsworn his Catholic roots." Culbertson elaborated on that remark by noting that Moratino had used his own money to found a convent school for girls in India. In Culbertson's view Sonya Klepper DeLisle was also a "good Christian," a woman who had "raised three fine children and stood by her husband during his final long illness."

Only two of the suspects had left reunion-specific memories in his mind. He had spoken to Amanda Everson at either the dinner or the reception before it. She had struck him as "brittle or maybe she was nervous. Wouldn't talk about her late husband. In any case, she wasn't quite the easygoing girl of high school days. But then," he added, his mind perhaps on his own remarkable transformation, "Who among us hasn't changed? God works in wondrous ways."

The classmate who loomed largest in his reunion memory was Trish Ridgway. He hadn't actually talked with her one-on-one as far as he could recall, but as the evening had proceeded, she had become louder and sillier, and in the process of making a spectacle of herself had intruded into the consciousnesses of everyone present. "Just ask. I'll bet everyone remembers Trish. She was sloshed, and that's why, when she came bursting in with her report of having found Tony, I didn't believe her at first. And I'll bet others were also dubious. She had spent the evening becoming increasingly obnoxious." (Shrug recalled reports that Culbertson himself had irritated many with his reiterated efforts to win converts to Christ.) "And I figured she was just trying to outdo herself in winning attention." Culbertson added that shortly after the reunion he had sent Ridgway information about how she might contact Alcoholics Anonymous, but that the message had not been acknowledged.

After finishing with the roster of suspects, Shrug and Culbertson talked for ten more minutes, for Culbertson was curious to learn scuttlebutt about classmates, and Shrug was interested to find out when Culbertson might again visit Humboldt. They briefly discussed the work of Cyclists for Christ, and from the tenor of the conversation Shrug concluded that Culbertson had learned since 1998 to tone down the counterproductive missionary fervor that classmates had found so off-putting at the reunion. Toward the end of the conversation Culbertson surprised Shrug by declaring that he had an interest in running for class president. It was close to a quarter to twelve when the call ended.

"Only two to go," Shrug commented as he set the phone down. The silence from Amanda Everson was not entirely unexpected: New Zealand was both geographically and psychologically distant from Ohio. But the silence from Sonya Klepper was a bit more puzzling. She lived just over the state line, in eastern Indiana; and while a letter writer ordinarily had no reason to assume that someone would reply immediately to a letter, an inquiry about a murder seemed a subject sufficiently unusual to warrant making an exception to that expectation. *Ah well*, Shrug thought as he prepared a bologna sandwich for lunch, *she could be out of town or ill or busy. I guess I can wait a bit longer before beginning to prod.*

"Back to work." Muttering and stumbling briefly on his slippers, Connie swung out of bed on Monday morning. *Work was what retired folks needed*, he thought. *Work, or at least a good hobby.* His mind was on the prerequisites of happiness because he had spent the previous evening at Tuscan Court leading the members of the Well-Being Club in a discussion of various readings about aging that he had suggested to this group of positive-thinking seniors. In their eighties and nineties *(I feel like a lad in their midst,* he realized) they had seasoned their reactions to Cicero, Montaigne, Shakespeare, and Glückel with ample doses of a common sense that long life had instilled, and the lessons they had endorsed were the truisms of timeless wisdom. "Don't count too much on your children." "Don't run out of money." "Accept advancing infirmity with charity of spirit." "Nourish your friendships."

Since a breakfast with a former student lay immediately ahead of him, Connie consumed only a glass of orange juice before dressing. He then dispatched the duty of e-mailing to Abe Steinberg the locations and dates associated with Claire Van Tassell's letters to Tony. Looking forward to the forthcoming breakfast conversation, he thought back on George Stolz's student days, when the bespectacled young man had proved himself to be earnest and hard-working, with a gift for writing. A double major in English and Philosophy, he had graduated *cum laude* and gone on to a career in war reporting. He had now returned to town to give a talk in Humboldt College's summertime Public Events Lecture Series about his coverage of the Yugoslav wars. Because Connie's commitment at Tuscan Court had prevented him from attending the lecture the previous evening, the two men had chosen an early breakfast at Bob Evans for a moment of catching up before Stolz flew back to Washington to resume life as a journalist.

Connie met Stolz at the restaurant, where, cheered by warm eggs and warmer rolls, he eagerly asked about Stolz's post-Humboldt life, and the former student filled his former professor in on the outlines of his professional travels. But when Stolz began talking about the strange warrior ethos of some of the Serbs, Croats, Bosnians, and Kosovars he had met, of their "rooted belief in the righteousness of their clan/family/race and of their cocky acceptance of the privilege of force," Connie recognized a personality type that sounded very congruent with Fritz Kramer's.

"We see it as an atavism," Stolz said, munching on an English muffin. "They see it as God's expectation for humankind. Two very different world views."

Stolz's student driver picked him up at 9:30 to take him to Port Columbus International Airport. Connie was feeling so stimulated by the line of conversation that had unexpectedly brought Freddy Kramer back into view that he decided almost as soon as Stolz left to take the unusual step of canceling his barbershop appointment (happily, he was almost bald) so that he might pay a visit to the local hate monger. Curiosity, he realized, was his prime motive: repugnance, yes, and a measure of anger, but chiefly curiosity. *I've never known a Nazi. I'd like to get a bead on this guy before Shrug and I discuss the investigation this afternoon.*

Connie's gamble paid off, for when he knocked on Freddy Kramer's front door at about 10:00 A.M., he found his quarry at home. His first thought on seeing Shrug's infamous classmate was modest disappointment. Kramer was wearing a white T-shirt that was slightly too small for his paunchy torso, and his glossed-down, dark, and graying hair conveyed little hint of Aryan blondness. He stood quietly in the open doorway, waiting for Connie to introduce himself.

"Mr. Kramer, I'm Connie Haydn, a friend of Shrug Speaker's, and I was . . ."

A smile that hinted at contempt flickered briefly across Kramer's face. "I know who you are. You're the philosopher. I'm flattered you've come to visit me. Please come in." To Connie, the words sounded like an invitation to combat.

The floor of Kramer's front room was littered with books and magazines. Other books filled the shelves along two of the walls. The computer screen featured the Web site of a newspaper with French headlines decrying the advance of *Islamisme*. As Kramer swept two magazines from an easy chair to clear a seat for Connie, he welcomed his visitor to "my library. It's small. But it has the important works."

Connie had spent the previous twenty minutes sorting through various opening gambits that he might use in launching his conversation, but none had seemed to catch the right tone. Walking up the driveway, he had realized that his difficulty was his inability to imagine what the term "right tone" might mean for a man as alien from his own experience as Kramer. So he struck out into unknown territory. "Shrug has told you what he and I are doing. I'm here to follow up on your conversation with him. Would you be willing to tell me what you can remember about the evening of the reunion?" If nothing else, this opening was bland.

"Yes," said Kramer, who had taken a seat at right angles to Connie's. "Tony Travers. A brave man." He fell silent for several seconds. "Shrug thinks I killed him, you know. I'll bet you do too. But I didn't, you know. I admired him. He was courageous." Kramer sounded almost wistful. "He was not afraid to fight. I think that if he were alive and young today he would have contempt for his native Britain. The land of Churchill has become the land of Blair, you know. The strong have become the weak, you know. And people from Pakistan and Jamaica and Uganda are overrunning the country. Black people are inferior, you know."

Connie ran his tongue across his upper lip. Deciding it was pointless to take on Kramer's views when it was information about Kramer's actions he was interested in, Connie asked about the evening of the reunion.

"Why don't you believe me?" Kramer's face turned serious. "I never lie. Since I've come to see the truth—that race is the controlling factor of history. I've never felt the need to resort to lies. So when I say that I didn't kill Tony Travers, that means I didn't kill Tony Travers."

"That's not the question I asked." Connie felt irritated. "I asked about the evening of the reunion. Do you have any recollections of the evening that might be relevant to our inquiry."

"Your 'inquiry.'" My, my. Aren't we taking ourselves a little too seriously?"

"Are you always this rude with your guests?"

Kramer leaned back, inhaled deeply, and stared at Connie. "I'm sorry. I *am* being insufferable, you know. Sorry. I don't have many guests. I'll try to guard my terrible tongue. Now, what are you asking?"

Connie repeated the question, and Kramer began a wandering, free-association excursion through his recollections of the evening of Tony Travers's death. He explained that he'd chosen to attend the reunion both because he lived right in Humboldt ("it was easy") and because he wanted to see what forty-five years of life had done to some of his classmates. In general, he'd been very disappointed. All of them, even the few who in high school days had shown the potential for rebellion, had become good bourgeois. "But then," he added by way of commentary, "I shouldn't have been surprised, since Nietzsche is very clear about the power of the herd mentality. Even Cole Stocker, who had the body of a god in his high school basketball days, has settled for the respectability of health care."

Kramer remarked that Shrug had seemed fixated on Eddie Moratino. "That's not surprising, you know. Two pudgy guys, obviously unable to find female companionship, perhaps *gay*." (His intonation indicated that he wanted Connie to know he was quite ready to use alternative terms.) "And fond of music. They embody the death throes of the bourgeoisie."

"That's outrageous, Freddy."

"'Fritzy,' if you please."

"That's outrageous, Freddy, and on many levels. First, as sheer description. I don't know Eddie Moratino, but Shrug Speaker isn't pudgy. Or if he is, so are you." Connie immediately regretted his resort to schoolyard retort games.

"Second," Connie continued, "as innuendo. Again I don't know anything about Mr. Moratino, but Shrug isn't gay. And I have to add, even if only for my own satisfaction, not that it would matter if he were. In fact, since you seem to be living alone and since I happen to know you've blown two marriages, you hardly seem like the model preacher for good relations with women. Third, music is one of the glories of civilization, and an ennobling glory. Just because I don't understand and relish it the way Shrug does, and I take it you don't either, doesn't make it a sign of decay. Fourth, your understanding of history is cliché-ridden." Connie stopped. He was embarrassed at his inarticulateness. And even worse, he had lost his cool, which was probably what Kramer had hoped would happen. He could only hope his wince wasn't visible.

"I'll continue," Kramer said quietly, apparently savoring his quick victory. Sticking with just the persons about whom Shrug had inquired, he told of brief conversations with the Grunhagen sisters, one of whom had dated Tony in high school. He recalled a particularly disappointing exchange with Denny Culbertson. "The guy was smart, real smart, and now he's truckled under to the vapid foolishness of what Nietzsche calls a slave morality. He's a loser, you know." He smiled in relating the insubstantial contents of a brief conversation with Amanda Everson. "She can't be a murderess, you know. She's too conventional."

Determined to avoid further outbursts, Connie stuck to his listening mode and noticed how often quasi-poetic allusions to Tony Travers flavored Kramer's recollections. Travers had "held himself erect even with his cane." He had "borne his pains without complaint." His smile had "reflected the confidence of a life lived boldly." His choice of words had "shown little deleterious effect from decades of engagement with the effete classes of society." Connie quickly decided that Shrug was right: Tony Travers exercised some strange effect on Fritz Kramer, an effect that Kramer seemed unaware of.

Finally Kramer's monologue of reminiscences came to an end. Connie took the opportunity to pose a question that Shrug hadn't asked. "If Tony was in fact murdered, who do you think did it?"

Kramer laughed unpleasantly. "He wasn't murdered, at least by a classmate. To put the question is to answer it. To commit murder you need guts, balls, cajones. You do know what 'cajones' means, don't you? Of course you do; you're a scholar. No, no one in the class of 1953, Tony Travers excepted, had the requisite courage to kill another person. They'd all been emulsified in the great gray laxative of mediocrity. They'd all forgotten, or maybe they never knew, that society rests on someone's being willing to be courageous. Maybe Tony killed himself. Maybe he tripped and fell down the stairs. Maybe some old enemy stole into the school and struck him down. But you can be sure of this, you know. He wasn't murdered by a classmate. They are all effeminate cowards."

"Those are strong words, Freddy, and deeply unfair ones, too."

"It's 'Fritz,' Connie. Or perhaps you'd prefer to be called 'Connie-boy.' And the words aren't unfair. You're a philosopher. I'd expect you to know your Nietzsche, even if most people don't."

"It strikes me," said Connie, still determined to stay calm, "that you're misunderstanding your philosopher hero. Nietzsche's view of life consists of much more than a few outrageous aphorisms. In fact, at his core he is an epistemologist, not a critic of morality."

"Wrong, friend, wrong. That may be what grad schools teach. That may be what your loosey-goosey, pomo-spouting colleagues teach, but they're engaged in the fundamentally dishonest task of trying to trim Nietzsche to politically correct specifications. To make him presentable to a bourgeois audience. To transform . . ."

"Scholars know he hated the bourgeoisie." Connie couldn't help himself, even if yet again he suspected he was being caught out by one of Kramer's mind games.

Kramer ignored him. "They're being dishonest. *You*'re being dishonest. And that's not surprising. Any fan of Kant's is a fan of Plato. And Plato taught the nobility of lying. Well, I don't lie. Do you know what Henry Ward Beecher said about Kant? He called him 'the twin sister of hypocrisy.'"

Connie was stunned. He knew the quotation. It was standard jocular fare during the lighthearted moments at gatherings of Kant scholars. He therefore knew that Kramer *didn't* know what he was talking about. "Beecher was referring to 'cant,' Mr. Kramer, not Kant. To falsely pious words, not to a German philosopher." He refrained from calling his host a numbskull.

It was as if Kramer hadn't heard him. "At the heart of your philosophy, Connie, is a refusal to acknowledge the primary empirical social truth of our time—that there are basic and ineradicable differences between the races. Look at performance in schools. Then look at performance on athletic fields." Connie noticed that it was Kramer, stammering as he tried to speak rapidly, who now seemed to be losing his cool. "Whites are better at thinking and hence at leading. People of African descent"—again there was the sense that Kramer was flaunting what he would regard as a euphemism— "are better at jumping around and following orders. Ergo, whites are the superior race."

Instantly Thomas Henry Huxley's exultant thought, "The lord has delivered him into my hands," flashed upon Connie's mind.

Kramer had now left himself open to several lines of counterat-
tack, and whether they were empirical or logical in character, they
would be based on grounds that Kramer himself had legitimized.

"How then should we interpret the data that show that, on average, Asian-Americans are abler at intelligence tasks than whites?
That Jews are abler than non-semitic whites? By your reasoning
aren't these groups therefore *more* superior than the group you
place at the top? Are you pleased with that conclusion?"

"Easily explained," Kramer replied calmly. "In some cases the
data are simply false. In others they reflect a measurement of an
intelligence that is soft rather than hard. And in any case, remember, Asians and Jews often have the advantage of being raised in
families that encourage hard work in schools. Their scores reflect
in part a hothouse upbringing."

"You're dodging the question," Connie continued. "Which
suggests that you don't like the conclusion that your logic leads
you to. In any case, what does intelligence have to do with courage?"

"Not much at all. That's why, instead of Plato's philosopher-
king, I'd prefer Nietzsche's warrior-king. After all, only the culti-
vation of a warrior culture can save us from the corrosions of liberal democracy." Kramer stared directly into Connie's eyes. "Yes,
you heard me right, you know." Kramer drew himself up proudly.
"Democracy destroys a society. Strong leadership saves it."

"Well, I'm glad you've made that clear, Fritz. At least we know
where we stand. In a day or two I'll send you a reading list from
which you might profit, not, I suspect, that you'll pay it any heed.
Meanwhile, thank you for an enlightening morning." Connie got
up to leave.

"You're always welcome to visit me again, Connie. I think
you detest me, but you're smart enough to pay heed to evidence.
Truth has its way. And remember: I don't lie."

"Good day, Fritz." And Connie left, feeling not unlike the angry English gentleman seen in numerous films, withdrawing from

an unpleasant situation neither victorious nor defeated, but at least with his dignity intact and his temper under control. He had only his baseball cap to slap on his head, not the derby of the scene he was imagining, but he did it with such force that it slid off to the ground. At that point he could only chuckle at himself. That, and mutter something under his breath about Freddy Kramer being a nasty piece of work.

———

Shrug received Connie with beer and crackers when he arrived at 1:30 that afternoon. The languid, warm morning was yielding to a breezier afternoon, and Connie was glad he had remembered to pull out his red Humboldt jacket before leaving home.

"One of your neighbors has a new blue Camaro," he remarked, as he made his way through the entranceway to the living room.

"Sorry, I'm not a car guy. I hadn't noticed. Why do you say so?"

"It's parked up the street a ways, just like yesterday. I noticed only because most people along here park their vehicles in their driveways."

Vaguely curious and juggling a tray of crackers, Shrug stepped back outside to look, but saw only the empty street. "They're gone now. Maybe they were visiting."

The two friends sat down at the familiar card tables, eager to begin a substantive discussion on the struggling investigation. "I wish more evidence of some sort were turning up," Shrug said, thumbing through the note cards in his hands. "If we were to go before a grand jury now, we couldn't even meet the 'ham sandwich' criterion."

"Maybe. But if we haven't uncovered a crime, we've sure unearthed a perfect villain. I visited Freddy Kramer this morning—and I'm wicked enough to admit I took pleasure in calling him by that name—and came away with the same reaction you did: a very unpleasant man." Connie related the highlights of the conversation to Shrug, who enjoyed the tale.

"If Cole Stocker's medical training were psychiatric rather than orthopedic, we could invite him to give us some diagnostic thoughts about Freddy's thing about Tony," Shrug remarked when Connie had completed the narrative. "Only I don't think we need to probe too deeply to get a sense that Kramer was or *is* almost mesmerized by his war-hero classmate. Mesmerized and perhaps (though this lies beyond my well-honed competence) enraged."

"Yes, there's the question, isn't it. Is Fritzy just a hero-worshipper? Or is he also pathologically fixated? Didn't someone say the distance between love and hate is very small?"

"Sounds deep. But, just because someone said it doesn't make it so."

"And I just love that change from Freddy to Fritz. From the effete to the rugged. That's what they called Frederick the Great, you know. Fritz. Or maybe it was 'Old Fritz.' In any case, I'll bet your classmate hoped to add an aura of masculinity to his persona by trying to change his nickname."

"Odd that you should mention Frederick the Great," Shrug commented. "As I lay on what I feared would be my deathbed four days ago, I spent some time trying to figure out who Tony's 'the Great' might be. Probably not Alfred, I concluded. Or Peter or Ivan." His eyes were twinkling.

"Don't forget Charlemagne: Carolus Magnus."

"Have you noticed how generally it's males who win the title? Mary the Great, Doris the Great, Joanie the Great. It doesn't ring right. In fact, the only woman who comes quickly to mind is Catherine. Which leads to the question: Have you come across any Catherines while rummaging through Tony's correspondence?"

"Not that I recall. He had a number a lady friends, but nary a Catherine, nor a Kate nor a Katie nor a Kit nor a Kitty."

"Don't forget Cathy or Katrina. You're a copious cascade of catalytic concatenations."

Connie hoisted his beer glass in a sign of mock-appreciation. "But we need to get down to business. Putting noisome nomenclatural nonsense aside, where exactly do we stand?"

Thus prompted, each man summarized what his investigations had thus far uncovered. Some of the information had been mentioned the day before, when Abe Steinberg had been present. But for the sake of thoroughness and context, each reporter included the familiar nuggets again. When Connie mentioned Bunny Grunhagen's remark in Tony's yearbook, Shrug immediately caught the allusion to *Sense and Sensibility* that Connie had missed and proposed that it constituted strong evidence that one of the twins was quite fond of the visiting Brit. Freddy Kramer had said as much. "And if that's so, we can't ignore the likelihood that, with Tony being twenty-five or twenty-six and a man of strong sexual appetites, the relationship was physical."

"I suspect most high school relationships are physical these days," Connie opined. "I know that most college ones are."

"Maybe. But less so back then. At least if I can trust my memory of my distant, rather celibate high school days. Remember, I was their classmate. Of course, maybe you guys on the West Coast had an easier time of it."

"I plead the fifth amendment," Connie replied with laugh. "And now, on to business. Where do we stand?"

"I think . . . ." said Shrug haltingly, "I think that Freddy Kramer has to be at the top of our list of suspects. I don't say that because I dislike him, though I do. I say it both because, despite his emphatic denials, he has both a possible motive, which he also denies, and more important, because he has revealed a temperament that suggests he would not be averse to recourse to violence. And we can't forget his odd fascination with Tony."

"Well, I guess so," Connie replied, equally hesitant. "But it's a pretty shaky list of suspects if Freddy Kramer rises to the top by virtue of an ideological tic and a psychological quirk."

With that remark, the friends surveyed the other candidates. Trish Ridgway had a motive. She had been drunk the evening of Tony's death. She had even found the body. Might her inebriation have led her to give a shove to the man whose recognition five years earlier she had begrudged? That possibility struck both men as plausible. But the sending of a threatening note seemed incongruent with a deed perpetrated in the fog of intoxication.

One of the Grunhagens? It told against them that they had apparently kept silent about the fact that one of them had dated Tony in high school. And if Bunny had been the sister who dated Tony, then his frequent appearance in a yearbook that she edited might be more explicable. Finally, since both sisters had been out of the dining room for part of the window of opportunity, they might have ganged up on Tony. But even though Shrug remained fascinated by the possibility that one twin could alibi the other in some thus far fog-enveloped murder plot, neither Connie nor Shrug really thought either of the Grunhagens to be the "murdering kind," whatever that might mean.

How about Eddie Moratino? Nothing remotely like a motive had been uncovered so far. And everyone seemed to like him. In fact, the only thing that left even a trace of suspiciousness attached to his name was the international character of his business, which provided a number of exotic locales where he and Tony might conceivably have met. To impute guilt to him on the basis of evidence so inconsequential would seem to argue more for the parochialism of the detectives than the guilt of the merchant.

And then there was Denny Culbertson. Odd, yes. But more levelheaded than the reports of reunion conversations had suggested. He might not like abortion-providers, but nothing that the friends knew about him suggested a readiness to countenance murder. And where was a motive? Aside from the fact that Tony and he *might* have been in the Pittsburgh area about the same time, there was no reason to believe the two men had ever crossed paths since high school days. Was it strange that Culbertson had no recollection of a conversation that Kramer recalled clearly? Probably not, for memories are funny things, and a conversation that lingered with one participant might easily have seemed unimportant to the other.

"Is it suspicious," Shrug finally asked, "that we haven't heard from either Sonya Klepper or Amanda Everson?"

"Why should it be? We don't even know whether Everson has received your letter yet. And in any case she may be too busy supplying fashion ideas to the Kiwis to reply right away. As for Klepper, I think your good luck in hearing from Moratino and Culbertson this morning has given you excessive expectations about responses to letters. She could be traveling. She could be sick. She could even be dead. Most likely, though, she's just waiting until she has time to contact you. If you're worried, you could give them calls later this week. A few days of delay can't hurt since we've got other things to do. And other information may come in."

On that point both men agreed. They had high hopes for the reply from Claire Van Tassell. And although Connie had not yet written the three wives, he would do so promptly, an initiative that held out the promise of unleashing a flood of useful information. They needed a new conversation with Bryan Travers, to see whether the mention of the wives' names, or of Van Tassell's, awakened any memories. And to see if he knew the full names of any of his father's friends from his military days. Connie set for himself the task of coordinating the information that could be gleaned from Tony's memorabilia boxes with the biographical scaffold that Abe Steinberg had provided. "We need to flesh out Tony's life story," he added. Shrug replied by volunteering to find out about the effectiveness of the security arrangements that the class had put in place for the night of the reunion. "If *anyone* could have gotten in, then this whole exercise of ours is basically pointless. I should have made this my first step."

As the men allotted their tasks and expressed their hopes, they came finally to acknowledge their mutual sense of letdown. "At some point," Connie said after mid-afternoon, as he slipped his shoes back on and carried his glass into the kitchen, "we may have to face the fact that, aside from Less's letter, we have nothing—absolutely nothing—to suggest that a criminal act occurred. That's depressing. And even Teresa's cheerleading can't overcome the implacable force of facts. If there are no traces, there are no defensible conclusions. Period. Bloch and Hume would agree."

"Not only that," Shrug replied, "but at this point I'm realizing that I'm propelled chiefly by the rather unworthy motive of hoping to stick it to Freddy Kramer. What happened to the disinterested pursuit of truth and justice?"

"Yes, thank goodness for Freddy. If we weren't consumed with a rarefied sort of blood lust, our rage in the Zocor set, we might be ready to fold. But hope springs eternal." Connie was laughing aloud now. "That's why we go to chess club to get beaten more often than not. And that's why we'll persevere in this investigation for at least a bit longer. After all, there's still a lot of ground to cover. We may just have been unlucky in the allocation of our energies. Besides, as always, it's fun. So let *les bons temps roulez*-on!"

On that cheering thought, Connie pulled on his baseball cap and headed out the door. *Yes, I would enjoy the opportunity of skewering Freddy Kramer. And . . . yes . . . yes . . . that blue Camaro was again parked up the street. Odd, isn't it?*

7

Tuesday, June 12, 2001

"Shrug, you won't believe this. I think I've identified your murderer! And, it's incredible! She's even confessed."

"What the hell are you talking about, Allan?" Though the speaker hadn't identified himself, the rector's voice was unmistakable. "And do you know what time it is? Is this any way to start a Tuesday morning?"

"Yes, I know the time. 8:15 isn't all that early. I've been up since 6:00, longer than you, I can see. But did you hear what I said? Aren't you interested?"

Even as Clark had been engaging in this bout of modest one-upsmanship, Shrug had pulled out a pen and pad, eager to jot down notes about the startling declaration. "Yes, of course I'm interested. You have my attention. Who are you talking about and what's this confession? Nothing vouchsafed under some expectation of confidentiality, I presume."

"Hardly. She wrote about it in a magazine. Can you believe it?"

"She did *what*?" That was certainly not an answer Shrug had expected. "And who are you talking about? Who is this *she*?"

"That's the tricky part. I don't know." And with that somewhat deflating acknowledgment, Clark filled Shrug in on the full tale. "As you know, I try to read lots of periodical literature published by various religious denominations. It's a way of scouting the competition or, to put it more politely, a way of keeping up with what's deemed hot or relevant in other confessional communities. Well, one of the magazines I track is *Guide to the Faithful Life*. It's a weekly put out by the Unitarian-Universalists, and I imagine its circulation is tiny, like *really* tiny. But it has a monthly series titled 'Ethics in Action.' A different author appears each month." Shrug sighed quietly and settled back in his chair, waiting for Clark to move to the point at his own pace.

"Three months ago," the rector continued—"I thought I'd remembered it when we spoke earlier, but didn't want to say anything to you 'til I'd checked my memory out—Three months ago there was a piece by someone named Saunders Cleaver, who reported that he had received a letter with a moral inquiry. It's in this letter, as related by Cleaver, that the unidentified writer admits to killing Tony Travers."

"Okay. Tell me about it."

And Clark proceeded to explain that the letter writer was seeking advice on whether she had done the right thing. In her letter she told of meeting an old love at a high school reunion. Shrug's attention started at that term. Travers was deep into failing health, and, in a private hallway rendezvous, she found him desperately sick and wanting to die so as to avoid the pain and debilitation that inevitably lay ahead. He was, however, unable to muster the courage to take his own life. He didn't exactly ask the letter writer to do the deed for him, but she claimed she knew him well and understood his heart, and out of love and pity decided to grant him his desire. They were talking at the top of a steel staircase, which offered the letter writer the opportunity of conferring a swift death upon her old flame on the spot, and so she abruptly pushed him down it. As he'd fallen backwards, he had briefly looked back up at her, gratitude on his face. The writer then left the building and the reunion. Her subsequent letter to Saunders Cleaver asked if what she had done can be regarded as right.

"That's appalling," Shrug gasped.

"What disgusts me most," Clark continued, "is the gloss this Saunders Cleaver puts on this terrible action. After pretending to discuss the complexities of the situation, the fact that the law doesn't look kindly on murder, the requirement that Christians must not take lives, the desperate future lying ahead for the longtime love, the obligation to help others deal with their problems, he concludes that Ms. I-prefer-to-remain-anonymous had taken an action that probably should not be called wrong and might even be called right. It all depended on her mind and heart at the time she pushed her old love to his death. How's that for a waffle? 'Probably not wrong, maybe right. It all depends on whether your heart was pure.' There's moral incisiveness for you." The rector's tone was angry.

Shrug agreed completely. But he was more interested in the article itself. "Can I come by to pick the magazine up right away? The event it describes is too close to what may really have happened at the reunion to be dismissed out of hand as a mere coincidence. The writer was almost surely there. And *our* question is: how do we identify her?"

Clark's grunt didn't convey much information, but he said he'd be happy to lend the magazine to Shrug. And within twenty minutes the extraordinary issue of *Guide to the Faithful Life* lay on the front seat of Shrug's car as he drove back home.

Shrug placed a phone call to his co-investigator when he reached home and twenty-minutes later Connie arrived at Shrug's house, deeply curious about the unexpected turn that the investigation had now taken. "What a great way to be greeted after a morning jog. Haven't even showered. Hope you don't mind." His broken diction showed his eagerness to proceed.

Connie read the article. Then Shrug, with the advantage of more than an hour's earlier notice, spoke. "I'm gonna cut to the chase. We can't take this at face value, whatever 'face value' might mean with this unusual piece. I'll bet that there is no one named Saunders Cleaver. In fact, I'll go further. I'll bet that Sonya Klepper is the ostensible letter-writer and in fact that she's the author of the entire piece. I'll bet that Saunders Cleaver is just a pseudonym that Sonya Klepper adopted. Just say the names aloud: Saunders Cleaver,

Sonya Klepper. A pseudonym adopted to create a margin of distance between the do-er of the deed and the supposedly independent commentary upon it."

"Sounds plausible. More important, it ought to be easy to confirm or disconfirm." With those words, he moved to Shrug's computer, searched for "Saunders Cleaver" and came up empty. "Not proof positive perhaps, but certainly supportive of your theory. If he were a real counselor and author, he wouldn't be escaping a Web sweep."

A brief silence fell on the conversation. Then Connie spoke. "So our initial take on a recasting of the article would be that Sonya Klepper pushed Tony down the stairs in 1998 and at some later point, for reasons not clear to us, decided to acknowledge that she was the perpetrator of his death, but to do so in a context that allows her to distance herself from the identity of the murderer and to reason her way through to her own absolution." Connie wiped his sweaty forehead with his sleeve. "But why be so complicated? Why be so oblique? Denny Culbertson said she was a good Christian, but that isn't the first term that comes to *my* mind when I think about this sequence of events. However, I defer to your far deeper understanding of the theological issues involved." He wasn't smiling. "Is that how you read this situation?"

"No it's not. But you first. I want to hear how you deal with these complexities."

"Okay," Connie grunted. "I'll go first, if you prefer. And in fact, I'm pretty sure that just as we can't take it at face value, we can't take it at what I just called an 'initial take' at a recasting. We've got to go deeper." He sipped the cold Coke that Shrug had supplied, while again using the sleeve of his sweatshirt to dry his flushed cheeks. Shrug brought him a towel before he continued. "The difficulty for me is that it presents a Tony Travers I don't recognize. His son, his physician, and his attorney, just about everyone who commented on his state of mind, all described a man who, though certainly in precarious health, enjoyed the challenges of life. That such a man would suggest to a high school classmate whom he probably hadn't seen in forty-five years, even if they *had* dated in the good old days, that he wished he could kill himself seems . . . well . . . implausible. No, it's worse. It rings false. Especially with that grateful look beaming from his face as he clattered down the stairs."

"That's good," Shrug replied. "I agree with your analysis. And I hadn't really thought of that angle, though it probably explains why I was feeling queasy with the psychology of the story. My own concern, however, lies elsewhere, in the improbable convenience of a meeting at the top of a staircase. Why aren't there some chairs? Why not a lounge? After all, Tony wasn't comfortable standing up. I can understand a desire for privacy. But then, all the more reason to find a comfortable place to talk. And so I don't think it is a conversation that belongs at the top of a stairwell. In which case, the story, and the motive, are at least a *little* more complicated than Sonya would seem to allow."

"So then," Connie said, "are we saying that Sonya is lying?"

"She's lying about something. There's no doubt there. The question is what?" He hesitated, his eyebrows and cheeks tensing. "Sorry. That's not very helpful. Still . . ." He was hesitating. "Still, I'll tell you what I think. I suspect she may have killed him, but for motives quite different from the disinterested ones she now broadcasting. Waddaya think?"

"That doesn't strike me as likely," Connie replied. "Why confess at all? It's very dangerous and as far as we know, at least when she was writing a piece that was published three months ago, completely unnecessary. No. I suspect something else is going on. And from what little we know of Ms. Klepper, it could be she's protecting someone else."

"But who needs protection? Protection from what? Do you suppose someone else is looking into this matter, someone who, in Klepper's view at least, may be getting close to the truth?" Shrug felt embarrassed by his inability to articulate his various questions crisply.

"Damned if I know. If that's it, she's sure using a roundabout means to divert attention from someone else. A Unitarian publication, for God's sake! You can't get more obscure than that. With a circulation of —what?— five hundred? No wonder the police somewhere haven't gotten more curious. Who's going to read *that?* It doesn't make sense." His curiosity alerted by Shrug's suggestion that someone else might be on the case, Connie walked to the window to see if the mysterious blue Camaro was in sight but it wasn't. "There's probably only one way to get the answers we need. Do you feel like a road trip?"

"Great idea! I was moving that way myself. And Richmond, Indiana, is only three hours away. A pleasant summer's drive. Let's see if I can get her on the phone." Although cautious on many matters, Shrug was quick to move to action when only a single course recommended itself. And Connie, seeing no ready alternative, made no effort to stop his friend from taking a step that, while it might gain them quick access to Sonya Klepper, might also send her into hiding. "I'm not going to give our game away," the host mumbled as he dialed the phone number provided by the class of 1953 directory. "We'd just like to stop by for visit, right? As part of our inquiry, right?"

Sonya Klepper DeLisle answered after the third ring and, while sounding surprised at hearing from Shrug, acknowledged receipt of his letter. "I was going to reply this weekend," she said, adding that she'd welcome a chat with the two investigators. They set 1:00 P.M. the following day for their visit. "Remember," she cautioned as the call was ending, "although we're in the eastern time zone in eastern Indiana, we don't go on daylight saving time. It's a silly system. And so now we're an hour behind you Ohioans. I suggest you leave for Richmond a tad before 11:00 your time." Shrug thanked her for the practical advice.

"Nary a word about any role she might have played in Tony's death," Shrug said after hanging up the phone. "So it sounds like she's going to play it cool. Of course, we could be wrong on our operational assumption. Maybe Sonya Klepper *isn't* Saunders Cleaver, has never even *heard* of Saunders Cleaver."

"Nonsense," Connie exclaimed. "We're right. The story has too much relevant detail. The only real danger now is that we have given her almost twenty-four hours to skedaddle if she's so inclined."

"Don't be a party pooper. Look on the bright side." Shrug briefly whistled the blithe tune. "I think we'll learn a lot from this conversation. But we need to be prepared. And to me, that means, first of all, reviewing the video on the reunion dinner."

Connie agreed with the idea, and within minutes the two friends were again studying the now-familiar closing hour of the video that recorded the evening of Tony Travers's death. At 7:45 P.M., as the class started to applaud the work of the planning committee, Amanda Everson moved in beside Tony Travers to speak with him briefly and then returned to her table. "I wonder what *that* was about?," Shrug muttered. Shortly before 8:00 the general singing began, with Rosey Thomas at the piano. After the *alma mater,* the selections turned to football fight songs. At 8:05 P.M., five minutes before Tony left his table to disappear from sight and life, Sonya Klepper, who had been seated several tables away from Travers, rose and departed, walking directly behind Tony on her way to the door. Her pink dress was somewhat more formal in its effect than the attire most women wore to the dinner, but her hair seemed oddly disarrayed, as if she had walked in front of a fan. "And look!" said Connie suddenly. "Do you think she spoke to Tony on her way out?" They ran the video again, and still could not be sure. There was certainly a small turn, maybe no more than a twitch, of the head as she passed behind him. And her lips may have moved, but the shadows and the camera angle obscured the lower part of her face at the critical moment. "Well, maybe not," Connie concluded. "It's just too hard to tell."

Even though they knew Klepper would not return, the friends kept viewing, transfixed by the knowledge of what lay ahead. At

8:06 Freddy Kramer walked slowly out of the room, limping slightly. At 8:10 Tony Travers made his exit (*his last exit*, thought Connie), supported on his cane. Connie made a quick note to contact the three classmates who had been seated at his table: Joanne Ducey, Kit Stephenson, and Jerry Albrechtsberger. At 8:14 one of the Grunhagen sisters left, speaking briefly to the other as she rose from her chair. At 8:16 Kramer returned, still limping and, in the brief moment when the light was right, showing an inscrutable face. A minute later the other Grunhagen sister rose quickly and left. They both returned five minutes later, arms linked and cheerfully chatting to each other. At 8:23, as the singing turned from football encouragement to nostalgic pop tunes of the 1950s, Denny Culbertson stood up and made his way to the door, pausing en route to bend down and speak to three classmates. The clock over the door registered 8:24 when he finally left. Only a few seconds later, and moving very quickly, Eddie Moratino made his exit. A minute after that it was Amanda Everson's turn, and while she wasn't as swift as Moratino, she still seemed to be a woman on a mission. At 8:26 Trish Ridgway exited, somewhat unsteadily. Two minutes later, with the second verse of "Auld Lang Syne" ringing through the room, Culbertson and Everson returned together, but conversing less vigorously than the Grunhagens had. Finally, at 8:31, Ridgway came rushing back into the dining room, and pandemonium ensued.

When the viewing was finished, the friends were silent for a few seconds.

"It's rather inconvenient," Connie mused, "that people who left the dining room might have gone in any of three directions. I know that two of the routes were hallways that were not well illuminated. But still they weren't inaccessible. Had there just been one straight pathway facing them, we might expect to get some tales of them meeting each other outside the dining area."

Connie's remark solidified Shrug's emerging conclusion about the choice of an inquisitorial strategy, and he pulled the conversation back to the subject at hand by declaring that asking Klepper what she had done when she left the dining room might be the best opening gambit. "We'll keep the secret of knowing about the magazine article to ourselves until we see how she responds to a presumably innocent question."

"Isn't that a bit underhanded for a friend?" Connie asked.

"I'm hoping for answers. Asking that question seems to me a good way of getting at them quickly. Besides, didn't you know that 'deviousness' is my middle name."

Connie bowed his head. "I'll follow your direction, oh master of cunning. The path toward truth leads circuitously upward. Let's just hope we haven't made fools of ourselves in conflating Saunders Cleaver with Sonya Klepper. And meanwhile, on to afternoon assignments."

——— ——— ———

At 1:30 that afternoon Connie walked into the large brick Victorian structure that now served as the county historical society. The well-lit front room contained mannequins garbed in the apparel that the nineteenth-century founders of Humboldt had brought with them from Germany. Small information posters identified the items. Farm clothes. Social attire. Frocks for little girls. Leathery pants for little boys. A minister's stiff clerical uniform. A faded wedding dress. Given his interest in local history, Connie was familiar with the display and knew many of the benefactors who had supplied the old clothes to the museum. But his purpose today was more recent history, for when he had phoned Abe Steinberg to let him know that Sonya Klepper had abruptly vaulted to the top of the list and to inquire if Steinberg had uncovered anything of interest about this obscure Indiana widow, the archivist had replied by inviting Connie to the museum. "About Klepper," he had said, "I've found almost nothing. Sorry. But I've fleshed out the sickening story of Freddy Kramer even more. I'd like you to see what I've accumulated. And all of sudden I've got information that links Tony Travers with, of all people, Denny Culbertson. I think you'll be interested."

When Connie entered Steinberg's small and cluttered office, he saw that a display table had been shoved to the center of the room and that the archivist had laid out several documentary exhibits for him. Steinberg immediately handed him the slim Klepper file.

"After graduating from Humboldt High, Ms. Klepper attended Wheaton College in Illinois, got an education degree at the University of Kentucky and taught at two Kentucky high schools before coming to Humboldt High in 1981. She left in 1987 when her family moved to Richmond, Indiana. Her husband, whom she had married in 1959, died in 1990. They had three daughters. End of easily accessible story. Her life seemed pretty straightforward, and so I didn't turn any special investigatory efforts her way."

Connie thanked him and took the file. "Tell me about Kramer and Culbertson."

To tell the Kramer story, Steinberg picked up a pile of papers from the bench. They were printouts of material found on the Web. "Edify yourself with these."

Connie saw immediately that they were essays. The one on top identified "Fritz Kramer" as its author, and Connie presumed the others had the same honor. Their titles, visible as Connie thumbed through the pile, told the story of their purpose: "The Holocaust: Truth or Myth," "The Jewish Plan to Control International Finance," "America and the Crisis of Color," "Race and History: The Key to Understanding the Human Past," "Where Hitler Went Wrong," "What We Can Learn from Nietzsche."

"Well," Connie said, "I see I've been a bit laggard in my education."

"It's not funny." Steinberg's remark was clipped and angry. "I know you mean well, but to see anything humorous in this rancid stuff is to abandon one of the defenses which stands between civilization and the barbarism of hate. We have a duty to revile it, to revile and despise and decry it, and to never allow it, even through the slippery backdoor of irony, into polite company."

Connie was stunned. "Sorry," he mumbled. He felt ashamed, recalling again that Steinberg had lost his parents and at least some of his siblings in the final inferno of Nazi hatred in 1944 and 1945.

"It's okay." Steinberg took Connie gently by the elbow. "You're one of the good guys. I know." He laid the pile down and picked up the other. "Here, let me show you the evidence I've found of a Travers-Culbertson connection. Except, 'connection' isn't exactly the right word. To put it candidly, these two gentlemen had a confrontation back in 1970."

Connie accepted the sheets of paper, thankful for the gracious way Steinberg had changed the subject and quite curious to see what unexpected crossing of life trajectories Steinberg had uncovered. But when he realized that the printouts were copies of newspaper articles, replete with repetitions and rich in details, he looked up to the archivist. "Give me the skeleton story. Then I can make quicker sense of all this information."

"Actually there's less here than you might think. Lots of redundancy and lots of angry but probably irrelevant quotations. You need to recall that back in the late 1960s Tony Travers lived in Brockton, just outside Pittsburgh, and managed a successful construction company. And you need to recall that Denny Culbertson was then in his pre-Damascus-road days"—a joke from one non-Christian to another—"and probably much like the famous Mr. Gordon Gekko." Steinberg then told how Culbertson had invested in a firm that wanted to develop a large tract of land north of Brockton, how Travers had been a leader of the local group that opposed the proposal, and how the opposition had finally managed to protract the proceedings for so long that the investors abandoned their plan and set out to look for a more receptive community. "Ultimately, during the 1970s," Steinberg explained, "much of the land was turned into, of all things, an animal preserve where large fauna, endangered in their native African or Asian habitats, can roam free, except of course for the perimeter fences."

"And the 'confrontation'?" Connie asked.

"At two public meetings, Travers and Culbertson wound up shouting at each other. Maybe Culbertson thought that Travers, as an old high school classmate, would be willing to help out. In any case, he may have tried to purchase Travers's support or at least that's one interpretation that can be put on Tony's declaration that 'your money can't buy my conscience.' It probably really pissed Culbertson off that within a month or so of leading the successful opposition to the project Travers moved away from Brockton. And while I have no idea how much money Culbertson invested in the scheme, or whether the investment finally paid off in the long run, he must have been mad as hell that his Pittsburgh-area project was being blocked by an old acquaintance."

"Yeah," Connie concluded when Steinberg's account was over, "that might constitute a motive. But by all accounts, Denny Culbertson is a changed man. He's repudiated his old life. Why should he want to revisit an affront that happened three decades ago? Still less, use it as a justification for murdering someone?"

"Sounds like a question you'd want to put to him. But you might want to make sure you've got an exit route when you do. He wouldn't be the first con man to use religion as a highway to influence. Still, my money and heart are on Fritzy-boy. Bring him down and you'll make me one happy guy."

Connie thanked Steinberg for his help, gathered the assorted files that had been prepared for him, promised that Kramer's pieces would be kept for the day they could be used against him, and set out into the mild June afternoon, his mind back on the puzzle of Sonya Klepper. So deep, in fact, was his immersion into the world of Klepper-speculation that it wasn't until 2:15 that he recalled he had a 3:30 appointment with his ophthalmologist in Columbus. As it turned out, he was only a few minutes late for the appointment, and the only casualty of the moment of forgetfulness was his self-image, since he was of that age when every incident of memory misbehavior occasioned worries that the onset of Alzheimer's was at hand. Happily, a good evening of chess, capped by a rather masterful bishop-rook combination that led to an unexpected victory, eased his fears and allowed him to believe that he had a few more months of cognitive health left.

———

Shrug used Tuesday afternoon to revisit the Grunhagen sisters. It seemed quite clear that they hadn't been candid with him during the earlier conversation, and he hoped he could extract a more truthful account of their friendships with Tony Travers than they had chosen to present the previous Wednesday. He still thought them unlikely murderers, though he recognized the very silliness of that sort of thought the moment it took shape, but he also remained intrigued that they might somehow be prepared to pull the twin-stunt if the investigation should somehow wind up pointing at one of them. And the fact that they had kept the truth about their relationship with Travers away from him didn't help to nourish their general aura of innocence.

Bonny and Bunny met him at the door, attired in identical long yellow dresses. They smiled endearingly at him but clearly were curious at what turn of events had prompted Shrug to request a second conversation in less than a week.

"You must find us attractive, Shrug . . ."

". . . to grace us with another visit so soon." They giggled.

Shrug returned their smiles as he entered the house, and allowed the tone of conversational sprightliness to hang in the air for just a moment longer before abruptly dissolving it with his opening declaration. "I know now that you two weren't candid with me last week." His face was now severe. "And worse, your effort to mislead me touches upon a matter that is central to this investigation, the relationships that various classmates, you two included, had with Tony Travers."

Bunny tried to interrupt, but Shrug, who had planned his opening gambit in advance, did not want to be diverted from his goal of establishing a new set of ground rules. "I cannot make you tell me

147

the truth. I am not a policeman. But I can say with real assurance that if Connie and I conclude that Tony was murdered, we will tell all that we know to the authorities. And among the points we will make are that you two were uncooperative and bent upon concealing something. In the eyes of law enforcement officials, that kind of information will move you to the top of any list of possible suspects."

Bonny opened her mouth to speak, but Shrug waved her off. "So if you had nothing to do with Tony's death, I think it would be best if you reconsidered some of the things you told me last time and let me hear the true story."

Shrug fell silent, privately admiring his ability to assume the role of the stern dispenser of disapprobation, while the normally chipper Grunhagen sisters stood staring at him wordlessly.

"Will you please excuse us for a moment?" Bunny finally said. And the twins left the room arm in arm, upright and dignified. Shrug, who had been left standing by the entrance, stepped into the living room and took a seat on the couch. Clearly he had shaken them. A long ten minutes passed before the sisters returned. Their expressions struck Shrug as opaque, but Bonny began by declaring that after consulting with each other, they believed they could be more useful to Shrug than they had been the previous Wednesday. "You need to know first," she said, "that neither of us had anything to do with Tony Travers's death. But the story I'm about to tell will show why we might have wished an unpleasant end for him."

Sensing that he had won the day, Shrug immediately shifted from the stern to the avuncular—*if it's possible to be avuncular*, he thought, *with someone your own age*—and, smiling benignly, told the sisters that he was sure their tale was complicated and their sentiments warranted.

With that encouragement, and very uncharacteristically for two sisters who had mastered a talent for speaking stereophonically, Bonny alone told a tale of the Grunhagens and Tony Travers, while Bunny and Shrug sat back silently to attend to it.

"Tony Travers was a rat," she began. He had, she explained, been fully aware of how attractive he was to sixteen- to-eighteen year-old girls. "A rugged war hero, or so we all assumed. Not handsome in a Van Johnson sense, but strong and chiseled. Older, wiser, more experienced, and we soon had good reason to be confident that that last judgment was correct. And that wonderful voice, a British accent that rolled around in his mouth. I'll bet that almost every girl in the class had a crush on him. And that included Bunny and me."

With that introduction out of the way, Bonny told of how Travers had set out to capture Bunny, had dated her frequently across much of the senior year, and had led her to believe she would soon be Mrs. Anthony Travers. He had asked that she keep the relationship a secret, and confident that he loved her, she had gladly complied. She knew, of course, that he was "dating" other girls, but *that*, he assured her, was just a ruse, a way to keep their own deep love "uncontaminated by the tawdry scrutiny of an uncomprehending world." "Those were his very words," Bonny said bitterly. "And Bunny trusted him." But suddenly, in April, shortly before graduation, he told her that they were through.

Two weeks after Tony broke the relationship off, Bunny learned that she was pregnant. Bunny felt that there wasn't a chance in the world their parents would have understood, and so she asked her sister—"I'm the older one, by about six minutes"—to help her arrange a "procedure" right after commencement. "That much was easy," Bonny continued, "but thanks to the abortion, Bunny became incapable of having children. That was devastating to her. She was left feeling both betrayed and victimized."

Shrug glanced at Bunny, who was sitting quietly in her straight chair, face down and hands in her lap, scarcely moving as Bonny's tale unfolded, the very antithesis of the ebullient and lively woman he had talked with five days earlier.

"But it's even worse," Bonny continued. "Bunny and I were best friends. We had formed our special bond by sixth grade. We

shared, we laughed, we cried, we griped—together, always together. And at this crucial moment, I let my sister down. I didn't
stand by her." She stopped, apparently trying to figure out how to
make her next point. Then she began again, obliquely. "You may
have noticed that the only time the two of us have been apart for
any significant amount of time in our lives was our college years.
That's because I was so angry at Bunny that I refused to accompany her to Ohio State."

Shrug didn't want to interrupt, but he needed to be sure he
understood what Bonny was saying. "You were angry with her for
dating Tony? For getting pregnant?"

"Oh no. Not at all. I could understand her attraction to him. I'd
probably have slept with him too if he'd asked. *That* I could understand. What I couldn't understand was her decision to have an
abortion. To kill her baby."

Shrug saw Bunny cringe as Bonny reached this point in the
tale.

"It was selfish and pompous of me," Bonny continued, "to be
so judgmental, so totally insensitive. But because I needed a few
years to grow up, we stayed apart through most of our college
years, each missing the other so much that it hurt.

"Finally, in the summer before our senior years, when we had
no choice but to live with our parents in the same house here in
Humboldt, we began reaching out to each other again. Or rather,
Bunny forgave me."

"No," Bunny murmured, speaking for the first time. "You forgave *me*." Bonny laid her hand over her sister's.

Bonny then told how the two of them had decided that hence-
forth they would live together and have nothing to do with men.
And that's what they had done. Whether as airline hostesses or
gardening columnists, they had stayed celibate, forswearing all
relationships with men in order to remain true to each other. "We
know that people think we're lesbians, but we're not. It's just that
we've rediscovered what Renaissance nuns knew: that women are

freest when they avoid all entanglements with men. Maybe that's unfair. Maybe *you* were a great husband." Even before he could check himself, Shrug shook his head negatively. Bonny didn't seem to notice. "But for us it has been the best life possible."

And so, she explained, they preferred to devote themselves to their work and to helping each other. When Tony attended the reunions in 1993 and 1998, they stayed away from him. "Check your video," Bonny said, "you won't find us going near him in 1998." Even when he had won the award at the fortieth reunion, they refused to congratulate him. "It's likely he never even noticed our inattention, of course. Chances are he didn't even remember us. Men are like that. And we tried to make sure, and I think we *did* make sure, that Tony never learned that Bunny had been pregnant or had an abortion. He probably would have approved, but what she did was none of his business."

Over the years their feeling about Tony had undergone a subtle shift, assuming in the end the form of contempt rather than anger. And there was reason for that. They had seen too many of their high school and college girlfriends squander good futures to please mediocre husbands. "Men have little regard for women. They don't see the sacrifices women make." Shrug was beginning to feel uncomfortable, but Bonny had developed her own momentum. "They . . . well . . . they *presume*. Yes, if there's anything that characterizes your sex, Shrug, it's your innate sense of entitlement. Bunny and I decided to play the game of life by our own rules, not yours."

She stopped talking, and Shrug briefly considered defending the male sex from this assault. But he quickly decided that it would make him appear unduly defensive and do no good anyway. So, sounding as if he were bringing a trivial exchange of pleasantries to an end, he thanked the sisters for their help and candor, shook hands with each, and saw himself to the door. His last view of them, seized as he briefly turned his head back before entering the warmth of a perfect June afternoon, was of Bonny putting her arm around Bunny's shoulders. They'd certainly testified to the existence of a motive, he thought, but it's increasingly hard to see them as killers. Or, he continued, is that the point? On balance, he concluded, for all the sympathy their tale evoked, the information he had now learned made the likelihood of their guilt somewhat higher. But they were still eclipsed by the suddenly enormous puzzle of Sonya Klepper.

Shrug reached home by the middle of the afternoon, his groin sore and his legs aching. He was, he decided, just plain weary. He didn't feel up to chess that evening, and while he was tempted to phone Marilyn to fill her in on the development that had suddenly elevated her former teacher to the top of the suspect list, he decided that he would put off making that call until after the next day's visit with Klepper had provided an opportunity to cast a clarifying beam on the shadowy situation. So Shrug poured himself a beer, put a recording of *Die Winterreise* on the CD player, and let the wonderful voice of Dietrich Fischer-Dieskau—*has any singer been so suited to performing Schubert Lieder?*—soften his pains and tranquillize his soul. After dinner, feeling uncommonly mellow, he let his fingers wander through the sad and lovely first movement of Beethoven's "Moonlight Sonata." Then, having made all right with the world and offered thanks to God for His bounty, he retired, eager to be rested for what promised to be a difficult interview the next afternoon.

8

Wednesday, June 13, 2001

Though the calendar said mid-June, the early morning warmth radiating from the pavement suggested that the season of sultry summer days had arrived. Happily for the two friends as they headed toward Indiana, the air conditioning of Connie's Regal protected them from the oppressive heat. Connie promptly told of the decades-old contretemps between Tony Travers and Denny Culbertson. Shrug passed on the revised version of the Grunhagen-Travers relationship of almost fifty years earlier, adding that Bunny's pregnancy left no doublt that Travers could father a child. "So much for Abe's worry on that score." Then, as the Ohio landscape rolled past, the men fell silent.

For Connie, whose topographical preferences had been shaped by a West Coast childhood, the flatness of much of central Ohio was uninteresting. No spectacle, no grandeur, no Wordsworthian vistas. For Shrug, a lifelong Ohioan, it testified to the nuanced character of the charms of the Buckeye State. Sure, there were no snow-brushed mountains, lofty forests, or wave-besieged seacoasts to treat the eye and quicken the imagination. But there were times, he often thought, when the ostentation of soaring peaks and craggy abysses cheapened the sensitivity of the soul. Better, sometimes, the chaste harmonies of a rolling hillside, the stark shadows of a rural Midwestern evening, the delicate modulations of a breeze-stirred cornfield. Just as there were days when Haydn (Franz Josef, of course, not Connie) was to be preferred to Beethoven, so also were there days when Ohio hill country was to be preferred to the Alps or the Devon coast.

"I had another of my classroom dreams last night," Connie suddenly said as they cruised past Columbus. "I was lecturing on Sartre. But the weird part is that the students were all animals: horses, frogs, cassowaries, lizards. Or maybe the really weird part is that I wasn't bothered by this strange assemblage. I just kept prattling on about existence preceding essence. And they kept nodding their heads and taking notes. An intellectual bestiary. Do you ever dream about your days as an investment adviser?"

"Nothing so exotic, that's for sure. In fact, I'm not sure I ever strictly dream about my career at all. But I often daydream about it. Or rather reflect back on it. Sometimes I think about how I helped the people who came to me for advice. But too often I think of those I failed. And those aren't pleasant reminiscences. The only consolation in the latter instances is that, since I generally followed my own advice, if others were hurt by it, so was I."

"That's not quite what I meant. After all, a dream in which I'm lecturing to note-taking animals hardly suggests that the career that the dream is based on was a very serious one. It all sounds rather cartoonish. And yet I know I regarded it as serious at the time, and important, too."

"And it was." Shrug wasn't clear where Connie was going with these remarks, and so he offered a bromide that might encourage his friend to elaborate. But Connie fell silent.

Several miles flowed by before Shrug decided to extend his reply. "On balance, I've found retirement wonderful. As long as I have health and am not overspending, I have time and opportunity to play any games I want to." He paused, aware that Connie was listening with care. "But the downside, and maybe this is what you're feeling, for I do, is precisely that *everything* now seems to be a bit of a game. Our generation of middleclass males was raised to be serious and responsible people, brought up to think that we had jobs, schedules, and, above all, obligations. As long as we were being paid to perform these tasks, we felt that we were fulfilling our side of the implicit contract of life. But when compensation stopped, when we started being able to call our own shots, to use our time more exactly as we wished, the veneer of seriousness faded from life. We were returned to the games of childhood. Or so it seems to me. Some people, I guess, can rejoice in this situation. But others, and that seems to include you and me, miss that matrix of accountability that made adult life seem serious, unduly so, I should probably add." Again he paused, before suggesting how these remarks might be relevant. "Your dream may be nothing more than your present state of mind passing a silly and jealous judgment on your vocation. The happy thought is that you and I had useful careers and yet we, like everyone else, are more than our careers."

"Well," said Connie, "it's certainly clear who's going to play the role of being a philosopher today." He smiled at his own pass at humor. "And on the subject of role-playing: I think you should play at being the questioner today, too." It was the first time that morning that either man had mentioned the purpose of the trip. "You're the one who knows Sonya Klepper. Moreover, she knew your daughter. And you've got a clearer sense of interrogative strategy than I do. Everything points to you." Shrug nodded his assent to his friend's reasoning, adding only that since the two of them had proven themselves rather adept at pulling off a good cop/bad cop routine in the past, Connie should feel free to jump into the coming conversation at any point if he felt his intervention might nudge Klepper toward telling the truth.

An hour later, as they pulled off the interstate to drive into Richmond, both men noticed that a blue Camaro exited two cars behind them. "I think," said Connie, with deliberate understatement, "someone is uncommonly curious about what we're doing." But the Buick's mirrors afforded them no useful view of the driver of the Camaro, and the traffic left them no immediate opportunity to pull over.

A few minutes later Sonya Klepper welcomed Shrug and Connie at the door of her small white bungalow. It sat in a mixed commercial/residential neighborhood, with a barbershop on one side and a tanning center on the other. She hugged her former classmate, Shrug, and shook Connie's hand, saying, "I'm Sonya." A short woman with gray hair and an angular face, she wore a beige blouse and a blue skirt, and struck Connie as a person who carried her years well. Grandmotherly, yes. But handsome in a matronly way. She guided them through the entranceway to a family room that featured an array of photos, and even before getting them seated, she offered them lemonade and a tray of small brown sweets. Shrug had hoped that he could choreograph the seating of the trio into an arrangement that would be suitable for confrontation if necessary, but Klepper's initiative trumped his hope, and Connie and he wound up nested side by side on the short wine-colored couch, while Klepper sat at right angles to them in a uncomfortable-looking captain's chair.

"I haven't had gingersnaps in years, Sonya," Connie said, both as an authentic compliment and as a way of launching conversation. "These bring back happy memories."

"Thank you. And yes, I'm so happy they do."

Shrug briefly considered using the unprompted appearance of nostalgia in the conversation to move promptly to the main topic, but decided to stick to his game plan. So he told of how he had recently spoken to Marilyn, who in turn had had many nice things to say about 'Mrs. DeLisle' as a teacher. "Bless her heart," smiled Klepper, seizing the compliment to speak fondly of her teaching days at Humboldt High School, remarking that it was unusual for a teacher to have the opportunity to return to a school she had attended while growing up, and adding that she had always regarded herself as very fortunate that God had been so kind to her.

Shrug asked about the many pictures in the room, and Klepper took the bait, rising to direct their attention in turn to her late husband, her children, and her grandchildren, fleshing out each photograph with a relevant and affectionate story or two. When they resumed their seats, she offered them more refreshments, and Connie, playing his role to the hilt, commented on the deep satisfaction cool lemonade afforded on a hot day.

"I guess," said a smiling Shrug, sipping from his newly-fortified glass, "it's time we turned to business." He reminded Klepper of the "unhappy conclusion" to the reunion dinner in 1998 and then went over the information—chiefly, Bryan Travers's discovery of a warning note and the class committee's approval of a quiet investigation that his letter to her had imparted.

"I'm sorry I didn't respond right away. I was curious, of course, but I thought I'd wait 'til the weekend. I'll bet everyone else replied right away."

Shrug thought she seemed suddenly nervous, but said simply that Amanda Everson was also being a little slow to write, and no doubt for similar reasons. "We all have busy lives. So Connie and I thought we'd give ourselves the pleasure of a nice summer drive. Besides, I enjoy introducing him to my high school friends."

Connie smiled benignly. He was savoring the performance of Shrug at his most ruthless.

"Did you talk with Tony that evening?"

Klepper shifted slightly in her chair. Her "no" was soft.

"We've been told, and I can't recall by whom, that you dated Tony in high school. Did you?" Shrug knew he was quickly moving onto difficult terrain, and he wanted the advance to be swift enough to keep Klepper off-balance.

"No. That's silly." She giggled and twisted. "Who would say a thing like that?" She suddenly seemed to be finding her skirt uncomfortable.

"Do you recall anything about him that evening?"

"No. As I said, we didn't talk." Her voice was now unmistakably edgy.

"We've noticed from the videos of the evening that you left rather early. Were you feeling ill?"

Klepper hesitated, sensing (Shrug assumed) that the questions were beginning to focus on the crucial period when Klepper and

Tony—if the hypothesis drawn from the Saunders Cleaver article was correct—had their meeting. "No . . . I don't recall, really. I wasn't sick. Just tired . . . tired."

"Do you recall seeing anyone as you left?" Shrug was trying to press ahead relentlessly.

"No."

"Do you recall which hallway you took when you left the dining area?"

"No. Why are you asking questions like this?" Her voice sounded almost strangled.

And at this point Shrug struck. "Have you ever heard of Saunders Cleaver?"

The look of terror that seized Klepper's face was unmistakable. In a flash the friends' hypothesis was confirmed and the atmosphere of the room transformed from tense to electric. A barely audible "no" was her reply.

As he feared would happen, Shrug was now feeling deeply uncomfortable about the ordeal he was forcing his hostess to submit to. But, he reminded himself, she might be a murderer; and she certainly had information that they needed. So he kept drilling. "Well, Saunders Cleaver seems to know more about that evening than anyone else."

"Oh." Klepper gave every appearance of hoping to recede into invisibility.

"He has even written about the evening, though indirectly, in the role of an ethical counselor. His piece appeared in *Guide to the Faithful Life*, a Unitarian publication."

"Oh?" Klepper's eyes were wide open, staring blankly at her guests. Connie thought that she looked liked a frightened, trapped, helpless animal.

"He said he'd received a letter from a woman who confessed to committing a fatal attack much like the one we're forced to envision Tony Travers having suffered—that is, if his death wasn't accidental."

"But what does that have to do with me?" asked a suddenly emboldened Klepper.

To Shrug, this remark was a sign that his prey had seen a glint of hope, desperate perhaps, but still a final chance to avoid being the target of the imminent final and crushing blow. He moved quickly to forestall any sense that an opening was at hand. "Well, Sonya, we are struck by the coincidence of names. Saunders Cleaver. Sonya Klepper. Say them aloud." He did several times. "It's odd how similar they are, isn't it?"

"In fact," said Connie, his appointed moment now at hand, "I've told Shrug that I think *you* are Saunders Cleaver. And given the character of the article, I think it only reasonable to conclude that *you* killed Tony Travers." He stopped.

The two men watched as, over the next five seconds, the already agitated woman dissolved into a moaning and writhing wretch. She twisted herself into a ball and seemed to be trying to shrink into nothingness. Sounds kept coming from her shaking body, but since she managed to bury her mouth under her arms and was convulsed with sobs, most of the muffled utterances were incoherent, although Connie thought he could pick out a "damn" and a "stupid" and a particularly wretched "why?"

Shrug waited about two minutes, as the paroxysms swiftly mounted and then slowly subsided, before moving to console his miserable classmate. He reached across the space between them, took her shaking hands in his own, and in a gentle and reassuring voice asked her to tell them what happened. Klepper looked up, her eyes red and moist, her blouse and sleeve wet, and her lips trembling. "Oh, Shrug . . . oh, oh, Shrug." He squeezed her hands tightly, tilted her chin up, and said "Tell us about it."

Unexpectedly, at that moment Sonya Klepper untwisted herself, rose, and straightened her dress. Then, as Connie and Shrug exchanged apprehensive glances, she moved quickly to the kitchen to recover the pitcher of lemonade, with which she promptly refreshed everyone's glasses. Then, wiping her eyes and nose with a towel she had acquired during the kitchen visit, she returned to her seat, smiled at her astonished guests, and finally spoke, quietly and clearly. "Yes, I am Saunders Cleaver. You two are good detectives. But no, I didn't kill Tony." She waited for those words to sink in. "So you'd probably like me to tell you what I *did* do that evening, right?"

She leaned forward and rearranged the items on the coffee-table. Then, sitting back, revealing eyes that were now bloodshot and swollen, she began. "There's one piece of background information you need to know. My deep secret. For the happiest moment of my life, the very happiest moment, came on the evening I had a date with Tony Travers in high school. It's a terrible thing to confess. But I have to, for it will give context to everything else I'm going to tell you."

Connie and Shrug settled wordlessly into the couch, and Klepper told her tale. Although she had loved her husband and she certainly continued to love her far-flung children and grandchildren, the evening with Tony Travers—an innocent evening ending in a chaste kiss, so far as the friends could infer—had been the enchanting centerpiece of her life, and she had spent the next forty-five years cherishing its memory and clinging to foolish dreams spun from it. "I was obsessed. I know that's probably a clinical word and I'm probably misusing it. But that's how I felt—obsessed, and often giddily so."

Tony had not been in the practice of attending reunions, she explained, and so, when he'd returned for the fortieth in 1993, Klepper had been thrilled to see him. More important, she had wanted to speak with him. To see his face close-up. To find out whether he treasured a memory of the magical evening the way she did. But her courage had failed her, and she had stayed silent and distant, applauding her award-winning "hero" from afar. For days afterwards she had felt miserable and foolish about her faintheartedness.

When she learned that Tony was planning to attend the forty-fifth reunion, she vowed not to play the coward a second time.

And since she had heard that his health was poor, she realized that the forty-fifth might be her last opportunity to talk with him. He was, after all, past seventy. So she left a note for him at the hotel registration desk, asking him to leave the Saturday dinner to meet her shortly after 8:00 "by the old fire door," an out-of-the-way site in the north wing of the building that had been a recognized place of rendezvous in high school days. He hadn't spoken to her at the reception before the dinner—an alarming sign—but she kept to the plan, even whispering to him as she passed behind him on her way out of the dining room. Then she exited and waited at the appointed spot.

Some time passed. She grew fretful, alarmed. But just as she was on the point of leaving, he appeared. She introduced herself, and he seemed surprised to see her. She asked if he had gotten her note. Somewhat embarrassed, he said he had but that he'd thought it was a joke. He said that he was sorry but that he'd come out of the noisy dining area to meet someone else.

"I should have run at that point, but I'd come this far and one further step into humiliation wouldn't matter. And so I asked him if he remembered our date. And with a goofy, apologetic smile he said he didn't, adding the final insult: that he'd dated so many girls in high school he couldn't really remember their names. I stared at him for a moment or two. My forty-five year-old edifice of myth was dissolving on the spot. And then I ran away. I was crying. You've seen how I can gush. I was ashamed. I felt contempt for myself. I felt like an idiot. It's hard to find words for the self-revulsion I felt. And I just had to escape."

Klepper's voice had begun to quiver as she told her story, but she had never totally lost self-command. And at that point she drew herself up and declared, "When I left him, Tony Travers was alive. He was lighting a cigarette, mumbling an apology, totally alive, and waiting for someone." But the words were scarcely out when she began sobbing again.

Connie glanced at Shrug and then asked, "Why did you write that article then? What purpose was there to confessing to a crime, or an act that you hadn't committed?" He wished he could have made his voice sound less annoyed.

Before Klepper could answer, Shrug interceded. "I think I know why you did it, Sonya. You saw Tony seeking release from the distress of old age and infirmities, and you wrote about what you wished you'd had the courage to do."

Connie gave Shrug an astonished look. But submitting to a quick, commanding glance from his friend, he said nothing.

"No," said Klepper, "that's not it at all. I felt as if I'd killed him. After all, if I'd stayed, he'd probably still be alive today. I left him. Deserted him. Whatever happened to him wouldn't have happened if I'd been there. Can I ever be forgiven?"

Shrug moved to kneel before the seated Klepper, at the same time awkwardly trying to enfold her in the comfort of an old friend's arms. "It's not your fault, Sonya. You didn't do anything wrong. Connie and I are trying to find out what happened. And you've helped us a lot. So there's nothing to forgive. Besides, as you know, God is always forgiving."

Connie realized that he had been inclined to believe Klepper. How could such a doleful, self-lacerating story not be true? He took Shrug's words as a sign that his friend, too, was inclined to accept it. If true, of course, it had implications for the investigation. "Do you remember what time it was when you left Tony?"

Klepper looked up, a strange smile on her face. "What a silly question. How could I know the time? All I can say is that was after 8:00. Probably after 8:15. As I said, I'd waited longer than I'd expected. But I wasn't looking at my watch. I didn't give a shit about what time it was."

The expletive startled both men. "Can you guess?" asked Shrug.

"Why? Why is the time important?" Klepper seemed genuinely unaware of the importance of timing to the investigation.

"We're trying to eliminate suspects, Sonya. Anybody who's on our suspect list but can be accounted for when Tony was still alive is no longer a suspect."

"Oh." The voice was bleak. "I wish I could help but I can't."

"But maybe you can." Connie's voice was explosive with sudden excitement. "Did you walk past the dining room when you left?"

"Of course. I had to. That was the way to the exit."

"Do you remember what the class was singing as you walked by?"

"Singing? Oh yes, of course, they were singing, weren't they? All happy and sentimental while I was bitter and forlorn. And the song made it worse, for it was . . . ." She paused, seeking to solidify the wisps of memory that she had retained of her ignominious departure from Humboldt High School that evening. " . . . it was . . . 'The New Year's Eve we did the town.'" She hummed a bit with the words. ". . . it was . . . it was 'Moments to Remember.'" The title came out with a note of triumph. "There couldn't have been a more stinging song for the occasion. What a moment to remember!" The words were spit out. "I began crying all the harder and almost ran to the exit door so that no one would see me."

"Thank you, Sonya," Shrug said. "You've been an enormous help to us." He hugged her again, both to comfort her and to let her know he was grateful. "I think Connie and I should go now, but I'll stay in touch."

Connie offered Sonya his hand, which she took. "I'm sorry we've brought back so many painful memories for you."

"It wasn't your fault. It was mine. I know that people do stupid things, but I hate it when I'm the one who does them." She smiled wanly through swollen eyes. "As they say, any friend of Shrug's is a friend of mine." And unexpectedly she gave Connie a hug.

"You were magnificent," Connie said once the two friends had cooled the sun-baked car. "In top form."

"I wish I felt a little better about it," Shrug replied. He waved his hand to brush off the remark he anticipated. "I know, I know. It's all in the line of duty. But we're not law officers. It's not our duty to squeeze out truth. It's our hobby. That's a different thing altogether."

"We've been through this before," Connie reminded him. "We live in an imperfect world, an argument against God's existence, by the way, and sometimes we have to adopt imperfect means to serve the goal of truth."

"Do you see a blue Camaro?" Connie asked. They were pulling on to the interstate as he spoke, but two quick and simultaneous glances offered no signs that their mysterious shadow was still interested in them. They settled back for the relaxing return drive to Humboldt.

"I take it," said Shrug after a while, "that we accept Sonya Klepper's new account of the evening of the reunion dinner."

"Well, yes, I do. Though we need to keep alive the possibility that she has tried to con us—no, make that '*has*' conned us—with a brilliant bit of acting. Also, I suppose there's the remote possibility that Sonya's role was to lure Tony outside so that someone else could dispatch him."

"Aha! The epicycle gambit. No, I think it's unlikely that Sonya lied. Marilyn told me that she was always feeling guilty about the failings of others and assuming responsibility for them. And so when I offered her an alternative explanation for writing that silly piece . . . "

"Aaah. I knew you were up to *some*thing."

". . . She rejected it for a far more characteristic explanation, that she felt guilty that she was responsible for his losing his life. And in any case, all our earlier speculations about motives were wrong-headed."

"You realize what this implies then," continued Connie, as, with one free hand, he pulled out his time line from the reunion evening. "If Tony was alive when the class was singing 'Moments to Remember,' then he must have died in the last five minutes or so of the window of opportunity. And that in turn means," he consulted his notes, "that only Denny Culbertson, Eddie Moratino,

Amanda Everson, and Trish Ridgway remain as viable suspects. And we just passed up an opportunity to ask Sonya Klepper about them."

"And no Freddy. Abe Steinberg sure will be disappointed." Shrug sighed.

"Me too," said Connie. "I would have loved to pin the whole thing on that scumbag." He pointed to a McDonald's sign to indicate that he planned to turn off. "Of course, we could always *frame* him."

"Don't tempt me."

Over a hamburger and fries the friends agreed that their failure to have had any exchange with Eddie Moratino or Amanda Everson now loomed larger than ever. "As of this morning," Connie remarked abstractedly, "we had contacted 75 percent of our suspects. Now we've contacted only 50 percent. That doesn't sound like progress."

"Count on a philosopher to concoct weird arguments like that."

Once back on the road, they sorted through the four remaining suspects again. Ridgway had the most obvious motive, namely, anger or disappointment that Tony had "stolen" the class award from her in 1993. It might also be telling that she was the one who discovered the body, "a fairly easy task for the murderer," Shrug remarked. Denny Culbertson also had what might be construed as a motive, but unlike Ridgway's, it was distant in time, so distant, in fact, that it lay on the far side of his religious conversion. Connie reminded Shrug that Culbertson was also the only one of the four who, by the testimony of the videos, didn't speak to Tony during the dinner; but whether that fact had any relevance was, for the moment at least, unascertainable.

For the other two suspects there was nothing. Moratino's activities in the Far East might invite speculation, but there was no hint whatsoever that he had ever spoken to Tony after their graduation in 1953. The only thing suspicious about Everson was that she hadn't been heard from, and this silence could easily be accounted for by her residence in New Zealand. "Maybe," said Shrug as they drove southeast of Columbus, "we need to return to the likelihood that his death was a natural one and the warning letter merely a—for *our* purposes at least—a red herring."

"Oh, I don't think so," said Connie. "The single most interesting fact imparted by Sonya was that Tony was *waiting* in the hallway to talk to someone. His words imply prearrangement. And prearrangement at least invites speculation that someone was setting up an opportunity for mayhem."

After a few minutes of silence Connie declared, firmly and proudly, that he didn't want to "wimp out" just yet. *If* there had been a murder, they had made real progress that afternoon. If none of the remaining four looked particularly suspicious, that fact might reflect the craftiness of the killer, not the absence of a crime. Or it might indicate that Teresa Espinosa was right in suspecting that someone not associated with the reunion class had snuck into the school. "At any rate," he added, "at least until we've tried to reexamine Culbertson's and Ridgway's stories for the evening and heard the tales of Moratino and Everson, we should proceed."

To which remark Shrug appended a promise to immediately fulfill his pledges to find out just how "secure" against intruders the safety steps of the class had been, and to contact Tony Travers's three surviving ex-wives. He would, in short, start acting on the possibility that someone not from the reunion class had made their way into the school. He also smiled, for, as usual in these matters, he could not disguise that he was enjoying investigating more than was seemly and had no desire to throw in the towel yet either.

So in an impromptu War Council session, held in the front seat of Connie's Buick rather than the comfortable living room of Shrug's home, the friends modestly reallocated responsibilities. In addition to looking into the security arrangements for the reunion and contacting former spouses, Shrug would stay on top of the silent duo of Moratino and Everson. In fact, he declared he would start pestering them. Connie, meanwhile, would take over the task of looking more closely into the lives of Culbertson and Ridgway. New interrogations would be his first steps. "Never let it be said," declaimed Connie, holding an invisible cup aloft, "that the Second-Best Club are quitters." A car-sore Shrug joined the mock toast.

But the day wasn't over. A cold front had blown through Humboldt late in the afternoon, and so Connie decided to take advantage of it for a relaxing jog. But as he was tying the laces of his running shoes he noticed the blinking red light on his answering machine. He pressed the button and picked up a pencil to jot down forthcoming information. "Hello," came a raspy but efficient female voice, "this is Claire Van Tassel. I'm calling at 11:30 A.M. Eastern Daylight Time on Wednesday, June 13, in reply to a letter from Connie Haydn." She gave a phone number she could be reached at and said she expected to be in all day.

Excited by the unexpected call, Connie dialed the number immediately, and Van Tassel answered during the fourth ring. After a quick exchange of introductions and a brief explanation and apology from Van Tassel for the quality of her voice—it seems that she was undergoing treatment for throat cancer—she turned to the subject of Tony Travers.

"I had known Tony had died. Well, of course, you knew I knew that, didn't you? Such a shame. Seventy-two is so young." She seemed distracted. Connie wondered if she were older than Tony. "And then to hear that he might have been murdered. Poor Tony. Poor Tony."

"We still don't know that yet, Ms. Van Tassel." Connie expected her to encourage him to call her by her first name, but she didn't. "But we *are* making some progress in figuring out what happened on the evening of his death. As a longtime friend of Tony's, would you be willing to answer some questions we have about him?"

Van Tassel agreed and Connie began.

"How did you come to know of his death?" Connie decided to begin obliquely.

"Linda wrote me about it several months after . . ."

"Linda?"

"Linda Dremminger, his former wife. Bryan's mother. She knew Tony and I had been close for many years." The tone was matter-of-fact, neither coy nor proud. "And she thought I'd want to know. She even apologized for not notifying me sooner. That's when I wrote the note to Bryan that you found."

"How did it come about that you knew Tony?"

"It's not a complicated story," she began. But the tale she told turned out to be far from simple. She was much younger than he, born in 1950. "Yes, I know I sound much older than that. It's this damn disease that's eating away at my throat." They had met in 1972 in Bogota. He was piloting planes for a company that ran drugs, and she was trying to make a living as a free-lance photographer. They had a good year together before he returned to the States. They met again, not entirely by accident, in Washington, D.C., in 1978. This time their relationship was an off-and-on one, for he had a wife who worked in the West, and he was sometimes with her. When a job opportunity took Van Tassel to Brussels in 1979, they parted on friendly terms. "We enjoyed each other's company, but we had no desire to encumber each other's lives." Their third time together came in 1984, in Lexington, "when Tony was getting over the collapse of his fourth marriage and concluding that, just maybe, he wasn't suited for marriage." Van Tassel's croaky laugh, a cross between a cough and a gasp, sounded painful to Connie's ears. After that, she explained, they stayed in touch by mail, though they never got together again.

Connie had been jotting down information furiously, noting in passing that two holes in Tony's biography had now been partially filled in. "What can you tell me about Tony? In particular, did he have enemies?"

"Oh, he probably had *loads* of enemies, dear. You don't run drugs, smuggle jewels, or play the spy game without annoying people. And Tony had killed more than a few people in his lifetime."

Wow! thought a dumbfounded Connie. *In ten brief seconds she has entirely recast our image of Tony Travers!* "I have to tell you, Ms. Van Tassel, that much of the information you've just passed on is new to us. We knew that he'd been in the British army and that he'd traveled a lot but we. . . ."

"You have it wrong, dear. He wasn't in the army. He was in a highly secret intelligence unit that operated in France during World War II and then in Malaya after the war. He used to share experiences with me during, well, pillow talk." For the first time she sounded coquettish.

"I hope," said Connie, "you'll be willing to share some of these conversations with me. And I hope you'll believe I'm not asking out of prurient curiosity."

"Oh, I haven't heard that word in a long time. How delightful. And don't worry, dear. I'm *pleased* you've encouraged me to reminisce. Tony was a charmer, a real man. He was an important part of my life. And he was proud of his own life. Even if you didn't think the information might be helpful I'd be inclined to rattle on." Her voice was stronger. "And *with* your encouragement, well. . . !"

The reference to drug running, she said, alluded to his days in Colombia, though at some point he had also flown drugs across international borders in southern Africa. The reference to jewels, she explained, was misleading, for although he had occasionally conveyed precious stones out of places like Hanoi and Bangkok, he had preferred to work with contraband archeological artifacts. "He was very good at passing himself off as an authority on art, and he explained that while any kind of smuggling operation involved the bribing of corrupt officials, precious stones were riskier to move than artifacts because the ease with which they could be hidden increased the likelihood that a bribed official might double-cross the smuggler. Did that sentence come out right?"

She's really enjoying herself now, thought Connie. "It was fine. What about the espionage?"

Because it was part of Tony's pre-Van Tassel life, she knew less about this aspect of Tony's past. But this much she *did* know. In France in 1944 and 1945 he had worked in league with the Communists who were resisting the German occupation. In Malaya in the late 1940s he had worked against the Communists who were trying to bring down British rule in that domain of the Empire. "Tony really had no political leanings. He thought life was a game, an adventure, even a lark. He loved being alive and taking risks."

"Did he ever mention names from those days? Colleagues? Friends? Co-conspirators? Whatever?"

Van Tassel laughed. "All of a sudden, dear, you sound very bourgeois." She fell silent for a moment, and then mentioned several unfamiliar names that Connie jotted down.

"Does the name Eddie Moratino ring a bell?" Connie decided to force the conversation ahead.

"Never heard of him. And my memory is good."

"How about 'Sandy'? We've been told he was Tony's wartime commander."

"*He?* That's funny. Dear, you have been sorely misinformed! 'Sandy' was a woman. Yes, she was the commander of the secret unit. Yes, she was tough as nails. Yes, she was Tony's wartime lover. And that's all I know. But it's clearly more than *you* knew." The tone again was matter-of-fact, neither subdued, triumphant, nor annoyed.

Connie took down a few more names, all new to the investigation and in every case of persons whose lives had intersected with Tony's across five continents and thirty years. Finally, sensing from her wheezing that Van Tassel was becoming weary, he said he had three concluding questions.

"Did he ever mention anyone named 'Less'? That's L – E – S – S. Less."

"Never heard of him."

"Well, maybe you've heard of 'Chucklehead Clancy'?"

"Who?" Van Tassel's amusement was clear.

"Chucklehead Clancy. Believe it or not, he whoever he is, this unknown person is a major beneficiary of Tony's will. But he's never been identified to claim his legacy."

"Well, good luck to him then. But no, I've never heard the name."

"How about this? And this is awkward, so I'll just ask it. He told his son that he had had one great love in his life, someone whom he called 'the Great.' Could that be you? Are you 'the Great'? Or if not, do you know who she is?"

"Well, that *is* an awkward question, isn't it?" Her laugh was both loud and raw. "You can probably get away with it only because you know you're posing it to a dying lady. But again I can't help you. If he thought *I* was the great love of his life, I'd be surprised. We amused each other; we had fun together. What does love have to do with sex? No, I'm quite sure it wasn't me. And as for telling me about his greatest love, well, all I can say is that, while we may have been close, we weren't *that* close, darling."

Connie wasn't sure what to say, so he simply thanked her for her candor and assistance, and said he'd be in touch again if further questions arose.

"Don't take too long, dear. Tony was right: I should have given up smoking long ago." They exchanged good-byes.

Connie's first impulse on hanging up was to phone Shrug. But he recalled that his friend was at Evening Prayer and so he belatedly undertook his jog instead. The flood of news he had received was deeply interesting, but it didn't oblige him to do anything immediately. And exercising in the cooler evening air would give him a chance to try to get his mind around the implications of Van Tassel's stories. That they opened up many new investigative possibilities—drug-running, smuggling, spying, killing: the man had led a rich life—was clear. Whether their consequences extended even further was a matter he wanted to give more concentrated thought to.

9

Thursday, June 14, 2001

Shrug woke up on Thursday feeling sore. *I guess I don't bounce back from surgery like a thirty-year-old.* His groin hurt, but so did his legs and back. He quickly decided that on the previous day he shouldn't have spent six hours on his butt, another hour or so on his feet, and a little evening time on his knees. The flesh, he reminded himself, was weak. *Perhaps I should stay in bed a bit longer.*

Then the phone rang. Shrug rubbed his eyes, saw that the clock registered 8:14, and picked up the extension by his bed, half-expecting to hear Connie's voice. Instead a woman with a foreign accent, sounding distant and somewhat indistinct, asked for "Meestair Shroog Speak-AIR, please." Puzzled, Shrug identified himself as the person beingasked for. *"Merci,"* replied the strange voice, *"excusez-moi un moment while I koe-nekt a call from de 'otel Continental in Dakar."*

About thirty seconds of silence followed. The line clearly wasn't dead, but Shrug had no idea what the various mechanical sounds meant, and then a strong male voice with American diction came on the line. "Hello, Shrug. This is Eddie Moratino. I hope I haven't waked you. It's early afternoon here in Senegal, and since my African trip is taking longer than my secretary and I thought it would, I decided I should give you a call from overseas rather than keep you waiting until I get back to the States. Especially since it's Tony Travers's death you're looking into."

During the half-minute of silence Shrug had stumbled out of bed and found a pad and pencil. He told Moratino how pleased he

172

was to hear from him, and when Eddie encouraged Shrug to talk a bit about himself, Shrug decided that Moratino was not squeezing the call in between important meetings and allowed himself to talk briefly about life in Humboldt. "I suspect that you're the most cosmopolitan member of our class," he added after relaying a few anecdotes about classmates still resident in the town.

"Well, now that Tony's dead, that may be so," Moratino replied. "Please tell me about the investigation and how I might help." Shrug appreciated the gracefulness with which Moratino shifted the conversation onto message and he filled him in on the course of the inquiries, mentioning while hoping to underplay the fact that Moratino stood with only three other classmates as still among suspects in the class.

Moratino laughed heartily. "Well, let me tell you right away that I didn't kill Tony. He was a good guy, but I hadn't seen him in maybe twenty-five years before he died at our reunion."

Shrug did some quick subtraction in his head and realized that Moratino was implying that Travers and he *had* met in the early 1970s, well after high school days. This was very interesting. "What brought you and Tony together back in 1973?"

"It was '73 into '74. We met in Southeast Asia, as the Vietnam War was winding down. Not long after Nixon's trip to China. I was bopping around from city to city, looking for opportunities to purchase pottery for American collectors, and one day in Bangkok I heard of an ex-pat Brit named Tony Travers who was working for a private building contractor in the city. On the off-chance he was Humboldt's Tony, I looked him up, and sure enough, he was. We had beers that evening (Siamese beers are really bitter, by the way) and swapped lots of stories; and because we felt we could help each other, we decided to stay in touch. I suspect he was more helpful to me than *vice versa*, however, for he introduced me to two reputable dealers but I never connected him with anyone wanting construction done. We last saw each other in Sidney in early 1974. I was sorry we fell out of touch. He was a lively guy, full of wild tales, some of them perhaps even true, and generous with his time and energy."

"That's a fine endorsement, Eddie. And in many ways it's consistent with our emerging picture of Tony. But you need to know that we think he may sometimes have walked on the far side of the law in his pursuit of interesting jobs." Even though Shrug as yet knew nothing of Claire Van Tassell's revelations to Connie, he felt confident his guarded terms were apt.

"I'm not surprised. After all, Southeast Asia isn't the U.S. In particular, the administration of law in that part of the world has its, well, its *quirks*." Moratino could be every bit as guarded as Shrug. "I'm an honest man by inclination and upbringing. And since my buyers are Americans, subject to American law and relevant international agreements about artifacts, my professional success rests on staying well on the *near* side of the law, as you might put it. So character and necessity prompt me to be honest."

Shrug was listening attentively, enjoying the instruction he was receiving and anticipating an imminent 'but.' He was not disappointed.

"But the business ethos of the East is more flexible than the code-dominated ethos of the West. More ambiguous too. Plastic is less frequently used in business transactions. There's an ambivalence about standards, a greater readiness to let ends justify means," said Moratino.

Shrug was uncertain where Moratino might be going with this reflection.

"Let's just say that while I've always tried to adhere to exemplary business practices, I've met many people who, for perfectly understandable reasons, have played fast-and-loose with the relevant trade statutes. And I will not judge them, unless their transgressions exceed the limits set by natural law," said Moratino.

The unexpected invocation of a concept likelier to be heard in theological than commercial circles startled Shrug, reminding him that his caller was a Roman Catholic.

Moratino continued. "It would not surprise me to learn that Tony engaged in some smuggling. Lots of foreign nationals in those parts do. And he did love adventure. But the people he got me in touch with were honest businessmen, their items were authentic and of determinate provenance, and so, in my experience, he was an honest man."

Impressed by Moratino's arguments and tone, Shrug found himself liking, even admiring, his former classmate in Senegal, and so he dropped Southeast Asia to inquire about the evening of the reunion dinner. "Why did you leave so soon after the dinner was over, well before the singing was completed?"

"Easy. I was flying out to New York and on to Copenhagen the next morning. I wanted to get back to my hotel in Columbus that night so I'd be ready for the flights."

Shrug asked if Moratino recalled anything about Tony that evening. He replied that they'd chatted at the predinner reception, chiefly about a display of ancient Khmer art that had been on exhibit at the National Gallery a year or so earlier. Moratino had seen it; a hobbling Tony hadn't, because the condition of his legs made even trips of modest distances too painful. "He was in good spirits, and I clearly recall my pleasure in seeing him again. But I don't think we discussed the old days in Thailand and Australia at all."

After receiving assurances that Moratino had time to answer a few more questions, Shrug inquired about the reunion behavior of three other suspects. Moratino recalled all three. Not surprisingly, he remembered Trish Ridgway as being drunk. But in addition he remembered her as being agitated simply because she had seen him talking with Tony at the reception. "That's when I learned of her sense of grievance toward him. She felt that because *she* was angry, we should *all* be angry. Seemed awfully petty, but for her it was clearly serious. She also told me of several new garbage trucks that her company had bought to serve Humboldt better. I tried to sound interested, but I'm afraid I found the herky-jerky character of the conversation more off-putting than engaging."

Like many others, he recalled Amanda Everson for her sense of style. But it was less her attire than her hair and make-up that impressed themselves on him. "She did an astonishingly good job of covering up the inevitable ravages of time. I tend to look closely at women's hair and eyebrows. They are excellent guides to age. Amanda knows how to deal with those cues, to modify and adjust them. In high school she was good with clothes. Now she's good with make-up." When Shrug reminded him of the conversation he had had with Everson and the Grunhagens about the difficulties of receiving medical treatment in the wild, Moratino sighed, "Yes, I came out sounding too much like an exponent of conversational one-upsmanship. I didn't mean to be rude, for she had just been telling tales of enjoyable visits she'd made to the Pacific Northwest and New England. If I'd had my wits about me, I'd have kept my mouth shut."

Of the three suspects, however, it was Denny Culbertson who figured most prominently in his memory. He and Denny had talked at length about Moratino's hopes to educate young girls from Gujarat. The school that Moratino had established there provided an education through twelfth grade, and for the past six years Moratino had been funding an American college education for a small number of academically able graduates from that school. He explained that, much as he admired Humboldt College, it was too secular for the kind of schooling he had in mind, and so he sent the young women to Sacred Heart or Marymount instead. Culbertson's contribution to the plan was a proposal to raise money in the States to support the college education of a larger number of Indian girls. "He's an evangelical Protestant, but on many important issues Catholics and Evangelicals stand by side. We've both been moving forward with his proposal, and with luck and God's blessing, the first students will arrive for college in the fall of 2002." In light of this story, Shrug was not surprised to learn that Moratino thought very highly of the businessman-turned-missionary.

"I'm really impressed with your ability to summon up all these three-year-old memories," Shrug commented when the account of the discussions with Culbertson was over. "Most of the classmates we've talked to have had trouble recalling anything at all about the evening. They plead incipient Alzheimer's, of course, or maybe they invoke a 'senior moment.' And since I'm in their league, sharing their sense of a sometimes recalcitrant memory, while you're in a league of your own, I say again that I'm impressed."

"First off, I don't really believe you. Sleuths don't have bad memories. But you're right, neither do I. Ever since I was a kid I've retained information. I seem to hold lots of observations in my mind. And I'm fortunate in that I like talking with people and I'm usually genuinely interested in what they have to say. So I hear a lot, and it tends to stick." The tone was not boastful, but Shrug sensed that Moratino was proud of his powers of recall.

"I understand you tune pianos," Shrug said, deliberately moving to a potentially shared interest. "Do you play too?"

"For my own pleasure only, and maybe for good friends. I played in a small jazz band in Bangkok for a while. But we weren't together for long. When I'm by myself I get a kick out of ragtime. Now *there's* music!"

Shrug heard a sudden beeping over the line, and Moratino quickly announced that he needed to go. He added that he'd instructed his secretary to let Shrug get in touch with him promptly if the investigation took a turn that suggested input from the class's art collector might be in order. Then the call ended, and Shrug moved to the breakfast room thinking that only Amanda Everson remained unheard from. As he prepared his coffee, Shrug found it difficult to imagine that Eddie Moratino was a murderer. *And there's another thing*, Shrug smiled. Once again Moratino had negotiated his way through an easy and relaxed conversation without talking at all about his personal life. The former class clown remained a man of mystery, though whether any of the mystery bore upon the investigation was itself an independent mystery. Shrug prepared a piece of toast and, his wound aching more than it had since Monday, decided to spend much of the day off his feet. He put a call through to Connie's number to report on the conversation, but the line was busy. He decided the news could wait. Within half an hour he was back asleep in bed.

Connie had learned many years earlier that insights often came to him overnight. It was as if sleeping lent clarity to intuitions as his slumbering mind wove connections that his conscious mind had been too cabined to spin. On the previous evening the information that Tony Travers had been a British intelligence agent had seemed merely interesting, a further fleshing out of his biography. In the bright light of a chipper June morning it seemed potentially transformative. Secret intelligence agents, Connie assumed, made enemies. And unlike the enemies that gunrunners and drug-traffickers might make (people who were angry simply because someone had interrupted their hope for pecuniary gain) the enemies a spy might make could potentially be ideological, and hence lifelong, foes. Or so Connie thought. And if Claire Van Tassel's account was correct, Tony Travers might well have irritated either Nazis or Communists, or both! *No sooner do we exculpate Fritz Kramer than all of a sudden the Nazis are back. Maybe.*

These thoughts led to an inevitable additional implication. If Tony was killed because of something he had done in France or Malaya, then it hardly seemed possible that one of his Humboldt High School classmates had killed him. And *that* meant that all of Shrug's and his own investigative efforts thus far had been irrelevant, and that Shrug's nagging worry, and Teresa's admonition, that someone else had snuck into the high school on the evening of the reunion dinner could be true. Wow!

Connie realized that he was musing over improbables. The likelihood that Tony Travers's espionage days had come back to strike him down at the remove of half a century seemed remote. But Connie's curiosity was piqued, in large measure, he realized, because he knew nothing of what a secret spy unit might actually have done. Fortunately, and this was one of the perks of being an academic, he knew someone who might be able to help. Jimmy Brackett was an expert on British espionage operations in World War II. A friend of Connie's brother Donald in Korea, Major Brackett had retired from the armed forces to devote himself to learning all he could about how the cunning British intelligence machine had operated on the various fronts of the "War against the Axis" (as he always called it). He might have settled anywhere in the country to do his work, but he had chosen Columbus because of the strong military history tradition at The Ohio State University. Thus over the past twenty years, though not a formal member of the OSU faculty, he had been given an office in Dulles Hall and become an informal adviser to numerous doctoral candidates working their way through the vast and labyrinthine documentation of the great mid-twentieth-century conflict. More to the point, he had a reputation for knowing more about British intelligence operations during the war than any other scholar on the western side of the Atlantic.

Connie gave Brackett a phone call, ascertained that the major, his curiosity aroused, could meet him at his Columbus office at 10:30 that day, and then wolfed down a Danish. As he was about to leave the house, he suddenly recalled that he had assumed responsibility for filling in the information holes on Denny Culbertson. He paused to phone through to Pittsburgh and, though not reaching Culbertson himself, learned that the leader of Cyclists for Christ was holding a "faith gathering" in Zanesville, late that very afternoon. Connie made a quick calculation, and realized that if he managed the clock well, he could make his appointment with Brackett *and* get to Zanesville in time to talk with Culbertson. *This is truly my lucky day.* Grabbing another Danish, he headed out the door and, by driving faster than was his wont, was almost on time for his meeting.

Major Brackett's office was a smoke-filled cubbyhole, made smaller still by the presence of filing cabinets and great mounds of boxes, papers, and tapes that lay in apparent disorder about the room, clogging corners and climbing walls. His signature pipe was at his lips. "How's your mum?" he asked when Connie entered, reminding his visitor that Brackett had been the only serviceman to visit the Haydn home after Donald's death in 1952 who had personally known Connie's older brother.

"She's doing okay. Happy, to all appearances. And for some reason, quite sure I'm Donald."

"Take it as a compliment. Your brother was a fine person. I won't say losing a friend is like losing a brother, but still he's the only person from those distant days in Wonsan that I sometimes think of. That's a major confession from a non-sentimental old bastard like me." Then, regathering himself from this unexpected revelation of a streak of tenderness, he gruffly asked for more information about Tony Travers. Connie filled him in on the little he knew and asked what it might mean. Brackett beamed. "I can humbly say you've come to the right place—the world's expert."

Over the next hour, despite several interruptions from phone calls (which Brackett handled with impressive dispatch), Connie's host provided a wealth of information about the kinds of activities that British intelligence units in Europe carried out during World War II, both before and after D-Day.

Some, he explained, were assassination squads. "You'd be surprised how many high-flying Nazi shitheads met quiet ends at the hands of the sneaky Brits." Others were under orders to link up with French or Dutch resistance cells. "The Belgies weren't much into resisting their Gerry overlords, but the Dutch were, and so too, despite the bad rep that Vichy France has come in for, were the Frogs." Others were assigned the task of sabotaging German facilities. "These guys seemed to have the most fun, and I've heard great stories of the Brits chortling as the Gerries got blown into their discrete body parts while sitting on the can." Still others were spies pure and simple, sent out to insert themselves into French society and learn what they could about the German occupation and troop movements. "For this kind of work, the military needed lads who spoke French or German, or Dutch or Danish, like a native. And again, counter to stereotype, the Brits had a fair share of people who could go native."

The aspect of intelligence work that most fascinated Brackett was the psychological pressure it put on the people who undertook it. They needed, he explained, to be able to make quick decisions of a truly life-or-death nature, to dissimulate with abandon, to kill without remorse, to sacrifice friends to higher purposes. In short, they needed nerves that never betrayed them and a very flexible sense of morality. "And, since the Gerries were doing the very same thing, the Brits—like all spies—needed to be perpetually suspicious. When you do that kind of work, you can't completely trust anyone, anyone at all." Brackett added that he thought John Le Carre had done a reasonable job of conveying the tensions of the life of an intelligence agent. "But remember, Smiley and his lads were operating in an era of ostensible peace, not on a foreign battlefield. It *does* make a difference."

Brackett was skilled at multi-tasking, for even as he spun out his tales and handled the phone calls, he was pulling out boxes and cabinet drawers, shuffling his way through folders and envelopes. His searching ended when, as he began his discussion of Le Carre, he pulled out a battered sheet of paper and began waving it about to punctuate his analysis of *Tinker, Tailor*. Connie hoped and suspected the sheet had some information that pertained to Tony Travers.

"I think," Brackett suddenly said, proudly blowing his first smoke ring of the morning, "I've found Travers's unit." He scanned the sheet again. "Hmm. The 'Mefisto' Squad. That's the kind of name these units liked to give themselves. And here, I suspect, is the lad you're looking for—A. Travers." Connie wanted to check the list himself, but Brackett continued to study it. "No Lesleys or Lesters, or, for that matter, Leczenskis or Leicesters, as in Robert Dudley, of course." Controlling his impatience, Connie remained quietly seated. "And," continued Brackett, speaking quietly, "no sign of a woman at all, a 'Sandy.' You're sure the unit leader was a woman? That would be unusual, almost unheard of." With that remark, he finally passed the piece of paper to Connie.

To Connie's disappointment, the sheet contained only a penciled list of last names and first initials, and it appeared that Brackett's attentive eye had already culled all the immediately relevant information from it. But he knew that any of the names might later turn out to be useful, especially since he had already compiled a partial list of first names from Travers's memorabilia boxes, and so he asked if he might have a copy. Brackett quickly obliged, needing only to shove a previously unnoticed cat and a few books onto the floor to get to a small copy machine hidden behind the door to the room. As he handed the copy to Connie, he motioned to a bearded young man who had been visibly standing outside the office door to come in. Brackett introduced him as an OSU doctoral student from Bulgaria working on Soviet-British cooperation in the Balkans in 1942. "I'll keep searching for additional information. 'Less' and 'Sandy' and the very memorable 'Chucklehead Clancy' will keep me awake at night. Meanwhile, good luck on your search. Let me know how it turns out. Maybe some day you'll be adding some information to my files."

As he left, Connie thanked Brackett, explaining in passing that the wartime espionage angle was not the only track that he and Shrug were following in this investigation. "So whether any of this has been relevant, I just don't know. But I'm grateful for your sharing your time and knowledge, and in any case it's been good to see you. I'll tell mother about our talk." As he walked to his car, Connie realized that Veronica Haydn almost surely wouldn't remember Major Jimmy Brackett. But at least, he mused, he'd finally have a reason to bring Donald into their conversation.

After a lunch at a deli near the OSU campus, he picked up State Route 315 down to Interstate 70, and began his drive eastward toward Zanesville. For the first half hour his mind was on what he had learned from Brackett. The life of men in these intelligence units, he thought, sounded very much like the kind of life that Tony Travers would have relished. But after a while, Connie decided to direct his mind to the task immediately ahead. After all, as he reminded himself, this would be his first meeting with Denny Culbertson, the man whose money-making ambitions had been thwarted by Tony Travers about thirty years earlier.

———

Zanesville was a gritty town, known for its resilience and pride, if no longer for its industrial clout. The extensive display of the Stars and Stripes along its streets reminded Connie that June 14 was Flag Day. As the product of a military family, he approved of American patriotism, and found his academic colleagues who were squeamish about endorsing love of country oddly detached from the legitimate sentiment of the nation.

He had little difficulty finding the Open Worship Church, the site and sponsor of Denny Culbertson's evangelical visit. He didn't know what to expect. It had been decades, at least five, he had calculated, since he had attended a church gathering for purposes other than weddings, funerals, lectures, or concerts. And even back then his mounting doubts about revealed religion had already smothered the attractiveness of the pious teachings of his mother, and he had attended simply as a dutiful teenage son. Summerlike heat was again baking central Ohio, and the only thing he felt confident of was that the gathering on this day would be hot and sweaty.

The large blue tent pitched next to the church building was the first object to catch Connie's eye. A group of people, later swelling to about 150, was seeking relief from the sun by gathering under the canopy, some standing and others sitting on folding chairs. It might have been any midsummer outdoor wedding reception except for the multitude of bicycles, either propped against the church exterior or standing independently, all glistening in the bright sunlight. On a small stage at the front of the tented space an electronic piano and an amplification system were being tested.

Connie stood watching for awhile, trying to figure out which of the various men who seemed to be exercising some sort of supervisory responsibility might be Denny Culbertson. He had no intention of interrupting his quarry while the preparations were under way. But he wanted to be sure that Culbertson would know he was present and leave time for him before returning to Pittsburgh. (*By bicycle? Really?* Connie wondered.) Eventually he identified the energetic, ponytailed person who was being called "Denny" and approached him.

"Hello, are you Denny Culbertson?" The man he addressed turned to see who had spoken to him. "I'm Connie Haydn, a friend of your high school classmate Shrug Speaker. I'm hopeful I could have a few minutes of your time after your meeting." Connie didn't know whether to call it a 'service.' "I'd like to discuss our investigation into Tony Travers's death."

"God rest his soul, poor Tony," Culbertson said. Then, removing his frameless glasses and wiping his sweaty brow with his hand, he welcomed Connie to the "gathering of the faithful" and said he'd be glad to talk with him in about two hours. With a quick smile, he returned to his work. He was, thought Connie, a man of surprising strength, energy, and agility for his age.

Half an hour later the formal part of the "faith gathering" began. Joyous hymns rang across the church green, many still familiar to Connie though he hadn't sung them in over half a century. "It is Well With My Soul," "Love Lifted Me," "Shall We Gather at the River," and the ubiquitous "Amazing Grace," the *Pachelbel's Canon of hymnody*, Connie thought.

These strains reminded Connie of many of the reasons he found religious belief unacceptable. The hymns were attractive, of course, with singable, memorable tunes and beguiling lyrics. But they were completely unreasonable, their messages grounded solely on what was written in a book that its adherents held to be beyond challenge and hence, from Connie's point of view, beyond engagement. The hymns were, Connie thought, nothing more than a grand tool in a game of psychological manipulation, a way to bind people together in a feel-good movement of blind faith. A "gathering" indeed!

He immediately remembered that Shrug was a Christian. *Why then do I regard him as different?* The answer was easy: *he* could *be engaged.* Yes, he knew the gospels and the letters of Paul. But he was also familiar with the works of Augustine, Anselm, Aquinas, Pascal, Schopenhauer, Kierkegaard, Tillich, and Barth. And Hume! *Yes. Wasn't that remarkable.* Shrug actually admired David Hume—as close to a secular saint as any person could be, in Connie's view—and come away with his faith still intact. Shrug was a serious Christian. It was possible to discuss religious faith with his friend in a way that would be rewarding to both of them. *Why couldn't all Christians be as intelligent and well-read as Shrug?* And then Connie smiled at his unpleasant train of thought. *What an intellectual snob I am. What a perfect, obnoxious, insufferable, pompous, condescending, patronizing snob!*

When the hymn-singing was over, Denny Culbertson, with his sleeves rolled up and his glasses perched precariously, addressed the gathering. He spoke of the mission of Christianity to rescue the world from itself. He said that the task of rescue rested on the shoulders of the common folk, of people like the cyclists who had come together on this hot day. He emphasized how bicycle enthusiasts had many occasions to talk of the good news of Christ to their friends, co-workers, colleagues, children, relatives, and spouses. He emphasized, however, that mere talk, in and of itself, was insufficient; that people came to know the joy of faith by seeing the happiness it brought to others, by seeing how it shook people out of their shells of narrow self-regard, by seeing how it transformed lives. When Culbertson was finished, Connie adjudged the remarks, though marred by clichés, to have been well-delivered and wholesome.

More hymn-singing followed the address, plates were passed to encourage donations, and shortly before 6:00 P.M. the gathering came to an end. Connie couldn't help feeling as if he had attended an entertainment. He couldn't exactly take it seriously, but he had found the afternoon's proceedings diverting and instructive. Perhaps, he speculated, this is how an anthropologist feels when observing the rites of an exotic tribe. And then he again kicked himself for what he could only regard as the elitist spitefulness of his thoughts.

He gave Culbertson fifteen minutes to assist in the dismantling of the stage and electronic equipment and then moved forward. Seeing him approach, Culbertson spoke briefly to one of the men assisting in the work and then came over to meet Connie. "Did you feel the Spirit touch you?" Connie explained that religion was not his cup of tea, adding that he had found Culbertson a bracing speaker. Culbertson in turn, noting Connie's trim build, asked if he were a bicycling fan. Connie replied that he jogged rather than cycled. Then he turned to the business of the trip to Zanesville.

"I'm following through on some new information we've just received. And it's information you kept to yourself when you talked with Shrug." Culbertson frowned. "I'm talking about your quarrel with Tony Travers in Brockton, Pennsylvania, in 1970 over a tract of land that you and some fellow investors wanted to buy." Culbertson stared back at Connie, removed his glasses, and said softly, "That wasn't me."

"Oh?" Connie was surprised at the disjunction between tone and meaning. "My evidence says it *was* you." Connie realized he was sounding more adversarial than he meant to, but he didn't know how to throttle back. "And in the context of a possible murder investigation, even one as informal as the present one, the fact of the altercation, compounded by your earlier silence, make this land project a matter that Shrug and I have no choice but to pursue."

"Let's sit down," Culbertson said, pointing to two folding chairs still enjoying the protection of shade. Connie joined Culbertson on the seats.

"I cannot answer questions about those events in 1970," he repeated after they had settled in. "That was not me. I simply cannot speak for that man."

Connie began to discern the point Culbertson was trying to make. "Would I be correct in assuming that what you mean is that the Denny Culbertson who traded insults with Tony Travers in 1970 was a pre-Christian Denny Culbertson? That you are a new man, perhaps a born-again man, and that you have repudiated your preconversion days and ways?"

"Well put, Connie. I am deeply ashamed of my life before coming to Christ. But I have come to terms with my shame. The Denny Culbertson of those days is a man I scarcely recognize. He is not me. I realize that the law might not see matters this way and that some court might even want to hold me responsible for crimes I might have committed before I saw the light of Christ. But I didn't commit any crimes back then—lots of sins, but no crimes—and I didn't murder Tony Travers three years ago. So the courts can have no interest in me. Which means in turn that I need not talk about events which don't involve the current Denny Culbertson, the true Denny Culbertson. And I won't."

Connie thought the line of reasoning preposterous, especially since the Culbertson he was talking to, for all his protestations about not being the Culbertson of thirty years earlier, clearly retained memories of the events Connie was interested in. But in the face of the preacher's resolution to keep silence, and in the absence of any power to subpoena him into talking, Connie found himself stymied. And so after about twenty minutes of fruitless expostulation, in part to avoid completely losing his temper at Culbertson's remarkable display of calm obduracy, Connie bade Shrug's classmate good-bye and left the grounds of the Open Worship Church, irritated as much with himself as with Culbertson.

Whoever would have thought, he mused as he headed for his car, *that a worship service would unmask so many of my unpleasant traits?* And on the subject of Culbertson, Connie remained suspicious. Clearly the encounter of 1970 continued to trouble him. The major question, the question that Culbertson refused to talk about, was whether the events vexed his conscience or stirred his resentment.

Connie stopped at a Wendy's for dinner in Zanesville, then began the drive back to Humboldt, a bit more than an hour away. Connie's mind drifted indeterminately from hymns to baseball to Nietzsche to the queen's gambit. He paid attention to the road in the way that most drivers do who have their minds on other things did. But about halfway home he noticed that a blue Camaro was several hundred yards behind him, often visible in the rearview mirror on the straighter sections of the winding state highway. He slowed down, and so did the Camaro. He speeded up, and so did the Camaro. Angry that this stalker was spooking yet another day, Connie decided to try to find out who sat behind the wheel. He pulled off on the berm behind a sign and prepared for the snoop to speed past. When the stalker obliged, Connie took off in pursuit. But about a minute later the Camaro began to speed up, and though Connie was prepared to hit 80 miles per hour in pursuit, when his game continued to pull away, Connie backed off.

He was curious. But not curious enough to risk drawing the attention of a state trooper. He wished he had remembered to look for the Camaro when he had driven to Columbus to talk with Jimmy Brackett. Had he been followed on that trip too, he wondered. Yes, he must have been. How else could he have been trailed to Zanesville? *Well at least our stalker now knows we're on to him.* Still, the key question dogged him: who is this mysterious Camaro-driver? On that matter, as on many others in this odd investigation, Connie was clueless.

Shrug awoke from his nap about noon. It was unusual for him to sleep during the day, and the consequent panic of disorientation was briefly acute. But the sense of surcease from physical discomfort and the memory of a phone conversation with. . .? *Who was it with? Oh, yes, Eddie Moratino,* pulled him back into the world of real time. He then stretched, enjoyed the soft coolness of the bed, and cast his mind over the previous day's encounter with Sonya Klepper. He was glad he believed her—glad that she no longer loomed as a major suspect for Tony Travers's murder. If, he reminded himself, there had actually *been* a murder. Lying abed early on a sunny June afternoon, he felt buoyant and sloppy in his thinking, disposed at last to believe that Tony's death had been nothing more than the natural result of the carelessness of an elderly man suffering from poor health. Life, he thought, is too pleasant to spend it scurrying around in search of nonexistent criminals. Then he realized he hadn't eaten since his small breakfast. And duty called too, for he needed finally to find out about the security system that was protecting the high school against intruders on the evening of the reunion. *Yes*, he sighed, *it really is time to get up.*

As Shrug dressed and then padded downstairs, he assessed his postsurgical discomfort. *Much better than this morning*, he concluded. Sleep was truly a restorer. He prepared a fried-egg sandwich, an apple, and a rich coffee, then phoned Craig Brownlee, the classmate who had been charged with assuring high school officials that the returning class of 1953 wouldn't trash its facility when it celebrated its forty-fifth reunion. As a graduate of Humboldt College and for many years the spokesman for the security office of that institution, Brownlee had been a natural for this assignment.

The call interrupted Brownlee's own lunch, but he was glad to talk with Shrug, for he had, like all classmates living locally, heard of the investigation and had expected to be contacted. "What the class committee and Connie and I really need to know," Shrug explained, "is how easy it would have been for a complete stranger to enter the high school, hide somewhere, meet with Tony Travers to kill him, and then leave the building, all without being noticed."

"Well," Brownlee began, in the richly reassuring tone that had helped make him such an effective security officer on a college campus, "hiding would have been easy. Lighting in most of the school building was dimmed that night, to discourage wandering. So all sorts of hiding areas were available. Leaving would also have been easy. By regulation, the exit doors, though locked from the outside, had to remain unlocked from the inside. As for how easy it might have been for an unknown person, having somehow snuck into the building, to link up with Tony. . . . Well, I can't have an informed opinion on that, can I? And I'm guessing that's a major part of what you and Connie are looking into. Sounds to me like prearrangement would have been necessary."

"It's clear you've expected a phone call of this sort." Shrug appreciated Brownlee's concision. "So what about getting *into* the school in the first place? That's the key question, isn't it?"

"That would have been harder, not impossible, but harder. The system we set up involved hiring a retired police officer, Andrea Michaels, to serve as gatekeeper to the one entry door. It's the big, wooden main door that was open to outsiders. She came on the high recommendation of the superintendent and in fact is often employed by outside groups who want to keep gate-crashers out when renting or using high school facilities. I already knew Andrea. When you're in the rule-enforcement business, you get to know others with similar jobs in town, and I was delighted at the suggestion."

"What exactly did she do?"

"Well, days before the reunion she and I got together to identify the groups of people who would need admission. The classmates, of course. Their spouses or partners or guests. You'll recall that everyone could bring one additional person. Members of this group were admitted when they showed Andrea an e-mailed communication of welcome they had received from the reunion committee, acknowledging their registration. We called it 'the entry ticket.' In a few instances, when classmates didn't use the Internet, we used snail mail. In any case, classmates needed this credential to get in. If anyone forgot their ticket, Andrea wouldn't admit them until a class member already inside vouched for them." Before Shrug could pose the obvious next question, Brownlee pushed ahead. "But that's not all. A few other people also needed access, in particular the caterers and a few members of the maintenance staff."

"How would Andrea Michaels recognize the legitimacy of these people, since they didn't have that entry ticket?" Shrug quickly asked.

"Boy, you really are suspicious and thorough. Well, in the case of the maintenance staff members, about all I can say is that they came in uniforms and, in effect, vouched for each other. Ditto for the caterers. They, too, were uniformed. Maybe you'll recall the blue-and-orange shirts they all sported. Most of the catering team were quite young, too, probably hired for the job. We weren't, after all, thinking of keeping potential killers out."

"Hmm." Connie paused to take in the import of what he'd been hearing. "It's as I feared, I guess. It sounds like a determined stranger could have found a way around these precautions and gotten in."

Brownlee considered that formulation for a moment. "You're technically right, of course. But you probably shouldn't minimize the difficulties a gate-crasher faced either. First off, unless there was an accomplice to unlock one of the other doors, the only route of access was the front door. And it was patrolled by Andrea Michaels, a responsible person who never had cause to raise an alarm during the entire evening, until, of course, the body had been discovered. Second, putting aside the classmates and their guests, you're left only with people who were marked by the uniforms they wore. How could a stranger have secured a uniform and yet passed unnoticed among his uniformed colleagues?" Brownless paused to let his explanation sink in. "Far be it from me to give Connie and you advice, but if you mean to pursue this murder angle, I think you need to figure out how someone who's not a class member could pass himself off as a classmate or classmate's spouse. And good luck with that." Shrug could almost hear Brownlee smugly chuckling. But he still saw a few problems with the security system just described and confined his reaction to thanking him for his counsel.

During the call Shrug had heard the unmistakable sound at the front door of the day's post being shoved through the letter slot. So after ending his call with Craig Brownlee, he walked to the door to find out what the deliverer had brought. The pile contained the predictable items, a few advertisements, a few catalogues, a few magazines, and a letter from Dunedin, New Zealand, with Amanda Everson's name in the upper left-hand corner of the envelope! *So the last culprit has reported in,* Shrug thought. *It's about time.* He padded into his living room while prying open the envelope, taking care to protect the stamp for his philatelic grandson. *This is my international day—a phone call from Senegal in the morning and a letter from New Zealand in the afternoon.* A photograph promptly fell out with the letter, and he bent down to pick it up, noting in doing so that his groin remained sore. He began reading the note with the softness of the afternoon still cocooning his mood. And then he got into the second sentence.

"Dear Shrug,

"It was so lovely to hear from you and to learn what old friends are doing. But you must be mistaken, for I didn't attend the forty-fifth reunion. . . ."

What? Shit! Shrug's eyes fixed on that clause. *She didn't attend the reunion. She wasn't there!*

A flood of implications filled his mind. But almost instantly they boiled down into one: *If Amanda Everson wasn't at the reunion, who was the woman pretending to be Amanda Everson? Yes, there's the mystery. Craig Brownlee's formulation doesn't go far enough. For we need to identify not only* how *someone managed to pose as a classmate but also* who *the damned impostor was.*

It was as if the world had been changed—as if the very frame of the investigation had been instantaneously recast.

For it had.

10

Friday, June 16, 2001—Saturday, June 17, 2001

Connie placed the two sheets of stationery back on the table. The blustery storm rattling Shrug's breakfast room window on Friday morning mirrored his mood. "I feel like a damn fool," Connie mumbled. "It never occurred to me that one of the reunion attenders might not be who she said she was."

Shrug laughed sharply. "*You* feel like a fool! What about me? I was there and talked with her. Moreover—and this is what has gnawed at me all night— I'm the one who kept reminding us that a stranger might have been in the building that night, and yet I never made the leap to the obvious possibility that the stranger might have come in disguise and passed as a classmate."

"The trouble is, it *wasn't* all that obvious." Connie stared across the room with tightened eyes. "That's what messed us up. Since everyone we've talked to, that's twelve people now, including the very respectable class committee, said Amanda Everson was at the reunion, talked about her, reported on conversations with her . . . since all these people (not just you) assumed that the woman who was passing herself off as . . ." Connie took a sip of coffee before continuing. "I'm bailing out on that sentence," he chuckled, "because I'm clearly so flabbergasted I can't keep my grammatical constructions in order. Let's just say we were all fooled because whoever impersonated Amanda Everson was very good at it. At least you've finally found your German augmented sixth chord." He tipped his invisible cap to Shrug.

A War Council during the morning hours was unusual, but the arrival of the unexpected news from New Zealand on Thursday seemed to require an irregular scheduling. In fact, if Connie had gotten home from Zanesville the previous evening any time before 9:00, the friends might have met immediately. As it was, they had chosen to wait until the next day, and their reward was the window-rattling weather that was bringing an abrupt end to the unseasonable heat wave.

Connie picked up the letter again, glanced from it to the photograph, and then read a paragraph aloud:

> "I hope the enclosed photograph is useful. It's the closest thing I have to evidence that I was in New Zealand at the time of the reunion. It shows me—I'm third from the right—with my daughter, her husband, and several of their friends on ANZAC Day in 1998. ANZAC Day is celebrated on June 6. That's why the banner is waving. If you have questions, please phone me. We are currently 16 hours ahead of Ohio, and I'll try to stay in on Sunday morning, which is Saturday afternoon your time."

"Now if we wanted to be truly picky," Connie said, "we might find this evidence less than completely successful. After all, we don't know who this photo is really of. And even if the woman identified is actually Amanda Everson, we don't know when the photo was really taken." Shrug remained silent, waiting to see how far Connie wanted to push playing devil's advocate. "But I don't feel like being a scoffer. If there was a plot that somehow extended all the way to New Zealand in 2001, the smart thing for the conspirator to do in response to your letter would have been to remain silent and incommunicado. For just think: how likely would it have been for an informal investigator to fly halfway around the world just because a letter wasn't answered? No, I think the odds are very high that this letter is genuine."

"In which case," Shrug finally said, "we have a whole new can of worms. And all our efforts so far have been beside the point."

"Not quite, my friend. In the process of our investigation we've gathered a number of impressions about the faux-Amanda. Up until now they've been scarcely more than curiosities, amounting (if my memory is right) to the reiterated impression that she had a good sense of style. But now we need to look at them more closely and try to gather more of them."

"So you think it's likely that Ms. X—to give her a name—was up to no good at the reunion." Shrug found himself amused at his own formulation, and answered his own question. "Of course you do. And so do I. Does that add up to being a murderer?"

Connie said that while it might be premature to adjudge Ms. X a murderer, her decision to attend the reunion under a false identity almost certainly meant that she was trying to do something that she would not want attributed to her.

"After all, it's not as if you all were a bunch of politicians or celebrities, and Ms. X was a photographer or newspaper reporter who needed to go under cover to get information. No, I think it's reasonable to surmise that she was up to something shady. And since we were already asking ourselves if a strange death that occurred at the reunion was a murder, I think we ought to treat this new information as a powerful reinforcement of the conclusion that the answer to the question is yes."

"Spoken like a philosopher," said Shrug, as he returned the tip of a nonexistent hat to his friend.

The subsequent discussion, sprawling over an hour, established four important points on which the two friends agreed. 1) That since Ms. X presumably wasn't a classmate passing herself off as another classmate, Tony's pre-high school career was no longer to be deemed unimportant. 2) That since Ms. X knew a lot about Amanda Everson's life, including all those "memories" of her high school days, Ms. X must have had friendly conversational relations with the real Amanda Everson at some point. 3) That their local investigation should now focus on gathering as many recollections of Ms. X's activities at the reunion as possible. And 4) that Shrug should place the invited phone call to the real Amanda Everson as soon as possible to see if she could point them to a possible suspect.

"This is really a very thoughtful and intelligent note," Shrug commented. He read aloud another section from Everson's letter.

> You might wonder why I hadn't learned earlier that old friends had thought they'd met me at the reunion. As I think back on it now, it was a function of some accidents. I got sick within a week of arriving in New Zealand—in fact just two days after the photo was taken—and spent a long hospitalization. I don't use e-mail (my daughter tells me I must learn) and so I'm not quickly in touch with old classmates. In fact, I just haven't stayed much in touch with old friends in any case. And finally, I have known for about a year that a few people were saying I was present at the 45th, but I treated it as a joke or a confusion.

"An admirable succinctness and organization," Connie commented. "If only *all* letter writers commanded their mind and pen so efficiently."

The morning meeting broke up at 11:15, with the stormy weather abating and the spirits of the Second-Best Club again high. They reminded themselves that there were still some independent trails that needed attention. Finding the identity of "Less" certainly, and perhaps the identities of "the Greatest" and "Chucklehead Charlie" and "Sandy." Evaluating Denny Culbertson's refusal to talk about his run-in with Tony Travers. Exploring the possibility that Eddie Moratino's relationship with Travers had been less benign than Moratino's story suggested. Tracking down the driver of the persistent blue Camaro. But the two friends agreed that discovering the identity of Ms. X, and thereafter some assessment of her motive for impersonating Amanda Everson, was the central issue before them. Since Shrug had a follow-up appointment with his surgeon scheduled for that afternoon while Connie planned to visit Tuscan Court, there was nothing they could jointly do during the rest of Friday. But before Connie drove back home in the cool, light drizzle, they blocked out a busy Saturday for themselves. The German augmented sixth had changed the key signature of the investigation.

As Connie nibbled at his lunch, he entertained the hope that a mention of his visit with Jimmy Brackett might prod a glimmer of a memory in his mother, and he was eager to hear Teresa Espinosa's take on the latest twist in the investigation. But neither anticipation panned out. Veronica Haydn didn't remember the officer who had visited her shortly after Donald's death. Indeed, Connie continued to be "Donald," and Veronica stayed happily submerged in a pre-1945 world that on this day included Carol Lombard, Bugsy Moran, Mrs. Tomashito, the building of the Golden Gate Bridge, and Mr. Bradley. Even more disappointingly, Teresa Espinosa had fallen and broken her nose the previous day and, while pleased to see Connie, was feeling the effects of her pain medications and confessed to a light-headedness and inability to concentrate. He congratulated her on having intuited that an outsider might somehow have intruded into the reunion festivities, but her only new contribution to the inquiry was the possibility that Ms. X.—"I like that coinage," she commented, "a woman of mystery"— might have been working in collaboration with a real classmate.

At midafternoon Connie caught up with Trish Ridgway in her large office at the front of Humboldt Waste Removal Services building. When he had called on Wednesday evening for an appointment, she had suggested he could find her there after 2:30 on Friday. In light of the new information about Amanda Everson, Connie's interest in Ridgway as a suspect had diminished. But she was still on his agenda and could not be completely ignored.

"So nice to meet you at last, Connie. You know, the reports that proceed you are correct: You're by far the handsomer member of the detection team."

Connie had been forewarned, but the sheer brazenness of Ridgway's approach to men had to be experienced to be believed. He noticed that her hair touched the shoulders of her peach blouse, which was open enough to reveal more than a hint of cleavage. The aromas in the room briefly puzzled him, but it didn't take him long to distinguish between a perfume that was too sweet and a bourbon that was too heavy. *How,* he wondered as he accepted her offer of a seat, *can a lush like this be a successful business woman?* Ridgway's chair sat at right angles to Connie's, close enough to allow her left knee to bump his right knee whenever she leaned forward. Which she did often, showing off the looseness of the blouse.

"How can I help, Connie? Are you and Shrug making progress?"

"We think we are, and so I'd like to follow up on some of the things you told Shrug when you two met a week or so ago." Connie had decided that he wouldn't be specific about new developments, but since he would need to focus his questions on Everson, Moratino, and Culbertson (and, of course, on Ridgway herself), his host would have to be very unperceptive not to notice the narrowing of the investigation. "We've found your memories of the reunion dinner very helpful. And your comments about the personalities and characters of some of your classmates struck us as unusually acute. You are a good observer." Connie hoped he wasn't piling on the flattery too thickly. "But first, about you. You got sick that evening. That's why you left the dining room. Do you know what made you ill?" Connie thought the question clumsy, but Ridgway strode right in.

"Probably the food. I have this problem with eating too much. It sometimes comes back to haunt me at parties."

Connie was amused at the reply, but decided to move in a different direction. "You said that Amanda Everson was a stylish dresser. Do you recall anything else about her that night?"

"I didn't know her well in high school, but she was one of the girls whose clothes I studied as I tried to acquire a sense of style myself. And friends tell me now that they trust my instinct for clothes." She told of how she had recently helped someone named Suzy buy a mother-of-the-bride outfit, and Connie let her rattle on for a few minutes, hoping to put her at ease. When she got back to Everson, she asked Connie to remind her of his question. His reply allowed her to amplify the remark she had begun with by saying that Everson's sense of style had matured over the years. "I don't mean just that she knows how to dress her age, that of course is essential, but that she knows how, for example, to dress beautifully for a woman in her early sixties and still give the impression, subtly but unmistakably, of a woman who is younger." Connie knew nothing of fashion, but the comment struck him as more insightfully nuanced than he might have expected from the tipsy Ridgway.

"It's interesting," he said tentatively. "Everyone speaks of her flair for clothes. Is there anything of a nonapparel nature that you recall about her."

"Well, I remember her saying that she was fond of older films. She collected them on VCRs." Ridgway appeared to be trying to summon up memories of the reunion conversation. Meanwhile her knee continued to graze Connie's. She smiled softly. "The person she most admired was named something like 'Wells.' Maybe it was H. G. Wells."

Connie suggested Orson Welles.

"Yes, yes, that's it." Ridgway was suddenly sounding a bit giddy. "Orson Welles—the big fat man. She called him the greatest actor or director or producer or something in the history of American filmmaking. Movies aren't my bag, as you can see. But Amanda was really into these Welles's flicks. In particular one about a chase in a sewer system."

"*The Third Man*," Connie said.

"What?"

"That's the name of the film you're thinking of—*The Third Man*."

"Oh." The remark was dry, reinforcing Ridgway's claim that she wasn't interested in film history. She didn't continue the thread of the conversation, and so Connie decided to direct her attention to Denny Culbertson. "How did you come to know that his religious conversion came about in the Middle East?"

Ridgway told of Culbertson's efforts to press a New Testament upon her at the reunion, "as if I'd never read the Bible," she said indignantly; and of his explanation that Jesus had appeared to him in the shadows of some church he visited in Jerusalem. "He said he'd always scoffed at religion before that, but from that moment on he knew Jesus as a friend."

Connie asked why, if Culbertson was not a believer, he had gone to Jerusalem in the first place, and Ridgway replied that the trip to the Middle East had been an effort to work up a partnership with some Israeli businessmen. "He said that after his encounter with Jesus he flew back to America without even meeting the Israelis. He knew his life had been changed."

Finding Ridgway rather loquacious, Connie inquired if she recalled anything else about Culbertson, and she spoke of his strong dislike of perfumes. "You may have noticed that I like perfumes," she said, "and friends have complimented me on this, too." She bent closer to Connie. Her knee nudged his somewhat more vigorously. "Well, it turns out that Mr. I'm-more-pious-than-you-Culbertson disapproves of scents. Most men like them, you know." With a toothy smile Ridgway signaled that she was moving into true Rue McClanahan mode.

Growing distinctly uncomfortable, Connie asked if Culbertson ever explained his disapproval of perfumes. "It had," Ridgway explained, "something to do with being willing to accept what God had given us by way of our bodies. But it seems to me that if God gave us beautiful bodies, then it makes perfect sense to adorn and draw attention to them." Yet another nudge prompted Connie to get up as if needing to stretch, and to walk around the room. Ridgway smiled broadly.

"You told Shrug you thought Eddie Moratino was gay. What led you to that conclusion?"

"Oh, his body language, I suppose. I can always tell if a guy is gay. It wasn't just that he didn't talk about his wife. Lots of married men who are out on the town take off their wedding ring. No, it was other things." She rose, straightened her trim slacks, and unsteadily took a seat in her desk chair. "It was, I suppose, his interests." Ridgway went on to explain how Moratino's curiosity about "ancient crockery" and other old artifacts was a clue. So too were his fondness for travel and his caution about making any self-revelatory statements. Finally, Ridgway added that she didn't recall Moratino ever dating in high school. "None of these things alone seals the deal, but if you take them together, well, a woman gets to know the signs. He's hiding something. And in this day and age, that's so needless. As I told Shrug, and as I'm sure he told you, I'd gladly join Eddie on one of his world trips if he'd ever invite me. Fat chance of that, of course." For the first time in the conversation, Ridgway seemed to be laughing at herself. "He'll take his boyfriend, whoever that lucky guy is."

"Did he say anything about his travels to Southeast Asia?"

"Well, I suppose he might have. He *was* fun to talk with, and full of stories. What an exciting life he's led! But I chiefly remember him talking about trips to Africa, elephants, mosques, people with funny names. Yes, I think he talked chiefly about Africa." Connie noticed that Ridgway seemed a bit uncertain about standing up.

Feeling safer as he stood on the far side of the rather warm office, Connie let her proceed with her happy recollections of her conversation with Eddie Moratino, a man she clearly found to be pleasant company. Then at 3:15, pleading the need to let her get back to the work of running Humboldt Waste Removal, he said he would be going. Ridgway said she was sorry he hadn't asked her about finding the body on the evening of the reunion dinner, and Connie replied that since Shrug had already covered that ground, he had felt it unnecessary to return to the unpleasant subject. She seemed disappointed but didn't protest, saying only that she hoped she'd see him again. She didn't rise. And with that brief exchange, Connie escaped the tigress's lair.

At 2:00 P.M. the next day, Saturday, Connie and Shrug sat in the high-tech home office of Bryan Travers. On the previous afternoon, before driving to Columbus for the meeting with his surgeon, Shrug had alerted Bryan to the dramatic change in the investigation, asking if he would arrange a quick meeting with as many of the class officers as possible. The result of his efforts was, Connie thought, very impressive. Two were present in person, Cole Stocker having driven out from Upper Arlington, and Dirk Glass having left his antique shop in his wife's hands for the occasion. And while neither Cheryl Bollinger, vacationing in South Carolina, nor Gertie Heintzelman, working in Washington, could make herself personally available, both had arranged to be on phone lines that connected them with the Humboldt meeting, their voices amplified throughout Bryan's studio by a speaker phone. Shrug could readily imagine that some combination of curiosity and a desire to be useful had prompted them all to make themselves available.

Deliberately leaving the contacts with Claire Van Tassell and Major Brackett unmentioned, Shrug began by stressing that the letter from Amanda Everson had reshaped the investigation. It was now clear that some stranger had attended the reunion, persuasively impersonating a member of the class of 1953. Though no one participating in this conversation was now surprised by that information, since it had been communicated the previous day as the explanation for the emergency meeting, they all took a few moments to express their total astonishment that they had been so fooled, avowing to a person that they never even had doubts that

"Amanda Everson" was who she said she was. "After all, she knew all the stories about life at Humboldt High," Heintzelman declared. "I guess there'll be no more jokes about Amanda bringing couture to Kiwis in Christ Church."

Shrug continued by saying that later that same afternoon Connie and he would be talking with the real Everson in New Zealand. With that call they hoped to begin the job of identifying who the impersonator might have been. But they needed, he went on, to revisit the weekend of the reunion and recover as many recollections as possible about conversations with, and consequent impressions of, the woman pretending to be Amanda Everson.

At that point Connie took over the task of explaining the friends' plans. He said that they would take a new look at every conversation they had notes of, aiming at identifying the interests of "Amanda Everson." They would recheck the video tapes, trying to figure out what she was doing at every moment she was on screen. And they would start consulting additional classmates—people who had thus far been outside the scope of their questioning—to see what other memories might be recoverable. "We now have good reason to believe that something strange was happening at the reunion, a reunion at which one class member unexpectedly and perhaps mysteriously died. Moreover, we now have a single person to direct our attention to. That's just the kind of refocusing and reenergizing that this investigation has needed. So we're going to push very hard at getting all the facts we can about that weekend."

The assembled group, aided by the two distant-participants, reshared various memories of "Amanda Everson" at the reunion, but the stories were in every case variations of tales that Connie and Shrug had already heard. To Connie the poverty of novelty underlined the importance of widening the pool of classmates being consulted. Surely someone, he thought, was impressed by something other than her flair for dress.

"Shouldn't you turn the matter over to the police?" Cole Stocker suddenly asked.

Connie turned to Shrug, for they had anticipated the question. "At some point, yes, Cole," Shrug said. "Bryan asked the same question yesterday, and Connie and I have pondered it. But I think it can't really become a police matter until more is known, who Ms. X is, for example, or what motive she might have had for attending the reunion incognita, or evidence conceivably that a crime had been committed. With matters as vague as they are now, the police wouldn't devote remotely as much energy to the matter as we would. And while they have far more technological fire-power than we do, at this point the investigation needs plods to go around asking questions, not bells-and-whistles equipment. The police certainly wouldn't devote manpower to investigate a three-year-old death that aroused no questions at the time. That's some-thing we can supply—manpower." He looked over at Bryan Travers. "What's most important, however, is that Bryan has asked us to stay on the case." Shrug smiled inwardly at how well he could spout the jargon.

Shrug then spoke specifically to Gertie Heintzelman in Wash-ington, asking if she had located the reunion records that Bryan Travers had asked her to try to find. Her report was succinct. Amanda Everson had never attended an earlier class reunion. As plans took shape during 1997 for the forty-fifth, she was living in Connalton, Texas, a suburb of Houston. Her first correspondence with Heintzelman, about a year prior to the reunion, indicated that she was tentatively planning to attend. Then in March of 1998 she had written to say that she wouldn't be able to be there because she'd be moving to New Zealand in late May or early June to be near her daughter. But then, on May 16, she wrote again to say that her moving plans had changed and that she could attend after all. With that letter she included a new e-mail address, adding only that it was temporary. With that explanation, Heintzelman handed a copy of the address to Shrug.

"Did you keep these letters?" Connie asked quickly, but Heintzelman replied that she had merely recorded the information in her computer files and discarded the letters. "Unless the notes were personal, I saw no need to keep them. Sorry."

"Not your fault," Connie said lamely.

Heintzelman then disclosed what she knew about Ms. X's brief stay in Humboldt. She had taken room 3 at the Andrew Strett Bed and Breakfast, the most expensive of the various hotels and inns that the class had used. It was located conveniently close to the high school, and Heintzelman added that Cole Stocker and Cheryl Bollinger, as class officers, had lodged there too, in rooms 5 and 6. "Oh, wasn't *that* cute," Connie mumbled before he could catch himself. "Sorry," he muttered. Stocker did not look amused. Heintzelman continued that on her preliminary information sheet "Everson" had not checked off the square that indicated she was bringing a car, but perhaps the B&B would have records that could help. (Shrug immediately realized that such records, though potentially useful, were probably inaccessible, since only official authority could subpoena the documents, if they still existed at a distance of three years. He sighed.) Heintzelman concluded by noting that "Everson" had made no contact with her whatsoever after the reunion. "That was unusual. Most classmates sent me thank-you notes, or had questions, or just wanted to reminisce. But I didn't think anything of it, probably didn't even notice it, until yesterday, when I got your request to start pulling up this information."

Dirk Glass had spent the interval of Heintzelman's report scribbling in his pad, and when the report was concluded he joined the conversation to suggest that a note he had been composing be sent to all classmates. He read it aloud, and everyone approved his focus and phraseology.

"I like your clever choice of words in notifying our old friends that we had an impostor in our midst," said Cheryl Bollinger from South Carolina. "And you were right to recognize the value of our receiving *photographs* of the fake Amanda," added Connie. "I'll bet there are a number of them. And with their help we'll be able to get a sense of what Ms. X looks like."

Glass proposed to e-mail the note that evening to all class-mates who were on-line, with a follow-up note to everyone in the class to go out in Monday's mail. "Of course, it's summer," he added, "and so some of our classmates may be on vacation. But that can't be helped." The proposal received approval.

Because Cole Stocker had a medical meeting in Columbus requiring his attention, the conversation broke up soon thereafter, with Shrug promising to keep the class committee informed, and Bryan Travers thanking them again for their readiness to be helpful. Before taking their own leaves, however, the two friends sought information from their host. He looked through the list of names that Connie had accumulated, chiefly from Jimmy Brackett, and found none that rang a bell. But, though unable to vouch for their currency, he was able to supply Connie with addresses for Tony's wives. And he confirmed Connie's surmise that he was the one who had stuck Claire Van Tassel's condolence note into the packet of love letters.

Satisfied with those replies, Shrug and Connie headed for Shrug's house so that the phone call to New Zealand, to be placed (by Shrug's plan) on a Saturday at 5:00 P.M. Eastern Daylight Savings Time in Ohio, would arrive in Dunedin, New Zealand, at 9:00 A.M. Sunday morning local time. Although an obliging Amanda Everson had said she would stay at home that Sunday, Shrug wanted to start his efforts to contact her as early as seemed reasonable.

———————— ———————— ————————

It was 5:05 P.M. when Shrug heard Amanda Everson's voice at the other end of the phone line. A quick exchange of authentic pleasantries followed between the two acquaintances who hadn't seen each other in almost fifty years. But because both were eager to discuss the imposture, Shrug had no difficulty moving the conversation onto the subject that prompted the call.

Everson said that she had known for about a year that someone pretending to be her had attended the reunion. In general, she had thought it odd that someone would have impersonated her.

But in the overall picture, it hadn't loomed large in her mind. After all, her life in New Zealand was busy, she hadn't stayed in close touch with high school friends anyway, and from the perspective of Dunedin, famous for its haggis ceremonies, penguins and rugged scenery, the distant world of Ohio seemed almost inconsequential. "A world that scarcely touches me anymore," she said.

Shrug thanked her again for sending the photograph and asked if her appearance in the picture was similar to her appearance in the years before she left the United States. She replied that the image reflected the way she had worn her hair for many years prior to leaving the States, adding however that her struggle with breast cancer and chemotherapy over the past two years had significantly altered her looks. The mention of the disease, which had been diagnosed within days of the taking of the photo she had sent to Shrug, prompted him to inquire about Everson's health. She replied that she guessed her cancer was "slowly making inroads" but that she no longer allowed it to consume her life. "As long as I can, I'll live the way I want to, not the way the invader would like me to."

Shrug explained that he and Connie were confident that the impersonator had known Everson. "She could readily talk with your old classmates about things that happened in high school."

"That's weird. No, it's scary."

"Actually, we think it's the consequence of someone having carefully, and probably subtly, milked you for information about your high school days. We have no idea why someone would *want* to do that, however. By the way, did you ever live in New England or find employment as an agent for literary manuscripts?"

Everson laughed. "Shrug, you probably don't remember, but I wasn't much of a reader in high school and never became one afterwards. So I'm an unlikely one for a literary agent. As for New England, no. I left Ohio State after my sophomore year to marry Harry, and we lived in Kansas for a few years before moving to Connalton. He finally wound up working at Enron, a wonderful employer. But, as you may know, he died in 1995, before I came to New Zealand. That's sort of why I came. Melinda, my daughter, married a New Zealander and wanted me closer at hand, to keep an eye on me, to make sure I didn't become a misbehaving merry widow." Shrug liked the sense of fun he heard in Everson's voice. He also stored away the possibility, and now maybe the likelihood, that if Ms. X had talked about New England and a career as an agent at the reunion, she could very well have been drawing on her own experiences, not Amanda Everson's.

"I've been thinking about this whole thing ever since your letter came," Everson continued. "And you know, your suspicions may be right. In the years before I left Connalton I did begin talking about high school days. And what makes that interesting is that there was one woman who prompted me to do it, Harriet Murray."

At last, a name!

With Shrug's encouragement, Everson told how she and a number of her friends had formed a weekly sewing circle which they called "Stitch and Bitch." Shrug groaned inwardly, wondering if they couldn't have come up with something cleverer than that old chestnut. Murray had been a member and had often tried to get Everson to discuss her years at Humboldt High, even saying that Everson's stories were so amusing and interesting that she ought to consider writing her high school memoirs. "I see now that it was absurd flattery. Maybe I knew it then, too, but I didn't mind being made much of in the years right after Harry died. It gave me occasions to meet people. That's when I stopped using my married name of O'Neill, not as a mark of disrespect for my late husband, but as a rather extravagant gesture of reasserting autonomy. And that's when I began tentative outreaches to neglected friends from Humboldt days."

Nudged along by Shrug, Everson told how Murray had asked about Everson's high school activities: field hockey, Spanish Club, choir, a short effort at acting, Future Homemakers of America and boy friends. "She liked to hear me talk about teachers, too. Miss

Corping, who, remember, we used to call 'Miss Corpulent,' and Mrs. Redding, and old Dr. Stephenson." The names brought back quick and vivid memories to Shrug. Murray had also asked about Everson's best friends, what she did after school, pranks she may have pulled, anything else that might have made high school memorable. "Now that I'm telling you all of this, it sounds spooky and, in light of what you now know, suspicious. But at the time, and I'm talking about something that happened weekly, over months, maybe years, it just seemed that she was trying to be a helpful and friendly and curious neighbor."

"Did Harriet Murray ever borrow your high school yearbook?" For Shrug, this was a crucial question. If Murray had systematically been trying to learn about Everson's high school days, the yearbook would have been vital reading.

"Yes, she did. In fact, I had to remind her to return it to me before I moved down here."

Shrug was now immensely interested in this Harriet Murray and asked for more information. Everson described her as childless, maybe eight years younger than Everson herself, with long brown hair (Shrug knew from the photo that Everson's hair was short and brown) and a roundish face, "sort of like mine, I guess," and an inch or two advantage in height on Everson. She dressed well and spoke with a very slight foreign accent; she was well-mannered, cheerful, and good company. Everson said she couldn't recall what Murray did for a living and speculated that she maintained herself on alimony payments. Nor could she recall anything about Murray's earlier life. "I guess I should have been puzzled by that asymmetry: she wanted to know so much about me, and yet she revealed so little about herself."

Wanting to gather additional information about Harriet Murray, Shrug asked for the name of some of Everson's friends in Connalton. "You should get in touch with Elinor Burroughs," was her prompt suggestion. "She's a dear, and she'll be glad to help out. Gossip is one of her hobbies."

When the phone call ended, with promises from Shrug that Everson would be kept informed, Shrug felt that he had uncovered a treasure trove of useful information. Connie had sat silently during the call, curious but patient. Once Shrug had filled him in, the two friends called Abe Steinberg to ask him to search the Web for information about Harriet Murray, who as recently as three years earlier had lived in Connalton, Texas. They also asked him to check out the "temporary" e-mail address that Murray had presumably used to secure the "entry ticket" to the reunion. Then Connie had to leave, for he had an umpiring assignment ahead of him that evening at a Police Athletic League baseball game. But the two members of the Second-Best Club were beginning to feel pretty cocky: they had identified the likely impersonator with unexpected ease and could reasonably expect to receive pertinent information and photographs in the coming days. Where this all might lead was still very unclear. But the developments of the day had the unmistakable feeling of progress.

Connie had served as an umpire at PAL games over many summers. He enjoyed helping the local league, which consisted of six baseball teams of ten-to-twelve-year-old boys and girls. He used the opportunity to provide occasional tips to the young players, and his enjoyment in watching baseball games, whatever the skill level of the participants, never diminished. On this evening Connie had responsibility for the base paths, while his fellow umpire, Tim Lucas, was behind the plate. The timeless banter of the childhood diamond—"good eye," "force at any base," "a walk's as good as a hit," rang across the field.

But base path duty was not arduous, allowing time for his mind to wander. So Connie's thoughts drifted back to baseball nicknames. Today he was struck by how the most celebrated players often had more than one nickname. Joe Dimaggio was "Joltin' Joe" and "the Yankee Clipper." Lou Gehrig was "the Iron Horse" and "Larrupin' Lou." Ted Williams was a one-man nickname industry: "the Kid," "Teddy Baseball," "the Thumper," and "the Splendid Splinter."

His mind turned to Grover Cleveland Alexander, the remarkable pitcher who had won 373 games in the National League. He was both "Old Pete" (*Where did that "Pete" come from any way?*) and more naturally "Alexander the Great." The last nickname brought back to mind the conversation about historical figures bearing "the Great": Frederick, Alfred, Catherine, Ivan, and Peter. But it rang other echoes as well. One of Tony Travers's lovers, the most eminent in that long list, if Bryan was to be believed, was "the Great." Someone called "Less" had urged him to seek protection from the authorities. A woman named "Sandy" had been commander of his unit in 1945. *What is it about the name Alexander that summoned up all these shards of thought?*

And then, like jigsaw puzzle pieces clicking into place, it came! The female version of Alexander was Alessandra. "Alessandra" might readily yield two nicknames: Sandy and Less. "Sandy" was the obvious, conventional one, suitable for general usage. "Less" would be personal, the unexpected usage appropriate, say, for an intimate friend. And anyone named Alessandra might easily be styled, by an admirer, Alessandra the Great. That had to be it! Tony's greatest love, the woman who had been his commander in wartime espionage, the woman who had urged him to seek help, they were all one and the same: they were a person named Alessandra.

Connie was awakened from his reverie by a tangle of shouting boys and girls standing around him, with many other young players, several coaches, the raucous fans, and his amused fellow umpire all awaiting his call on a play that had just eventuated in a runner, several fielders, and a baseball arriving at second base almost simultaneously. He could only confess that he hadn't been paying attention and ask Tim Lucas to adjudicate the play. He felt his face turn red. But at the same time he felt that he had possibly, and he had to admit to himself that "possibly" was the operative word, solved three of the nickname questions by conflating them into one person. Alive with excitement, he was eager to share his insight with Shrug. Only "Chucklehead Clancy" remained as the unknown outlier.

Three more innings of diamond activity lay ahead before he could get to a phone. His sense of self-reproach assured that he would not let his mind wander again during those three frames. So he was safe from the prospect of further embarrassing episodes of inattention. *Still*, he thought, *it's a good thing I'm not always a prisoner of duty. My God! Look what a free-associating mind can do!*

11

Sunday, June 17, 2001—Monday, June 18, 2001

Connie tried to jog daily. It was a point of pride with him. But only on Sunday mornings did he usually set aside enough time to run a longer circuit. Out to Grandison Park. On past the old Indian mound site. Turning at the water tower on Schultz Hill. Back along the edge of Old Critters Creek. Past Mabel Lawrence's farm produce store. And finally back into Humboldt. The course stretched out for a bit more than seven miles, and Connie, who had retained his teenage weight of 150 pounds, completed it in about an hour. His clocking hadn't changed much in eight years, and he was quietly very pleased with his physical condition. Too smart to believe that he could forever defy Father Time, he nevertheless harbored the jogger's hope that he might find a way to extort a few extra years from the old gentleman. His part of the bargain, he thought, was to run as regularly as possible.

Sunday dawned foggy and chilly, but the forecast promised a quick burn-off, and the cool dampness of the morning obliged Connie to don a Humboldt College sweatshirt over his National Baseball Hall of Fame T-shirt. Then, as most of his Humboldt neighbors were preparing for a morning of indoor worship, Connie set out to celebrate the great god Pan, to suck in with each measured breath an exalting sense of unity with the still-exploding trees and the thickening grass, the jubilant song birds and (once beyond the city limits) the lowing cows. And as the lonely run continued and the fog slowly lifted to reveal the shining early-morning fields of rural Ohio, Connie felt the glow of the poet's famous declaration of contentment: all's right with the world.

He knew that in part his sense of satisfaction arose from his conviction that he had cracked the mystery of the nicknames the previous evening. He was pleased to note that even with the passage of a night, his reasoning still seemed to be plausible. He also knew that in part his sense of pleasure with the world was the natural consequence of the sudden emergence of this person named Harriet Murray as the probable key to anything odd that might have happened at Shrug's reunion. Now the investigation had focus; now there was a suspect; now the odds favored a crime over an accident. What Alessandra might have to do with Harriet Murray was yet to be determined, but the investigation had definitely moved into a new stage.

The metronomic pace of his run was steady and reassuring. Left, right . . . left, right . . . left, right, soothingly robotic in its regularity. The roadside scenery flowed by. Thoughts passed in no particular order or pattern. He approached the water tower from its right, shifted direction slightly to avoid the maintenance shack, turned the corner of the shack, and . . . with his left leg suddenly blocked, he found himself lying face down on the ground!

Before he even had a chance to think that he had stumbled and lost his glasses, he felt a heavy force land squarely in the middle of his back, driving the air from his lungs and making any effort to scramble back to his feet impossible. Stunned, gasping for air, Connie lay face down, dirt and grass in his mouth and the pain of his abrupt fall swelling through his body. A voice barked, "Don't try to get up." When, a few seconds later, Connie made an effort to defy that command in order to see who had tripped him up, the weight on his back pressed down all the harder. He submitted, his knees shrieking and his stomach suddenly nauseated.

A hand from behind slipped under his forehead, raised his head a bit, and quickly guided a piece of cool cloth across his eyes. He immediately felt the cloth being tied tightly behind his head. *I've been blindfolded*, he thought, sensing even as he did so that he had been rendered almost helpless. And that it had happened so quickly that he had not even resisted in any significant way. Immediately thereafter, and again from behind, the assailant gagged him, stuffing a cloth in his mouth and securing the cloth with some sort of strap that was knotted behind Connie's head. Connie could no longer hope to cry out. Then, and only then, did Connie begin to feel afraid—deeply afraid. Someone, he realized, was trying to hurt him, maybe to kill him; and he had no idea why he had become anyone's target.

The assailant turned next to Connie's ankles, aiming to tie them together. Connie kicked out backwards in protest. Almost immediately the heavy force landed again in the middle of his back. He now recognized it as a foot. Not a word was spoken, but Connie, gasping and shaking with pain, understood the command and lay silent as his ankles were bound.

When the attacker turned to the task of tying Connie's wrists together behind his back, he didn't resist. Instead, even as he was being made still more helpless, he began to consider his situation— to think, as he would later say, like a philosopher. Resistance at this moment seemed pointless. Conveniently, since he lay sightless on his stomach with his limbs immobilized, it also struck him as impossible. So he found himself puzzling over the identity of his attacker. Who is he? For that matter, could he be a woman? Could a woman trip me and tie me up? What did the voice sound like? And with that question Connie realized that he couldn't recall the voice clearly enough to know whether it was a man's or a woman's. Just five words had been spoken: "Don't try to get up." All else had passed, quite briskly, in silence. *I can't even know whether it is a man or a woman who is doing this to me. Christ Almighty!*

After tying Connie's wrists, the assailant moved away, leaving a panting Connie lying on his stomach. He could be heard rustling around in some bushes or undergrowth, and then returning. He grabbed Connie by his shoulders, turned him over, sat him up, and dragged him from behind for some uncomfortable distance, only to leave him propped against what felt like the trunk of a tree. Connie found the situation physically uncomfortable, for with his arms bound behind him, he could find no satisfactory way to lean back against his support. Despite his wiggling, his lower back and his shoulders began to cramp; and his neck, jerked about while he had lain on his stomach, ached with each movement of his head. All he could do to ease his discomfort was pull his legs up by bending his knees.

A minute or so passed, as Connie tried to glean information from the attacker's heavy breathing. Unexpectedly, the unknown person steadied Connie's head and placed on his nose and around his ears what could only be his glasses. Blindfolded, Connie could not use them. In fact, of course, they had not been designed to fit over a blindfold, and Connie felt the assailant twist them to get them to sit in place. Still, he experienced a small surge of relief that his glasses had been recovered. But then, equally abruptly, the attacker snatched them from Connie's face and quite audibly snapped them in two. He then pushed the two halves of the glasses into the breast pocket of Connie's sweatshirt. The attacker was breathing hard now—*it* must *be a man*—and tied something around Connie's left forearm. And then, to Connie's astonishment, the attacker left, his footsteps receding quickly into the still-twittering calm of an early summer morning.

So that's it; I'm not to be killed after all. Although sweat was dripping from his forehead and tickling his arms and back, Connie tried to relax, catch his breath, and will the waves of nausea to recede. After a little reflection, he decided that the assailant would probably not return. After all, with each passing minute, the likelihood that someone else might appear on the bucolic scene increased, and the assailant would not wish to be found continuing his crime. The thought brought modest relief to Connie. So did his success at finding a sitting posture (with his head bent far forward) that gave some ease to his back and neck. He tried to wriggle his hands free from their bonds, but the effort was unavailing. He had even less room at his ankles and quickly concluded that they, too, would remain confined until a rescuer arrived. *All I can do*, he concluded (in both anger and resignation), *is wait until I'm found.*

The wait seemed like a long one. He had been dragged, he guessed, behind some bushes or trees, for on two occasions he heard people pass fairly nearby, and yet he was not seen. Unable to speak or move about, he couldn't draw attention to himself. In his isolation he sometimes started to yield to the pangs of self-pity. He fought off despair by forcing himself to summon up various lists that had come to inhabit his memory over the years: the periodic table of the elements, the books of the Old Testament, the senators of the fifty states, the annual batting champions, the capitals of the countries of the world. He also puzzled over whether the attack could be related to the Travers' investigation. He was able to imagine connections, but all seemed ridiculously implausible.

His rescue, when it came, was a quick one. He was scarcely aware of someone's approach on the nearby path when a bark, a panting breath, and a wet tongue told him that a dog had arrived to slobber over him. Two voices cheerfully called out "Kino!" But the voices quickly turned to distress when they saw what Kino had found. Within minutes Connie was unbound and thanking his saviors, who turned out to be Wesley Preston and Kimberly Stolz, two Humboldt seniors whom he actually knew because he had taught them in introductory philosophy several years earlier. Despite his wariness about canines, Connie reached out to thank Kino, too. His blood-smeared knees ached in protest, but he felt an unexpected welling of fondness for the inquisitive mutt.

After cautiously grunting his way back into a standing posture, he reached into his sweatshirt pocket to extract the two pieces of his glasses, noting right away that the assailant had taken a moment to scratch the lenses. "Bastard," he muttered. Reminded by the stares of his saviors that a card was hanging down from his arm, he pulled it up close to his myopic eyes. The message, in large and inked block letters, was brief: "Stop looking into the death of Tony Travers." *Well, that answers* that *question.* Otherwise the card, an unlined 3" x 5" card available in any stationery store, was unmarked. The message was attached to his arm by a piece of twine; it too looked conventional, though Connie was less a connoisseur of cords than of cards. He placed both into his sweatshirt pocket. Then he gathered up the pieces of cloth that had blocked his vision, silenced his voice, and bound his limbs. He assumed that all of them might be regarded as evidence.

The very word "evidence" brought his mind back to a plan of action he had been conjuring up even when he had no substantial reason to link the attack to the investigation. And the adventitious circumstance that some former students were his discoverers gave him a realistic opportunity of acting on the plan. He would deliberately defer reporting the crime until he had had time to confer with Shrug. An attack of this sort was so unexpected—so at variance with the developing shape of the investigation—that Connie wanted to compare impressions with his fellow-investigator before notifying law officers, a step that would trigger the intrusion of some measure of police curiosity into what they were doing. Although his rescuers offered to drive him to the hospital in their car, parked only a few hundred yards up the path, Connie had no trouble persuading them that they should help him get to his home instead. Like most Humboldt students, they were disinclined to contradict the wishes of a professor, even, Connie smiled, a bruised, bloodied, and retired one. When they reached his house, he invited them in for coffee or cocoa, but they said they needed to get Kino back on his walk. "Besides," Stolz said, "you look like you could use a shower, Professor Haydn." She was right, of course. But what struck Connie as the two students walked back to their car was the fact that no one had addressed him as "professor" in two years.

Shrug stared at Connie across Connie's kitchen table. He had driven to the home of his friend as soon as he had returned from church and found the voice mail message waiting for him. "You look awful," he remarked. Connie couldn't dissent. He was wearing his battered back-up pair of glasses. His face was blotchy and sore, his lower lip was swollen, and he sported Band-Aids above his left eye, on his right cheek, and across his chin. Although not visible at the moment, his legs, which he had grimly shown to Shrug earlier when he had told the tale of his assault were similarly swathed. "I'm glad, however," Shrug continued, "you're now thinking with that wonderful and celebrated Haydn-esque coolness. As some-one said, 'Revenge is a dish best served cold'."

"It comes from *Les liaisons dangereuses*, you twit," Connie laughed. (He was still stung that he hadn't picked up the reference to *Sense and Sensibility*.) "And besides, it's not revenge I want, it's justice—hot, burning, searing justice." He dwelt on each of the adjectives, and both men laughed.

"Spoken like a true Kantian," Shrug teased, earning a frown and arched eyebrows from Connie.

They sipped their coffee in silence for several minutes before Shrug asked the inevitable question. "What do you make of this?"

"Right now," Connie replied, "I just have random thoughts. That's why I wanted to give us a chance to prod each other." Rub-bing various bumps and bruises as he spoke, he explained that he thought it likely that his assailant was a man because a woman would have been unlikely to have had the strength to tug his bound body about. Shrug disagreed, noting that Cheryl Bollinger, either of the Grunhagens, and Trish Ridgway, "just to mention some women we've recently met," were far from feeble damsels. Ignor-ing the interruption (and sticking with the male pronoun), Connie added that the conspicuous silence of the assailant suggested that he didn't want his voice heard, which in turn suggested that he feared that Connie would recognize the voice. It seemed quite clear, he noted, that the assailant hadn't meant to kill him, and that therefore the whole point of the attack, underscored by the note, had been to frighten them off of the investigation.

"Yeah, that was my immediate conclusion, too. But why? It seems to me we had just pretty convincingly shown that the person who did Tony Travers in—if that's what happened, I know—was not anyone connected with Humboldt's class of 1953. So who in Humboldt would object to us looking for this unknown Harriet Murray?"

"Well, it's possible we've gotten everything wrong, of course. That we've misread evidence or misinterpreted the facts. Or overlooked something. In short, that someone in the class of '53 is involved in Tony's death, perhaps as an accomplice with Harriet Murray." Connie paused, his tongue gently stroking his sore lip. "But in fact, I don't think so."

"Oh?"

"No. And this is what came to me as I leaned against that damned tree. I think that this new Harriet Murray line is rich with possibilities and quite likely to lead us to the explanation of Tony's death. But I also think that, quite independently of that matter, someone is trying really hard to get us to back off—and doing so for reasons that we haven't yet got a clue of."

"So we have *two* mysteries. I like that. But why now? What led your attacker to strike now?"

"I wish I could be sure," Connie replied. "It might, of course, be that the attacker hadn't acted earlier simply in the hope that the whole thing would fizzle out. Then, as the two nosy old farts kept pushing ahead, he finally decided that he needed to take action. And an isolated and predictable early-morning jogger made a convenient target for delivering a warning."

"If that's the case," Shrug interjected proudly, "he sure misunderstands old farts. The trouble with trying to scare codgers like us is that we've already lived our lives, we're less scared of dying than the middle-aged are, and we assess risks pretty brutally."

"All true," Connie said approvingly, "but on the timing question there's another possibility. What if we have done something in the last few days that set off an alarm button? What if we have crossed some sort of threshold and thereby *provoked* the warning?"

"But what sort of threshold?"

"I don't know. But one that comes immediately to mind is my conversation with Jimmy Brackett. Maybe someone is unhappy that we've picked up on Tony's intelligence ties."

"Oh, that really seems unlikely. Could the long arm of MI6, or whatever agency it is or was, actually reach into rural central Ohio? And at this point, fifty-five years after the war, who would care?" Shrug smiled at the foolishness of his last remark. "But of course someone *does* care. That's what this whole new line of inquiry presupposes. Sorry."

Again they fell silent, as Shrug prepared himself another piece of honeyed toast. Then he spoke. "Here's an idea. Maybe the impatience-with-old-farts theory and the threshold theory can be combined. For something else we've done just recently is tell Brian and the class committee that we're going to redouble our efforts, recheck our sources, and reevaluate each step we've taken. Now it's true we said all this in the context of trying to learn more about the fake Amanda Everson. But maybe, for reasons we don't yet understand, it sounded ominous to someone on the committee. And that would explain," Shrug was becoming visibly excited as he spun his suggestion out, "why your attacker didn't want to speak. Why an effort to scare us off, risky as it would inevitably be, was now called for."

"Sounds plausible, I guess. But we'd need to spread the net of suspected assailants wider than the class committee. Dirk Glass presumably got his e-mail message out to all members of the class of '53 last night. Some of them live right here in Humboldt or nearby. Some of them have been our suspects! Some we've talked to. Any one of them might have decided that hesitation was no longer an option and acted on the news."

"But they'd have had to know your running habits," noted Shrug dubiously.

"Yes, and if whoever assaulted me had always had a warning attack in mind as a back-up plan, he might well have tracked my movements. Remember: there's that blue Camaro." He frowned. "Except, of course, that we've only seen it when we've been driving places, often to out-of-town places. If I'd been followed on a jog, I'd have noticed."

"Okay, okay. So the theory doesn't answer all our questions. It has some flaws. Maybe we can work them out. It still strikes me as useful."

"Or maybe the theory is just plain wrong." Connie was smiling broadly and laughing aloud, even as the soreness in his ribs prompted a wince.

"Well, I'm glad your spirits are feeling better," Shrug mumbled.

"There's something else I'm feeling good about." And Connie proceeded to explain how the name 'Alessandra' would solve three different problems.

Shrug was impressed. "That's a very nifty insight, Sherlock. It's too bad we haven't seen an Alessandra anywhere during . . ."

"That's because people call her by her nicknames, and, on this hypothesis, she has at least three of them."

"I know. All I'm trying to say is that we need to get our hands on some sorts of documents which give the full, legal, birth names of the people who consorted with Tony. But where to turn to get them is a bit of a mystery. It makes sense, I suppose, to ask Abe's help. But even he might not be able to do much with a single first name."

"Especially since Alessandra is almost surely a Brit. Of course, maybe Jimmy Brackett will come up with something. But the list he gave me doesn't include any persons with the first initial of A except for Tony—Anthony—himself."

Shrug's sigh at that remark was audible. "Maybe the list is incomplete. Maybe it's a list of just unit members, *not* including the leader." He groaned. "We're sounding pretty feeble right now. Maybe. I suppose. Counting on friends. Those are what is known as pious hopes. And so. . . ." Shrug stopped, then abruptly declared: "That's why I'm going to seize the other horn of the dilemma."

Connie knew immediately from Shrug's tone and expression that something was afoot. "And just what *is* this other horn of the dilemma?"

Shrug paused for a dramatic instant, and then declared with a small smile that he had new information. "Abe Steinberg left me a voice mail message this morning saying that Harriet Murray was no longer to be found in Connalton, that she may have taken flight. And that means that we can't waste any more time here in Ohio. So tomorrow I'm going to get a ticket for a Tuesday flight to Texas. Then I'll start asking questions about Harriet Murray. We need to find out where she's gone to. Which probably means that we need some dirt on her, stories about her interests, tales of her peculiarities. And the only efficient way to gather that information is to go talk with the people who knew her."

Connie approved without hesitation. "Your absence will give me an excuse to get some guiltless rest. I think I'll need a day or two to shake off my soreness."

"Longer than that, I fear."

"But speaking of soreness, I need to report the attack to the sheriff. He'll probably be annoyed I took so long to come by the office, but, tough, right? It's my body and my victimhood. And I've got a card, a string, and some cloth strips to give him as evidence. Plus the testimony of my two rescuers." Lighthearted as the remark was meant to sound, Connie still winced and groaned as he struggled to rise.

Shrug drove him to the sheriff's office, where, it being Sunday, he dealt not with George Fielding but with a rather bored deputy while Shrug bought some groceries. Shrug then drove Connie to Trinity Hospital, where X-rays confirmed that his tumble had not broken any facial bones. After leaving the hospital, the friends agreed that while Shrug was in Texas seeking leads on the Harriet Murray angle, Connie would spend his recuperation in

Humboldt trying to get leads on the identity of his assailant and probing into the relevance of the mysterious blue Camaro to any of these other matters. "It's not clear," Connie said summarily as Shrug dropped him off at his house, "whether we have three strands or two or conceivably just one. But we've riled someone up, and that must mean we're making progress, right?" To which Shrug replied, with raised eyebrows: "where have I heard *that* before?"

The Humboldt Herald & Examiner was delivered to subscribers midafternoon on weekdays. Shrug found the Monday edition on his stoop at 3:45 and as he picked it up he was thinking that within little more than eighteen hours he would be on his way to Texas. Getting the plane reservations had been easy that morning. So had getting new glasses. But persuading Elinor Burroughs to talk with him had been much tougher, for even though Amanda Everson had been a friend of hers before moving away, the same claim could be made by Harriet Murray. In the end, Shrug had won her cautious willingness to meet him only when he had promised that he would show her Amanda's letter. It didn't mention Murray, of course, and Shrug had explained that omission to Burroughs, but at least it confirmed the fact that someone pretending to be Amanda Everson had taken her place at an occasion at which a mysterious death had occurred. Shrug hoped he could supply enough confidence-inspiring peripheral information, seasoned with winning smiles, to get Burroughs to open up. That, and the universal human fascination with mysteries, might induce her to share some thoughts and perhaps even, he could hope, encourage her friends to contribute their recollections as well.

Shrug opened the paper to the column of police reports, where he found the expected terse summary of what had happened to Connie the day before. But catching his eye right below the reports was a small headline: "Local man attacked." The assault on Connie, it seemed, was important enough to have earned treatment in a separate article.

Humboldt resident Dr. Connie Haydn, professor Emeritus of Philosophy at Humboldt
College, was attacked Sunday during an
early-morning jog at the water tower. An unknown person knocked Dr. Haydn down and
left him tied up, blindfolded, and gagged.
Two Humboldt College seniors, Wesley
Preston and Kimberly Stolz, found him later
that morning and drove him back to his residence. Although Dr. Haydn sustained no serious injuries, he visited the hospital on Sunday afternoon for treatment for bruises and
lacerations.

The sheriff's office believes the attack is connected in some way with the probe that Dr.
Haydn and Shrug Speaker, another local resident, are conducting into the death three years
ago of Anthony Travers at the forty-fifth reunion of the Humboldt High School class of
1953. It bases this belief on the contents
of a message the assailant tied to Dr.
Haydn's arm. Since their probe has involved the questioning of individuals as far
away from Humboldt as Zanesville and
Richmond, Indiana, the range of possible
suspects for the attack must be regarded
as wide. The sheriff invites persons with
information relevant to their investigation
to contact his office. He is not saying at
this time whether his office will now begin
to investigate the death of Travers.

Shrug read the piece through twice, puzzled by its cast and
contents. Either Connie had been remarkably talkative while Shrug
had shopped or the reporter had had access to additional sources
of information.

The phone rang. Guessing and gambling, Shrug lifted the receiver and with his best British accent intoned, "Dr. Haydn, I presume."

"We've obviously been sharing the same reading matter, my friend," Connie grinned in reply.

Shrug inquired about Connie's health. "Sore but sound," was the reply. He then turned to what he assumed was the subject at hand. "Just how much information did you supply to the police, anyway?"

"Just the facts, ma'am. Nothing more. And *nothing* whatever about towns our investigations have taken us to. It's as if the first paragraph had been drawn from public information available through crime reports and the second had been drawn from some sort of supplementary source. It's very odd." He hesitated. "And yet it's *not* odd." He was excited. "After all, there's at least one person who knows all the extraneous bits in the article, and that's our mysterious friend in the blue Camaro."

"Of course!" Shrug exclaimed, feeling foolish that the thought hadn't come to him right away. "But why should that person talk to some reporter at the *Herald & Examiner*?" Even as he asked the question, he felt the answer.

But Connie beat him in articulating it. "Because the reporter and the driver of the Camaro are one and the same person!"

"Bingo!"

"Still, it seems hard to believe that Barry Imhoven, the paper's editor, would countenance reporting via stalking."

"Oh, I don't know. He's never exactly been our ally. And he may have enough respect for our successes now that he wants to try to figure out what we're up to. After all, news of our latest investigation is scarcely a secret. But then again," he paused, "maybe he has an ambitious, less-than-scrupulous rogue reporter on his hands. Maybe . . ." Shrug stopped because he'd run out of ideas.

"There's only one way to find out," Connie interrupted. "Let's go see him. I'll meet you at his office in ten minutes."

"Can you drive? I mean, are you feeling up to it?"

"Damn straight. We may be about to identify the person who's been tracking us. Let's go for it!"

It took fifteen minutes to gather themselves and reach their destination, but at 4:20 Connie and Shrug strode into the office of Barry Imhoven, longtime editor of *The Humboldt Herald & Examiner*.

"Shrug. Connie. How nice to see you." Imhoven was a large man, a football player in college. His tie was loosened, his cigarette was fresh, his appearance was hassled, and he looked in need of a shave. A large computer sat on his desk. The air conditioner rattled in the window. The rug featured a rich palette of food stains. The office was not large, and it was stuffed with so many books and files that it made Shrug feel faintly confined and reminded Connie of Jimmy Brackett's lair. The setting also struck Connie as coming straight out of a film noir from the 1940s about a courageous local editor waging the fight for justice against some unscrupulous mill operators.

"You're working too hard, Barry," Connie said quickly, "and we've come to make your life just a little bit harder still."

Imhoven frowned as he immediately gave them his full attention, asking them to sit down in the two chairs in the office. "That sounds ominous. What's up? Aside from your getting beaten up, that is." His expression suggested that he hoped that guy-to-guy levity would defuse a potentially awkward scene.

"Your article about the attack on me," Connie began. "It contained some information that couldn't have been picked up from the police blotter. Where did it come from?"

"Are you asking me to reveal my sources?"

"Oh, come off it, Barry. This isn't an issue of confidentiality. Your writer knew some things about us that only someone who has tailed us would know. And wouldn't you know, by the strangest of coincidences, someone *has* been tailing us, in a less-than-inconspicuous blue Camaro. What do you think of *that*? Do you know anything about it?"

227

Shrug had rarely seen Connie so obviously angry, and he remained silent, allowing his friend to set the pace and tone of the conversation.

Imhoven's hesitation confirmed what Connie and Shrug had suspected. "You know we've got you nailed, Barry. Why did you allow someone to slink around like that to spy on us? Is that what's called good journalistic practice?"

The editor took a big breath, punched out his cigarette, and leaned forward in his chair, elbows on his desk. *He's not going to take space from me*, thought Connie, who leaned right back toward the editor.

"The reporter was Peter Truman, a new guy. About a week ago, maybe earlier, I asked him to keep an eye on the Tony Travers investigation that you two were getting involved in. You know, local man dies under suspicious circumstances. Lots of local suspects. Two local sleuths with a good track record asking questions. It seemed like something the *Herald & Examiner* ought to be following. He asked if it would be okay if he followed you when you left town. Something about him looking for an unexpected pattern in the kinds of people you were talking to. He hasn't found anything yet, but I thought that if . . ."

"But why didn't you ask us about it, Barry? That's what both common sense and common courtesy dictate."

"Would you have told Peter anything if he'd asked?"

"What sort of a question is that? Are you suggesting the end justifies the means?" Suddenly Connie felt like he was back in a philosophy classroom. "You're right. We probably wouldn't have told him diddly-squat because, one, we didn't *know* much, and two, we didn't want to tip off our hand in case we were finding out more than we realized. But so what? You're not *The Washington Post* investigating a high finance scandal in competition with the *L.A. Times*. You're a hometown newspaper, with a monopoly on local press overage, and the community expects you to operate like a responsible neighbor. Snooping on people isn't nice."

Connie wasn't sure whether Imhoven would accept his effort to frame the issue as one of community responsibility and good neighborliness; and the editor's long silence suggested that he knew full well he had the choice of going in either of two directions in responding to Connie's berating. In the end, sociability won. "Okay. I'll change Peter's guidelines and ask him not to follow you two about. But how about you promising me that when you have something—assuming the authorities aren't obliging you to drop the investigation—you'll give us a full story?"

Pleased that he had prevailed, Connie assured Imhoven that he had every reason to want to cooperate with the local media and that Shrug and he would talk to Peter Truman when the pieces had fallen into place, or when the whole matter had turned out to be a silly goose chase. Imhoven grimly thanked him for the vote of confidence and for his willingness to forgive his own thoughtlessness.

Hitherto silent, Shrug cleared his throat and asked, as decorously as possible, if Imhoven could assure them that Peter Truman had not been responsible for the attack on Connie.

Imhoven seemed astonished by the question. "Why would he want to do that? What a bizarre idea."

"It's not bizarre," Shrug continued, "especially if Peter Truman should turn out to be more than just a reporter. Maybe he has his own agenda. You say he's new. How did he get this assignment anyway? At *his* suggestion or yours?"

"Well," said Imhoven, his brows bunched, "I think it was at his suggestion, not mine. As I said, he's ambitious. And he heard the scuttlebutt in town. But I *know* he wasn't out at the water tower yesterday morning because he was with me. With the whole *H&E* staff at our monthly Sunday breakfast-slash-assessment meeting." Quiet anger crept into Imhoven's voice. "So you'll have to look elsewhere than to my staff for your assailant."

"Thank you," said Shrug quietly. "I felt I had to ask. And I feared Connie wasn't going to."

The friends left Imhoven to his rueful reflections. "Well," said Connie, "we've finally solved one mystery. Chalk the blue Camaro up to an overzealous reporter."

"And an addlepated editor. What a careless decision!"

Shrug drove home to make final preparations for his trip. He was delighted to discover that the first replies to Dirk Glass's message were arriving via e-mail, and one included a photo of the faux Amanda Everson. *That's just what I need, for now Elinor Burroughs will see I'm not a mad man.* He immediately downloaded and copied it. Then he dialed Marilyn, wanting to tell her why he'd be out of town for the next few days. But it was Guy who answered, explaining that Marilyn was at the office. Shrug left the message with Guy, feeling oddly empty as he always did when an effort to speak with his daughter was unexpectedly thwarted. He recalled how his relationship with his own parents had been, well, awkward—he hadn't yet found the adjective that captured its bonds and difficulties—and how he had consequently labored hard as a single parent to serve his daughter better than he believed he had been served. He hung up the phone and, sensing the need of a pick-me-up, put a disk of Brahms's First Symphony on the CD player and settled down in his favorite chair with an iced tea. *I believe*, he thought as the symphony surged toward its triumphant close, *we're on the verge of breaking this case.*

Connie showered when he returned home, poured himself a beer, and eased his aching body into the couch. He tallied up the post-attack scorecard. His back was looking more bruised than it had the day before, and his lip was very sore, but his neck was feeling better and various wounds were healing. On the whole, he was improving. Still, he was glad that he didn't need to gird himself for a flight to Texas the next morning, concluding that a few days of rest would certainly be of benefit to his body. Besides, there was much he could do while sequestered—get back in touch with Jimmy Brackett and pore through Tony's memorabilia again to see if there was any hint of someone named Alessandra. The thought that gave him the greatest satisfaction, however, was the realization that, unlike during an earlier case, an effort to intimidate them had been dismissed without even a discussion. *In fact, the attack on me was so stupid, so likely to have precisely the opposite of its intended effect, if not from us then from the authorities, that it smacks of desperation. Who in the world of Humboldt could possibly feel so threatened by what we're doing? That's a question we'll need to explore even as we track down Harriet Murray.* He was confident that both tasks could be accomplished.

12

Tuesday, June 19, 2001—Wednesday, June 20, 2001

Shrug pulled himself out of bed before dawn on Tuesday to catch his flight to Houston. He scarfed down coffee and a doughnut, drove to the oddly named Port Columbus airport, and two hours after rising he was in the air, mulling over the list of possible suspects in the criminal attack on Connie. By casting through the known facts he persuaded himself again that it almost surely *had* to be someone local. Nothing else made sense. But who? A man? A strong woman? And for what purpose? In light of the evidence implicating the mysterious but presumably distant Harriet Murray, the whole matter was oddly vexing. The working hypothesis that the attack was not directly related to the task of identifying Harriet Murray, that there were two separate mysteries, seemed the soundest for the moment.

Knowing that the logistical logic of the airline hub system decreed he should spend two hours in Atlanta, Shrug had brought along a pad of legal paper so that he could use his time to begin to block out the article he was planning to write for *Christian Living* on the intellectual deficiencies of a purely materialistic view of life. It was not a defense of theism that he had in mind. That was a more complicated task, and one he feared he might not be up to, but rather an attack on the beguilingly simple idea that matter and energy were the only constituents of the universe. The subject had preoccupied his thought for many years, during which time his sense of the issue, and of the character of an appropriate answer,

232

had undergone many permutations. He had recently come to feel that he now needed to commit his ideas to paper, even though, as he knew from past writing experience, it was likely that he would no sooner do so than he would regret the prematurity of his resolve to give them the aura of fixity. *Thoughts are ever-shifting things,* he mused, as he settled at midmorning into a corner seat in Hartsfield Airport, with pen in hand and as distant from the pervasive television screens as he could manage.

"What are you doing?"

The soft words startled him, and he looked up to see a round-faced boy staring down at him. His expression was blank, he wore blue shorts and a red Atlanta Braves tee-shirt, his brown hair was cut in bangs, and he was nibbling a chocolate bar.

"I'm trying to write an article," Shrug declared, immediately suspecting that his reply was too remote for a ten-year old to grasp.

"What about?"

This question was even worse. Shrug felt a combination of annoyance and panic. *How should a query of this sort be responded to?* He decided to trust his hunch that sailing over a child's head was better than cruising under it, a hunch, he knew, that had received some empirical confirmation in his interactions with his grandson Brandon, and he explained that he wanted to show that there was good reason to believe that the universe of existing things consisted of more than mere matter. He winced as the abstractions that studded that statement came clattering out.

The boy seemed to ponder Shrug's words for moment or two. Then, taking a bite of his candy bar and declaring to no one in particular that grown-ups wouldn't be so confused if they opened their eyes to see all the evidence, he walked off, perhaps to interrogate another isolated passenger-in-transit in the vast airport.

Shrug thought about the parting remark. In a sense, the boy was absolutely correct. How, Shrug wondered, could anyone in his right mind hold to materialism. Such a belief left consciousness, the most immediate experience of humankind, inexplicable.

It left rational discourse and logical demonstration to be understood as products of the interplay of atoms (or whatever physical entities one chose to regard as fundamental). It reduced imagination, the power to create, to the anomaly of matter somehow bodying forth alternative worlds. It left humankind without a basis for ethical actions. And because it ran counter to the usual human experience of having plan and intent precede creation, it left the existence of the physical universe inexplicable. Any theory of the world that was so at variance with the way humans confronted that world would make sense only to a madman, or to an intellectual. Recalling Orwell, Shrug smiled.

What is it, he wondered (not for the first time), *that makes intellectuals, especially the college-teacher type, so inattentive to evidence? That's easy*, he answered (not for the first time), *they look only at* part *of the evidence, at that selective segment that suits their prejudices or their convenience. And that's why* . . . Shrug suddenly checked this self-congratulatory line of thought. *Wait a minute. That's exactly what I've been doing with this Travers investigation. We've had that second tape of the reunion dinner for two weeks now. The tape that shows the head table, and I haven't even studied it. And I've ignored it for the worst possible reason, because I assumed it would be irrelevant. But how can I come to that judgment without viewing it? Especially now that there is evidence for some sort of local angle? How careless. How unprofessional. How . . . how . . . stupid.* Stung by that final and apt term of self-reproach, Shrug vowed to check the head table tape as soon as he returned to Humboldt.

At that moment the first call for his Houston flight sounded through the terminal, and he made his way to the gate.

———— ————— —————

It didn't take much to convince Elinor Burroughs to talk about Harriet Murray. A perusal of Amanda Everson's puzzled letter from New Zealand and an examination of a reunion photo that showed, in the identifying annotation of the photographer, "Amanda Everson" standing with three classmates at the reunion sufficed. Muttering "hell, that's Harriet all right," the petite Burroughs scrambled to the kitchen to get herself a cold beer, offered one to Shrug (he accepted), and asked her visitor how she could help.

They sat in a large and cool family room in a modern suburban home in Connalton. Shrug had arrived about midafternoon in what struck him as midsummer heat. *Texas*, he thought, removing his tie, *sure isn't Ohio*. The flight had been on time, but the car rental agency had found something odd about his Ohio driver's license and detained him for fully half an hour before finally entrusting an Escort to his road skills. As he sat appreciatively sipping his beer, he wondered what it cost to air condition a home this large.

"How do you know it's Harriet?" he asked, after they settled down. "We're pretty sure she had longer hair when she lived here in Texas."

"Oh, she did. She surely did. But the face is unmistakable. The chin, especially, and the nose. Oh, that's Harriet, all right, that's Harriet, a pretty girl in an offbeat sort of way. Do you have a picture of Amanda?"

Shrug pulled out the photo of Everson taken on ANZAC Day in 1998 that she had sent him with her letter. Burroughs placed the two images side to side and began pointing out to Shrug the differences between the two women's eyes, chins, cheeks, and postures. Shrug was impressed by her ability to describe distinctions that to his untrained eye seemed fairly minor. "They were about the same height," Burroughs said, "and it was easy enough for Harriet to adopt Amanda's hairstyle. But they really didn't have the same build. Look at the wider shoulders on Amanda, and their eyes weren't in the same places on their faces." Once the dissimilarities were pointed out to him, Shrug admitted he could see them.

"So," he said, "not that I'm in doubt but . . . you're sure that this woman who called herself Amanda Everson at the reunion three years ago is really Harriet Murray."

"As sure as my momma's name isn't Tabitha."

With that response, any lingering suspicion that the mysterious impersonator might have been some other woman from Tony Travers's multifaceted past disappeared. As far as Shrug was concerned, the search for the impersonator's identity was over.

"Then, in answer to your earlier question, Elinor, you can help by telling me all you can think of about Harriet Murray. For I'd sure like to be able to track her down."

Although Shrug wasn't adopting the accent of Texas, he heard himself slipping into the more casual locutions of the region. As for Burroughs, she needed no more encouragement than that nudge, and after inviting Shrug to call her "Ellie," began unfolding a set of reminiscences about an old Texas friend who for some unknown reason had wound up disguised as another old Texas friend at an Ohio high school reunion.

Murray, she said, had moved away from Connalton several years earlier, not long after Everson had left. Burroughs didn't know where she'd moved to. "I don't know whether I never knew or whether I've forgotten; I just remember her suddenly being gone one day." And she had no forwarding address for Murray. On a more hopeful note she added that perhaps another of Harriet's friends would have that information.

As for Murray's life before her Connalton days, Burroughs was not very helpful. "She didn't talk much about herself, as I remember. Though she *was* divorced. I remember that. She *was* divorced." To Shrug's question about children, Burroughs replied with sheepish ignorance. "But I'll bet another of the girls knows. Would you like me to gather a bunch of them here tomorrow afternoon to talk with you about her?" Because he had planned to propose such a gathering himself, Shrug accepted that invitation on the spot.

As Burroughs continued her recollections of Murray, she shifted from biographical data to subjective impressions. Murray had been a lively woman, she said, possessed of a big and inviting laugh. She had loved clothes. (Shrug sighed inwardly on hearing that familiar remark, as Burroughs amplified it with several illustrative tales.) One of her favorite magazines was *Vogue*, copies of which she often brought to the stitching club meetings. "Oh yes, she was crazy about knitting." And her favorite television personality was Oprah Winfrey. Like most of her friends, Murray had joined the local Baptist Church soon after arriving in Connalton and had been a moderately active participant in the social life of the congregation. She had enjoyed reading, often recommending books and showing a particular fondness for an author named Clarkson. "Yes, that's it I think, Clarkson . . . maybe Catherine Clarkson." When Shrug suggested that the name might be Cookson, Burroughs assented, but with no enthusiasm. Shrug pointedly asked if Murray had dated anyone while in Connalton. "I don't think so," was the muted reply, "or rather, no one special. She once said one marriage was enough for her."

Ultimately the stream of recollections ran dry, and Burroughs was reduced to lamenting that her memory was "so defective." Shrug assured her it wasn't, settled on 2:00 P.M. the following day for the meeting with some of Murray's circle of friends, and left in time to catch a steak dinner at a Tex-Mex restaurant recommended by the desk clerk at the Holiday Inn he was staying at. All in all, he thought as he retired that night, the Texas visit had begun well.

The following afternoon, Wednesday, Shrug returned to Elinor Burrough's home. His hostess introduced him to four women, ranging in age (he guessed) from forty to sixty-five, and all eager to talk about Harriet Murray. Burroughs explained that she had enticed them to attend the conversation "with the handsome man from Ohio" (Shrug squirmed slightly) by sharing the remarkable tale of how one of their old pals had apparently impersonated another of their old pals in order to commit a murder. Although in Burroughs's telling the story was rather more lurid and definitive than Shrug would have preferred, it had certainly accomplished its goal of attracting the guests.

The women were eager to see the photos that Shrug had brought, and so he passed them around. Everyone agreed that the person pretending to be Amanda Everson was Harriet Murray. Shrug then explained that he and a friend were trying to locate Murray. "She is probably in hiding," he added. He said he hoped that information from her Connalton friends might provide clues about her whereabouts. "I don't suppose," he added, "that any of you know where she is living now?"

As he expected, no one did. But Sandra Chang, a dark-haired Caucasian woman presumably married to an Asian, surprised Shrug by saying she had received an e-mail from Harriet about eighteen months earlier. "She just said, 'Hello, hope the gang is still knitting—I'm fine.' That sort of thing." But she said she'd changed her name. And she signed the message 'Helen Magnuson.'"

The other women were surprised to hear this news, and one chided Chang for not having shared the message when it had arrived. After confirming that Harriet Murray/Helen Magnuson hadn't said where she was living, Shrug asked Chang not to send her an e-mail about the current conversation or about the sudden interest in her whereabouts, lest it prompt her to run to a new hiding place.

Chang agreed to honor the request, but noted, a point Shrug was pondering himself, that if Murray/Magnuson was trying to hide, then it had certainly been odd of her to send out an e-mail to a former Connalton friend in the first place.

Shrug could only agree. For someone presumably in hiding, it had been reckless behavior. "Perhaps," he suggested, "now that her mission, whatever it was, is accomplished, she is relaxing a bit and cautiously letting her guard down. She may have concluded that her assuming Amanda's identity is now a safely undetectable secret. But it's no longer undiscovered." Shrug was hoping to pull the discussion back to his agenda. "So what else can you tell me about Harriet Murray?" At the same time he drew out his notebook, looking directly at each woman in turn to secure silent approval for taking notes.

Brenda Quintero, a bleached blonde who had probably undergone cosmetic surgery, said that Murray had been a good friend of Everson's and had seemed sad after Everson moved away. "Harriet was the sort of person who liked to help shy people become more engaged in life and activities. She was always doing things. And Amanda was a bit shy, so the two of them complemented each other."

"Complemented! My foot! Christ, it was a *creepy* relationship." The speaker was Carol Lively, who until this moment had struck Shrug as the least lively of the quartet. "And you girls will remember that I commented on that even back then, how Harriet was peculiarly nosey about Amanda, how she'd prod Amanda into talking about her life before her Texas days. Amanda in grade school. Amanda in high school. Amanda in college. About boyfriends and school clubs. Even back then I felt that there was something twisted about this relationship. It wasn't natural."

"But it wasn't creepy at all, Carol," said Yvonne Didinger reproachfully. "Remember how they both loved clothes and loved talking about clothes and shopping for clothes. 'Shop 'til you drop.' That was their motto. They'd go to Dillards together all the time. And they both had good taste. A touch on the boisterous side for me, of course." Shrug could tell that Didinger was the most conservatively dressed of the five women in the room. "But classy and stylish. Yes, that's what they were, stylish. And there's nothing creepy about wanting to look good."

Shrug suspected that Didinger had missed Lively's point, but as Lively didn't choose to defend her assertion, Shrug let it pass, listening instead to an animated discussion of clothes, stores in Connalton, and the annual charity fashion show. Harriet Murray was never entirely absent from their minds, however, and so Shrug gleaned from the rambling conversation that Murray often changed her hairstyles, seemed to be wealthy though no one knew exactly where the wealth came from. "Maybe a nice alimony settlement," Quintero speculated. "And liked bright colors, especially yellow."

He finally interceded, in an effort to pull the colloquy back on subject. "Aside from her interest in clothes and knitting, do you know of other interests she had?"

"Well," said Quintero with a smile, "there was always cooking."

This remark elicited chuckles all around, and Burroughs explained that Murray had acquired the unhappy reputation for being a poor cook. "She enjoyed cooking and she seemed to think she was good at it. Goodness knows, she certainly invited friends in for dinner often enough. But the main courses were either overdone or underdone, overseasoned or bland. And her sense of presentation was horrible. It was just amazing, that someone with such a fine eye for attire had no sense of how to make entertaining friends with a meal a successful occasion." The other women nodded in agreement

"Did she have pictures around the house?" Shrug inquired.

"Not many," Quintero answered. "None of her former husband, of course, a louse as far as I could tell, though she rarely spoke of him. There were a few black-and-white photos of a young man whom I took to be an adult son, but I don't remember her saying much about him either, and I gathered they weren't often in touch with each other. I don't recall any pictures to suggest grandchildren. Do you, girls?" All agreed that Murray's house had revealed surprisingly little about her family.

Discussion then led to other interests and foibles. Although a fitness buff and frequent dieter, Murray had a famous fondness for key lime pie. She played a good game of bridge, though she occasionally bid too exuberantly. She liked the theater, often driving into Houston for productions; and she had even joined the Connalton Players for one year, serving (as best as anyone could remember) on the publicity committee. She was a Republican in a town that was still generally Democratic by registration, even if many of those Democrats had voted for George Bush both for governor and for president. She enjoyed travel, both in the United

States and abroad, and she spent some of each winter somewhere in the North to go skiing. Didinger thought she had in fact been raised in the North, maybe Montana or Maine or Michigan or Minnesota, but wasn't sure.

"And do you remember," asked Chang, "her funny little accent? It was barely noticeable, but it was there. And it told me she had been raised speaking a language other than English."

"Spanish?" Shrug suggested.

"Oh no," Quintero laughed, "not Spanish. Her accent wasn't Spanish. I always thought it might be Welsh or Czech."

That combination seemed so odd to Shrug that he asked what Quintero based her judgment on.

"Not very much, I'm afraid. I've seen some TV shows set in Wales and Czechoslovakia, and her accent sounded to me just a tad like the voices I heard on the shows."

"Well," said Lively, again popping out of her silence, "I know for a fact she speaks German, for she gave me some lessons in basic, saving-your-ass German before Fred and I went to Bavaria. *Es tut mir Leid. Ich beheisse* Carol. *Wo ist die Klosett.* That sort of thing, like where is the toilet. She seemed quite fluent in it—at least she could speak it fast. And she had lots of German books in her house."

"So maybe," Shrug asked Quintero, "what you thought was a Welsh or Czech accent might have been German? What do you think?"

"No German accent I've ever heard," she replied. "At least not like Henry Kissinger or Colonel Klink."

Shrug was puzzled by the inability of his interviewees to identify Murray's accent, but he decided not to pursue the matter for the moment and asked instead if other memories were coming back to the women. They were, and in a flood. In a sprawling melee of recollections, the women told tales of Harriet's skill at needlework, of her fondness for movies, and of her remarkable vigor. They told how she enjoyed dancing, liked fast cars, and boasted an almost indecipherable brand of handwriting. They even recalled that she was a terrible singer, suffered from acne, and limped slightly. Once their tongues had been liberated by Shrug's encouragement and Burroughs's libations, the guests romped through a mélange of stories about Harriet Murray, some flattering and some rather less so. Yet as he listened attentively, Shrug heard an undertone of fondness for a woman who, whatever she may have done in Humboldt, had treated her Connalton friends with cheerful respect and had reciprocated their offers of friendship. After several hours Yvonne Didinger turned to her friends and said, "You know, girls, this has been fun. And the more I hear us chatter, the harder it is for me to believe Harriet killed someone. I think," she turned to Shrug, "I think you must be wrong."

The lateness of the afternoon and the growing repetitiveness of the gossip had already led Shrug to decide that the meeting had passed well beyond the point of diminishing returns, and so he seized Didinger's remark as an opportunity to say that, if he were wrong, it wouldn't be the first time, and to thank the women for their valuable help. Then he made his departure, extending private thanks to Burroughs for organizing and hosting the impromptu afternoon gathering. "I'll let you know how it all turns out," he said as he exited the house into the thick heat of a June day in Houston.

On his way back to his hotel, he realized, to his genuine surprise, that his mind had returned to the conversation in the Atlanta airport. "Out of the mouth of babes," he mumbled, the Bible being, as it frequently was for Shrug, the locus of ratifying quotations. *But is examining the unviewed video going to be a revelation or a waste of effort? Only time will tell.* And he didn't need scripture for that tag.

A sore and bruised Connie spent much of Tuesday digging again through the boxes of Tony memorabilia that he had pushed to the corner of his living room. Convinced that Sandy, Less, and "the

Great" were one and the same person, someone named Alessandra, he searched for clues among the letters and papers Tony had collected. But, as he suspected, his memory had not failed him on this point: an Alessandra was not to be found in their midst.

Off and on throughout the day he tried calling Bryan Travers, to see if his Alessandra-theory rang any bells with Tony's son. But after the third failed effort, Connie decided that Bryan was probably out of town.

After lunch he tried to phone Jimmy Brackett, hoping that that inveterate keeper of records might have the name of Alessandra somewhere in his files or that he might have a tip on how Connie could find her. But all Connie got for his efforts was a taped message saying that "Major Brackett" would be out of town for several days; and since it contained no information about how the major was to be reached, Connie had no choice but to exercise patience. June, he reminded himself, was a fine time for trips and vacations.

Toward evening, Connie felt discouraged. A day's worth of work had produced no detectable results. There was even a good chance, he told himself over a beer, that Alessandra was dead. After all, if she commanded Tony, she must have been older than he. If she was, say, twenty-five in 1945, that would mean she'd been born in 1920 and would now be eighty-one. And even if she were still alive, her mind might be slipping. (Like all elderly academics, Connie had an inordinate fear of age-associated mental decline, an apprehension intensified for him by his weekly visits with his mother.) *No, Connie*, he told himself, *you're not going to be successful in this search, even if your hunch was brilliant and correct.*

To pull his mind away from this lugubrious train of thought, Connie picked up the copy of Kant's *On Perpetual Peace* that lay on the table by his reading chair. Kant's heavy prose (which Connie was studying in the original German) never made for casual reading, but Connie wasn't looking for light fare. Rather, he had decided that if he couldn't find any tracks leading to the putative

Alessandra, he would turn to another project of his: the effort to argue that anyone who wanted to understand the *Critique of Practical Reason* needed to be familiar with the methodological assumptions underlying Kant's prescription for a world without war.

Connie knew he wasn't the first person to have suggested that the *Perpetual Peace* was a key to understanding Kant's tome on ethical reasoning. As a relatively accessible work, the essay was one of the philosopher's most widely read pieces. But Connie liked to link an author's theoretical works with his more political writings—his view that Hume's histories provided hints about his epistemology was his only major contribution to Hume scholarship—and he had cautiously come to the view that his fragmentary insights about Kant had merit and novelty, that no one had cast the relationship in quite the way he saw it, and that he might therefore have something constructive to contribute to the community of Kant scholars. Connie promptly immersed himself in Kant's hopeful work and soon forgot, as he scribbled new interlineations into the text, that the televised baseball game he planned to watch that evening began at 8:00 P.M. When he came up for air at 8:45, although annoyed with himself for forgetting the time, he found himself pleased to reflect that the charms of philosophy still could still beguile him. But he realized too that his brain needed relief, and so he set Kant aside and turned to a Cubs-Braves game.

During the commercial break after the sixth inning, as Connie walked to the kitchen to get an aspirin, he began reflecting on the fourth puzzling nickname: Chucklehead Clancy. *Who would allow himself to be known by such a humiliating sobriquet? Still, whoever he is, there's a lot of money waiting for him, if he can be found!* The wispy reflection on Clancy led Connie's mind to Tony Travers's will. And suddenly he stopped. Literally, in midstep, stopped. Almost falling over. Why, he suddenly asked himself, did Tony leave so much money to the Alliston Home for War Veterans? About fifty years earlier he had spent a brief time there for recuperation from a military injury. But obviously the place was still very important to him. The will testified to *that*. Could it be that its importance rested in the fact that someone dear to him lived or had at one time lived there?

Stunned by this thought, Connie pulled out his world atlas to find out where Alliston was. He was imagining a hamlet sequestered in southeastern England, but no, it turned out to be a village located about six miles from Inverness in Scotland. *Cold in the winter, but probably very pleasant in June. Could it possibly be worth a trip?* He smiled at the way his thoughts ran ahead of any evidence.

Knowing that the time was well past midnight in the United Kingdom, he returned to his baseball game. But his curiosity about the home for veterans kept tugging his mind away from the action on the screen, even as the Cubs mounted a late rally. Annoyed with his incapacity to command his turbulent brain, he turned the television off and headed for bed, carefully setting his alarm clock for 5:30 A.M. so that he could begin his efforts to phone the Alliston Home for War Veterans before too much British time had been wasted.

What Connie had forgotten was that he did not have the phone number for the veterans' home. And his efforts to discover it at 5:30 on Wednesday morning were thwarted by the wall of confidentiality in the British telephone system that protects private numbers. And so he had to wait until 8:30 A.M., when he called Axel Berlin to learn how the attorney who had drafted Tony Travers's will had contacted the Alliston Home for War Veterans after Tony's death.

"It was tricky, Mr. Haydn, I'll tell you that. It was tricky. It's a private place and doesn't have a listed number. Finally I had to write for it. Couldn't get it any other way. But I have it, I do, here in my records." At that point Berlin laid his phone down with a hard bang, presumably to pull up a record on his computer. And when he came back on the line, he gave Connie both the address and the phone number of the veterans' home. "By the way," he asked, after passing on the requested information, "have you had any luck figuring out who Chucklehead Clancy is? His money is waiting for him, and since it's accruing interest in the process, it comes to pretty close to $800,000 now."

Connie replied that, though he thought they were making progress on some fronts, the identity of Chucklehead Clancy had remained stubbornly inaccessible. "If we learn anything about him, we'll let you know. I promise. And thank you for your assistance." Connie tried to sound reassuring, for as he hung up the phone, he thought that one couldn't help but like Berlin, a friendly attorney who was obviously eager to be helpful.

Connie immediately dialed the Alliston Home for War Veterans, and after a short exchange with a woman whose heavy Scottish accent didn't disguise her surprise that a stranger should know their number, he was passed on to someone identified as "Major Constable." Connie had decided that the best way to begin was to contextualize his request with a reminder of the bequest that Tony had left the home; and his strategy paid off. Constable recalled in his clipped voice that "it was a godsend for us," and lavished praise on the expatriate who had beneficed his establishment. Connie followed these remarks with an adumbration of the puzzles surrounding Tony Travers's death, including a reference to the message of alarm; but he deliberately did not mention the name Alessandra. Not surprisingly, Constable was unaware of any of these matters and expressed his indignation that Travers might have been murdered. Pressing ahead, Connie explained what Shrug Speaker and he were trying to do. And then, reaching what he hoped was the climax of his presentation, he moved to his request. "I'm phoning to ask if you would be willing to send me a list of the persons who have been resident at the Alliston Home for War Veterans over the past ten years. I think one of them might have information that would help us identify the person who set out to harm Tony."

"You don't want to tell me this person's name, do you?" The tone was level and soft.

"No, I don't. I may be wrong in my reasoning. I don't want to cause distress to anyone."

General Constable hesitated a moment before replying. "You don't know about Alliston, do you?"

Connie acknowledged his total ignorance.

"We are not," the major proceeded, "a government-run organization. We are *private.*" He emphasized that word. "And our residents come here because they want seclusion. Some are alone and want to stay that way. Some are escaping unpleasant connections, if you know what I mean. Many have physical ailments and need the nursing care we provide. Some are scarred in mind, and need the protection of relative isolation. Some, believe it or not, hate their military past and want to be in a place where their wish not to be asked about it will be honored." He paused. "My point, Mr. Haydn, is that you are making an extraordinary request. We do not lightly issue the names of individual residents, much less a roster of our enrollment."

Connie's heart sank.

"But in your case I will make an exception." Connie could not believe what he was hearing. "Lieutenant Travers was a great friend of Alliston. His gift saved us from going under. If he was murdered, then of course the murderer must be found. And if you believe a list of our residents will be helpful to your enterprise, then of course you must have the list."

Connie thanked the major, but his bewilderment at Constable's decision to accede to his request was undisguisable.

"Don't be surprised, sir. I told you about Alliston because I wanted you to understand the seriousness of your request. I'm a military man, prepared, if necessary, to make prompt decisions. That's what I'm doing. You spoke with candor and purpose, and you spoke about a person whose life we honor. I'm not sure I fully understand your reasons for wanting to keep the name you're interested in a secret, but that desire suggests that you understand discretion. And discretion is always important. You sound like an

247

honest man. I hope I am not misjudging you. If you will give me a fax number, I will get the list transmitted to you within two hours. All I ask in return is that you treat the list as private and, if you discover the identity of Lieutenant Travers's murderer, you let us know. Does that seem fair?"

Connie was overjoyed, but fearing that an effusive display of his elation would cast doubts on his discretion, he couched his response moderately: "That's very satisfactory. Thank you." He read out the Philosophy Department's fax number, since he had none at home, and said he would be back in touch if the information on the list warranted a second call. The call ended with a crisp, "Good luck and God be with you, sir."

Two hours later Connie entered the office of the Philosophy Department. The secretary was nowhere to be seen, and a gum-chewing student intern whom he didn't recognize was on duty. When he said he had come by to pick up a fax from Britain that he was expecting, she pointed him to the fax bin without even speaking to him. *I guess the department is taking any majors it can find in these deeply unphilosophical times.* He picked through the pile of recently received faxes, finding the transmission from Alliston about three entries deep. It was four pages long. He knew that he should wait until he got home to read through it, but his driving curiosity won out. *No need for discretion here*, he thought. And so he sat down on a straight-back chair in the hallway just outside the office and began casting his eyes down the list of residents at the Alliston Home for War Veterans.

And there it was, toward the bottom of the second page. Alessandra Nicholson! Born in 1916, served in 'covert forces' in Germany in 1944 and 1945, began residence at Alliston in 1992. Not much information (at least compared to other entries: not even a rank) but more than sufficient. *Eighty-five years old and still alive!* Connie let out a whoop of joy, boisterous enough to penetrate even the nonchalance of the intern just around the corner and provoke an "is everything okay?" He was almost embarrassed by the swell of pride and jubilation he felt. His hunch had been right. Grover Cleveland Alexander, the old souse, had provided the key. And there she was: Less, Sandy, and (surely, surely, surely) the Great, all wrapped up into one. *Now we'll find out who threatened Tony Travers. Now we'll find out who Harriet Murray really is. Now, yes now, we'll get to the bottom of this.* On that exultant note he headed out into the bright morning of a glorious summer day, almost dancing (despite his bruises), and planning his next move.

13

Thursday, June 21, 2001—Saturday, June 23, 2001

Though the heat of Ohio at the summer solstice could not compete with the heat of Texas of the previous day, Shrug still found the enveloping warmth oppressive when he stepped outdoors at Port Columbus Airport just past noon on Thursday. His mood was not helped when he discovered that his Jetta, parked in the Blue Lot, would not start. When, half an hour later, the mechanic from AAA informed him that the vehicle was in need of a new transmission, he muttered a few words not usually heard from his mouth. Under these circumstances he was left with no short-term recourse but to call Connie and ask for a lift to Humboldt. This was a hard decision, sure to be inconvenient for Connie, for Shrug had talked with him by phone the previous evening and learned that his friend had pulled his weekly visit with his mother forward by a day, to this very afternoon. But the reason for the change in schedule—Connie's startling decision to fly out in the evening to Britain for a conversation with the mysterious Less—obliged the two to have a preflight exchange of information. And what better place for a good conversation than an automobile, especially when there was no alternative!

"You first," Shrug said somewhat over an hour later, even as he was climbing into Connie's Buick. But Connie refused to explain his plans until Shrug had told him about the fate of his Jetta, a sad tale whose effective burden was that the expense of a repair exceeded the value of the car, leaving Shrug with the task of buying a new vehicle and the necessity of making do until the purchase had been completed. Shrug discovered that telling of his woes was grand therapy and even concluded with the oft-heard moral about man proposing and God disposing.

With the parable of the stranded motorist out of the way, Connie turned to business, explaining that once he saw the name of Alessandra Nicholson on the roster of residents at Alliston, he knew he needed to talk with her, in person, right away. Because Bryan Travers was out of town, he could not be consulted on the matter. Still, since Bryan had promised to reimburse all transportation costs, even in the knowledge that such trips might involve overseas destinations far more distant than the United Kingdom, Connie had not hesitated to make appropriate plans. He was, he explained, scheduled to meet Nicholson on Saturday, and he hoped to return to Ohio on Sunday. A quick trip that promised to answer many questions. Shrug lavished appropriate praise on the intricate process of stitching hunches together that had led Connie to amalgamate the three persons of Less, Sandy, and "the Great" into one triune goddess and then to locate her. "Only a devout Christian," Connie noted, "could get away with a metaphor that outrageous."

The friends were well beyond the outer belt when Shrug's turn to reveal his successes came. Although he had secured lots of information that might help them track down Harriet Murray, and he passed much of it on, he said that the datum which loomed largest for him, and perhaps for Connie as he flew off to talk with Nicholson, was that Harriet Murray was now using the name of Helen Magnuson, a name that bore the same initials. "It's just possible that H.M. is of significance to her, especially if she had had another identity before Harriet Murray, and that may help us catch up with our mysterious impersonator." Connie agreed that more than coincidence might well be at play.

As suburbia morphed into a hazy farmland under the mounting heat of the afternoon sun, the friends turned from sharing information to analyzing their current situation. Thinking back on an earlier investigation, Shrug remarked that he was "certainly draw-ing the shorter straw when it comes to travel. "You get New York and now the U.K., while I get Arkansas and Texas." Connie pri-vately agreed but contented himself with noting that between them they were beginning to run up "a pretty big travel tab for Bryan. Our last-minute tickets do not come cheap. But at least, we both enjoy flying."

"I'll offer an amendment to that statement," Shrug replied. "Fly-ing itself is becoming less and less enjoyable. I'm not sure we enjoy it all that much any more. But we both enjoy travel. Flying is just a part, and now often the least pleasurable part, of travel."

Connie accepted the unremarkable amendment, and the two friends fell silent. For a while they simply savored the rural land-scape that floated past, with its annual June explosion of orange swathes of daylilies.

But as they approached Humboldt, Shrug resumed the conver-sation. "As I see it," he said thoughtfully, "we are currently work-ing on this investigation from two different ends. You're trying to move *downstream*, from the mysterious warning down to the at-tack, and finally down to the attacker. If you've correctly identi-fied the person who gave the warning, and I think you have, then we may make real progress in sorting this matter out, for we may find out what the threat was, why it was given, and who did the threatening. Meanwhile, I'm tackling the investigation from the other end, moving *upsteam* as it were; from your classmate who *wasn't* at the event, to the person who impersonated her, to, we hope, that person's new identity and hiding place. We're both hoping that as we chew away at our respective ends of the spaghetti string, and how's *that* for switching metaphors, that as we chomp toward the common center, we'll discover that the person who did the threatening and the person who is now hiding are one and the same."

"Same what? Piece of pasta? And why do we wind up kissing each other if we're right? That may be the most labored figure of speech I've ever heard. It tops even a triune goddess." Connie was chuckling. "But I take your point. And it's hard to know whether we're close to the end of the investigation or not. We seem to be assuming"—Shrug noticed Connie's tongue darting about outside his lips, a sure sign of serious and enthusiastic thought—"that the answer will be found in Tony's wartime experience. If I didn't think that to be likely, I wouldn't be flying off to Scotland. But in fact, I do see a problem with that assumption. What's the motive? After all, fifty years have gone by. What kind of grudge gets nursed that long? It's not as if Tony has been closeted away from possible retribution at the hand of an angry *Hitlerjugend* for the past half-century. So, while I'm flying off to Scotland because I think we've got a big opportunity here, I'm still not completely persuaded that we're on the right track. At the very least, there are still lots of holes yet to be filled."

When Connie pulled into Shrug's driveway, his friend thanked him for the lift and said that he'd try to use his weekend to work on some of those holes. "While you're gallivanting around Scotland, I'm going to revisit the possibility of exonerating, or perhaps implicating, the few members of the class of '53 who had still not been cleared. It would be nice to assure myself that I didn't go to high school with a future murderer."

"Don't forget the other loose end: that attack on me! I still recall it vividly, and so do my sore back and legs."

"Oh, don't worry. I won't. In fact, I feel like I'm operating under the terms of a nineteenth-century defense treaty. An attack on you is an attack on me. And I'm disinclined to think that diplomacy is the answer."

"You certainly are in a trope-tossing temper today. Just make sure, then, you're not in jail when I get back. There may be more important things for you to do than taking dubious satisfaction from punching out a bad guy."

"Yup. And one important thing for me to do right away is to phone Abe Steinberg and update him with the news that Harriet Murray might now be calling herself Helen Magnuson."

Which, he did.

As his 747 soared high above the Atlantic on its red-eye flight to
Scotland, Connie gave his attention to reading an Ian Rankin mystery, catching snatches of sleep, and soundlessly watching a silly
action movie that involved two impossibly attractive people trying
to accomplish some obscure task that involved lots of running while
holding hands, all to the accompaniment of spectacular explosions.
The quiet of the darkened passenger cabin was oddly eerie. Connie thought that he ought to be thinking about the investigation
and about his upcoming interview with Alessandra Nicholson, but
he didn't want to make the effort.

When the passengers deplaned at Prestwick Airport on Friday
morning, Connie's first impression was astonishment at the coolness in his lungs. The close heat of the American Midwest was
only a memory as he sucked in what seemed like the freshest air he
had ever inhaled. His passage through customs was uncomplicated.
I should always fly into the UK at Prestwick, he advised himself,
recalling Heathrow nightmares. Within two hours he had rented a
Ford and begun his drive north past Glasgow and on to Alliston.
Like most Americans, Connie enjoyed the novelty and challenge
of driving on the left-hand side of the road. The countryside became more rugged as he headed north. He began to see why the
region he was approaching was called the Highlands, and he did
not stop for a meal until he reached Fort William. He drove into
Alliston late in the afternoon and quickly found a room at a bed-
and-breakfast called The Stag's Arms. He put a short call through
to the veterans' home to confirm his meeting with Nicholson the
following morning at 9:00, and then, after a sandwich and a beer,
he set out on a walking tour of the small town in the bracing and
unearthly brightness that lingered until well past 10:00 P.M. at this
northern latitude on the second day of summer. When he got into
his bed at 11:15, he promptly fell asleep. He had, he dimly mused
as he drifted off, rarely spent such a mindlessly pleasant day.

Shortly before 9:00 the next morning, Connie drove his Ford along a tree-lined gravel drive across a sweeping expanse of lawn to reach the small, stony parking area in front of the Alliston Home for War Veterans. It was a four-story brick edifice, with asymmetrical wings that favored the right side of the building. He mounted the broad steps to the great wooden entrance door. A plaque by the door informed visitors that the structure had been built as a residence in 1875 by Sir Matthew Redding and had been converted to its current use in 1946 after the Redding family had sold it to a private organization that served the medical and retirement needs of select former members of Her Majesty's armed forces. Connie rang a bell that sounded surprisingly modern, and waited until, about twenty seconds later, an informally dressed young man greeted and admitted him. The entrance hallway was spacious, and Connie began to have the feeling either that many British movies he'd seen had been filmed here or that filmmakers had got the generic British country home down to a tee.

Major Constable came toward him from a room at the rear of the entrance hallway, and in the same crisp intonation that had snapped across the transatlantic line, only now sounding brusquer, said immediately that Colonel Nicholson was looking forward to talking with him. He said no more, and Connie, as he followed the major up a flight of stairs, was left to realize that for the first time he had heard a rank ascribed to Less. They walked down a quiet corridor to a room near its end. The nameplate by the door said simply "Nicholson." Constable knocked, and a male voice, clearly Jamaican, invited the visitors to come in. The speaker, a young, uniformed, and very black man, nodded at them both as they entered. He promptly left, saying he'd be outside. Constable led Connie across the room to the bed where a frail elderly woman lay propped up on pillows. "Sandy," he said, "this is Connie Haydn. He has come from America to talk with you about Tony Travers." That having been said, Constable turned around abruptly and followed the Jamaican orderly out of the room.

255

"Please pull up that chair," Nicholson said, pointing toward a corner of the room, "and come sit by my bed." Her raspy voice was louder than her appearance had led Connie to expect, and her British accent struck his American ears as impeccable. When he had complied, she stared at him hard, adjusting her glasses as she did so, as if trying to learn deeper truths from his features. "You're a *young* man," she finally said. "Did you know Tony?"

It had been many years since someone had called Connie "young." But he knew that from Nicholson's perspective he might easily have seemed, well, perhaps not young, but conceivably still in his prime. "No, I didn't know Tony," he replied. "But my friend, the man I'm cooperating with, whose name is Shrug Speaker, he knew Tony at Humboldt High School in the 1950s. They were classmates."

"I saw the school, once," Nicholson said, to Connie's surprise. "I used to visit him in the States occasionally, and on one occasion he gave me a tour of Ohio and his American high school. He remembered it fondly, though he had thought the girls rather immature."

"Well," said Connie, not wanting to miss a beat, "they were quite a bit younger than he. And they probably thought him an heroic figure, what with his service in the war."

"Oh, he *was* heroic, a god of a man." Nicholson's tone was wistful, and she turned her eyes to the window with its vista out on the lawn and the woods and the distant Grampians. Connie recalled that Freddy Kruger, Bryan Travers, and Teresa Espinosa had all used similarly extravagant language in describing Tony. *He must*, Connie thought, *have had an extraordinarily mesmerizing presence.*

"Growing up," Nicholson continued, "I always wanted to be a man. Men got to race the cars. To travel abroad. To go to war. To fight. I ached to do those things. It all seemed so exciting and glamorous. But as a female I was effectively disqualified. At least, that's what my father taught my sisters and me. But I overcame that handicap to become a leader in war." She smiled gently, perhaps savoring an unexpected memory. "And in one way at least I learned to be glad to be a woman. Tony made being a woman worthwhile." Her smile broadened, and while Connie suspected he knew her meaning, she added a definitively clarifying coda: "he was wonderful in bed."

Ill at ease when talk turned to sex, Connie wanted to change the subject. But the opportunity to confirm his nickname hypothesis was too good to pass up. "He called you 'the Great,' didn't he?"

Nicholson looked startled. "Yes, I was his Alessandra the Great. How did you make *that* out?"

"You probably haven't heard of Grover Cleveland Alexander. He's a famous American baseball player. Would you believe that it was when I was thinking of him that the various nicknames that were perplexing us all fell together. For he also called you Less, didn't he? Other people called you Sandy, but he called you Less."

"You're a remarkably clever and knowledgeable young man. How did you know that?"

"In part, luck. In part, deduction. But what got us launched on this investigation was a letter you sent him, signed 'Less' of course, in which you urged him to contact the police because he'd been threatened."

"Oh." Nicholson seemed annoyed. "When Major Constable said you were coming to talk about Tony Travers, I didn't realize that you had been privy to our personal correspondence."

"I've seen only one letter, your message of advice after he'd been threatened. If there were other letters, they aren't to be found in the files of papers and correspondence that Tony's son passed on to me. No one has read them." While allowing that assurance to sink in, Connie shifted his chair so that he could face Nicholson more directly. "I don't know what the major has told you about my visit to Alliston. It sounds like less than I'd expected, and so maybe I should fill you in before pushing ahead." When Nicholson rolled her hands as an invitation for him to continue, Connie began unfolding the tale of the investigation. Nicolson listened with an impassive face but clenched fists. "As a result of some recent evidence we've dug up," he concluded, "we think the odds very much favor Tony's having been murdered by a woman who disguised herself as a former high school classmate of Tony's. And while we don't have a motive yet, we tend to suspect that you might be able to help us out. After all, because you know *that* he was threatened, you probably also know *why* he was threatened."

Nicholson was quiet for a while. Connie studied the outline that her emaciated form gave to her bedclothes and suspected from the rumpled contour of the blanket that Nicholson's left leg had been amputated below the knee. He examined her face, wrinkled but ruddy, and her long, white hair. Tears suddenly appeared in her eyes, which she quickly wiped away with the sweep of the back of her right hand. Then, in an unnervingly deliberate voice, she declared that she was going to tell Connie some "wartime fairy tales. When I have completed my account, I want you to tell me if they seem relevant to your investigation."

"Fair enough," he replied.

With a grunt, Nicholson hoisted herself higher in her bed. Her arms, though dulled with crepey skin at the elbows, featured visible musculature. Connie offered to adjust her pillows, but she waved him away. "You need to remember that we were young and fearless and our enemies were Nazi scum."

With that beginning, Nicholson set out on a story of espionage, bravery, and betrayal. It was told in a firm voice, though long pauses sometimes punctuated the narrative. The small intelligence-gathering unit she commanded, which included Tony Travers, was dropped into a rural area in Lorraine late in 1944 to link up with a French resistance cell. Upon arrival, the five members of the unit were dispersed, each living in secret with a French family that had been vetted by the resistance. Their orders were simple: to lie low and to learn what they could about German plans in the region. And so, as the desperate German winter offensive against Allied forces in the Ardennes—"the Battle of the Bulge" in textbook lingo—raged to the northwest, the British unit remained discreetly invisible. Because they did not go out in the daytime, the families with whom they lived were their chief sources of information; each unit member met regularly with Nicholson, always at night, to pass on whatever tidbits of gossip about German activities he had learned from his hosts.

"Did Tony speak German and French?" Connie interrupted.

"Not well enough to pass himself off as a Frog or a Gerry. But that wasn't the point. He needed to understand what people were saying. And that he did." Nicholson's tone suggested that she had no more love for the French than for the Germans.

"You were called the Mephisto Squad, weren't you?" Connie threw that remark in chiefly to impress Nicholson with the background work Shrug and he had done, but she didn't respond to the query at all, moving instead to the resumption of her narrative.

In January of 1945 she was advised that the husband and wife with whom Tony was staying—Peter and Angela Moser—were in fact double agents, passing information about Allied intelligence activities on to the Germans. This was shocking news. It meant the whole operation had been compromised. It meant that the French resistance cell was unreliable. It meant that Tony was in danger. And it meant that Nicholson needed to take some quick actions.

"Were you living nearby?" Connie was trying to clarify his mental picture of the geographical distribution of the intelligence unit.

"About four miles away. No one in the unit was more than four or five miles away from me."

Reluctantly but promptly, Nicholson decided to withdraw the unit. The intelligence they were gathering wasn't very exciting, and since their existence was known to the Germans, the information could not be considered reliable. Besides, it was only a matter of time until the German authorities would stop toying with them and round them up instead.

Before leaving, however, Nicholson determined that the Mosers should be made to pay for their betrayal, both as an act of simple justice and as a notice to the Germans that the Brits had not been taken in. "I meant it as a message to the Frogs too: they needed to get their house of resistance in order." And so, just hours before the effecting of a prearranged extrication scheme and on orders from Nicholson, Tony Travers strangled Peter and Angela Moser to death. "We thought, of course, that *that* was the end of the matter. The people who betrayed us got what they deserved." The sense of satisfaction in her tone was unmistakable.

Since the narrative was obviously not at its end, Connie said nothing. Nicholson reached over to the table by her bed, opened a box of cigars, and lit one up for herself, not offering one to Connie. She is, he thought, very much in her own world of the past now.

"But that *wasn't* the end of it. Because, for starters, we'd been wrong. The Mosers hadn't betrayed us after all. That nugget of intelligence had been wrong, and I'd directed Tony to kill two friends. I didn't tell Tony the truth right away. But later on, well, later on, I did. He took it hard. No surprise there. He took it hard." She stared at an oboe that hung, incongruously, from a leather strap on the wall of her room.

"The Mosers had a son named Gaston," she abruptly said, resuming her tale. Gaston had been twelve at the time of the killings and witnessed them. Tony Travers considered strangling him, too. Connie winced at the thought. But he decided to leave the child unharmed, since he presumably was too young to be a player in the global struggle engulfing his parents. Gaston went on to become a university professor of history in France, but he died in 1968, a casualty of the semi-revolution of that year.

"They also had a daughter, much younger, who was named . . ."

"Wait. Let me guess at something," interrupted Connie. "Her name begins with H."

"Yes. It was Hanna. How did you know?" But before Connie could begin to explain, Nicholson continued. "Oh. I see. You and your friend have made some interesting discoveries in the States. You are already seeing patterns. That's good. That's *very* good. You must tell me about them."

"Not until you've told me about Hanna. But the initials are powerful evidence that we're talking about the same person."

"Actually," Nicholson continued, "I don't know much about her at all." She had been four when Tony lived with the Mosers. After the British intelligence unit left, its members saw no reason to keep track of the brat. She was a forgotten cipher until about 1995, "fifty goddamn years after the war!" Nicholson muttered. In that year she sent Travers a letter to say that she knew he had killed her parents and that she would track him down to avenge those deaths. "Tony wrote me about it right away, and at first I urged him to laugh it off. I said something stupid about ninety percent of threats being baseless. I invented that figure, of course." But the threats kept coming, not in torrents perhaps, but steadily, "maybe one every month or so. She was trying to unnerve him." So in the end, after five or six had come, Nicholson had urged Travers to notify the police. *That*, she surmised, was the note he had saved.

"I take it," Connie asked, "she didn't give any contact information?"

Nicholson laughed. "Maybe you *won't* go far in intelligence, after all." Connie felt properly abashed.

Nicholson asked Connie to get her a beer from the refrigerator in the corner of her room. He surmised she was thinking over what been said thus far and took his time opening the bottle, pouring the beer into a glass that she pointed to, and getting a beer for himself. When he delivered the drink to her bedside, she asked again how he had known that Moser's name would begin with H, and Connie explained how the friends had concluded that a woman named Harriet Murray aka Helen Magnuson, had passed herself off as an authentic classmate at the reunion. Nicholson then asked him to relate in detail what he and Shrug knew about the evening of Tony's death. He told her of the video tapes, the window of opportunity, and the reasoning that had ultimately led them to exclude all but four of the classmates. She had questions. Could more than one person have been involved? How secure was the school building? Was Tony taking precautions against an attack? And she wanted to know about Tony's health in his final days, a subject Connie pleaded ignorance about. In the end, and especially in light of what Shrug had discovered in Texas, she was inclined to believe that Hanna Moser had indeed somehow contrived to carry out her threat. "The fucking bitch got to him" was her mordant summary. "Somehow she got to him."

"I think we're going to track her down." Connie was trying to sound reassuring, even though he could not suppress a private sense that Hanna Moser's act of retribution did not merit unalloyed condemnation.

"If she's still in America, you might. You guys sound pretty good. But if she's fled the States—returned to *das Vaterland* or *la patrie*, for example—then you'll have trouble."

"You clearly knew Tony very well."

Nicholson smiled at the remark.

"And no," Connie added, "I'm not being coy, I'm probing for some insights here. You knew him well, it sounds like you knew how he might react to threats. Do *you* think he would have taken precautions, and if so, what?"

"Tony's problem," she began, almost analytically, "was that he liked women and trusted them too carelessly. I'm surprised he didn't leave half of Shrug Speaker's high school class pregnant." It was Connie's turn to smile. "What I'm getting at is that, if anyone might have gotten to him, penetrated his well-honed defense skills, it would have been a woman. And of course, with his health compromised, he must have been less agile, less quick, less ready to react than he was in the bloom of his marvelous youth."

Connie could no longer resist. "Can you tell me about your relationship with Tony?"

"He was," she began, "the kind of man women dream of. I know I sound like a silly teenager, but I mean what I say. I've given thought to it, much thought." She paused, twisting awkwardly to pull a photo out of a drawer in the table next to her bed. "Have you ever seen a picture of Tony?"

"Only his high school photo. He was probably twenty-six or so."

She passed the photo to him. A man of perhaps forty. Strong certainly but not obviously handsome. "Rugged" was perhaps a better term. A pleasant smile; a slightly bent nose; eyes that were, well, mysterious. Tousled brown hair. He was wearing a leather jacket and standing at the top of a hill. A wooded background scene that reminded Connie of Wordsworth's verbal portrait of the glen near Tintern Abbey lay behind him. Connie understood why Nicholson liked this particular photo.

"A fine-looking man," he said, handing the photo back to her. "I found it odd though," he added, "that in the collection of memorabilia I worked through there were no photographs. Did Tony not like pictures?"

"They made him sad. He knew that change was constant and inevitable, and he felt that photos were simply efforts to freeze time. He didn't want to participate in the fraud."

"Oh," was Connie's weak reply.

After a pause Nicholson resumed her account. "We had a lovely time during the war, simultaneously dangerous and romantic," she said, her voice suddenly wistful. "After he went off to Malaya, I left the Service and got married. It didn't last long. Knowing Tony had not been good for any future marriage. Though," she chuckled, "perhaps knowing me hadn't been very good for any of his marriages either." After shedding her husband, she had become a researcher at the Imperial War Museum. She and Tony had stayed in touch after the war, and she told Connie about visits she had paid him in the States in the 1960s and 1970s and of their travels in various parts of the world, especially Africa. She said that she had even met one of his wives, though she didn't remember her name. "We both liked zoos and animal parks, and so wherever we went we made a point of going to visit them, in Jo'burg, in New York, in Pittsburgh, in San Diego, in Berlin, in Vienna. Tony especially liked elephants, something to do with some gunrunning he did in Kenya once. They've got a great zoo in Vienna, did you know?" Connie knew little of zoological gardens, but he replied that Shrug knew Vienna well and was probably familiar with the zoological gardens there.

"We grew old, or maybe I should say older, neither together nor apart, and he never lost his magic. I last visited him, in Los Angeles, in 1988. I was his oldest and best friend," she continued, "and that's why he contacted me about the threats. I was the only person who could know the pressures we had operated under in that intense winter of 1944–45. I was the only person who could understand the primary operational rule for any close group in war-time: death to those who are deemed to pose a threat to the group. Little Hanna, little bitch Hanna, was barely four at the time, if that. What could she know of war? Nothing. Nothing, damn her!" Nicholson spat the last words out, her composure suddenly dissolving into rage as she struggled to raise her frail body from her bed.

But she immediately calmed down. "We live, Mr. Haydn, in a utilitarian age. Or rather, *you* do. I live in my past." She paused. "You know about utilitarianism and Jeremy Bentham, don't you?"

Although tempted to say he was a philosopher by training and quite familiar with Bentham, Connie realized that there was no way he could utter words to that effect without sounding both pompous and fatuous, and so he confined himself to quietly declaring his familiarity with the concept of utilitarianism.

"Well," Nicholson continued, "the morality of the soldier is grounded in honor, not pleasure. Pleasure undergirds a society based on commodification." Her contempt was audible in her tone. "Honor undergirds a society based on heroism. Tony was an embodiment of honor." Connie recalled that Fritz Kramer, *of all people,* had expressed similar sentiments. "That's why he earned my devotion."

The morning had gone by swiftly, and Nicholson was visibly tired. Connie said he needed to leave and thanked her for her help. He asked if he might get anything for her, a drink, perhaps, or a cigar, before he left the room, but she asked only for the *Times Book of Crossword Puzzles* that lay hidden under a newspaper on her dresser.

"You'll let me know if you catch that wicked woman, won't you?"

"Yes, Colonel Nicholson, I will."

"If you succeed, you have my permission to call me Sandy." She laughed at her little joke. "Yes, *then* you may call me Sandy. But never Less. Only one man calls me Less. And that's because he was *more.*"

Connie thanked her again. As he left, the young orderly, who had apparently been waiting outside the door of the room during the entire conversation, slipped back in, nodding wordlessly to the departing visitor. When Connie reached the entrance hallway of the Alliston Home for War Veterans, Major Constable reappeared.

"I hope your visit was successful, Mr. Haydn."

"I believe it was. I am now confident that a woman named Hanna Moser murdered Tony Travers, that she did it because he had killed her parents, and that he had killed them because intelligence reports had led him to believe they were betraying the Allied cause, though apparently they weren't. I strongly suspect she has assumed yet another identity in America, but with some tips that Colonel Nicholson has supplied and lots of information my friend back in the States has gathered, I think we may be able to track her down." Connie stopped talking and smiled knowingly at Constable. "You already know much of what I'm telling you, don't you?"

"That's satisfactory. You will inform me if you succeed in find-ing her?" The voice was as impassive as the reply was oblique.

"Of course. And thank you for your valuable help."

Connie left the building briskly. Even at midday, the air re-mained cool, and a light breeze swept in across the grassy lawn. Within fifteen minutes he was back at The Stag's Arms for a pub lunch. He had a few hours to kill before he needed to drive back south, and so he paid a quick visit to Inverness and the Culloden battlefield. War, he thought, his mind on his brother Donald as much as on Colonel Nicholson, confronted people with decisions he was glad he had never been forced to make.

Late that night his return flight to the United States took off from Prestwick. As he settled back to catch some sleep, for Sunday would be well advanced in Ohio by the time he got home, his thoughts drifted to the startling fact that Alessandra Nicholson and Freddy Kramer had seen the same virtue in Tony Travers. Honor. He had acted by a code of honor. The name of Kramer led him to reflect on how far the investigation had come. And it was turning out to be, as investigations go, a fairly simple one. For there had been no great motivational complexity in the crime. The task for the investigators had simply been to find the tracks that led to the revenge-seeking murderer. That had not been easy. But Shrug and he had managed to pull out the truth. All that was needed now was some more investigative grunt work, and the present identity of H.M. would become known. She could not evade them. Connie's final thoughts, before sleep brought relief to his body and brain, took him back to baseball. Dazzy Vance, the great Brooklyn hurler, had once declared his satisfaction at exacting revenge on a team that had traded him away. He could never, he said, whip them too often. The taste for retribution, Connie groggily thought, is rooted very deep in *homo sapiens*.

14

Friday, June 22, 2001—Saturday, June 23, 2001

Shrug was not one to suffer fools gladly, even when he himself was the fool, and nothing brought out his sense of doltishness more quickly than buying a new car. He disliked pretending he knew more than he did about automobiles. He disliked pretending that he didn't see that the dealer knew he was pretending. Haggling made him uncomfortable. Failing to haggle made him feel like a coward. There was, in short, no way he could make a visit to a car dealership anything other than a venture in self-abasement, self-contempt, and regret. The only course was to get the whole ordeal over with as swiftly as possible, and to that end he spent Thursday evening consulting issues of *Consumer Reports* at the public library and Friday morning purchasing a new Saturn. When he returned home for a quick ham sandwich lunch, he felt a modest sense of pleasure at the thought of owning a new vehicle. But above all, he felt sheer relief. It was astonishing, he mused, that someone who so relished the openness of the equity market was so discomfited by the openness of the automobile market.

Happily for his self-respect, he now felt free to turn his attention back to the investigation. And since Connie was in Scotland in search of information about the major target, he saw his task at home as the comparatively less important one of clearing up nagging loose ends. Why couldn't they find a way to formally exclude Denny Culbertson, Trish Ridgway, and Eddie Moratino from their list of suspects? And, a more important question, why had Connie been attacked? Shrug hated untidiness. And since there was little else he could do for a day or so, he returned to these nagging questions. Like the nuisance of unwanted background music when silence is sought, they defied ignoring.

As he often did, Shrug began an afternoon of sleuthing with a prayer, asking God to help him to understand how the pieces of evidence fit together. Then, following up on the prod delivered by the encounter in the Atlanta airport, he began studying the unviewed video of the head table on the night of Tony Travers's death.

The camera had been positioned near the middle of the room. Because it was only modestly elevated, its view of the short head table was sometimes obscured by classmates passing in front of it. But in general it afforded a fine view of the class officers and those who visited them.

The flow of events it revealed was pretty predictable. And since the tape was un-miked, it was dull, too. Still, since Shrug had been present during the evening, he was able to make out the general sense of what was going on. Cole Stocker welcomed his class-mates. Johnny Kettering, a Catholic priest, led the assemblage in a prayer for classmates who had died. Betsy Kugler, a meteorologist at a television station in Nebraska, told a few jokes. Several class-mates received awards that Stocker handed out. Only three persons from the list of suspects made appearances: one of the Grunhagens drifted in from the left to chat briefly with Cheryl Bollinger; Freddy Kramer whispered something in Gertie Heintzelmann's ear that brought a frown to her face; and just before Trish Ridgway's evening-ending entrance, Denny Culbertson arrived from the left to show to Dirk Glass a large stick of some sort that he was holding. Tony Travers never appeared, nor had Shrug expected him to, since the main film had already allowed his limping perambulations around the dining room to have been plotted.

Boring as it was, there was one particular point in this head table film that caught Shrug's attention. Cole Stocker and Cheryl

Bollinger were seated next to each other, flanked by Dirk Glass on the viewer's left and Gertie Heintzelmann on the right. And the evidence of the camera was clear: at various times during the evening, and despite the low skirt of the table cloth, Stocker and Bollinger could be observed playing footsie. The other video, the frequently-viewed main one, had offered only an oblique and distant view of the head table and had not revealed this *sub mensa* choreography. Recalling that Bollinger was unmarried and that Stocker had attended the reunion without his wife, Loretta Szek, this unexpected discovery seemed open to at least one potentially interesting interpretation, and so on his second viewing Shrug decided to focus on possible visual hints about the relationship between the class president and the class treasurer. That they were friendly and enjoyed each other's company was obvious. That they talked less with companions on their other sides than with each other was mathematically demonstrable. Shrug was most struck by the suggestions that they were not infrequently allowing their bodies to graze each other. This was public flirtation of a fairly high order.

Am I just becoming a dirty old man? Shrug asked himself. *Adults are free to do what they wish. Who am I to judge? And yet . . . and yet.* The trouble, he suddenly realized, was that Stocker was the esteemed head of the Columbus Christian Marriage Association. It was an organization that preached fidelity to spouses in the context of a Christian view of the holiness of matrimony. That's why Connie's sophomoric remark about Stocker and Bollinger having adjoining rooms at the Andrew Strett Bed & Breakfast had seemed slightly distasteful. *And remember this*, he told himself. *I'm not trying to figure out who killed Tony Travers. Connie is off in the UK following up on what may well be the decisive clue on that crime. No. I'm just trying to figure out who attacked Connie last Sunday. It seems likely it was someone local, someone who wants to scare us into backing off. Someone with something to hide.* Shrug let out a deep sigh. *Does this bit of wayward lustful-*

ness in the sixty-plus crowd have anything to do with a murder investigation? Probably not. But an assault? Is this about someone hoping to cover his ass? Well . . . conceivably!

Annoyed with himself after the second viewing, Shrug set aside the video and turned his attention to the written notes he had assembled from the statements that the various interviewees had given. If the three suspects as yet without alibis were to be definitively cleared, he thought, he would need to find something in their statements that might allow their professions of innocence to be confirmed.

Of the three, Culbertson seemed the most exposed to suspicion, for he had said nothing at all about what he had been doing during the crucial eight minutes he had been out of the room. In fact, he'd said he hadn't even recalled leaving.

Moratino had stated that when he had left the room, he had also left the building, in order to return to Columbus to catch some sleep before an early morning flight. Shrug could think of no easy way to confirm or disconfirm that claim. But since he also thought Eddie Moratino the unlikeliest of murderers, he noticed he wasn't much concerned.

Only Ridgway had made a specific claim—that she had left the room because she needed to throw up, and that in fact she *had* vomited shortly thereafter, not even reaching the women's rest room before the accident happened. *Now that,* Shrug thought, *is a claim that in principle might be susceptible to proof or disproof!* But how? As he glumly realized, at a distance of three years, the on-duty janitor was unlikely to recall if someone had disgorged the contents of her stomach in the hallway that night, especially since the truly attention-seizing event of the evening would surely have eclipsed all other matters in the minds of any persons who had responsibilities for readying the high school for students on Monday morning.

At that point, Shrug smiled, stretched his arms high in the air, and decided his afternoon was being poorly spent. He was getting nowhere in his probes, becoming unduly puritanical, and growing frustrated. He pulled out a CD of Beethoven's "Spring" sonata, inserted it into the player, and settled back in his preferred listening chair to enjoy the marvelous melodic interplay of piano and violin that made this work one of his favorites. His mind glided with the themes, and as he followed Beethoven's modulations, he was grateful again that his strict father had insisted many decades earlier that training in music theory was the foundation for intelligent listening.

At 4:45 Allan Clark phoned. He asked if Shrug could join him and his wife, Jacinda, for steaks that evening. He apologized for the short notice, but added that he wanted to discuss a parish business matter with him. "And just so you don't think later on that I ambushed you, I want you to know ahead of time that I'm going to make a request of you." Shrug accepted the invitation, happy at the prospect of escaping the vexations of the investigation for a few hours.

The rectory of Trinity Episcopal Church was a small white structure that sat adjacent to the church building itself. Clark met Shrug at the door and led him to the side garden, where green plastic chairs and a hot open grill awaited him. Jacinda smiled a greeting and they briefly hugged. Then Allan Clark spoke. "First, business. The parish has need of your financial skills." Shrug was not surprised. When people told him he might be needed, they usually had his background in financial matters in mind. "You remember I spoke last Sunday of how the health station in Abinjola, the one the diocese supports, had been destroyed by a storm. The people there now have no access to health care. Well, the diocese has determined that we need to reestablish the Nigerian station and give Dr. Asunjabe a new facility as quickly as possible. And that means we need to raise money here at Trinity. Will you lead our local fund-raising effort?" Allan Clark always got quickly to his point.

Shrug inhaled deeply, looked from Clark's face to the grill, and agreed. "Why not? It's better to be useful than useless. That's the Owen Meany rule."

Clark thanked him and asked him to come by the parish office during the next week to pick up the background information he'd need. *It's like two Gary Coopers talking to each other,* Shrug thought with a wry smile. But as far as he was concerned, crisp and no-nonsense decision-making beat hesitation and histrionics every time.

Clark turned discussion to the investigation, and Shrug filled him in on his recent trip to Texas and Connie's current visit to Britain.

"It sounds like Connie is recovering quickly from his injuries," Jacinda Clark noted. "I take it they weren't serious."

"Well, maybe you should ask the victim about that. But you're right about a prompt bounce-back. He does seem to be throwing off the effects of the attack pretty swiftly. He's a tough buzzard, Connie is."

"Like you," she smiled. "You seem to have recuperated well yourself, thanks be to God."

"A little sore, maybe, but generally quite comfortable, thanks."

"Do you know if the police are having any luck in their investigation into who attacked Connie?" Allan Clark asked.

"No. And I should check in with them about that while Connie's in Scotland." As Shrug replied, he jotted a reminder to himself. He continued by explaining that he was using Connie's absence try to sort out some of the unanswered questions still dogging the investigation. "That attack is the biggest. Whoever beat up Connie is some malicious dude."

"I inquired," Allan Clark continued, "in part because Cheryl Bollinger has just come back to town for a week or so and, as a former parishioner, came by the church yesterday to look me up." Shrug recalled that before she had given up direction of her fitness center and started dividing her time between Ohio and South Carolina, Bollinger had been an active member of Trinity Episcopal. "She wanted to know whether I knew anything about what the police were finding out. She subscribes to the *Herald & Examiner* even in Hilton Head, and so she knew about the assault."

Shrug considered mentioning what he had noticed in the video that very morning, but decided he didn't want to lower himself to rumor-mongering, at least, not yet.

"She was rather taken with your friend," Clark added, "and by that I mean she was impressed by the acuity of his mind and the cuteness of his eyes." Clark chuckled. "That's what she said, 'The cuteness of his eyes.' But she hoped he'd choose more flattering frames for his glasses this time around. She still strikes me as, well, restless, and . . ."

"She mentioned the need for new glasses?" Shrug was suddenly animated. "You're sure?"

"Oh yes. We were bantering, but in the context of the attractiveness of his eyes it was a natural subject, wasn't it?"

"No. You miss my point. How did she know he needed new glasses? How did she know they'd been broken? That information wasn't in the newspaper article about the attack!"

"Are you sure? It seems a small point."

"Oh, I'm very sure . . . very sure. And it's not a small point. For if it wasn't in the article, how could she know?"

Clark fell silent. The two men looked at each other. "You know what I think, Allan? I think she has an independent source of information about the assault. And I don't need to tell you what that means."

"Oh my." That was about as tart as Clark's tongue ever got outside of a sermon.

Shrug stood up. He was angry. But he was also puzzled. "Let's imagine," he began, talking more to the dogwoods at the edge of the yard than to Clark, "let's imagine that for some reason Cheryl Bollinger wanted to hurt Connie, even if he did have 'cute eyes.'"

"Sarcasm doesn't become you."

"Be quiet, Allan." Shrug was not too be put off. "Let's imagine she wanted to hurt Connie. She might have done it herself, but Connie suspects his attacker was a man. So maybe she figured out how to get someone to do her dirty work for her. The question is, why? Why would she want to hurt Connie?"

Clark remained silent, clearly uneasy about the subject of the conversation and apparently quite happy to let Shrug wrestle with the train of his own thoughts.

"No," said Shrug, after a few moments of thought, "I've put that wrong. Cheryl didn't need to convince someone. She already had her ally."

"What are you talking about?"

"Do you know Beethoven's 'Spring' sonata?"

Allan Clark nodded in a clearly perplexed negative. "No. And what does Beethoven have to do with Bollinger?"

"It's his Sonata number 5 for piano and violin. Not for violin *with* piano. But for piano *and* violin. I was reading the liner notes earlier this afternoon." The Clarks settled back in their chairs. There seemed little for them to do except listen to an instructive lecture on a masterpiece by the master. "I can't quote the text word-for-word, but in effect it says something like this: 'it's uncanny how the violin and piano never seem alone for very long. They are both frolicking with the melodies. They are inextricably bound together. That's why this is a sonata for piano and violin, not a violin sonata with piano accompaniment. The two are in it together—Cheryl Bollinger and Cole Stocker. They are inextricably bound."

Jacinda Clark interrupted. "Whatever *are* you talking about? Where did Cole Stocker come from?"

Without delay, Shrug told of what he had discovered from viewing the video.

"To tell the truth," Allan Clark said in reply, "that doesn't sound all that incriminating to me. Reunions can be a bit like cruises. People flirt. They may even misbehave. But it doesn't carry much meaning."

"Well," said Shrug, realizing he suddenly sounded somewhat defensive, "that's what I tried to talk myself into believing. But there's more." And he told of Connie's impressions that he had detected some odd current of sexual attraction and jealousy sparking between Stocker and Bollinger at their earliest investigation meeting. "They've been class officers for a while. They get together in Humboldt at regular intervals. The affair might be of long-standing."

"Still doesn't sound very damning. They were doing volunteer work, helping out. Happily for the health of society, people do that all the time. And remember: Cole Stocker is the well-publicized head of the Christian Marriage Association in Columbus. He'd be very unlikely to engage in conduct so at variance with his public position."

"Oh come off it, Allan." Shrug was suddenly annoyed with the rector. "I've always admired your ability to take human nature for what it is, a very messy hodgepodge of contradictory impulses and aspirations. And now you're suddenly going to claim that because Cole Stocker *espouses* principle A, he won't violate principle A? You know better than that. In fact, you've just given me a very plausible motive to explain what's going on." Shrug was reenergized. "Last Saturday Connie and I told the class officers that in light of the information about someone impersonating Amanda Everson, we were going to revisit the reunion weekend and explore every detail about it we could dig up. We emphasized how thorough we intended to be. Leaving no stone unturned. That sort of thing. That declaration of intent may not have alarmed Cheryl, but it portended possible disaster for Cole. He felt he *had* to stop us because he had to keep his secret affair, well, secret. The easiest recourse was to try to scare us off. And the attack on Connie, which occurred the very next day, was designed to do just that. What do you think?"

Clark stroked his chin and stared straight into Shrug's face. "I hope you get some more evidence before you launch into public accusations of sexual liaisons and physical assaults, my friend. Your hypothesis depends on several inferences which, though plausible, are scarcely irrefutable. And these two people you're talking about are friends of yours. Be careful. Don't go around hurting people just to placate your effervescent curiosity."

Shrug considered the rector's cautionary remark. "You're right, of course. Still another sign of why I trust your judgment. But I can and will do further exploring. For there's one point we can't ignore: *somehow, some way,* Cheryl Bollinger knew about the glasses." Jacinda Clark used that remark to artfully divert the conversation into less contentious channels. And the rest of the evening passed by quietly. But Shrug's resolve did not recede: Cheryl Bollinger had access to information not available to the public.

———————— ———————— ————————

Shrug had planned to sleep in on Saturday, but, awakened early by the chirping of birds, he found his investigation-obsessed brain churning away with ideas. Unable to return to the cocoon of slumber, he chose action; and by 7:15 he was at his breakfast, awaiting the arrival of the nine o'clock hour and its universally acknowledged sanctioning of phone calls.

Two lines of inquiry into the events of the reunion weekend had lodged themselves in his mind overnight. First, he wanted to discover what the long wooden implement was that Denny Culbertson had brought to the head table just before Trish Ridgway's disruptive arrival. It just might definitively clear his name. And second, he wanted to examine the character of interconnectedness of the adjacent rooms that Cole Stocker and Cheryl Bollinger had taken at the Andrew Strett Bed & Breakfast. Except for the mounting signs of trouble at Enron, the morning newspaper was poor company, and Shrug's restlessness made him impatient with the prospect of whiling away time at the piano.

Promptly at nine he placed a phone call to Denny Culbertson in Pittsburgh, and he quickly learned that he had been unduly cautious. The energetic Culbertson had been up since six. But the former classmate sounded glad to hear from his sleuthing friend, and Shrug allowed a few minutes of chitchat to pass before moving to his purpose.

"This may seem like an odd question, Denny, but it's one which has been nagging at me." Shrug wanted to make the matter sound unimportant, which, in a way, it was, even though it might prove to be the means of exonerating Culbertson. "Just before Trish Ridgway broke into the dining room on reunion night with news that Tony was dead, you had come up to the head table to talk with Dirk Glass. And you had what looks like a long stick in your hand. Do you remember what it was? Or how you got it?"

Shrug couldn't tell from the silence on the line whether Culbertson was worrying or laughing quietly. "Do you remember the stick?" he asked again.

"I can't believe this," Culbertson finally said, a tone of delight in his voice. "Of course! Of course!"

"Of course *what?*" Shrug had no idea what Culbertson was thinking about.

"Do you remember the old wooden lion that sits in the atrium of the high school building, we called him 'Leo,' the symbol of the Humboldt High Lions?" Shrug did. "Well," Culbertson continued with a barely suppressed guffaw, "that thing you're calling a stick was actually a part of Leo's tail, a substantial part, I'll add. I'd just gone out to the atrium, tugged and twisted it until I snapped the thing off, and then brought it back to the dinner. I met Amanda Everson as we approached the dining hall and showed it to her. She thought it was a grand joke. And then I walked over to Dirk because I thought he'd be tickled, too." The unexpected mention of Everson reminded Shrug that the two of them had returned to the dining hall together, but when asked, Culbertson couldn't recall anything else she'd said.

"It wasn't a very responsible thing for me to have done, if you know what I mean. I guess I'd had too much to drink and was feeling high-spirited." Culbertson hesitated for a moment. "Ooooh.

That's really embarrassing to think about now, for I was at my preachy worst that evening. But yes, that's what it was—the lion's tail. And even though I guess it was vandalism, I can't say that I'm sorry to have had such a lark. Though I should probably offer to reimburse the school, shouldn't I?"

With that final sentence Culbertson's tone grew more sober, as if the little boy within him were again ceding authority to the adult. But his explanation had set Shrug's mind racing ahead, and so, pausing only to note that he believed the school authorities would be grateful if Culbertson owned up to his prank even at this late date, Shrug thanked his friend and ended his call expeditiously.

The account, Shrug realized, had effectively exonerated Culbertson. For if he had used his eight minutes of off-screen time to walk to the front of the school building and snap the tail off of Leo the Lion, he could scarcely have had time to walk back toward the dining room and then on down a different hallway to a scheduled meeting with Tony Travers. The school was a large building with its side hallways darkened, and the tail presumably had initially resisted Culbertson's efforts to detach it. No, Shrug concluded, it simply didn't make sense to pack a be-tailing *(Is there such a word?)* and a murder into eight short minutes. And that in turn meant that Culbertson hadn't colluded with the fake Amanda Everson, not that Shrug had ever thought he had.

Culbertson's comments triggered other thoughts as well. His mention of "vandalism" reminded Shrug that among the papers in George Fielding's office related to Tony's death there was something called a "vandalism report." It might just be possible that, since Trish Ridgway had said she had vomited in the hallway rather than the bathroom, such a report would include a reference to the residue of the emesis. And if it did, that reference would help to clear Ridgway.

Energized by his success with Culbertson, Shrug wasted no time in heading out for two errands in Humboldt. His first took him to the sheriff's office, where he found George Fielding behind his desk, poring over papers. "You don't even take Saturdays off, do you?" Shrug often remarked on Fielding's impressive work ethic. In fact, on this particular morning he had been counting on it.

Claiming he was happy for the interruption in a slow morning, Fielding pulled the Travers file from his drawer. "I knew you'd want to see it again," he said and offered it to Shrug. The vandalism report was the fourth item in a not-very-full file of papers, and among its entries was exactly the reference that Shrug hoped for: "large pool of vomit on 1st floor of west wing, c. 20 feet east from girls bathroom." In a perfect world, Shrug might hope for a laboratory test of some sort that would prove beyond doubt that the pool was of Ridgway's making. But he in fact had no doubts. For the facts tallied with her tale—that she had left the dining room because she was ill, that she had lost her meal before reaching the bathroom, and that she had then discovered the body at the bottom of the nearby stairwell. Her window of opportunity consisted of five minutes: if she had used some of that time to purge herself, it scarcely seemed possible that she could have squeezed in a murder, too.

Feeling quite pleased with himself (and noting yet again the ancient truth about the ineradicability of pride), Shrug left George Fielding to his cluttered desk and headed off for a midmorning coffee before visiting the bed-and-breakfast. He wanted a caffeine interlude so that he could make a final decision about how to interrogate the innkeeper on the layout of the rooms without seeming to be either outrageously nosy or insufferably priggish. A bit of reflection, however, persuaded him that he was being too self-conscious, that hoteliers were interested in renting rooms, not judging behavior, and that he could easily secure the information he needed simply by asking to see rooms 5 and 6.

The Andrew Strett Bed & Breakfast sat about a hundred yards from Humboldt High School. It was a lovely late-nineteenth-century, multi-gabled structure that had belonged until the 1930s to the Strett family, founders and owners of the town's oldest Republican paper, the *Humboldt Herald*. The residence had subsequently fallen on hard times under a series of transient owners until, in 1966, the threat of a wrecking ball had induced longtime Humboldt residents Calvin and Rosemary Lovinger to purchase it, invest in its refurbishment, and turn it into Humboldt's most stylish inn. In the early 1990s their daughter-in-law, Paula Lovinger, had assumed management of the business.

Shrug had never seen the interior of the bed-and-breakfast before and found himself entranced by its artful juxtaposing of period pieces with modern conveniences. The light hand of a discerning interior decorator was evident throughout. He asked the young woman who was doubling as desk clerk and house cleaner if he might see rooms 5 and 6, and was handed the keys to both with the brusque notice that they were booked for that night but were available starting on Tuesday. He walked across what had once been the large living room of the residence to the bedrooms near the rear. Rooms 5 and 6 sat along the hallway.

He entered Room 5 and found what he expected: a door on the immediate right hand wall that connected the room with the adjacent Room 6. A single gravity bolt provided security against transit between the adjoining rooms. But, as Shrug thought to himself, what could readily be bolted could just as readily be left unbolted. He turned next to Room 6 and found the same security arrangement on the other side of the connecting door. A swift pulse of shame passed through him. *Am I becoming reduced to peeping-tommery in my old age?* No, he quickly reminded himself. The only reason he was probing into the private lives of two friends was that Cheryl Bollinger knew that Connie's glasses had been broken when he'd been attacked. Only someone with inside information would have been aware of that fact.

Shrug returned to the front desk, and leaving the two keys in a tray, shouted and mimed his thanks to the hard-working clerk who was vacuuming the adjacent dining room. He knew what he needed to do, and drove straight home to complete the unpleasant task.

Cheryl Bollinger's voice rang out with a cheerful "hello" when he phoned her shortly before 1:00 P.M. Shrug thought that the tone became more taut when he introduced himself, but he couldn't be sure.

"This is a business call, Cheryl. I need to ask you some questions."

Bollinger's silence suggested that her mood had shifted abruptly.

"When you were talking with Father Clark a few days ago, you knew that when Connie was attacked, his glasses had been broken. How did you know that?"

"Oh, Shrug, don't be silly." She giggled. "It was in the newspaper. I read about the attack in the *Herald & Examiner*. Everyone knew."

"No, they didn't Cheryl. That information wasn't in the newspaper article. It hasn't appeared anywhere."

"Well, then I must have heard it from someone."

"From whom? You'd just gotten back in town, hadn't you?" Shrug was trying to keep his voice level, dark, and slightly threatening.

"Well, I . . . don't . . . know. Maybe . . ." Bollinger had suddenly developed a nervous laugh. "Maybe it was . . . No, that's not it." She was audibly stumbling. "You know how people talk about things. Maybe. . . ."

"They don't talk knowledgeably about things they know nothing of, Cheryl."

She suddenly became strident. "Are you accusing me of something, Shrug?"

"I'm inquiring, Cheryl." Shrug sustained his flat tone. He was determined not to allow her to throw him off-stride by shifting to bluster. "You haven't answered my question."

"Well, I don't know where I heard about the glasses." She said huffily. "I just did."

"Do you see Cole Stocker often?" Shrug hoped to surprise Bollinger with the unexpected question, and he concluded from her long silence that he had succeeded.

"Cole is class president," she finally said, in a tone that could fairly be called icy. "I am class treasurer. We sometimes have class business to conduct."

"How often?" Shrug was hoping that by assiduously boring ahead he might get Bollinger to crack.

"Well, as often as necessary. Maybe a few times a year." Her voice tone came across as duller, perhaps even dazed.

"Do you transact the business at the Andrew Strett Bed & Breakfast?" *If this question doesn't do the trick*, Shrug thought, *she's going to brazen it out, and Connie and I will have to undertake a lot of ferreting to gather our evidence.*

"What do you know?" The unexpected reply was subdued and nervous.

I've succeeded, thought Shrug, with a simultaneous surge of victory and embarrassment. "I'll tell you what I suspect, Cheryl. You tell me how right I am." Shrug proceeded to explain the zigzag course of inference that had led him to believe that Stocker and Bollinger had somehow been responsible for the attack on Connie because they feared that the intensification of the investigation would bring their own affair to light and therefore do irreparable damage to Stocker's marriage and/or career and/or role as a counselor on Christian wedlock. "Do I have it right?"

Shrug realized that in posing the question, he was giving Bollinger one final opportunity to assume the stance of indignant denial. But he knew enough of humankind's general aversion to living painful lies to suspect that Bollinger would prefer to end her charade and, in effect, fall back on the mercy of friends.

"May we talk tomorrow, Shrug?" was Bollinger's surprising reply, offered in a cool, almost gentle, tone. "After church. With Allan Clark present. I think I can promise that Cole will be there, too. Will that be satisfactory?"

Shrug quickly agreed to the proposal. It was always possible, of course, that Bollinger wanted twenty-four hours so that she might run far away, but such an action seemed far too melodramatic for a friend whom Shrug had known for more than half a century. It was far likelier, he realized, that she wanted the intervening time so that she could talk with Cole Stocker about their situation. And since she obviously believed she could produce Stocker, she probably already had a pretty good sense of his feelings about the attack.

After the call, Shrug went out for a walk. He felt a bit tawdry. And he wasn't even sure why. Was it because he had browbeaten a friend? Was it because he'd gone snooping? Was it because he'd uncovered a private matter that two friends had hoped to keep secret? Was it *all* of the above? Fortunately, as he had hoped, the fresh air and light breeze of the early afternoon soon restored a sense of equanimity. He offered a quick prayer of gratitude for the revelations delivered to him during the past forty-eight hours. All he could do now was wait for the following day, when his meeting with Stocker and Bollinger and the return of Connie from Scotland promised to signal the opening of the final stage of the investigation.

15

Sunday, June 24, 2001

When Shrug arose the next morning, with the service at Trinity Episcopal in prospect, he found his curiosity at odds with his piety. Once inside the church, he decided that his piety would have to yield. Rather than taking his usual seat, about halfway back and on the right, he made a point of positioning himself almost covertly at the rear of the nave so that he might observe the movements of those who settled into the pews in front of him. As best he could, he wanted to study the two persons whose lives he might soon be shredding.

A primly-dressed Cheryl Bollinger arrived with about ten minutes to spare. Her dress was dark blue, her blouse was light gray. A small, white-lace bonnet covered her head. She was alone and took a place on the left. Aside from a brief moment of kneeling, she sat erect, staring (insofar as Shrug could judge from behind her) straight ahead. Shrug wondered if her isolation meant that Cole Stocker was not coming. But then, five minutes later, as families with children were beginning to fill up the empty pews and to smudge the harmonies of a Bach prelude with their greetings, murmurs, giggles, and shufflings, Cole Stocker and a woman about his age, his wife Loretta Szek, Shrug presumed, came down the center aisle and took seats on the right. They too were dressed more austerely than most in the congregation on this warm summer day, and their walk was rigid. Aside from a brief whisper as they moved into their pew seats, they did not appear to talk with each other.

The seventy-five minute service passed quickly. When Allan Clark delivered his sermon, focusing on St. Paul's second letter to the people of Corinth, he spoke with his customary vigor. It was the fourth in a summer series dedicated to the Pauline epistles, and whether by chance, choice, or divine interposition, he chose to place emphasis on Paul's message about the importance of reconciliation. (Shrug smiled at the thought that, had Stocker and Bollinger been pulled into a joint attendance a week earlier, they would have heard Clark talk about the first letter to the Corinthians and Paul's stern teachings on sexual morality.) Clark was an experienced clergyman, and so nothing in his demeanor suggested that he knew, even though Shrug had phoned him the evening before, that a potentially unpleasant post-service conversation lay just ahead.

With the pronouncement of the benediction, Shrug swiftly left the church and waited for one of the class officers to appear. To his surprise, Cole Stocker was the first to come through the church doors, his stern-faced wife at his side; and upon seeing Shrug, he left the line of congregants waiting to speak to Allan Clark and walked in his direction. "Where are we meeting?" was his only remark, and Shrug, hearing anger and tension in the voice, pointed him to a small building which sat between the church itself and the rectory. "The office is in there. I'll be coming very soon." Stocker and Szek then walked off toward the office.

Cheryl Bollinger appeared a few minutes later. She stayed in line to say some brief words to Clark and then walked over to Shrug. "Cole and Loretta are waiting in the office," he said. "I'm going to wait for Allan, but if you'd like, please go ahead and join them." Bollinger preferred, however, to remain outside until Clark was free to accompany her into the meeting. Shrug followed, alone.

Fully aware of his responsibility, Clark first introduced himself and everyone else, and then suggested that they all take seats at the table in the center of the small room. Then, adopting a tone and line that were clearly designed to soften rancors, he began the business of the meeting. "It is, as you all know, difficult circumstances that bring us together today." He cleared his throat. "But we need to get to the bottom of some recent and painful events, and I know from much experience with the recalcitrance of the human heart that conversation is a mechanism for promoting understanding and that confession is not only good for the soul but healthy for human relations." He nodded toward Bollinger, who sat on the opposite side of the table from the Stockers. "Cheryl has asked that I be present today, as has Shrug." His voice was deep and soothing, his pace gentle and reassuring. "My knowledge of the incidents that have led us to come together scarcely extends beyond what the newspaper has reported, but I have been given to believe that some of you may want to talk about them. So I invite you to begin our conversation." He extended his arms to encompass everyone seated at the table.

Several seconds of silence ensued, and then Cole Stocker spoke. "Let me get to the heart of the matter. I have been dumb . . . dumb . . . dumb." Each iteration of the word was softer than its predecessor, and having thus passed judgment on himself, he stopped. Loretta Szek meanwhile looked down in her lap.

"How have you been dumb, Cole?" Though he spoke soothingly, Shrug was trying to nudge him along.

"You need to speak up, darling," Szek said. "We all know what you need to say. It's better to get it over with." Whether her words were the counsel of an attorney or a spouse, or both, Shrug couldn't presume to guess. But they sufficed, and Stocker's halting confession limped into the world.

He was, he said, the person who had attacked Connie just a week earlier. He had done so because, as Shrug had surmised, he had felt backed into a corner by the renewed attention that the investigators had pledged to give to every last detail of the reunion weekend. He knew that Connie already nursed some suspicions about his relationship with Cheryl. (Szek's expression remained unmoved as the tale moved from generalities to the specific motive for the attack.) He knew that a thorough scrutiny of people's behaviors would lead one of the investigators to the Andrew Strett Bed & Breakfast, where, in all likelihood, the character of his and Cheryl's room arrangements would become known. He suspected that the scrutiny would also uncover their various private dining arrangements. (Shrug had no idea what Stocker was referring to here, but he remained silent.) Stocker continued by saying that he had felt he dared not let all these disclosures come out. And so he had stupidly decided to try to scare the friends off. He had been, he said again and again, desperate. He started crying.

No one moved to offer him comfort, and so after a few seconds, his composure partially regained, he began to stammer out an apology. "I'm so, so sorry. I didn't know what I was doing." (*That's the exact opposite of the truth*, Shrug thought.) "I was scared. I was foolish. I'm dreadfully sorry."

All sorts of thoughts crowded into Shrug's mind. What kind of a doctor must Stocker be if he loses control of himself like this? Who does he think he's apologizing to anyway, since Connie's not here? Isn't it likely that this act is just a con job—an effort to trick us yet again? But his question was advanced in a level voice. "Can you tell us about the attack, Cole?"

Stocker responded by telling how he had hidden behind the water tower, intending, he claimed, to confront Connie and beg him to back off.

"That's why I told him of Connie's Sunday jogging habit," Bollinger suddenly interjected. "He said nothing of planning to beat him up. He said he wanted to *talk* with Connie." Her tone came across as sharp to Shrug's ears, but he couldn't tell whether she was bitter or just disappointed.

Stocker explained that as he waited, he had a long conversation with himself and realized the foolishness of trying to talk Connie out of the investigation. Shrug and he were too deeply committed to their task to be dissuaded by a mere plea. And how could he justify making such a plea? All it would likely do was focus their curiosity. And so, at a moral crossroads, he abruptly decided to adopt a more aggressive strategy. Using a small branch he found lying near the water tower, he tripped up the unsuspecting runner. Then he jumped on his back to hold him down while he bound his hands and feet and blindfolded him.

"Wait! That doesn't make sense, Cole." Shrug spoke sharply. "If the idea of attacking Connie was a spur-of-the-moment thing, why would you have rope and a blindfold with you? And wasn't that small branch mighty convenient? Those tools tell me that you'd planned your attack from the beginning. Why can't you stop lying?"

Stocker remained silent for a few seconds, looked wanly at Szek, and then acknowledged the truth of Shrug's conclusion. "Okay . . . you're right . . . I'm sorry. I *did* know from the beginning that I was going to attack him but . . ."

"Oh, Cole," was Szek's half-swallowed judgment, registering disappointment at information that was new to her.

". . . but I deliberately didn't hurt him very much. I am a doctor, after all. I could have *killed* him. But it's my job to *protect* life and health." He described in some detail how he moved the trussed-up Connie off the path.

Bollinger got up from the table during this segment of the confession and walked over to the nearest wall, where she stood, her back to the room, until the conversation was over. To Shrug's eyes she was as immobile as a statue, her thoughts unreadable.

"I tied the note to his arm so he would know what was expected of him," Stocker concluded, "and I snapped his glasses frame because . . . because . . . because . . . I thought it was a gesture of intimidation that might intensify the message of the note."

Loretta Szek suddenly turned toward her husband, snapped his shoulder around toward her, and barked at him that she felt like screaming. "I don't know if I'll stay with you, Cole Stocker, but I can tell you this. I'll never trust you again. You bastard! You fucking bastard." A long silence followed this outburst.

Since she must already have known the outline of his story, Shrug inferred that her rage was a result of hearing him shift the narrative from his preferred and softer version of the assault, the one she had reluctantly accepted, to the more accurate and harsher version. With the others, he waited for Stocker to resume the tale.

Ultimately the humbled physician sighed and fell back on what Shrug could only see as a strategy of total abasement. Struggling to hold back tears, he promised to resign immediately from the presidency of the Christian Marriage Association. "Any connection with me would bring irreparable damage upon a worthy organization." (Szek sighed and Bollinger let out some sort of sound that Shrug could not interpret.) "I only hope," Stocker continued, his head hanging down and suddenly sobbing profusely, "that you might somehow find it in your heart to forgive me . . . to pardon me . . . to give me time and space to get my life back together again." He turned to Szek to say that it was *she* he had always loved, not Bollinger. He turned to Shrug to explain that he could still do much good for society, but only if his reputation was not publicly tarnished. He turned to Clark to plead for the counsel of forgiveness from the clergyman. The only person in the room to whom he had nothing to say was Cheryl Bollinger. *I wonder*, Shrug thought, *if Cheryl realized when she promised that she could produce Cole today that he would choose his wife over his girlfriend.*

After a few moments of silence, Shrug decided that the others were expecting *him* to be the one to offer the first response to this package of self-pitying nonsense. "I can't extend forgiveness to you, Cole," he began, "because I'm not the person you injured. Perhaps you didn't kill Connie, but you did hurt him. He went to the hospital. He is still in pain. And if he weren't in such good shape, it's likely that the injuries would have been more severe, a broken leg or broken ribs perhaps. It wasn't your doctoring skills that prevented a more serious injury. So don't look to me for forgiveness. It's not mine to extend. And if you're asking us to try to get the assault charges dropped, again it's not my call. It's Connie's. And I'll tell you right now that, if he asks my advice, I won't recommend leniency." He glanced at Clark to see if his priest disapproved of this hard-nosed reply, but insofar as Shrug could judge from his silence, the rector appeared to agree that the choice of turning another cheek was not Shrug's to make.

Abruptly Loretta Szek stood up. "We've taken enough of these good people's time, Cole. We need to go home." She took Stocker's hand and guided him to his feet. He was ashen and hesitated before taking a step. But with her encouragement they made their way to the door and left without another word. Shrug thought that the class president looked thoroughly broken. But he felt little sympathy for him. Embarrassment perhaps, but scant sympathy.

Not until the couple had left the room and audibly started their car did Cheryl Bollinger turn back around to face the two men left in the room. "It doesn't matter to me what happens now," she said. "After I leave town tonight I'll probably never come back to Humboldt again. But see if you can be kind to Cole." Shrug was startled at the request. "Loretta understands him and I do, too. And that's why I predict she'll take him back. Life is an adventure that's just too intricate for Cole. Things came to him too easy early on, and now, in the game of real life, he's in over his head. And so when pressures become intense, his brain becomes addled and he starts flailing about." She paused, her hand on the doorknob. "Besides, he's right, you know. He's a doctor. He can still do much good. Columbus needs him." And she left.

"Wow!" said Shrug. "Garbled eloquence on behalf of a broken and ill-deserving man. I felt tense the whole time."

"I've seen worse," commented Clark. "In my line of work you sometimes deal with people when their wounds are at their rawest and their sensibilities strained beyond the limits of self-control. But on the key point, you were right, of course. If anyone is to argue for mitigation, and I'm not saying it's a good idea, if anyone does it, it has to be Connie. And in any case it may be a matter out of his control now: the law doesn't take kindly to assaults, even if the victim is forbearing."

"Well," said Shrug with a deep sigh, "I'll report all this to him later this afternoon. He's back from the UK now, always assuming the flights were on time, and I'm hoping we'll be meeting to compare notes. If we do, *when* we do, at least I'll be able to tell him that we've solved the question of the attack of last Sunday. But I'll bet, if he's uncovered information that will let us solve the death of Tony Travers, the assault won't seem all that important. And that's probably the best Cole can hope for—assault being eclipsed by murder on the scales of crime and justice." Shrug thanked Clark for allowing himself to be conscripted as referee, witness, and confessor. Then he left to prepare for hosting a War Council.

Connie flew into Columbus shortly after noon on Sunday, tired, stiff and still a little sore from the attack by the water tower, but eager to bring the chase to its conclusion. He had caught snatches of sleep at Prestwick, during the transatlantic flight, and later at Kennedy; if anything, he felt deprived more of food than of slumber. When he got to his house at 2:30, he found Shrug's voice mail proposing a meeting that afternoon at 4:00. He freshened himself with a shower and shave, soothed his hunger with a grilled cheese sandwich, sorted through the mail that had been stuffed through his postal slot during his absence, and arrived at Shrug's house on time. He recognized the other car in the driveway as Abe Steinberg's unmistakable Hummer. *I guess we're going to get an intelligence report on Harriet Murray, too.*

Steinberg's presence meant that the arrangement for the fourth War Council was different from the set-ups for earlier strategy sessions. Instead of seating discussants across from each other at a paper-cluttered card table, Shrug directed his guests to cushioned chairs on his back porch, and he provided them with wooden lap trays for their papers. Side tables served as havens for the inevitable snacks: beer or Coke, pretzels or chips, and a pass-around bowl of dip.

Though Connie was eager to report on the successful outcome of his trip to Scotland, he understood that Steinberg should have primacy of place on the agenda, both because he was the authentic guest of the hour and because he had been acting at the behest of the two friends. And so, without much ado, for everyone was interested in hearing what the others might have to say, the subject of Harriet Murray moved to the forefront.

"I've had time to make a quick search," Steinberg began. "She has left some tracks. Not as many as I had expected, but enough to get an outline of her life." She was born, he reported, outside the United States, probably in France or Germany, but certainly early in World War II. She was orphaned during the war." Connie winced at that remark but stayed silent. "And adopted in 1947 by an American family by the name of Preston. John and Mary Preston named their new daughter Cynthia. They had no children of their own, and Cynthia lived with them in Brooklyn until the late 1950s. "At that point she apparently left her adoptive parents, maybe to go to college, though I find no evidence of her having attended college, and never returned to live with them again." Steinberg adjusted that remark to explain that he didn't mean to suggest that she had broken with the Prestons, just that she had never thereafter returned to live regularly in the family home. In any case, the adoptive parents died in the early 1990s, and their daughter received a modest bequest of about $25,000 on the mother's death.

"By that time Cynthia Preston had become Harriet Murray, for she had had her name legally changed in 1970." Pleased with his procedural skills, Steinberg took this moment to explain that although he was telling the tale of Murray's life from childhood to the present, he had in fact traced it largely in the opposite direction. Finding the moment of the name change had been central to his success. "I don't think the change of names was associated with any marriage. In fact, I find no evidence of her ever having been married at all. No children either, as far as I can tell." Steinberg concluded by reporting that Murray had moved to Connalton,

Texas, in 1993, had moved away in 1998, and had left no trace of herself in any reasonably accessible records for the past three years. "And that goes for Helen Magnuson too," he added. "I'd guess she's gone into hiding, and she may in fact have left the country."

Connie thanked Steinberg for his data-mining, expressing however some surprise that more information hadn't been unearthed in the search. Steinberg reminded the friends that he hadn't had much time for the assignment and returned to the idea that some of the gaps might be accounted for by trips abroad. "After all, that's where Tony Travers disappeared to for some of the time. In any case, there's no secret to my methods. Everything I've found out is available in public records. So in principle you could have gathered it all in too, if you'd traveled to New York City, Texas, and several places in between. My advantage is that I know how to milk the Web quickly for data in the public records. In a few cases, I have to admit, I called in some feet-on-the-ground, records-searching favors from some old pals."

The two friends, feeling the sting of the gentle rebuke, thanked him again. Then Shrug turned to Connie. "You've been looking a bit too smug over there. Why don't you tell us what you found out at the veterans' home?"

"Well," said Connie, adjusting himself in his chair to briefly prolong his moment of glory, "the big thing I found out is that our quarry's real name is Hanna Moser. You'll notice the HM motif again. I think we can safely conclude that Harriet Murray aka Helen Magnuson née Hanna Moser is always the same person."

"Which means," Shrug noted, beaming with satisfaction, "that my spaghetti metaphor was not entirely ill-considered." Steinberg looked puzzled, and Connie simply assured him that he "had to have been there."

He continued. "I've also discovered what is almost surely the motive for the killing. Revenge—pure revenge. And at this point the story gets murky." Although Connie would have enjoyed relating the fuller version of his conversation with Alessandra Nicholson, he chose to defer that pleasure to a more relaxed moment and moved immediately to the heart of the matter: how Alessandra Nicholson (aka Less, Sandy, and the Great) had commanded an espionage unit in wartime France, how Travers was assigned to the Moser family, how Nicholson instructed him to kill them because they were reported to be double agents, and how she later discovered that her information had been wrong. "Tony was doing his job, the Mosers were the luckless victims of poor intelligence or maybe of double-dealing in the morally treacherous countercurrents of war, and Hanna, at the distance of more than half a century, became the hand of avenging justice."

Shrug and Steinberg were briefly silent before the latter remarked that there were many wounds of war that could never be healed.

Shrug followed with the obvious questions: "How do we track her down? Where do we begin our search? What do we know about her that can help us identify her?"

The friends began listing the many items of information they had gathered about Moser. That she was a fashionista. That she came across as self-confident, or perhaps as brittle, depending upon the source. That she had a poor singing voice. That she had a slight and obscure foreign accent. That she had a slight limp. That she enjoyed hiking and winter sports. That she liked Orson Welles films. That she spoke of having been a literary agent. That, even as she changed names, she retained the HM motif. They also noted that, despite what she had suggested or told to the women in Connalton or to the members of the class of 1953 whom she had met, she had apparently never married and never had children. "At least we can understand," Connie concluded, "why some of your classmates thought she had changed less than the rest of them. She had an advantage. Colonel Nicholson said she'd been born in 1941. She was maybe seven years younger than they were."

In sorting through these factoids to determine which were most likely to be useful, Connie and Shrug did most of the talking. After some thrashing about, they decided that if she were still in the United States, "a dubious proposition, in my opinion," said Shrug, then the tidbits likely to be most useful in finding her were her liking of states that offered a lot of seasonal snow and her vocational interest in helping would-be authors find publishers. It was possible, they all admitted, that she would try to take a turn in the fashion industry, but after discussing that option, they concluded that while she might have had the interest, nothing in her past suggested that she had the networking ties that would have allowed her to enter the field at almost the age of sixty. "Let's put that one on the back burner for now," Connie advised. "We can test it out later if Plan A fails."

"But what's Plan A? I haven't heard any agreement about a strategy." Shrug was puzzled by Connie's remark, though, as always, he was prepared to acknowledge that his friend might well be ahead of him in seeing a pattern to this fragmentary puzzle.

"Sorry. I'm getting ahead of myself." And with that brief apology, Connie explained where his mind was going. "Do you remember Hanna Moser's story at the reunion about how she had been hiking in the wilderness and gotten injured at a location about fifty miles equidistant from two major hospitals?"

Shrug recalled the tale, but failed to see its relevance.

"Let's assume," Connie continued, "that when she left Texas, she returned to some locale she liked, presumably in the North. Let's also assume it's a rural place. On these assumptions it becomes possible to imagine our identifying the rural locations in northern states that lie about fifty miles *in different directions* from major hospitals."

"You're assuming the geographical information is accurate," said a puzzled Steinberg.

"You're assuming that the story she told was true," added a dubious Shrug.

"Well, not quite. But we have to start somewhere. And the story has verisimilitude. It has concreteness. Sure, it might have been a figment of her warped imagination. And so too might the talk of being a literary agent. But they're the best bits of evidence we've got right now. The most concrete ones. Let's run with them until they bring us success or we're certain that they're useless."

"Okay," Shrug replied, his reservations still apparent. "But . . . but . . ." His face suddenly brightened. Connie smiled, for he realized Shrug understood the mechanism of triangulation that he was about to propose. "I see where you're going. For quite independently of this search for locations that might fit the geographical description"—(Shrug was picking his way toward fleshing out the argument)—"quite independently of all that, we can see if we can find a literary agent with the initials HM. Maybe 'Harriet Murray.' Maybe 'Helen Magnuson.' Maybe by now still another variation on HM. If the two lines of inquiry come together, we probably have Hanna Moser. I like it! You're a genius."

Steinberg's expression suggested he was considerably less than convinced.

At this point, realizing they needed maps and guides to literary agents if they were to put this strange strategy to the test, the friends hesitated. It was Sunday. Where, they wondered, could these items be secured on the spot?

"How about the library?" suggested Steinberg.

"But it's Sunday evening," a frowning Connie noted.

"And *I've* got the keys," Steinberg retorted, smiling as he jingled them in his hand for added effect.

So, on Steinberg's invitation, the men drove over to the county historical society building in their separate cars. They stopped on the way for a quick dinner at the nearby Bob Evans restaurant, and without much prompting Connie was persuaded to flesh out the tale of his Scottish adventure while they dined. By 6:30 they were seated in the library conference room at a long table that was soon covered with atlases and smaller books. Connie and Shrug were trying to figure out how to identify rural areas in the northern United States that were about fifty miles in roughly opposite directions from good hospitals, while Steinberg was looking through various guides to literary agents, focusing first on those who specialized in romances.

After much discussion about how best to proceed, the two map investigators fell back on an unsystematic reliance on observational instinct. They would look at the charts and try to recognize rural areas that seemed to meet their rather loose criteria. "It all seemed so simple and obvious when it came to me at your house," Connie said, "but in practice it's rather more complicated, and we're missing the necessary algorithm." Shrug, who was studying a map of Minnesota, commented that "It's hard to figure out what constitutes a rural hiking area just from these maps." Yet they stuck to their task, moving slowly from west to east across the northern tier of states and marking various maps with green circles, red dots, and blue lines, all meant to suggest that HM might be sequestering herself in that vicinity.

Shortly after eight, Abe Steinberg closed his last guide and, after asking how the friends' study of maps was developing, said that he had compiled a list of twenty-three agents whose initials were HM. "It's a surprisingly frequent combination," he added. "Lots of common first names begin with H and lots of common last names begin with M. And it's a job that seems disproportionately represented by women, many of whom appear seem to favor pseudonyms." He began reading from his list. "Henrietta Maples, Hildegarde Merrywether, Helen Moore, Harvey Meissner, Hester Morgenstern, Holly Martins, Hermione Middlesex, Homer . . . ."

"Stop! That's it!" Connie's excitement bordered on exultation. "It's got to be Holly Martins. Where does she live?"

Steinberg shuffled through his notes, casting puzzled looks at Connie in the process. Shrug waited quietly, uncertain why Connie had seized on this particular name. "She lives," Steinberg muttered, "in Tompkins, New Hampshire, which is . . ." He moved to the atlases. "Which is . . . yes, yes, here it is . . . which is in south central New Hampshire."

"And probably," Connie interrupted, "about equidistant from Boston, with all its fine hospitals, and Hanover, with its Mary Hitchcock Hospital."

"Well, yes," Steinberg said, "but I'm sure there are good hospitals in Manchester. So the description doesn't really hold."

"She was just taking literary license," Connie replied. "Shrug and I realized an hour ago that her description of her wilderness adventure was too vague to be useful to us. Was fifty miles a precise distance or just a conveniently round one? What in any case constitutes a good hospital? As a way of locating a site it was a stupid idea, and I should have known that from the start. And yet it remains useful, as a token of confirmation. For the fact that Holly Martins lives in a place that might meet the vague definition Hanna Moser gave us in her Harriet Murray guise clinches the case. Holly Martins is Hanna Moser."

"But why is the name Holly Martins the key?" Shrug could no longer suppress his curiosity. "Why did that name leap out for you? A lot of them sounded contrived to me. How can you be so sure that that's the current version of HM she's using? What's so special about Holly Martins?"

"It's *The Third Man*," Connie explained. "She told Trish Ridgway that it was the Orson Welles film she really liked. And. . . ."

And Shrug caught on. "Of course. The Joseph Cotten character—the American. The friend of Harry Lyme's who goes out in search of him. He was Holly Martins. So triangulation *does* work."

Steinberg remained puzzled.

"It can't be a coincidence," Shrug continued. "Someone known to be a fan of Orson Welles films and seeking to change her name and identity while retaining the initials HM . . . choosing the name of a lead character from a Welles' masterpiece. It's an unusual name. It can't be a coincidence. No, we've found her. The pseudonym gives her away immediately. And she lives in Tompkins, New Hampshire, which, unless I miss my guess, we're soon going to visit, right, Connie?"

Connie smiled and nodded his total concurrence. "It's like the OPS stat in baseball," he remarked.

Shrug and Steinberg turned their heads in puzzlement toward him. "What are you talking about?" was the best Shrug could muster.

"There are," Connie continued, suddenly professorial, "several ways the value of a batter in baseball can be calculated. The most common is batting average, but people far wiser than I have shown its defects and have come to prefer the richer utility of combining the on-base average and the slugging average. Since each of these averages—and remember, they really represent ratios, not averages—since each of these averages is a percentage of 1.00, and since each is independent of the other, derived from fractions with different denominators, it makes no mathematical sense to add them together. In fact, of course, they measure different achievements. And yet the heavy hitters at SABR,"—Steinberg looked even more perplexed at the introduction of this term but Shrug raised his index finger, beckoning him to patience—"the heavy hitters at SABR have shown that the best rough guide to a batter's value is measured by adding the on-base average and the slugging average together. For convenience we call it OPS, on-base plus slugging. It's a way of allowing each stat to cancel out the deficiencies of the others."

"And these deficiencies *are*?" Shrug paused. "No. Never mind. I'm already lost. Just tell us what your point is." Even for someone indulgent toward Connie's penchant for diamond metaphors, this one seemed a bit labored.

"It's simple. Two logically unrelated baseball metrics, when conjoined, supply very valuable information. It doesn't make mathematical sense to add them. But it turns out to be an illuminating conjunction. And here today we have two unrelated facts, a fondness for Orson Welles and a familiarity with the life of a literary agent, that, when conjoined, have given us the location of Harriet Murray. It's the OPS method applied to the world of detection."

"Kind of careless of her, wasn't it?" Steinberg ignored a comparison that seemed merely to fancify the plodding task of linking clues, and returned to the more congenial task of trying to understand the reasoning that had brought Connie to his conclusion.

"Not really," Shrug replied, stepping in for his friend. "She probably felt quite safe. Maybe all of her *noms de guerre* have significance to her and we just haven't had the wits to see who or what Helen Magnuson or Harriet Murray might refer to. We just lucked out on Holly Martins." He paused. "No, that's not right. What happened was that Connie's remarkable memory and attentiveness to film history finally gave us access to the giveaway implicit in her idiosyncratic system of name-choosing."

And on that triumphant note, and handshakes, the meeting at the historical society ended. Soon thereafter Connie and Shrug, after heaping appreciation on the good work of Steinberg, stepped out into the coolness of the advancing evening, leaving the archivist to put the various reference books back in their proper places.

Connie and Shrug had parked their cars adjacent to each other about half a block from the museum. "I've cleared Denny Culbertson and Trish Ridgway," Shrug said as they turned up the block.

"I didn't know they were still under suspicion."

"They weren't, I suppose. But I don't like loose ends." And Shrug told how a wooden lion's tail and a pool of vomit had served to exonerate two of the remaining former suspects. "That leaves only Eddie Moratino still under a theoretical cloud. And since he's just about the unlikeliest murderer I've ever met, I'm not concerned that I can't readily confirm his alibi. Let's just call him the beneficiary of the 'good-guy alibi.'"

Connie congratulated his friend and concurred in the judgment of Moratino. "I think," he added, "we no longer have any need to contact Tony's ex-wives or Amanda's table companions at the reunion dinner either. They're all now irrelevant. Which in turn means . . . *more* loose ends have been tied up."

"Yup," was Shrug's terse reply. They walked wordlessly for a few seconds. Then Shrug broke the silence. "I know who attacked you."

"Oh?" Connie stopped walking and turned to face his companion.

Shrug pointed to a bench where they both took seats. Then he told the story of his main sleuthing activity during Connie's trip to Scotland, culminating in the tale of the awkward meeting held in Allan Clark's office after services earlier that very day.

"Nice classmates you've got," Connie muttered tartly as Shrug wrapped up his account. "Have you told George Fielding? Is Cole planning on turning himself in?"

"Actually," Shrug said with a small smile, "he's hoping you'll forgive him."

"He's what?" Connie made no effort to control his astonished anger.

"I'm just the messenger. Don't take it out on me."

"What a shit! He beats me up and he hopes I won't mind. Jesus Christ! I'll bet he's the one who suggested that you all meet in a *church* office. I'm not feeling much like turning the other cheek. And that's probably what you and Allan are advising. What a strange world!"

"I haven't heard you ask for any advice, and so I haven't offered any," Shrug said sharply.

"Well, I'll think about it." Connie's voice was suddenly calmer, though his anger was unabated. "There may be nothing I could do anyway, because I've reported the attack. The law may want to exact its pound of flesh, whatever I say. Let's walk." His tone was acid, as they stood up and resumed walking toward their cars. "What a shit! What an absolute shit!" By now, Connie was muttering more to himself than to Shrug. He suddenly stopped and turned to his companion. "Okay. I give up. What *do* you think I should do?"

"Glad you finally asked," replied Shrug with a smile. He took a moment to shape his sentence, deciding to avoid Connie's cauterizing noun. "I think you should throw the book at my classmate Cole Stocker." The words came slowly and deliberately. "Actions have consequences. And it's never too late for Cole to learn that lesson. I think he should pay. It's a fairly simple matter of justice."

A slow smile illuminated Connie's face. "Damn it! You fooled me again." He thanked his friend. "As I said, I'll think about it. But now I know that my thinking will have the advantage of your counsel. That helps. It may not be determinative, but it helps."

Shrug suggested that the two friends meet the following morning to plan for a trip to New England. Then, with a handshake and a cheery reference to the continued successes of the "Second-Best Club," they got into their cars. Even irritation over Cole Stocker's brazen hope for grace or condonation could not eclipse the psychological urgency both felt for bringing the Tony Travers matter to a prompt and proper conclusion. "Hanna Moser, here we come," were Connie's parting words.

16

Tuesday, June 26, 2001

Carrying small overnight bags, Connie and Shrug flew from Columbus to Boston via New York on Tuesday. During several hours in stuffy aircraft cabins and cramped waiting areas they shared news on how they'd spent the previous day. Connie told of his overdue visit with Teresa Espinosa at Tuscan Gardens. Her spirits were as reliably upbeat as ever, he reported, but her nose was still bandaged and her frame seemed, to his unskilled eye, to be shrinking. "An unhappy sign" was his realistic commentary. She had, of course, been fascinated by the tale of his visit with her similarly frail but tenacious counterpart in Scotland, and she expressed the fear that she herself lacked the "durability" of Alessandra Nicholson. Shrug reported on his phone call of the previous evening with Marilyn. Brandon, it seemed, had his first steady girlfriend, and Marilyn reported that Guy and she were not taking this significant moment in the life-trajectory of their maturing son with the equanimity they had assumed they would possess when the inevitable time arose. To Shrug's surprise she had not tried to talk him out of the coming encounter with Hanna Moser. "Maybe she's learned that her dad isn't easily moved from his purposes," he explained. "Or maybe she's just too fretful about Brandon to worry much about me."

When their thoughts turned to the case they were tackling, Connie mused on the twisted investigative path that had led them to bucolic New Hampshire. "Just think of all our false hopes," he said. "First we wanted to pin it on Freddy Kramer, and just because his fondness for all things Nazi made him such a perfect villain."

"No, that wasn't the first misstep," Shrug reminded him. "Even earlier we'd forgotten the possible importance of the veterans' home in Tony's will. That was dumb. Just plain dumb. Nor was Freddy our first false hope. Or rather, since I wasn't really *hoping* to incriminate the Grunhagen sisters, just tantalized by the murder mystery possibilities offered by identical twins, but the first false step, my syntax is totally garbled by now: help me out of this sentence, *my* first false step was to see Bonny and Bunny as possible killers."

Connie let the strangled sentence pass and continued his own line of thought. "Then there was Sonya Klepper. Not that we *wanted* her to be a killer either. But she virtually confessed! Wrong: she *did* confess. We couldn't ignore that strange story about Saunders Cleaver. It seemed that the solution had been handed to us on a silver platter. Poor woman. On the other hand, if I remember right, we at least had our doubts about her confession from the start."

"You know Tchaikovsky's Fifth Symphony, don't you?"

Shrug's question seemed to come out of nowhere, and Connie, accustomed to his friend's musical excursuses, plumbed his brain cells and pulled up a memory of the rich theme in the second movement. "It's the one with the beautiful horn solo, isn't it?" He was pretty sure he was right, and proud he hadn't been a total ignoramus.

"You've got it. The second movement. But, actually it's the fourth movement I'm thinking of," Shrug replied. Because he had long since schooled Connie on the relationship of the dominant to the tonic in chord progressions— "question and answer," had been one of his metaphoric explanations of the relationship, "anteroom and chamber" was another—he could move quickly to his point. "Deep into the last movement, Tchaikovsky thumps out so many successive chords in the dominant *boom, boom, boom, boom, boom!* that sometimes audience members mistake the section for a loud tonic ending and begin applauding when the subsequent extra-long pause in the score arrives. They think the piece is over. But it isn't."

"And now," interrupted a suddenly irenic Connie, "and now I think I see where you're going. On at least one occasion we've thought that the investigation was over. Only it wasn't. It turned out that we'd confused the dominant for the tonic."

"Well," said a pained Shrug, "that *was* my idea. But hearing it expressed like that, so baldly and sadly so accurately, makes me wonder whether it's a comparison I wouldn't have been better off squelching. I did better with the German augmented sixth. I should have quit while I was ahead. Music, I often tell myself, is not a guide to life; it doesn't have lessons. I should listen to my own advice."

Later on, as their plane was descending into Logan Airport, Shrug asked for Connie's thoughts on how much they should bill Bryan Travers for. "I've been thinking about that, too," was the reply. "We said we'd bill him for travel, and I think we should. Those were stiff costs we've incurred. Beyond that, I think we have to stick to our pledge to accept all other costs as our own."

"Agreed. But do room and board expenses count when they're part of the travel?"

"Of course. You're the accountant. You know that. And it's one of the first things a traveling academic learns, too."

Shrug smiled. "Just checking we both see it the same way."

Their flight landed shortly after noon, and by 2:15, having rented a Subaru, they were deep into the forested back country of southern New Hampshire. In the cooler New England air Connie had donned a light, brown sweater, and Shrug had covered his white shirt with a plaid lumber jacket. "It's beginning to remind me of Hanover," Connie remarked, thinking of a happy summer term he had once spent teaching at the still more verdant Dartmouth College. *Big Green, indeed.*

Only at this point did they try to work out their final plans for approaching Hanna Moser. It didn't much matter, they soon decided, that they'd waited so long to address this question. After all, once they had introduced themselves to her and announced their purpose, whatever subsequently happened would be up to her. In truth, there were so many different directions events might spin off in that they saw no reason to try to plot out the details of the coming confrontation.

Abe Steinberg had secured the home address of Holly Martins for them (though he assured them they could easily have managed the matter themselves), and a stop at the small and ragged post office in the woebegone settlement of Tompkins gave them directions to her residence, just outside of town. It was a modest rustic cabin of uncertain age, set on a plot of weed-covered earth among a stand of white pines.

"How can a respectable literary agent operate out of a dreary and isolated spot like this?" Shrug wondered.

"Who said she's respectable," Connie replied. "Besides, it probably takes only a computer, Web access, a post office box, and a fax machine to be an agent, that, plus two or three trips a year to schmooze at conferences. Though I admit I'd be put off if I thought any agent of mine was actually living this primitively. If I ever had need of an agent, that is," he added with a laugh, wondering what a bona fide literary agent would make of a manuscript that took the moral theory of David Hume as its subject.

They left the Subaru at the front end of the short dirt driveway, deliberately blocking in the old Chevy pickup that sat near the house. An ancient dog of uncertain breed was spread out in the shade of the pickup, watching their arrival with only a modicum of curiosity. Neither Connie nor Shrug felt comfortable with canines, but this animal did not appear to be capable of performing even the elementary duties of a guard dog, and so they proceeded to approach the house. They hesitated at the door, but then Connie raised the knocker and delivered two loud taps.

When the door opened, they immediately recognized the woman in the reunion photos. The brown hair was long again, but the nose, the eyes, and the shoulders all testified to her being the person who had impersonated Amanda Everson three years earlier.

She was wearing grey jodhpurs and a red jacket and had put on weight since her imposture at the reunion.

"Hanna Moser?" Connie's words were both a question and a declaration.

The woman they were facing hesitated less than two seconds. Then, violently shoving them to either side, she darted past the two friends and scurried toward her vehicle.

"Shit!" said Connie, incredulous. "She's trying to run away." Though still sore from his beating by the water tower, he was confident that he was in good enough condition to outrun any sixty-year-old woman, especially a chubby one with a slight limp. "I'll catch her," he explained to Shrug before setting off after her.

Moser paused at the door of her Chevy, looked down the driveway, realized that the Subaru and the pines effectively blocked her escape route, and, changing plans, headed for the nearby woods at a good trot. Connie stayed in pursuit. When Shrug cried out to ask if he could help, Connie turned around briefly to call back, "Don't worry; I'll catch her; she's got to leave tracks. You just follow."

Moser made for the pine- and birch-covered hill. At times she disappeared from Connie's view, but even when she was out of sight, he could hear her up ahead. And because he had seen her chugging pace, he also knew he was gaining. He quickly concluded that she had made a mistake in choosing to run uphill, for the advantage of his superior conditioning would assert itself more swiftly as she labored against gravity and out-of-shape leg muscles. He heard her gasping as she thrashed through the undergrowth, and he found the spot at which she had broken a few branches when she crossed through a wild hedgerow about halfway up the incline. Soon Connie came upon his prey, sitting on a log in a small clearing, heaving and gasping as she tried to fill her lungs with oxygen. He stared down at her for a few moments, somewhat breathless himself, and then, after reckoning that taking a seat beside her on the log was not a wise idea, sat down on the ground opposite Moser, his back leaning against a tree. He realized immediately that this was the same position he had found himself in nine days earlier. But today he was unbound.

"Why did you run?" was his first remark after Moser seemed capable of speaking. But before she could reply, the old dog he had seen on the driveway limped into view.

"Do you want to play, old boy?" Though hampered by her coughing and gasping, Moser spoke to her dog in a loving voice. She stroked him behind his ears and pulled a niblet of some sort from her pocket. "No games today, Cerberus," she grunted as she offered him the morsel. "But you can stay and listen to the grown-ups talk." Cerberus settled down, his eyes fixed on Connie.

"He's friendly?" Connie inquired, hoping he was masking his apprehension.

"Oh yes, he's too old to do anyone any harm. Though he might try if I asked him to. But I won't."

Connie heard Shrug flailing his way through the woods and called out the direction his friend should follow. Then he repeated his first question to Moser.

"I ran," she said, "because you obviously knew something I didn't think was known. I thought I'd hidden my past. I thought I'd left no tracks. Your arrival made it clear that I had. So I decided to try to escape. It was foolish of course. I'm sixty and not in par-ticularly good shape, and you, whoever you are, turned out to be in *great* shape. Wouldn't you know my pursuer would be a mara-thon runner! It wasn't long before I realized that I'd made a poor decision, and so I veered over to this clearing. If I was going to be caught, it would at least be in a place where I could sit down."

Connie detected the slight accent that several people had no-ticed, and he understood why nobody had felt confident about identifying it. Perhaps, he thought, it's the accent of someone who, though speaking almost-perfect English, had been raised bilingual, French and German, from birth.

Shrug emerged from the woods, perspiring and breathing hard. He took in the odd sight of the two gasping seniors seated in front

Death at the Reunion

of him and, despite his physical distress, pulled three bags of M&Ms from his pocket, saying that it looked like everyone could use a sugar boost. The speed with which the contents of the bags disappeared suggested he hadn't been wrong.

After Connie and Shrug introduced themselves and explained that they were from Humboldt, Ohio, Connie handed a reunion photo of "Amanda Everson" over to Moser. She studied it long and hard, and then wordlessly handed it back.

"We're here," Connie began, his breathing now slower, "to ask you about the death of Tony Travers."

Moser tightened her lips and turned her face away from her two interrogators and up toward the high afternoon sun. "Who is he?" she asked.

"Ms. Moser," Connie replied, mustering his sternest voice. "Please don't play games with us. I can assure you we haven't flown all the way from Ohio on a lark." And with that introduction, he revealed to Moser a portion of what they had learned over the past three weeks—about Tony Travers's death and military background, about Hanna Moser's wartime childhood, about her impersonation of Amanda Everson at the class reunion in 1998, about how she'd moved from Harriet Murray to Helen Magnuson to Holly Martins, and about how her most recent choice of pseudonym had given her away.

"That's amazing," she said when the narrative was over. "I never even knew I was being looked for. I never thought anyone would make the audacious connections you two have. I'm very impressed." Her tone suggested that the praise was authentic, not derisive. But her next statement, a question, actually, hinted at puzzlement. "Maybe this is obvious, but . . . you're not lawmen, are you?" She spoke with the confidence that they weren't.

"No," Connie answered quickly, "we're investigating the matter privately. We got involved because Shrug was a high school classmate of Tony Travers. And I take it you're not denying that you killed him." That remark brought a long silence, as Moser stroked the top of Cerberus's head and looked off into the shifting shadows of the low pines while the two friends stared keenly at the woman they had hunted down. Each was wondering whether she would make getting the true story out hard or easy.

"I didn't murder him," she finally said, her voice stern and hard. "I executed justice."

"Tell us about it," said Shrug in his most avuncular voice (even as he was beginning to suspect that Moser was immune to vocal manipulation).

"I could, I suppose, talk in hypotheticals," she began. "*Suppose* there was this little girl, *suppose* that her family hated the Nazis, you know the drill." She paused to get another niblet for the well-settled Cerberus. "But that's not my style. So I *will* tell you a story. And it will be true. Every word of it. Then you can form your own judgments."

Moser shifted her position on the log to make room for Shrug, who had thus far remained standing, his hands on his knees. A refreshing breeze was penetrating the woods and completing the cool-down of the three seniors.

"I was born in 1941 in Nazi-occupied France, in Alsace," she began. Her parents, Peter and Angela Moser, having grown up in such a culturally contested province, were bilingual and owned a small dairy farm near the town of Daunville. She and her brother Gaston, six years older than she, had spoken childhood French and German with equal facility. Her parents detested the Nazis, however, and after the Allied landing in June of 1944 had given them a reasonable hope that resistance might have some other outcome than certain death, they began offering assistance to the more formally organized groups that were opposing the German occupation. "They weren't deeply brave people, my parents. But they were good people. That's how it came about that they agreed to host Mr. Travers," she spat the name out, "whose authenticity as a British counterintelligence agent the local French resistance unit vouched for." Connie and Shrug were both struck by the ease with which she navigated her way through the syntactical intricacies of English, presumably her third language.

"But they were wrong, as Travers showed, when he killed both my parents on January 18, 1945. He was working for the Nazis, and his task was to infiltrate and destroy resistance cells. You didn't know that, did you?" Her face was proud but her voice was surprisingly dull.

Connie and Shrug glanced at each other and, practiced at reading their mutually exchanged eye language, remained silent.

"I was not yet four at the time," Moser continued, the words now coming forth in a steady drone, "and so I don't remember any of this. But Gaston *saw* it. He *saw* the brutal murders. And of course he told me about them." The story was indeed grim. The Mosers had pleaded for their lives, had begged to be allowed to continue raising their children. But a remorseless Tony Travers had tied them both up and then strangled them, killing Peter first and then Angela. The detail in the account was compelling, the evenness of the voice, chilling.

"So that," Moser suddenly declared, "is the first part of my story. And now you know why what I did over fifty years later was simple justice. But you're probably interested in that intervening half-century." And with that simple segue, she moved to explaining how an orphaned four-year-old in occupied France became a sharply dressed impersonator-cum-avenger fifty-three years later.

A ten-year-old when the killings occurred, Gaston had seethed with a desire for getting payback from that moment on. He urged the legitimacy of revenge on his younger sister. Rather than accept adoption by an American family, Hanna's route to the United States, he had stayed with an uncle in Alsace, growing up to become a tormented university instructor in Paris. Despairing of persuading Hanna that his message of *revanche* could be a code to live by, especially after she left for America, he almost stopped contacting her. He died in the Paris street battles of 1968, his fevered energies still seeking to rectify the wrongs of the world.

"That was when I began to realize what was at stake. My parents, and now my brother, had been killed for trying to do the right thing. The forces of oppression and cruelty were everywhere. And one wickedness stood out above all the others—the killing of my parents. With Gaston dead, the obligation to set the moral universe back on its proper moorings was mine." In an abstracted tone, in words that carried enormous emotional freight even as her voice suggested disengagement, Moser told of a determination for justice that gradually gnawed away at her until at the last, having ground her to morsels, it engorged her to make her its total captive.

As this passion came slowly to define her, she abandoned lesser gods. After a brief and unhappy marriage, she foreswore the distraction of having a husband. She gave up an advertising job in New York City and a banking job in Kansas City. She spent as much time as she could each day, such hours as she could carve out of the time she needed for task of earning the income that kept her going, searching for clues about the whereabouts of "Mr. Travers." She knew she was starting very late, almost a quarter of a century after the crime, but as the years passed, various nuggets of information fell into her possession—that at some point Travers had left Britain for America, that he had attended Humboldt College, that he was a perennial wanderer. And all the time she nourished and deepened her vision of what she would do when she confronted him in the final encounter. How she would remind him of what he had done to her parents. How he would counter by mocking her assiduousness and deriding her silliness. How she would then draw her weapon, a knife, perhaps, or a gun, and suddenly bring fear to his face. And then, having reduced him to whimpers and pleadings, how she would strike the death blow in such a way that it would inflict maximal pain before bringing death. That vision, she explained, had sustained her. "I wanted him to know *why* he had to die and I wanted his death to be agonizing."

"How did you finally track him down?" Connie asked cautiously.

"I tried the Humboldt College alumni office several times, but because he traveled a lot and was lax about keeping in touch with them, their information was always out of date. So I got my hands on phone books, big city phone books, generally, and looked for people with Mr. Travers's name. And then I called them. I did it for day after day, year after year. It was his tendency to jump around that stymied me. It's almost as if he knew I was pursuing him."

Connie sighed inwardly. The woman had to be mad. But even as that conviction grew in his mind, he also found himself, quite independently, puzzling over why this perfectly rational person was confessing to this terrible deed. *She knows very little of any evidence we might have, and she's not such a fool as to be bluffed by a mere photograph into needlessly acknowledging guilt.*

"And then," Moser continued, "I had the most amazing bit of luck." Quite by happenstance, she explained, she met Amanda Everson in Texas and learned from a conversation ("she was an inveterate chatterbox") that she had attended Humboldt High "in a class with Mr. Travers, no less!" At once, a whole set of scenarios came to mind, for even though Amanda Everson didn't know where Travers lived, she spoke of her intention of surprising her former high school friends by attending the next reunion of the class of 1953, which was scheduled for 1998. "Since I assumed that Mr. Travers would attend as well, I decided I'd be there, too."

"But at some point you *did* know where he lived," Connie reminded her, "for you sent him letters of warning."

"I'm coming to that," she replied, in a tone that sounded almost patronizing. "Once I started briefing myself on Amanda's classmates, I decided to get a Humboldt phone directory to see which of them still lived in town. And here was my second stroke of luck! Mr. Travers's name was right there in the directory. It made a kind of sense of course, since he was approaching settling-down age and it was a town he knew well. But I was still surprised because when I'd last checked out a Humboldt phone directory, several years earlier, it hadn't contained his name."

"And the warnings?" Shrug picked up Connie's line of questioning. "Why did you send them?"

"I wanted him to be uncomfortable. I wanted him to live in fear. Because I wasn't going to be able to act until the reunion, and it was still several years off, I wanted him in the meantime to know what it was like to be uncertain if he'd be alive the following day."

"But why did you have to wait for the reunion?" Connie remained perplexed. "Once you knew where he was, all you needed to do was go to Humboldt and, and, well, kill him." Connie was annoyed that the enormity of what he was discussing had compromised his ability to speak straightforwardly.

"Oh I considered it. I really considered it. I finally had all the information I needed. I might have flown from Texas to Ohio, confronted him, and flown back. But it seemed to me that the reunion, though still several years in the future at that point, offered me a better opportunity. He'd be off-guard, he'd be among supposed friends, he'd be, well, more accessible."

"And that's *it?*" Shrug couldn't suppress his astonishment at the feebleness of the explanation.

"Okay," Moser acknowledged. "I was still steeling myself. Besides, I could easily imagine that the letters I was sending him were making his life increasingly unpleasant, and that the few years that were elapsing were turning into years of quiet mental torment for him. And I guess they were, if he was seeking advice from friends." Her smile suggested that she found the thought pleasant.

Connie and Shrug remained dissatisfied but chose to let the subject drop. They could not pretend to understand Hanna Moser's twisted line of reasoning.

In her initial plan, she explained, she had envisioned just dropping in as an uninvited visitor on the reunion event, assuming that planners would not be worrying about taking steps to prevent gate-crashers from attending. To be a plausible visitor, however, she would need to know a lot about the class, and that's why she began milking Everson for all the information she could extract about her classmates, including Travers.

But when, several months before the scheduled date of the reunion, Everson decided she would skip it and move to New Zealand instead to be with her daughter, a new option presented itself: rather than playing a friendly stranger, Moser could pretend to be Amanda Everson herself. "We were about the same height, and we both liked to dress smartly. And since Amanda hadn't seen her classmates in over forty years, the actual dissimilarities in our faces seemed likely to be inconsequential. After all, who *hasn't* changed in appearance over four decades? And all that homework I'd done to learn about Amanda's classmates, all that silly chatter about dances and football games and parties I'd absorbed, all of that now equipped me to step into her shoes and relive an experience I'd never actually had. And the big bonus was that while Mr. Travers might have been suspicious of a stranger, he wouldn't suspect a classmate at all."

Moser was proud of the sheer number of facts she had assimilated and spent several minutes talking about proms, cars, French classes, the Raven's Cove, cafeteria accidents, Principal Crawford, Future Homemakers of America, the fire at the high school garage, and the Patriots Club. "How'm I doing, Mr. Speaker?" she asked, her voice unexpectedly twinkling with pride. Shrug nodded respectfully.

"Tell us about the evening of June 4, 1998." Connie tried to emulate the evenness of Moser's tone—to sustain the surreal disconnect between substance and manner that had characterized much of this silvan conversation.

"I'd found it even easier than I expected to pass myself off as Amanda," she began. She successfully "shared" memories and swapped "gossip" with "friends," even as she talked proudly of her post-high school "family." In order to get a moment alone with Tony Travers, she had first scouted out the floor plan of the high school building, determined that the top of the north wing stair case was likely to be an isolated spot, "though I'd have killed him even if a million people had been looking on," and passed a note to him at the pre-dinner reception requesting a staircase meeting during the dinner, at 8:25. He read the note, smiled, and said he'd be there.

"What did you say in the note?" Shrug was authentically curious.

"I just said I wanted to show him something from our high school days that he might be interested in. I suggested the north stair case. The note was vague, but I figured it would work, and it did, especially after I went by his table during the dinner to remind him of my hope. I got briefly alarmed when he left the dining room earlier than I expected, at maybe 8:10 or so. For a moment I didn't know what to do. But I didn't change the plan, and I guess he just left to take a whiz, his last, before meeting me. In any case, he met me where I'd requested."

"And then?" Connie couldn't help interrupting, even though it betrayed the intensity of his curiosity.

"Like I said, we met. What else? It was quick and sweet, though not, I confess, quite as satisfyingly sweet as I'd hoped. I told him who I really was. The name 'Hanna Moser' stunned him. He hadn't forgotten, of course. I'd seen to that. I'd hoped to see fear on his face but instead what I got was disbelief. Since I knew he was hobbling around with a cane, I'd already decided not to use the knife I'd brought. I chose the top of the stairwell because a fall down the stairs would accomplish my desired goal and, with luck, leave no hint of foul play. Since he'd had no idea of what was coming, it had been easy to position him at the head of the stairs before revealing my identity. And then all it took was a shove, a hard shove. As he bounced down the stairs, his head clunking regularly away, I shouted out, 'That's for Peter and Angela Moser,' and then I returned to the dinner, no blood on my hands or dress and no worrying fingerprints on any weapon. I met that crazy Denny Culbertson as I approached the dining area, muttering about some cult that, let's see if I've got his babblings right, worshiped Christ with wooden lions' tails. The only thing that really surprised me was how quickly the body was found. I guess the north wing wasn't quite as deserted as I had thought it would be. But no suspicion ever attached to me. In fact, so far as I knew, until earlier this very afternoon, when you two gentlemen arrived uninvited at my door, no one had even thought Mr. Travers's death was anything other than an accident."

"You then went into hiding?" Shrug wanted to know more about the three years since 1998.

"Not really. I'd fulfilled my mission. So I returned to Connalton. And for days afterwards I felt a triumphant sense of vindication. I'd finally brought justice upon a Nazi double agent who had murdered my parents. The satisfactions of revenge are reputed to be exaggerated, but in my case I'd have to say they're substantial. Still, I knew I had to leave Texas, if only because the real Amanda Everson might decide to return to the States and/or hear from high school classmates who had enjoyed seeing her at the reunion. Either eventuality had the potential of leading to problems. And so I settled back here in New Hampshire and changed my name to Helen Magnuson. But then I made the stupid, overconfident error of letting an old Connalton friend in on the new name. Careless. Dumb. Absolutely stupid. But then, I never really thought that anyone would be looking for me at all; or that, if they did, it would be *Harriet Murray,* not *Hanna Moser* that they'd be looking for. So the answer to your question is complicated. Yes, in some ways I was hiding. But in others, I was just being cautious. I cannot exaggerate the extent to which I felt safe. And therefore the extent to which your appearance today surprised me." She sounded genuinely impressed.

Then for the first time in well over an hour, Moser got up from her log. At her moving, Cerberus stirred enough to lift his friendly face. But she merely adjusted her jodhpurs and asked Shrug if he had any more candies. He did, and offered her a second bag. She resumed her seat next to him. Knowing that the time for elaboration was at hand, he and Connie exchanged glances. And then Shrug spoke slowly, hesitatingly, cautiously. "There is a tragic dimension to this story, Ms. Moser, that you know nothing about. It's something we've just learned in the past few days. Nothing, of course, allows the past to be undone. But our information recasts the events of 1945 and . . ."

"What the hell are you talking about?" Moser said abruptly, with obvious irritation. "Get to your point. What do you want to say?"

She has a quick temper, Connie thought.

Shrug apologized for beginning obliquely and recovered his customary directness. "The fact is, Tony Travers killed your parents because British intelligence had received credible reports that it was *they* who were the double agents, *they* who were working for the Germans even as they pretended to be aiding the French resistance."

"That's absurd." Her anger and disbelief were palpable.

"Yes," Shrug said quietly, "it *was* absurd." He heard himself hesitating again. "More to the point, it was wrong." He stopped briefly, watching the shifting reactions in Moser's hitherto largely impassive face. "But by the time the Brits knew they'd been misled, duped, stupid, it was too late. Your parents were dead. Killed by Tony Travers, who was operating under orders from his superiors and against his own inclination."

"How do you know this?" The query was quick and fiery.

"Straight from the mouth of the superior who gave the order. Or rather, Connie received the information that way. He visited Britain several days ago to talk with that officer." Shrug was being deliberately vague about gender, location, and rank. "And learned what I have just reported. The Brits regretted the mistake, of course, but dismissed it as one of those unfortunate 'fog of war' events. Tony was very upset, for he had liked your parents and appreciated their courage." Shrug wanted to conclude with some appropriately wise remark, but all he could think of was the bromide that "Tony Travers and your parents had been on the same side—the right side—after all."

Moser said nothing for a while, and Connie and Shrug chose not to interrupt her thoughts. As the afternoon had deepened, the air had continued to cool, and the dampness of their sweat-soaked shirts was leaving them vulnerable to the discomfort of the falling temperatures.

When Moser, her self-command recovered, finally asked for more details about the path of detection that the friends had blazed, Connie offered a fuller tale of the steps that had led up to his trip to Britain. But his narrative focused more on the generalized kinds of deductions that had prompted the two friends to conclude that Travers's commander was still alive than it did on details that might provide tips about their informant's identity.

Moser heard him out and then said, in a dull voice, "It doesn't matter. The politics of the killing of my parents lost significance for me decades ago. All that was important for me was that Mr. Travers was their killer and deserved justice. That was the Alpha and the Omega of the story. So I'm still glad I got him. The fact that the Brits got their information wrong doesn't change a thing."

Shrug was startled by the metaphor, pulled (he assumed) from the final book of the New Testament. But since the occasion did not seem suitable for conversation about Scripture, he simply said that he was surprised that this new information hadn't seemed to modify Moser's feelings about Tony Travers at all.

"You don't know human nature, do you, Mr. Speaker?"

That remark stung, for Shrug, steeped in Augustinianism, thought himself a good student of human nature. Christianity, after all (he had long told himself), provided a surer guide to understanding the more obscure recesses of the human soul than any secular doctrine. "Why do you say that?" he asked.

"I think," Connie interrupted, not interested in an analysis of revenge at this moment, "that Ms. Moser simply means that a desire for retaliation can be very strong in some people, especially when it is a wrong against a parent or child that is being avenged."

"You don't get it either, Mr. Haydn." Moser was speaking bleakly rather than sharply, her voice almost disembodied. "I wasn't seeking revenge. I told you just a minute ago what I was interested in. I was seeking justice."

That was too much for the trained philosopher in Connie. Almost against his inclination he blurted out, "Do you believe you have the right to be judge, jury, and executioner all by yourself?"

"Why not?" The voice was somewhat more energized. "Who better? Don't give me crap about the 'fog of war' or the 'indeterminacy of guilt' or the 'complicatedness of life.' Anthony Travers"— Connie and Shrug both noticed that, for the first time, she had given a first name to her victim—"Anthony Travers betrayed the two people with whom he was most intimately involved. The just penalty for capital betrayal is death."

"You didn't answer my . . ." Connie broke off his sentence when, at the same time, Moser twisted to turn her back toward him and Shrug waved his hand for him to stop. The three sat quietly for a few minutes, Moser perched on the log so that she needn't look at her interlocutors, and the two friends staring uneasily at her suddenly shriveled form.

Connie abruptly stood up. "Thank you for your time, Ms. Moser. Shrug and I will be returning to Ohio now." Shrug got to his feet more slowly, aware that his legs and back were sore, and impressed that his friend, so recently the victim of an assault, seemed so limber. Connie continued. "We will be reporting our conclusions to the authorities in Ohio. They may be in touch with you." Both men brushed themselves off. Cerberus raised his head to watch them. Moser however remained silent, and so, not wanting to delay their departure, Connie simply said, "Good-bye, Ms. Moser." And Connie and Shrug began making their way down the hill toward her cabin and their car.

"I'll deny everything, you know." The unexpected voice floated down to them at a distance of perhaps fifty feet.

Connie and Shrug halted their descent for a moment, and Connie turned to call back that they had expected nothing else. Then, since there seemed nothing more to be said, they continued their scramble down the hill. They felt satisfied in the knowledge that their investigation had succeeded, and although its outcome did not exactly invite a sense of triumph, at least it permitted a sense of accomplishment. It took them about five minutes to reach the cabin. Then, just before getting into their rented car, they exchanged high fives, and Connie, a small smile lighting his face, spoke for both in declaring that "the Second-Best Club has done it again."

They then drove off. No further words were spoken until they approached the Massachusetts border. It was Connie who finally broke the silence.

"In the past four days I have heard two different women describe for me how they developed elaborate plans for killing people. Whatever happened to the gentler sex?" Shrug knew that Agatha Christie had already answered the question, and so silence returned to the car.

Epilogue

June through August 2001

Late the next afternoon, comfortably back in Humboldt after their memorable visit to New Hampshire, Connie and Shrug reported their conclusions to Bryan Travers and George Fielding. Hanna Moser, they explained, posing as Amanda Everson, had pushed Tony Travers to his death during the reunion celebrations of June 4, 1998; her purpose had been to avenge Travers's killing of her parents in 1945. Bryan Travers thanked them for their "remarkable work," promised reimbursement for their travel, and urged Fielding to take action against Moser.

The sheriff was a careful man, however, and while committing himself to looking into the matter, noted that, unless she chose to confess, insufficiency of evidence might block efforts to proceed with a case against Hanna Moser. On the matter of Cole Stocker, however, his forecast was less cautious: "The good doctor will pay a price for assaulting a citizen of Humboldt."

That same evening Connie passed word of their success on to Abe Steinberg and Teresa Espinosa, while Shrug notified Allan Clark and Marilyn. The two investigators bestowed appropriate praise and thanks on these advisers and friends and received it in similarly appropriate measures. Steinberg declared that he was continuing his efforts to find "that damned Nazi" Freddy Kramer in violation of some law. Espinosa chortled that her intuition about the killer being an outsider had been "more right than wrong." Clark reported that Tuesday's *Columbus Eagle* had contained a brief notice of Dr. Cole Stocker's resignation from the leadership of the Christian Marriage Association. And Marilyn described to her father the awkward but bracing conversation about the dangers of unprotected sex that Guy and she had obliged Brandon once again to submit to the previous evening. Finally, before going to bed, Shrug wrote a letter to Amanda Everson in New Zealand to tell her that her impostor had been unmasked, and a separate letter to Elinor Burroughs with a brief and guarded account of the denouement of the investigation.

The next day Connie wrote a letter to Alessandra Nicholson, to provide the promised summary of their conversation with Hanna Moser. He did not disguise his pride that Shrug and he had contrived, despite many false leads, to sort their way through the variety of evidentiary tracks that the investigation had uncovered and thereby to discover the identity of the person who had killed Tony Travers. There was, he noted, and almost as a throwaway line, only one question they had not been able to answer: who the hell was this "Chucklehead Clancy?"

That afternoon Connie made the promised phone call to Peter Truman at the *Herald & Examiner* to report that the investigation into the cause of Tony Travers's death was now a police matter. When Truman pressed him for more details, he referred the reporter to the authorities for all further information. He hung up pleased that he had been able to be unhelpful. Meanwhile, Shrug spent the afternoon planning the parish fund-raising campaign for the Nigerian health station.

The next day a check for $5,000 made out to Connie Haydn and Shrug Speaker arrived from Bryan Travers. It more than covered travel expenses.

A week later an astonishing reply from Colonel Nicholson arrived. "Why didn't you say something about Chucklehead Clancy when you were here?" it began. "He is, or possibly I should now say 'was,' an elephant living in an animal park near Pittsburgh. Tony and I got a big kick out of him, for he had a lively personality, and since Tony always got on well with animals, he and Chucklehead Clancy seemed to be simpatico." Nicholson went on to describe how she and Travers would visit the park just to see Chucklehead Clancy, how Travers would wave at him and try to throw food to him, and how Travers had once said that Chucklehead Clancy was probably a more reliable friend than any human being. Connie immediately notified Axel Berlin, who in turn promptly initiated steps to see that Chucklehead Clancy, or more accurately his institutional owners (for the pachyderm *was* still alive), should receive the bequest that was his.

During a Tuesday evening chess encounter in mid-July, Shrug and Connie got to laughing and marveling about how ideas from their private passions had once again illuminated an investigation. Whether it was chords (of both the dominant and German augmented sixth variety) or the statistical monstrosity known as OPS or the legend of Grover Cleveland Alexander, their hobbies had either suggested solutions or provided them with metaphors of comprehension.

"To baseball and Beethoven," was Shrug's toast.

Early in August another mailing from Britain arrived. The postmark was smudged, but Connie thought it might be "Alliston, Scotland." The envelope contained a copy of a newspaper clipping from the Manchester (New Hampshire) *Free Press*, dated July 31, 2001. It told of the death of Holly Martins, a local literary agent, in a fire that had gutted her residence in nearby Tompkins. The article went on to say that Ms. Martins's pet dog had also perished in the fire, and that the cause of the blaze remained under investigation. Aside from the clipping, the envelope was empty.

Two days later the friends lunched quietly at Angelo's, their favorite local eatery. They were still thunderstruck by the capacity of the British, whether MI6 or the military or some sub rosa intelligence agency, to carry out swift covert actions at great distances. Their conversation focused not on means but on motive. Was it revenge that lay behind Moser's death? Was it justice? Was it loyalty? Was it love? Or perhaps some ever-shifting concatenation of all four?

Connie considered writing a chiding letter to Nicholson, but Shrug dissuaded him from getting further involved in a dispute that wasn't theirs. "Besides," Shrug said, "now Bryan doesn't have to worry about whether American law can deal with the complicated contours of this matter. He would probably agree with the thought voiced by Moser herself, when, commenting on Tony Travers's death, she opined that justice had been served." To which remark Connie appended, after a brief silence, his own take: "at least in a rough way." In the end, still stunned by this unexpected outcome to their labors, the friends concluded that the range, depth, and complexity of human nature were well beyond the capacity of their essentially sunny dispositions to grasp. And on that thought, cheering in its fashion, and with their stomachs feeling full and contented, they walked out into a warm and bright midsummer afternoon in Ohio, two old guys looking for new diversions.

Acknowledgments

As with the earlier Haydn and Speaker stories, it has been a deep pleasure nurturing this one into publishable form. In fact, taking a hobby seriously by working at improving my writing of mysteries has been a joy of retirement.

And to my deep satisfaction, friends have encouraged the effort by inquiring about the hitherto unrelated adventures of Haydn and Speaker. Taking the risk of making omissions I will regret, I wish to express my appreciation to the following friends: Robin Agnew, Fred Baumann, Phyllis Belden, Jay Bowditch, Bob Brusic, Karen Chakoian, Charlie Dankworth, Cindy Dilts, Cathe Ellsworth, Cynthia Enloe, Phyllis Evans, Pam Foster, JoAnne Geiger, Mark Geston, Janette Greenwood, Judy Hoffman, Pam Jensen, Dick and Jayne Johnston, Phil and Sheila Jordan, Chico Kieswetter, Bruce Kinzer, Jennifer Klein, Pat Leech, Judy Moffett, Tom Nicely, Borden Painter, Jeanne Paul, Ann Ponder, Ellen Price, John Price, Susan Richardson, Todd Rosenberg, Jim and Linda Salisbury, Carol Schumacher, Chris Schwarz, Will Scott, Harriett Stone, John Wahlert, Barbara Wright, and Victoria Wyatt.

Aside from being boosters, Jim and Linda Salisbury at Tabby House deserve special thanks for once again guiding me through the process of turning a manuscript draft into a published product.

About the Author

 Reed Browning grew up in Manhasset, Long Island, and is an alumnus of Dartmouth College. He did his graduate work at Yale University and the University of Vienna. He taught European and American history for forty years at Kenyon College before retiring in 2007. While at Kenyon he served eight years as provost and a brief stint as acting president.

In addition to writing mysteries, his hobbies include baseball history, song-writing, and opera.

He is the author of five books of history: *The Duke of Newcastle*; *Political and Constitutional Ideas of the Court Whigs*; *The War of the Austrian Succession*; *Cy Young: A Baseball Life*; and *Baseball's Greatest Season 1924*. He has also written three earlier Haydn-and-Speaker mysteries: *Trinity*; *What Happened to Joan?*, and *A Question of Identification*.

Reed lives at Kendal at Granville in Granville, Ohio, with his wife Susan.